More prai̶̶̶̶̶̶̶̶̶̶̶̶̶̶̶̶̶̶̶ ̶ ̶ond

"At once a folktale and a page-turner that acquires the dignity of tragedy. Samuel Perry has given us a new masterpiece, whose closing question is as urgent for us today as it was in 1934."

—Norma Field, author of *In the Realm of a Dying Emperor: Japan at Century's End*

"A vibrant account of the travails of Japanese colonialism, as experienced by workers and women, by the pioneering feminist writer of the Korean left."

—Andre Schmid, author of *Korea Between Empires: 1895–1919*

"How refreshing it is to have a good old-fashioned story, told without narrative tricks or artifice. Kang Kyŏng-ae's *From Wŏnso Pond* is a powerful novel that charts the struggles of her impassioned characters as they learn to live, work, and love. The questions Kang poses and the issues she tackles are as universal as they are enduring. This essential work should be required reading for anyone interested in Korean history and literature."

—Sung J. Woo, author of *Everything Asian: A Novel*

"This novel's canonical status will remain unchallenged for years to come. It is a rare blessing that the English-language version was produced by Samuel Perry, whose first-rate linguistic talent, literary sensitivity, and scholarly rigor are distinctively channeled through his passion for social change and aesthetic excellence."

—Kyeong-Hee Choi, associate professor of East Asian Languages and Civilizations at the University of Chicago

"*From Wŏnso Pond* is a powerful literary indictment of sexual and economic exploitation of the poverty-ridden farming population in 1930s colonial Korea."

—Yung-Hee Kim, professor of Korean Literature at the University of Hawaii at Manoa

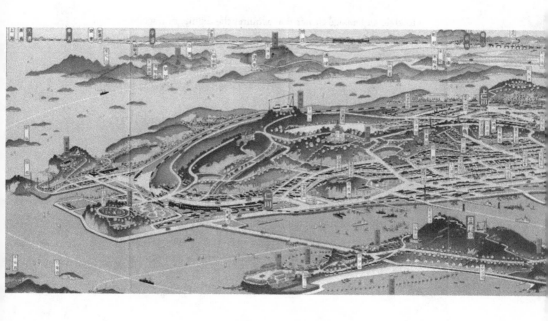

THE FEMINIST PRESS
AT THE CITY UNIVERSITY OF NEW YORK
NEW YORK CITY

FROM WONSO POND

KANG KYŎNG-AE

TRANSLATED BY SAMUEL PERRY

Published in 2009 by the Feminist Press
at The City University of New York
The Graduate Center
365 Fifth Avenue, Suite 5406
New York, NY 10016

www.feministpress.org

Publication of this book was made possible with support from the National Endowment
for the Arts, the Sunshik Min Endowment for the Advancement of Korean Literature at the
Korea Institute, Harvard University, and LTI Korea.

Cover and text design by Drew Stevens

Cover art: Detail of *Inch'ŏn* by Yoshida Hatsusaburō. © www.asocie.jp.

13 12 11 10 09   6 5 4 3 2 1

Library of Congress Cataloging-in-Publication Data

Kang, Kyŏng-ae, 1906-1944.
[In'gan munje. English]
From Wŏnso Pond : a novel / by Kang Kyŏng-ae ; translated by Samuel Perry.
— 1st ed.
    p. cm.
ISBN 978-1-55861-601-1 (pbk.) — ISBN 978-1-55861-602-8 (library cloth)
I. Perry, Samuel. II. Title.
PL991.38.K6I5413 2009
895.1'352—dc22

2008033701

Contents

Translator's Introduction

IN'GAN MUNJE is the second novel written by Kang Kyŏng-ae (1906–1944), one of several women writers active during Korea's colonial period.[1] Here, translated as *From Wŏnso Pond* (the literal translation of the Korean title is "Human Problems"), *In'gan munje* is one of Kang's most important works, one that provides a good introduction to the colonial history and literature of a nation still divided some sixty-odd years after its liberation from Japan. Given the paucity of women's works from this period that are available in English translation, Kang's novel helps in particular to illuminate the intersection of gender and modernity in colonial Korea and, more broadly speaking, in the Japanese Empire. Detailing both historical facts and human feelings, *From Wŏnso Pond* not only documents the daily lives of farmers, "new women," revolutionaries, and nouveaux riches, but also sheds light on how the violent shock of colonialism was experienced in the hearts and minds of Korean people and how writers attempted to shape that experience into part of the collective imagination.

As were most novels published at the time, *From Wŏnso Pond* was serialized daily in a Korean-language newspaper. It ran in the *Tonga ilbo* from August 1 to December 22, 1934, with each of its 120 episodes illustrated with a black-and-white picture of the main characters or setting. The novel was neither reedited nor reissued in book form during Kang's lifetime, and for some fifteen years it remained out of print, until the Labor Newspaper (*Rodong Sinmunsa*), where Kang's widowed husband worked as an associate editor, published a version of the book in 1949 in the Democratic People's Republic of Korea (DPRK, or North Korea). Not until decades after the Korean War, which ended only with a ceasefire in 1953, would Kang's novel be rediscovered in the Republic of Korea (South Korea), where it is now celebrated as an extraordinary achievement of Korean realism.[2]

Given the tragic events of twentieth-century Korean history—colonization, war, division, and sustained ideological conflict—most of Kang's original manuscripts have been irretrievably lost, and slightly different versions of *In'gan munje* exist in libraries today. In the absence of an extant original manuscript, I have, as translator of the novel, relied on the 1934 newspaper serialization to render it into English. The authenticity of this serialized version is nevertheless also in doubt, since little if anything ever appeared in newspapers without the official seal of a government censor.[3] Indeed, one year before *In'gan munje* appeared, Kang lamented police censorship in a short essay: "As for my own feelings, I cannot even pick up a pen and write! I have a mouth, but no words to speak!"[4] Like many colonial and especially socialist writers, Kang undoubtedly self-censored her writing, making careful decisions about individual words, scenes, and even plotlines that might have been deemed objectionable, and thus extirpated, by the publication police.[5] The flexibility of the novel form certainly allowed writers such as Kang some leeway. She begins her story with a traditional folk tale that amounts to an allegory for revolution, and throughout the novel Kang's irony mercilessly lampoons the hypocrisy around her—whether bureaucratic, corporate, or patriarchal. But the novel carries little exhortatory language, or ostensibly political commentary—certainly nothing overtly critical of the Japanese colonial regime.

How much of Kang's language was actually excised by censors from her original manuscript or changed by editors when it first appeared in the *Tonga ilbo* we will most likely never know. In episode 107 of *From Wŏnso Pond*, just as Ch'ŏtchae is imagining Sinch'ŏl being arrested by the police, the word "censored" appears in the newspaper edition, marking a deletion of unknown length. In two places in her text the letters "XX" appear—a common mark of censorship at the time—most likely in reference to the Communist Party, which few educated readers would have failed to grasp. This overtly visible mark of censorship, however, which had been used for some time in both Japan and Korea—sometimes preemptively by the authors themselves—was itself increasingly excised from publications. In any case, the colonial censorship bureau, staffed by both Japanese and Koreans, was still not as effective as officials might have hoped by the mid-1930s. Part of episode 106, which describes an uprising on the streets of Inch'ŏn, managed to find itself printed in the morning edition of the newspaper, though it seems to have been, after further scrutiny, deleted from the evening edition. This particular passage was carefully translated into Japanese and documented by the censoring authorities in a 1935 report of the Korean Publication Police—one of dozens of passages from Korean-language magazines and newspapers that were duly recorded each month by bureaucrats.[6]

While the 1949 DPRK version of *In'gan munje* also takes several liberties in the editing of Kang's novel—removing instances of abusive language that Ch'ŏtchae uses toward his mother, for example—there is little to suggest that even Kang's husband had access to an original manuscript to rely on when this first edition of her book was published. Perhaps with the opening of archives in the DPRK, future scholarship will piece together a more authentic version of *In'gan munje*, free from external censorship, but as it stands now our English translation of Kang's novel is based on the most complete version that can be verified.

The perils of translation also entail a kind of censorship, given that literary translation—as it has been practiced in the English-speaking world over the past century—often leans toward an emphasis on smoothness and readability. In principle, my efforts to translate *In'gan munje* have been guided mainly by a desire to capture the full range of voices in Kang's novel and to dignify the historical specificity of her use of language. Editorial demands however, have at times exerted their own particular pressures on her text as it appears in English—though only in what Kang Kyŏng-ae would have surely recognized as a sincere gesture to make her work more accessible. For readers unfamiliar with the cultures of East Asia, we have also included at the back of the book a brief glossary, which explains many of the Korean and Japanese words and place-names that appear in Kang's novel, though we have tried to keep the use of footnotes to a bare minimum.

WHAT SORT OF life experiences in colonial Korea could have led a woman such as Kang Kyŏng-ae to write novels that often featured the experiences of women and the poor? According to her accounts published in journals in the 1930s, Kang lived in close contact with both the haves and the have-nots in colonial Korea and neighboring Manchuria. Born the daughter of a poor farmer in Hwanghae Province, Kang grew up in the household of her well-off stepfather and was able to attend a Catholic boarding school in the city of Pyŏngyang.[7] Showing her rebellious colors as a youth, she was expelled from the school for participating in a student strike and would later scandalously run off with a young college student to Seoul, where she attended Tongdŏk Girls School and befriended many young Korean intellectuals. As Yang Chu-dong, the student she ran off with tells it, it was then that he lent Kang his copy of Karl Marx's *Capital* and introduced her to works of Japanese literary criticism.[8] While the details of her early adulthood are somewhat obscure, Kang is known to have dropped out of Tongdŏk Girls School to spend a year or two in Manchuria, working as a substitute teacher and—according to one North Korean source—hoping to join a group of guerrilla rebels. Newly radicalized, she returned to her home in Hwanghae Province, where she set up a night school and set her heart on becoming a writer.[9]

"Art is not something you place on a shelf and revere as 'Oh, blessed art!'" wrote the twenty-three-year-old Kang in 1929—in what is thought to be her first essay published in a national newspaper.[10] Echoing arguments being made by members of the influential Korean Proletarian Arts Association (KAPF), which sought to bring the voices of the oppressed into a popular form of literature, Kang was criticizing a particular version of aesthetic ideology being reproduced by the established novelist and critic Yŏm Sang-sŏp, who was more than a decade her senior. Mercilessly mocking the elitism of the Korean intelligentsia, Kang drew on classical Chinese diction to criticize writers "who wished to distance themselves from the *vulgar world* and rise high up into the clouds, where they might better amuse themselves like *hermits* amid the *steep slopes and secluded valleys.*"[11] In her essay Kang questioned Yŏm Sang-sŏp for his suggestion that the accelerated popularization of the literary arts had lowered the artistic value of Korean literature. "Isn't it precisely by means of popularization," she asked, "that we shall be able to create and promote an art of even greater value, and thus allow the life of the arts to become animated?"[12]

Published serially in the journal *Hyesŏng*, Kang's first novel, *Mothers and Daughters* (Ŏmŏni wa ttal, 1931–1932), grew out of this desire to popularize narrative fiction—to create characters and narrators with the perspective of hitherto marginalized people and to make literature something that appealed to a much wider spectrum of Koreans. With its detailed focus on the tribulations of women performing domestic labor, *Mothers and Daughters* also managed to put Kang on the map as a "new woman writer." A 1931 advertisement in the magazine *Sin yŏsŏng* ("New Woman") celebrated her as a rising star of the literary scene: "A Great Wonder of the Korean Literary World—A woman writer hidden away in a corner of Hwanghae Province ... [whose] bold one-thousand-page work has all eyes of the literary world fixed upon it." The editor of *Hyesŏng*, introducing the novel to readers, offered a mix of admiration and criticism: "In so many ways the craftsmanship evident in this work is something completely unfamiliar to us. In the way details are invoked with such precision in certain passages this novel indeed bears comparison to that of the great masters. . . I regret to say, however, that the novel does closely resemble American moving pictures in that the pace of the action is rather cheaply constructed."[13] After the publication of a 1933 short story called "Vegetable Patch," about a young girl who is murdered after siding with the workers on her family's farm, Marxist critic and KAPF member Paek Chŏl also praised Kang for her craftsmanship but called her writing "ideologically skewed," labeling her, not a proletarian writer, but rather a "fellow traveler"—a term made famous by Leon Trotsky's 1924 work *Literature and Revolution*.

Just before *Mothers and Daughters* began serialization, Kang married and settled down in Yongchŏng, Manchuria, just north of the Korean border, where her husband Chang Ha-il taught at a Korean middle school. It was from here that Kang built on her initial success as an author, continuing to write in a variety of forms: autobiographical sketches and travel accounts for women's magazines, tortured narratives of the self for intellectual journals, and carefully crafted portraits of the poor and oppressed for newspapers and literary gazettes.[14] Kang was most prolific between 1931, when she published her first short story, and 1936, when her first work was translated into Japanese and published in the Seoul edition of the daily *Ōsaka Mainichi*. In 1936 Kang also published her most famous, and most frequently anthologized, short story, "The Underground Village," a heart-wrenching account of a disabled teenager and his young siblings living in abject poverty.[15] In the late 1930s Kang worked briefly as a regional bureau chief for the daily *Chosŏn ilbo*, but by 1939, as the Japanese government heightened its wartime mobilization effort and banned the use of the Korean language in secondary schools and many publications, she abandoned fiction writing altogether. She died five years later at the age of thirty-nine in her home province of Hwanghae.

KANG'S SHORT LIFETIME coincided almost exactly with the forty-year period of Korea's colonization, during which Japanese capitalism took a heavy toll on the lives of most Koreans. An increasingly rich and powerful Japanese Empire had made Korea a protectorate in 1905, shortly after defeating Russia in the Russo-Japanese war, and then officially annexed Korea in 1910, only a quarter century before *In'gan munje* was first published. The rapid process of modernization that Korea experienced over the following decades is often cited as a reason for the nation's uneven, or "distorted," development. The Korean peninsula was originally seen by the Japanese as an agricultural "rice basket," a source of cheap labor and natural resources, and a market for Japanese goods. Although the rate of economic growth in Korea often exceeded that in Japan proper, colonial development was decidedly planned and orchestrated for the advantage of Japanese capital, not the Korean people.[16] By the time *In'gan munje* was published, more than two million Koreans were living in Japan proper, and several hundred thousand in Manchuria. Colonization had accelerated a pattern of migration caused by internal economic pressures that continued to separate families and break up communities, displacing people from ancestral lands into cities and villages throughout Korea, Japan, and Manchuria.

From the beginning of Japan's occupation of Korea, the South Manchurian Railway, the premiere instrument of Japanese expansion and mobility, ran from the port city of Pusan in the southeast, through Seoul and Pyŏngyang in the northeast, and on to the cosmopolitan cities of Manchuria, making many of Korea's cities important centers of trade and government. Over the course of some twenty years, from 1910 to 1930, Korea's largest urban center, the colonial capital, Seoul, doubled to a population of more than half a million, including a large group of Japanese, and grew into a bustling city of department stores, cafés, movie theaters, and an imperial university. A colonial policy shift in the 1930s, which led to an emphasis on building up industry, led to the creation of massive factories such as the Tongyang Spinning Mill in the port city of Inch'ŏn, which employed close to two thousand workers and most likely served as the model for the factory where Kang's characters Sŏnbi and Kannan work in the second half of *From Wŏnso Pond*.

Despite the population shifts caused by efficiencies in rice production, taxation policies, and dangerous fluctuations in the marketplace, the population in Korea still remained a primarily rural one throughout the colonial period, with 80 percent of Korean men involved in agricultural labor in 1930.[17] Once urban centers began to grow, however, the differentiation between country and city became more prominent in the mass media, and writers in the 1930s began to look nostalgically at the countryside as the locus of an authentic, romanticized past, which Korea was thought to be in danger of losing with the onset of its rapid modernization. In the realm of literature and the arts, a mature craftsmanship gradually took shape in the hands of young writers and artists, who, like Kang Kyŏng-ae, were drawing on the techniques of realism, modernism, popular fiction, drama, and film to create imaginative experiences in response to Korea's unique confrontation with colonial modernity.[18]

After the 1919 failure of the Korean independence movement (the March First Movement), political opposition to Japan's colonization expressed itself as part of a cultural nationalism, which the Japanese government tolerated for more than a decade. Historians have normally divided this opposition into that of the nationalists and that of the socialists, neither of which is normally seen as having made much room for women to politicize their own agendas. Confucianism had for centuries served as the ideological foundation of patriarchy in East Asia, limiting women's participation in the public sphere in China, Japan, and Korea. Even educated Korean society, however, seemed to remain particularly entrenched in a Confucian patriarchy well into the twentieth century, in part because of the experience of colonization.[19] Christian missionaries seeking converts and Enlightenment-oriented Korean intellectuals set on building a strong nation had begun to promote women's literacy at the end of the nineteenth century, but the first public school for Korean girls was not established until 1908, only two years before Korea's annexation by Japan, where, by contrast, almost all girls were enrolling in elementary school.[20] Under the subsequent humiliation of Japanese colonization, the need to reconfigure traditional gender relations tended to get short shrift from male intellectuals in Korea, many of whom supported the general idea of women's equality, but only insofar as it worked explicitly in the interests of national liberation and did not require much change in their own behavior.[21] Kang Kyŏng-ae was part of a new generation of educated young women who not only were becoming well versed in modern politics, economics, and the arts, but also were gaining strength in numbers by the late 1920s as they began to contribute, as active journalists and creative writers, to public discourse on women's role in society. Although the economics of publishing were such that no women—or even men for that matter—could support themselves writing novels alone, other notable women writers of fiction at the time included Pak Hwa-sŏng, Paek Sin-ae, Song Kye-wŏl, and Ch'oe Chŏng-hŭi.

All these women were affiliated in one way or another with institutions connected to socialist theory and activism, which, alongside the Christian Church and nationalist organizations, played an important role in asserting women's equality and enfranchising a new generation of women writers and teachers. Before her own career as a writer blossomed, Kang Kyŏng-ae had been a member of the Kŭnuhoe, an association of women activists of varying political and ideological persuasions, who had come together in 1927 with the goal of "abolishing all social and legal discrimination against women" and with a special emphasis on promoting the education of poor women through lecture tours and night schools. Founding member of the Kŭnuhoe and an editor of the magazine *Sin yŏsŏng* ("New Woman"), Hŏ Chŏng-suk (1908–1991) drew on a language of women's liberation that was indebted to the work of Frederic Engels, and like many Korean socialists, she was convinced that women's emancipation could come only as part of a socialist revolution that would reform the family system.[22] Leftist women such as Kang would not have called themselves feminists, but their politics were certainly molded by a combination of class-, nation- and gender-consciousness.

Despite censorship and publication laws that banned many books from the colony, such diverse texts as Engel's *The Origins of the Family*, August Bebel's *Women and Socialism*, Alexandra Kolontai's *Red Love*, and the feminist writings of the Japanese socialist Yamakawa Kikue were all available in colonial Korea. Kang Kyŏng-ae would have been familiar with many of these works, whether in English, Japanese, or Korean translation. In a passionate 1930 letter to the editor published in the "Women's Column" of the *Chosŏn ilbo*, however, Kang offered more practical advice to women in the colony wanting to reform the family and to make a contribution to Korean society at large. Referring to the success of an anti-British campaign initiated by the wife of Mohandas Gandhi, she encouraged women to make use of their economic power as producers and consumers by buying only Korean-made goods, limiting their husbands' consumption of alcohol and cigarettes, and abandoning their own use of cosmetics and perfume. Embracing what she viewed as the supportive role that all women could play in the home as wives and mothers, Kang also exhorted all literate women to read the newspaper every day, and to teach at least twenty other women to read.[23] While the opportunities for women to venture outside the domestic realm and join the workforce as telephone operators, waitresses, shopkeepers, and secretaries were increasing, the vast majority of Korean women—more than 98 percent—were still illiterate. The challenges that socialists identified in the reconstruction of gender boundaries might be summed up in the words of the prolific writer Yi Ki-yŏng. In an essay addressed to members of the Kŭnuhoe, encouraging women to become writers, Yi embraced as part of the proletarian struggle women's efforts "to fight against the feudal ideology of 'honoring men over women' [namjon yŏbi] and to liberate women from the prison of the household, from illiteracy, and from a contemporary social system that enslaved women to men."[24]

IN THE 1920s the Japanese authorities had tolerated a kind of cultural nationalism in the Korean colony, but by the time In'gan munje was published the colonial police had begun cracking down severely on members of the socialist opposition, including those involved in the broader proletarian cultural movement. With its attention to issues of class and political enlightenment, Kang's revolutionary epic In'gan munje in fact marks the end of a decade of proletarian culture in the Korean colony. For inciting a student demonstration in Seoul, Kunŭhoe cofounder Hŏ Chŏng-suk had been sentenced to a year in the infamous Sŏdaemun Prison—where Kang's character Sinch'ŏl is jailed in In'gan munje—and many members of KAPF had already served, or soon would serve, long prison sentences. Not an official member of KAPF herself, Kang Kyŏng-ae had participated in the literary movement from a distance, though once she moved to Manchuria she seems to have kept in close contact with Korean communists in exile. Along with the government crackdown on socialist institutions, however, print culture in general settled into a more entrenched gender conservatism, most evident in a cult of domesticity that fetishized women's roles as mothers, housewives, and consumers.[25] Portraying working-class women who venture outside these identities—as housemaids, factory girls, and underground activists—is one of Kang Kyŏng-ae's major strengths as a novelist responding to her particular moment in history. If her novel draws on common tropes of victimization and desire that might be seen as feeding conservative anxieties about women's new roles in society, *In'gan munje* also shapes gender as a place where the contradictions of colonial capitalism are poignantly portrayed and dignifies its women characters as agents of self-, and social, transformation. [26]

Although few literary critics commented on *In'gan munje* as it was being serialized, many male critics and journalists in the mid-1930s were often equally scornful of commercial culture and women's literature, both of which were considered frivolous or overly emotional. And yet by all accounts, popular fiction written by and for women was becoming a major source of newspaper revenue.[27] Increasing literacy rates were accompanied by the unprecedented expansion of the marketplace for print culture. The daily *Chosŏn ilbo* nearly tripled in sales from 1930 to 1937, while the leading daily *Tonga ilbo*, which constituted more than 40 percent of all newspapers read by Koreans throughout the Japanese empire, more than doubled its circulation.[28] The growing literacy rates and a burgeoning market created a new demand for fiction, and the 1930s became, in the words of Korean poet and essayist Kim Ki-rim, "the Olympic age of the newspaper novel."[29] Media companies were shrewdly making use of the serialized form to attract and retain subscribers, who might get hooked on a particular story line and continue to purchase their newspaper, but they were also using the popular stories to sell advertising space—huge ads for Japanese medicine, leather shoes, chocolate, cosmetics, and candy often appeared next to episodes of serialized works such as *In'gan munje*. Aware of the context in which her novel would be published, Kang produced a masterfully hybrid form of the serialized novel, dutifully creating a desire on the part of the reader to consume the coming episode while at the same time reinserting into the noise of the marketplace important ideas, elsewhere discounted, about the relations between labor, class, and gender.

On July 27, 1934, several days before *In'gan munje* began serialization, an editor at the *Tonga ilbo* introduced Kang's novel to readers with a short teaser, noting that the inspiration for her novel came from a local legend about a pond called Wŏnso. He went on to summarize what would appear to be the first half of Kang's story line.

And, oh, how the man's carnal desires knew no end! A fatherless young girl soon poised to become victim of his lecherous fangs and paws. The son of a sharecropper for whom this girl is his first love. And then the son of a gentleman, visiting from Seoul over summer break, who develops feelings for . . . this very same girl. What we have here in this tiny village is a love triangle pitting father against son. And while the whole village places its hopes in the benevolence of its legendary Wŏnso Pond, the twisted world of human passions, sparked by conflicts of the heart, finally overwhelms the human soul as this village meets with a night like death.[30]

The present-day reader may justifiably find this synopsis of Kang's work over the top, but its distortions of her overall story line perfectly illustrate the melodramatic reading practices that were being fostered by this new form of popular fiction. What did Kang Kyŏng-ae herself have to say to her potential readers? In an author's introduction printed adjacent to the teaser, Kang sang an altogether different tune.

Human society continually witnesses new problems, and it is as human beings struggle to solve these problems that human society charts its development. Human problems can in general be divided into major problems and minor problems, and by capturing in this work the major problems in the world today, I have tried to suggest which human beings are endowed with the strength and requisite qualities to solve these problems and to show which path as human beings they will have to tread. Let me end by asking that you read to the very end of the story and that you offer me your sincere reproof on the errors and contradictions I have allowed to proliferate in the pages that follow.[31]

The abstraction, the earnestness, the staid humility of Kang's formal introduction all speak of a public voice almost stripped of the real passions that animate *In'gan munje*—passions somewhat different from those the newspaper was promising its readers. Kang's words can be read, perhaps, as those of an intelligent woman distancing herself from the stereotype of a shallowly sentimental or melodramatic women's literature. But her use of the terms "human beings" and "human problems"—poignantly evoked in the authorial interjection that ends her novel—also reminds us of the colonial censorship that forbade a more radical lexicon of "proletariat" and "revolution." And it serves to underscore a moment in Korean history when socialist women saw their own specific struggle, as that of women, as inseparable from that of a much broader effort to liberate all people, an effort to fundamentally shift the dynamics of a society newly reorganized around the principle of profit accumulation. The struggle between the structures of colonialism, patriarchy, and the marketplace on the one hand, and the passion and commitment of women resisting them on the other, is part of what makes *From Wŏnso Pond* such a fascinating work to read some seventy-five years after its first publication.

Almost a decade now has passed since the "Complete Works of Kang Kyŏng-ae" was published in South Korea, where Kang has become cherished as an important writer of the colonial period among students and scholars of literature, history, and feminism. For some thirty-odd years after the Korean War, the Republic of Korea banned all books by writers who "fled north" (*wŏlbuk*) to the DPRK, an example of the Cold War anticommunism that for decades prevented even writers such as Kang, who died before liberation, from entering either popular consciousness or the literary canon. With the now frequent republication of her work and a renewed interest in the colonial period, Kang's reputation as a writer has grown over the past twenty years in Korea, as well as abroad. Ten years ago, in an area of northeastern China, where she lived for more than a decade and where more than a million people of Korean heritage still live today, a stone memorial was erected in the foothills of Mount Piyan to commemorate Kang's "literary spirit and achievement" as one of Korea's representative women writers. The English translation of *In'gan munje* adds to a growing library of Kang's works now available internationally in English, Russian, Chinese, German, and Japanese. The proletarian cultural movement to which Kang made such a significant contribution has also become a lively topic of academic discussion in recent years, throughout East Asia and around the globe, as scholars have begun to reexamine—and reconnect—the international contours of a cultural movement that saw literature as indispensable to revolution.[32] One might say that Kang's novel remains an eloquent testament to that belief today—that fiction can and must have a role in social change.

Samuel Perry
Providence, R.I.
February 2009

Notes

1. Following Korean practice, I use the author's family name first, followed by her given name. The "a" of "Kang" should be pronounced as "Ah."

2. For an account of the internal divisions following Korea's liberation that developed into the Korea War, see Bruce Cumings, *Korea's Place in the Sun: A Modern History* (New York: W.W. Norton, 1997).

3. For more information on the relationship between censorship and the development of Korean literature, see Kyeong-Hee Choi, *Beneath the Vermilion Ink: Japanese Colonial Censorship and the Making of Modern Korean Literature* (Cornell University Press, forthcoming).

4. Kang Kyŏng-ae, "Iyŏk ŭi talbam," *Sin tonga* (December 1933), reprinted in *Kang Kyŏng-ae chŏnjip*, ed. Yi Sang-gyŏng (Seoul: Somyŏng Ch'ulpan, 2002), 743-745.

5. The draconian Japanese Peace and Preservation Law, for example, in 1928 made criticism of the imperial system and of private property newly punishable by death.

6. *Chōsen shuppan keisatsu geppō*, Kuksa P'yŏnch'an Wiwŏnhoe (National Institute of Korean History), Kwachŏn, South Korea, 1996, microfilm.

7. Hwanghae Province is now part of the DPRK.

8. Yang Chu-dong, "Ch'ŏngsach'o—munhak sonyŏ K ŭi ch'uŏk," in *Insaeng chapgi* (Seoul: T'amgudang, 1963).

9. Yi, *Kang Kyŏng-ae chŏnjip*, 846.

10. Kang Kyŏng-ae, "Yŏm Sang-sŏp ssi ŭi nonsŏl 'Myŏngil ŭi kil' ŭl ilgo," *Chosŏn ilbo* October 3–5, 1929; also in Yi, *Kang Kyŏng-ae chŏnjip*, 705–9.

11. Yi, *Kang Kyŏng-ae chŏnjip*, 705; emphasis mine.

12. Ibid., 708.

13. Editor's note prefacing *Ŏmŏni wa ttal, Hyesŏng* 1 (August 1931); Yi, *Kang Kyŏng-ae chŏnjip*, 13. When the journal *Hyesŏng* was discontinued, Kang's novel continued its serialization in the journal *Cheilsŏn* ("Front Line").

14. Yongchŏn is now also known as the city of Longjing, located in the Yanbian Korean Autonomous Prefecture within Jilin Province, People's Republic of China.

15. An English translation of "The Underground Village" ("Chihach'on") is available in Suh Ji-Moon, *The Rainy Spell and Other Korean Stories* (Armonk, N.Y.: M. E. Sharpe 1998).

16. Cumings, *Korea's Place in the Sun*, 148.

17. For more information on colonial development in Korea, see Kyeong-Hee Choi, Michael Edson Robinson, and Gi-Wook Shin, eds., *Colonial Modernity in Korea* (Cambridge: Harvard University Press, 2000).

18. For a discussion of Korean modernism, see Janet Poole, "Late Colonial Modernism and the Desire for Renewal," in *Korea under Japanese Colonialism*, ed. Andre Schmid (forthcoming).

19. For a comparative account of East Asian women and patriarchy, see Anne Walthall, "From Private to Public Patriarch: Women, Labor, and the State in East Asia, 1600–1919," in *A Companion to Gender History*, ed. Teresa A. Meade and Merry E. Wiesner-Hanks (Malden, Mass.: Blackwell, 2004).

20. Chŏn Chŏng-hwang, "1920–1930 yŏndae sosŏl tokja ŭi hyŏngsŏng kwa mun-hwa kwajŏng," *Yŏksa munje yŏn'gu* 7 (2001); cited in Samuel Perry, "Korean as Proletar-ian: Ethnicity and Identity in Chang Hyŏk-chu's "Hell of the Starving," *Positions: East Asian Critique* 14, no. 2 (2006).

21. Kenneth Wells, "The Price of Legitimacy: Women and the Kŭnuhoe Movement, 1927–1931," in *Colonial Modernity in Korea*, ed. Kyeong-Hee Choi, Michael Edson Robinson, and Gi-Wook Shin (Cambridge: Harvard University Press, 2000), 191-220.

22. Hŏ Chŏng-suk would later become a high official in the DPRK.

23. Kang Kyŏng-ae, "Chosŏn yŏsŏngdŭl ŭi palbŭl kil," *Chosŏn ilbo*, November 28–29, 1930; Yi, *Kang Kyŏng-ae chŏnjip*, 712.

24. Yi Ki-yŏng, "Puin ŭi munhakchŏk chiwi," *Kŭnu* 1 (1929): 63–66.

25. One of the earliest extant films from Korea, now available with English subtitles, is the 1936 "Sweet Dream" (*Mimong*), which dramatizes the figure of the Korean "new woman" in the context of this cult of domesticity. See the DVD set *The Past Unearthed: The Second Encounter Collection of Chosun Films in the 1930s* (Seoul: Taewon Entertain-ment, 2008).

26. Part of my language here is highly indebted to that of Barbara Foley in her book *Radical Representations* (Durham: Duke University Press, 1993).

27. "Sinmun sosŏl kangjwa," 1-8 *Chosŏn ilbo*, September 6–13, 1935.

28. Han Wŏn-yŏng, *Han'guk kŭndae sinmun yŏnjae sosŏl yŏngu* (Seoul: Ihwa Mun-hwasa, 1996), 452.

29. Kim Kirim, "Sinmun sosŏl 'olimp'ik' sidae," *Samchŏlli*, January 1933.

30. *Tonga ilbo*, July 31, 1934.

31. Ibid.

32. See *Positions: East Asian Critique* 14, no. 2 (2006) for a collection of scholarly essays on the proletarian cultural movement in East Asia, including one that focuses on the work of Kang Kyŏng-ae. In particular, see Ruth Barraclough, "Tales of Seduction: Factory Girls in Korean Proletarian Literature."

FROM WONSO POND

1

What a fine view of Yongyŏn village that is, once you've climbed up this hill. The big house pointing up over there—the one with the western-style shingles—that belongs to Chŏng Tŏkho, who also owns the farmland in front of it. The tin-roofed building over to this side is the township office, the one right next to it is the police station, and those dark spots forming a circle around them are farmhouses.

And that blue pond down there? That's Wŏnso Pond, the very lifeline of the village. It's the reason the village was settled here in the first place, and the reason the fields were later cleared. Everyone, even the dogs and wild animals, depends on it for fresh drinking water.

Now there won't be anybody around, of course, who knows just how and when the pond actually got there. But the farmers in the village have a legend to tell about it. To the villagers this is their one source of pride, and it's become an article of faith for them.

If you listen to their story, this is what they'll say:

Long, long ago, before the pond was ever formed, a rich official lived here, or so the story goes, with countless numbers of slaves and fields and well-fed livestock. Such a miser was this man that when he failed each year to eat all the grain he harvested, he preferred to see it rot in his storehouse rather than offer it to the farmers suffering around him. Begrudging even a spoonful of rice that the occasional beggar wandered by in search of, he made sure his front gate was locked up tight before letting anyone in the household begin cooking.

After several years of poor harvests, when the local people began to die of hunger, they came to plead with the official several times a day. But the man did little more than turn a deaf ear, and shooed them off with a scolding before they could pass through his front door.

Under these circumstances the farmers felt they had no other choice but to band together and raid the official's house, which they did one night, taking away his rice and livestock.

Within a few days the official filed a petition with the local authorities and had all the local farmers arrested. Those who weren't subjected to cruel punishments or execution were banished from the area, so the story goes.

The children in the village who had lost their mothers and fathers and the elders who had lost their daughters and sons called out for their loved ones until their throats were raw. They cried in the man's courtyard, refusing to leave.

They cried and cried, and cried even more, so that in the course of a single night they transformed the official's splendid mansion into a pond of tears. This pond, according to the story, is the very same blue pond you see down there.

Now anyone can guess with a glance at its surface how wide the pond is, but there's not a soul around who knows how deep it goes. There's talk of someone long ago who let several spools of silk thread down into the water in order to measure its depth, but none of the spools reached the bottom.

Whenever new people move into the village, the first thing the farmers tell them is the legend of Wŏnso Pond, and as soon as children learn how to talk, their parents teach them the story. Little children and adults alike, they all know the legend by heart. And even if the facts remain somewhat obscure, they hold a certain hope in the pond.

It's for this reason that the farmers seek comfort from Wŏnso Pond whenever they're distressed or tormented by something—one glance at Wŏnso Pond and their troubles are gone, they say.

On the four major holidays the farmers used to carry down white rice and rice cakes and bury them beside Wŏnso Pond, sometimes even offering their clothes or shoes to the water. Such was the extent to which they once showed their devotion. Even people on the verge of death, they say, would come to pray at the pond and be cured of their illnesses.

As the years passed, their blessed Wŏnso Pond notwithstanding, increased suffering and misfortune for some reason fell upon the villagers. And, in recent years, with little more than wheat gruel and acorns to eat, it was a rare soul indeed who could bury white rice and rice cakes near the banks of the pond.

Still, the villagers were convinced that Wŏnso Pond alone could cure their pain and sorrow, and they continued to make a practice of looking out over the pond for comfort.

Today, as ever, the water in the pond is as blue as blue can be—so blue that all who see it want to dye their white clothes the color of the water.

Down below the pond, where the eulalia reeds grow sky high, Wŏnso's water trickles gently out into a stream come springtime. The ancient willow trees encircling the pond seem dead at first glance, but fresh, green buds are emerging.

Out of nowhere a single beetle jumps onto the surface of the pond, glides freely in a circle, and flies off once again. And then, from somewhere in the distance, comes the faint sound of footsteps approaching.

2

The footsteps grow closer, and a girl comes bounding down the hillside. It appears as though she is being chased by something—or someone— for as she runs down the slope out of breath, she keeps looking behind her.

She is wearing a blouse dyed pink with the bindweed flowers that bloom throughout the village; her complexion is somewhat pale, but bright and unblemished. The basket of wild herbs she carries seems something of a burden, for she keeps switching it between her right arm and her left, and eventually balances it on her head. But here, too, it seems troublesome, and with a frown she finally holds the basket against her chest with both arms. She glances back up the hill every so often.

Soon afterwards a woodcutter—hardly more than a boy—appears waving a long stick at the girl.

"Stop it right there, you stupid girl!"

Shouting at the top of his lungs, the boy races toward her with incredible speed. The girl lifts the basket onto her head and runs down the hill as though her life depends on it, until she falls head over heels and tumbles to the base of the slope. The basket keeps rolling and rolling.

Finding this quite amusing, the woodcutter steps up to the girl with a snicker.

"Now why didn't you just give me some right away instead of running off like that? Did you really think you could beat me? Well, it serves you right! Happy now?"

The sniffling girl jumps to her feet, looking around for her missing basket. She spots it at the edge of the barley field just beyond them, then glares at the boy. She slowly turns her back to him. The boy quickly runs off, then brings back her basket.

"Look, you stupid girl! I'm going to eat all your sourstem. . . ."

Standing right in front of the girl, with the basket in his arm, he sticks his hand inside and takes out a piece of the sourstem. He starts to chew on it, smacking his lips all the while.

"Give it back, you jerk!" she says, still glaring.

She takes a step toward him and snatches away the basket. "Hah, ha!" The boy snickers, thinking her pouting funny. Then the mole on her eyebrow catches his eye. "Hey, what's that?" he asks, poking his finger into the girl's eyebrow.

"Ouch, that hurts! You idiot."

"Hey, you're pretty tough for a girl . . . Just give me one more . . . ?" The boy sticks out his hand with a sniffle.

Her fears eased by the gentle sound of his voice, she picks out one more stalk of sourstem and tosses it in his direction.

The woodcutter turns to pick the sourstem off the ground, and without bothering to peel off its skin, begins chewing on it, sucking out its juices. Sensing something missing, he turns to find the girl is gone. He looks around him and sees she's made her way well past the pond.

"Stupid girl! Going back all alone."

The words roll off his tongue unthinkingly. Staring out at the black dot of the girl's distant figure, suddenly he, too, wants to return to the village.

Shouting "Hey, Sŏnbi! Wait for me," he runs to catch up with her, but the girl is nowhere to be seen. "The nerve of that girl! Going back all alone . . . " he grumbles. "Where the heck did she go?"

After a brief rest, he happens to look down, and spots a scruffy-looking figure clearly reflected in the water. Surprised by what he sees, he bursts out laughing. As he stares into the water he swings his arms and legs and stretches out his neck. Just then the mole on the eyebrow of the pouting girl flashes into his mind. "Who's that?" He quickly spins his head around. Nothing there. "I'm telling you, that girl is just . . ." he

4

mutters under his breath as he looks out over the grove of willows into which the girl has long since disappeared. Suddenly thirsty, he peels off his sweat-soaked shirt, and flings it into the grass as he goes to the pond for a drink of water.

Lying flat on his stomach, he stretches out his neck and drinks thirstily. The water passing through his throat is oh, so sweet. After drinking his fill, he jumps to his feet and takes a deep breath of air.

Sweeping over Wŏnso Pond, a light breeze picks up the strong scent of grass in the distance, refreshing him as it dries the sweat beneath his arms. Then all of a sudden the boy spins around.

"My A-frame...?" he mutters unconsciously, as it dawns on him he's followed the girl far from where he left his pack. He scrambles back up the hill to his wooden pack, picks up his sickle, and goes into the woods where he starts cutting trees again.

Once he has returned with his newly cut wood, he sits down on the ground and leans against his A-frame. The scent of grass still strong in the air, he feels completely refreshed inside. Ready for a bit of a nap, he closes his eyes.

Suddenly he hears someone calling, "Hey, Ch'ŏtchae!"

3

Having just drifted off to sleep, the startled boy jumped to his feet. He quickly looked to either side of him, and there—gasping for breath— was Yi Sŏbang, hobbling toward him with the aid of a wooden crutch.

"Yi Sŏbang," the boy cried. Seeing the man, he felt happy, and also hungry.

"So this is where you've been. I've been searching all over for you, boy."

Leaning heavily on his crutch, Yi Sŏbang looked affectionately at Ch'ŏtchae. The shadows of the man and boy stretched far down to the base of the mountain. With a grunt Ch'ŏtchae lifted his load of wood onto his back.

"You were looking for me?"

"You bet I was. The sun's going down already! Now, listen to me, no more talking back like that to your mother."

Ch'ŏtchae laughed sweetly, as he walked side by side with Yi Sŏbang.

The strong light of the low sun was so blinding it was hard to tell if it was morning or sunset.

"Your mother cooked rice, you know. She's been waiting all day for you."

Yi Sŏbang kept mentioning his mother so that the boy's anger toward her might subside.

"She made rice?" asked the boy. Stopping in his tracks, Ch'ŏtchae looked over at Yi Sŏbang, and then stared into the distant paddies, lost in his thoughts. In the light of the setting sun the fields look as soft as silk.

"Yi Sŏbang, I sure hope I can start working in the fields this year."

Yi Sŏbang felt the boy's words pierce his heart. How can he want to work in the fields? He's just a boy, he thought. But he remembered how he himself, long ago, had been just as anxious to start working. Yi Sŏbang let out a deep sigh, staring out at Mount Pult'a with vacant eyes.

"I can be out weeding, Yi Sŏbang, and you could bring me lunch in the fields. . . And then . . ."

The boy was all smiles, happy just to talk about it. "And just what fields do you have to weed?" thought Yi Sŏbang, suppressing the impulse to speak his mind right then and there. Something surged up uncomfortably inside him.

"Then you won't have to go out begging any more, 'cause you can eat the rice that I grow in the fields . . ."

Yi Sŏbang stopped short in his tracks, and leaned heavily on his crutch. In all likelihood he had never in his entire life been touched so deeply. He had certainly never resented this heartless world so much as he did now. A servant ever since he'd been a child, he had suffered every kind of abuse until finally he'd had his leg broken. But, oh! How could any of that matter given what the boy had just said?

Ch'ŏtchae, meanwhile, continued to talk with excitement as he walked along, then turned to find that Yi Sŏbang wasn't following him any more.

"Yi Sŏbang, why are you crying?"

Wide-eyed, Ch'ŏtchae walked back toward the man. Yi Sŏbang wiped away his tears, then he set his crutch back into motion.

"Mom said something to you again, didn't she? Let's just kick her out of the way!"

6

The boy's eyes flashed with anger. Yi Sŏbang, shocked by his words, stared back at Ch'ŏtchae. Could he still be angry about the fight they'd had earlier? Why else would the child be so hateful towards his own mother?

"Ch'ŏtchae, don't let me hear you talk like that again."

As he spoke Yi Sŏbang wondered if the boy already sensed something about his mother's bad behavior. He thought of the men who visited her: Yu Sŏbang,* Yŏngsu and then the blacksmith who'd also been coming by recently. Yi Sŏbang lost the courage to speak any further.

The two entered a narrow path along the bank of a wheat field.

"Yi Sŏbang, how much money did you earn today?"

The man had the courage to take on this one.

"Come on, boy, what money? There was a party over at the tavern today. I stayed there all day long, and only just got back."

"A party .. ? So you brought back rice cakes, didn't you? You brought back rice cakes!"

Tapping his stick on the ground, he stared up at Yi Sŏbang.

"Yeah, I brought some back with me."

"How many?"

The boy licked his lips and moved up closer to the man.

"Not too many."

"You didn't give them to Mom again, did you?"

"No, I still have them," he replied, not wanting to disappoint the boy, but fully aware of the nervous twitch in his own eye.

"Yi Sŏbang, wouldn't it be great if all we had to eat was rice cakes?"

The boy's mouth was watering.

"This spring I'll bring you so many rice cakes your stomach will explode! How about that?"

Ch'ŏtchae laughed and struck a few rocks on the ground with his stick. At times like this, when the boy lowered his eyes, he looked more lovable than ever.

They arrived home in the dim light of dusk. Ch'ŏtchae's mother was standing outside the front door when she saw them coming.

---

*The reader should note that there are two characters with similar names in the novel: Yi Sŏbang, who lives with Ch'ŏtchae and his mother, and Yu Sŏbang, who works for Tŏkho.

"Why can't a tiger carry off that little brat!"

She spoke without thinking, and was horrified by what she'd just said. How long she had waited for the boy to come home, and now these nasty words escaped her lips.

Ch'ŏtchae let down his load of wood and sprang back up on his feet.

4

"My rice cakes!" cried Ch'ŏtchae, looking back at Yi Sŏbang, who had followed him into the room.

Ch'ŏtchae's mother quickly took down from the upper shelf a gourd bowl filled with rice cakes.

"You little brat, why are you always so hungry? Well, there's plenty, so eat your fill."

Snatching the bowl, Ch'ŏtchae grabbed a rice cake and began chomping away. His mother and Yi Sŏbang stared at the boy and felt pity for him, he must surely be famished to eat like this. In no time at all Ch'ŏtchae had finished them off.

"No more?"

Ch'ŏtchae's mother lit the lamp.

"No. Haven't you had enough already?"

"Just have some rice," said Yi Sŏngbang, who kept his eyes fixed on Ch'ŏtchae's mother, her face scarlet in the light of the flame.

"Mind you, Yi Sŏbang." Ch'ŏtchae's mother slipped back into the shadows. "You've spoiled the brat rotten with everything you give him. He doesn't know what it means to have a full belly. The greedy little thing will eat us out of house and home if we let him."

She had wanted to savor one more rice cake herself, and had left it in the gourd, hoping to eat it later with her son. But watching the hungry boy devour the treats made it hard for her to stick her hand back into the bowl. Now that she realized Ch'ŏtchae hadn't left a single piece for her to eat, she felt somewhat offended.

"Come on Yi Sŏbang, let's go to bed!" Ch'ŏtchae's eyes were heavy with sleep. However pleasant it was sitting across from Ch'ŏtchae's mother like this, Yi Sŏbang couldn't refuse the boy, and he managed, though just barely, to raise his stubborn hips off the floor. Leaning onto his crutch, he pulled himself to his feet.

"All right. Let's go."

Ch'ŏtchae got up as well, and hand in hand they went into the room across the hall. The boy quickly sank down into the warmest corner of the room, and after tossing his limbs a few times was fast asleep, gently snoring. Looking over at Ch'ŏtchae in the darkness, Yi Sŏbang thought about what the boy, all smiles, had said to him earlier so innocently. He let out a deep sigh.

Perhaps someone had already come into the inner room. His ears now seemed to pick up the sound of whispering voices. "I wonder which bastard's in there tonight?" he mumbled, bending his ear to figure out to whom the voice belonged. But they were speaking in whispers, and no matter how hard Yi Sŏbang tried to listen, it was impossible to identify tonight's visitor. All he could make out, from time to time, was the giggling voice of Ch'ŏtchae's mother.

He kept his eyes closed in an effort to fall asleep, but the whispering in the next room kept him wide awake, and instead of sleep it was anger that overcame him. He simply had to get out of this woman's house! What sort of life was this, anyway? Yi Sŏbang lost his temper almost every night, just as often as he was forced to witness this abomination.

He jumped out of bed, lit some tobacco, and took a seat by the window. Beams of moonlight streamed through the torn paper window like a rainbow. He took a drag on his pipe and exhaled very slowly. Billowing up through the air, dissolving into the moonlight . . . that smoke seemed just like the bitter feelings surging up inside him!

Without thinking, he began to gently stroke the wooden crutch he'd placed on the floor beside him. Whenever he was upset he caressed this wooden leg of his . . . this leg with no response! This stiff and heartless crutch! And yet, this wooden crutch was his one and only true companion.

"The nerve of that girl . . ."

Yi Sŏbang turned around in surprise at the sound of Ch'ŏtchae mumbling in his sleep. Could the boy really be thinking about some girl already? he wondered. If he'd had the power to keep the boy from growing up, he would have made sure Ch'ŏtchae remained a child forever. Perhaps it was rather selfish to think so, but he knew Ch'ŏtchae's future path in life looked no different from the one he himself had taken.

Yi Sŏbang moved over to Ch'ŏtchae's side and stared down at the boy. He was still breathing heavily in his sleep. This moment in time would be the happiest, it seemed, that Ch'ŏtchae would ever see. "I wish

I could work in the fields, too," Yi Sŏbang remembered the boy saying. He then laid his cheek down on top of the boy's.

Oh, the warmth that passed from Ch'ŏtchae's cheek to his own! And these heaving lungs full of life! If the boy had been made of his own flesh and blood, could Yi Sŏbang possibly have been more deeply affected?

Without thinking, he drew his arms around Ch'ŏtchae's neck and embraced him. "I'm nothing but a cripple, my boy, but from now on I live for you, and for you alone," he said, repeating the pledge several times over.

Just then, Yi Sŏbang lifted his head at the sound of something crashing.

5

"You filthy whore!"

The very pillars of the house seemed to shake with these thunderous words. Yi Sŏbang went to the door and crouched down beside it.

"What's gotten into you? Why say something like that?" said Ch'ŏtchae's mother.

"Shut up you tramp, you filthy slut! As if shacking up with that crippled beggar isn't enough. Now you're screwing around with this moron. You no-good bitch!"

Yi Sŏbang then heard someone spit. But it was the words "shacking up with that crippled beggar" that rang in his ears. The life seemed to drain right out of him, and he lost the strength to lift even a finger.

"Oh, my, they're really going at it."

He could hear the rough sounds of a scuffle. Yŏngsu and the new one, the blacksmith, seemed to be at grips with each other.

"They say, 'New-born pups don't fear a tiger.' Well, they must have made that one up for morons like you. You pathetic fool! Did you really think she was was pure?"

Whatever happened next, it was followed by a blood-curdling scream.

"I'll slice you up into pieces, you bastards!"

"No, not a knife! Not a knife!"

Hearing Ch'ŏtchae's mother scream, Yi Sŏbang jumped to his feet in alarm, grabbed his crutch, and dashed out of his room. The door to the inner room had fallen into the dirt hallway, but without a lamp on it was too dark to see inside.

Ch'ŏtchae's mother ran out into the hallway.

"Take this! Take it!"

Gasping for breath, she thrust the knife towards Yi Sŏbang. He took it and rushed into the kitchen, but not knowing where to put it, he shuffled back and forth for some time, finally hiding the knife inside a bundle of firewood. Then he returned to the inner room.

"Why are you two doing this? You're both decent men. Please control yourselves!" he shouted, trying to break apart the two men.

"Stay out of this, you fool . . . Oh wait, you're the cripple! So maybe you're just looking for a beating."

One of them gave Yi Sŏbang a powerful kick and he crumpled to the floor. His crutch had flown to the side, and he began searching for it in vain. Only after crawling frantically over the entire dirt floor did he manage to find it. The bitterness that had built up inside him for many years was now at the point of exploding. He did his best to suppress the feeling, grabbed his crutch, and hurried outside.

Normally, there would have been a crowd of spectators gathered outside, but tonight there was no one, perhaps because it was so late. He made his way over to the woodpile, where he stood staring into the sky.

There, soaring high above dark Mount Pult'a, was the brilliant moon! Even that moon, it seemed, had come out in order to ridicule his crippled leg.

"Yi Sŏbang!"

He turned around at the sound of Ch'ŏtchae's voice. The boy came running outside and stopped to relieve himself, squirting a long stream of urine to the side. Yi Sŏbang thought of Ch'ŏtchae's bad temper and was suddenly frightened. "What if that boy ups and . . ." he thought, panicked. He rushed to Ch'ŏtchae and managed to grab onto him by the seat of his pants.

Having finished peeing, Ch'ŏtchae was on the point of running back to the house in a rage.

"You fucking idiots!" The boy was screaming at the top of his lungs, but Yi Sŏbang had been quick to grab onto him. The boy responded with several violent blows, yelling, "Let go of me!"

"Ch'ŏtchae! Ch'ŏtchae! Don't do it! You'll get hurt, do you hear me?"

"I don't care. Those bastards!"

This time the boy rammed his head into Yi Sŏbang's chest and kicked at him mercilessly. The man tumbled over backwards again. Ch'ŏtchae flew over to his wooden pack, picked up his sickle, and ran into the house.

"No! No!"

Yi Sŏbang saw this was a matter of life or death. He scrambled inside on all fours until he managed to grab hold of Ch'ŏtchae's ankle. Ch'ŏtchae's mother, dashed out of the inner room and snatched the crossbar off the front gate.

"You little brat! Why aren't you in bed, instead of causing all this trouble?" she shouted at her son.

"Me? Those bastards in there are the ones causing trouble!" He yanked on his mother's long hair, pulling her head downwards.

The crashing sound from the inner room grew more and more violent. Yi Sŏbang felt goosebumps all over. If the men came any closer, Ch'ŏtchae would likely end up with a broken bone. Yi Sŏbang vividly recalled how he'd gotten his own leg broken by fighting with the master of the household long ago, and he feared the boy was dangerously close to meeting a similar fate.

Yi Sŏbang took several good kicks from Ch'ŏtchae, rolling this way and that on the ground, but he never lost his grip on the boy's ankle. A trickle of bright blood now ran from his nose.

"Ch'ŏtchae! You keep this up and I'll never give you another rice cake again!"

He'd said the words without thinking.

"Do you mean it? Yi Sŏbang!"

His chest heaving breathlessly, Ch'ŏtchae twisted to face him. Yi Sŏbang sprung from the ground and swept the boy's head into his embrace. Within an instant, tears were rolling down the man's face.

6

As she plaited thatch in the backyard, Sŏnbi's mother was filling a bowl at her side with grains of rice she'd removed from some straw. Sŏnbi came bounding toward her.

"Mom!" she shouted.

She looked up curiously at her daughter, who ran into the yard short of breath.

"Don't tell me you got into trouble again?"

Sŏnbi shook her head emphatically, then put her lips to her mother's ear.

"Guess what, Mom… Sinch'ŏn Taek and the Missus up at the big house got into a huge fight, and Master scolded them something terrible."

Sŏnbi's breath tickled her mother's ear, and the woman cocked her head slightly to the side.

"Those two are at each other's throats day and night. Did anyone get hurt?"

"Remember how Master used to beat up his wife? Well, this time he beat Sinch'ŏn Taek just horrible. I felt so sorry for her."

Looking rather sad, Sŏnbi stuck her hand inside the rice-filled gourd without thinking and swished the kernels of grain.

"A concubine needs a good beating now and then, you know. Is it fair for his wife to get it all the time?"

The woman stared at the face of her daughter, who seemed somewhat distant. There was a pink hue to Sŏnbi's cheeks, which had blossomed with the arrival of spring.

"But Mom, Sinch'ŏn Taek told me that she didn't even want to come here. She said her father sold her for a lot of money and that she had no choice in coming here."

"Well, I do remember hearing that … Just goes to show, money's the most frightening thing of all."

Sŏnbi's mother pictured Sinch'ŏn Taek sitting on the floor in tears, and once again she began worrying about the future in store for Sŏnbi, this beautiful bud just beginning to flower.

"Now, you get on back to work. What are you doing just sitting there, anyway? You've got laundry to starch today, don't you?"

"I guess so."

Sŏnbi reluctantly rose to her feet at her mother's words, then took another look inside the gourd. She smiled.

"Hey, Mom! If you hull all this rice, I bet we'll get a good quarter bushel."

"Okay, enough from you. Now go on!"

Sŏnbi put down the bowl and headed out of the yard. Her mother watched as she walked away. How fast time flew by, she sighed. She realized with a broken heart that she couldn't keep Sŏnbi living with her for much longer.

The woman let out a deep sigh, stuck out her hand to grab another bunch of thatch, then stared at her hands for a while absentmindedly. Her fingers had been scraped by the straw and were covered with tiny red scratches. Thoughts of her husband immediately came to mind.

As poor as they were while he was still alive, she had never done outdoor chores this like before, whether it was plaiting thatch or rebuilding reed fences. She had gone about her own business unconcerned with these repairs, which she'd assumed were somehow naturally taken care of by springtime.

But after losing her husband, she'd had to do everything with her own two hands. Not only did it take her twice the effort to complete the chores, but she was never satisfied with her handiwork.

The housework was, well, housework, and even in a small two-room hut, the tiniest stone had to be returned to its proper place, and not a single husk of grain could be wasted.

While her husband was alive, she had never appreciated the gray loam with which they used to plaster the walls or the brooms with which they swept out the backyard; she had used them as necessary and then thrown them away. But these little things she had once taken for granted, she now could not use as she pleased. She had nothing unless she made it with her own two hands.

With so much on her mind, Sŏnbi's mother worried herself no end trying to figure out whose help she could enlist to climb up her roof and rethatch it. She had stayed up for several nights to make the straw rope she would need, and she had only just managed to finish four coils of it. By tomorrow she would be finished plaiting the thatch as well, but she still needed to ask some of the men in the village to help her. The ridge thatch placed along the center of the roof had to be cut in a special way; the thatch itself had to be laid out over the roof; and then all of it had to be tied in place with rope.

She'd gone over and over in her mind whom she might get to come help her. But in the end, she reconsidered. Oh, hell, expert or not, I'll just try doing it myself, she thought, glancing up at the roof once again.

She had neglected the job the previous year, which explained the green tufts of grass she saw sprouting here and there where the thatch had given in.

"Why did he have to go and leave me all alone?" she said softly, jumping to her feet. She spun her head around and looked out at the other

14

houses around her. Well-kept houses, all around! Big or small, each of them was neatly thatched with brand new straw!

The sunshine now bathed them in a brilliant, yellow light.

7

Roof after golden roof, glowing in the brilliant spring sunshine! How soft and lovely they were!

She closed her eyes tightly, but the roofs appeared even more vividly in her mind. And then among them appeared an image of her husband's rugged hands, followed by the face of the dead man himself. He had refused to close his eyes on his family even as he gasped for his last bit of air.

Kim Minsu had been such a good man, so gentle and honest. Though he'd worked under Chŏng Tŏkho for close to two decades, he was the sort of person who had never pocketed a single copper. And no matter how tired he was, if Tŏkho gave him an order, he would rush off to work, be it rain or shine.

Everyone in the village, came to trust Minsu, even Tŏkho. And that was why Tŏkho entrusted to him, and him alone, any jobs that required the collection of large amounts of money.

Eight years ago this fall Tŏkho had sent him on just such an errand. Sŏnbi at the time was seven years old.*

That morning huge snowflakes had been falling gently from the sky since dawn. Minsu rose early as he always did, and went to Tŏkho's. He had just swept out the house and the courtyard and was boiling feed for the cows when Tŏkho came up to him.

"Can you go over to Pangch'ukkol for me today?"

Minsu bowed his head submissively.

"Yes, of course."

"Well, come inside then."

Passing through the cauldrons of cow feed, Tŏkho made his way into the living quarters, with Minsu following. Tŏkho rummaged through a stationary chest placed in the warm corner of the room, took out his account book, and looked through it for a moment.

---

*In Korea children are normally considered one year old at birth, and add a year to their age with each passing of the New Year rather than with the passing of a birthday.

"This idiot in Pangch'ukkol owes me a good fifty wŏn . . . I wonder if you'll get much out of him, though. He's a tough one."

Minsu said nothing, his head still bowed.

"So you'll go? If you can't get anything out of him, I'll have to send Kkoltchi's father over. Come on now, speak up!"

Minsu didn't know what he should say; he just sat there hesitating as the color rose in his face.

"Why do you have to be such a fool? Just go, will you? Oh, and another thing. Make it perfectly clear that if he doesn't pay up this time, I'm pursuing legal action. And shake him up a bit, will you!"

Tŏkho stared at Minsu with bloodthirsty eyes.

"Stop by Myŏngho's house, and Iksŏn's, too, on your way over there."

"Yes, Sir."

"Be sure to go today."

Having pressed Minsu one last time, Tŏkho put his account book back into the chest and stood up. He cleared his throat a couple of times and then went outside. Minsu followed right behind him. The pleasant smell of the cow feed boiling in the work kitchen had already filled the air. By the time Minsu had scooped out all the feed from the cauldrons and carried it into the stalls, the cows had already caught a whiff of it. They were gently lifting themselves off the floor and moving to the side of the feeding troughs. Among clouds of warm rising steam, they happily chomped away at their meal.

After shoveling all the feed, Minsu headed outside. The snowflakes were still falling heavily, without even the faintest sound. He looked up at the sky anxiously.

"In this snow . . ?" he mumbled.

When he arrived home, Minsu scraped the snow from his shoes. Sŏnbi's mother looked at her husband with a questioning eye.

"You're not going out again, are you?"

"Yes. To collect some money."

"What? On a day like this?"

"There's nothing to worry about. When the flakes are this large, it means it's warmer outside."

Sŏnbi had been staring at her father, bright-eyed, but at this, she jumped up and ran into his arms.

"Daddy, can I go too?"

She looked up at him imploringly. Minsu gave his daughter a hug, then sat in front of his dinner tray. He made a gesture of eating some food, but then stood up again.

"I'll be gone for a few days, so keep a good eye on Sŏnbi. And keep the fire going so it's nice and warm."

"What is he doing sending you out on a day like this? Does he think the rest of us are built of iron?" muttered Sŏnbi's mother, picturing Tŏkho before her eyes.

"Watch what you say in front of . . ."

Minsu glared at his wife. Her face colored and she took her daughter's hand into her own. Then Minsu stroked Sŏnbi's head a few times, opened the door, and went outside. His eyes were blinded by the brilliant white snow.

"Come back safely, dear."

He could just make out his wife's farewell as he set out with long strides. With his eyes cast to the ground he walked for a bit, but then turned suddenly at the sound of Sŏnbi crying. She was running to him through the snow.

8

Minsu unconsciously took several steps toward Sŏnbi, before her mother grabbed her from behind. Minsu signaled with his hand for them to go back inside, then turned around.

The snow was falling more heavily than before. The giant, flower-like flakes landed on his lips and melted into his mouth. Each one felt like a refreshing sip of ice-cold water.

What path there was to follow had been completely buried by the snow, and the familiar trees alongside the road were obscured by the falling snowflakes. Even Mount Pult'a, high up there in the sky, was nothing more than a faint shadow.

When Minsu strayed from the path he would walk in the furrows of fields, or on the banks of rice paddies, until he located a village and managed to find the trail once again. His snow-drenched shoes had by now frozen solid, and they crackled as he walked.

Trudging through the snow like this, Minsu just barely made his way to Pangch'ukkol after stopping off at several houses along the way. It was now dusk, two days after he had first set out.

"Hello? Is anyone home?"

The doorframe was stuffed with rags to keep out the wind. When the man of the house opened the door, his face seemed to turn a shade paler.

"You've come all this way, in this weather? Please come inside."

Minsu entered the room, but it was so dark inside he couldn't see an inch in front of him. He sat with his eyes closed for a while. Slowly opening his eyes, he found it difficult to breathe in the stuffy room. He should never have come here, he thought, with regret. It didn't look as though there would be food to serve for dinner here.

"You've come so far in this snow . . . I've been meaning to pay you a visit, but I've given only empty promises for so long now that I . . . It must have been awfully cold out there."

The man was at a total loss as to where to begin.

"Set out a dinner tray, dear. Though we haven't much to offer."

Smoothing down her hair, his wife slowly stood up and left the room. Minsu, trying to pull himself together, noticed something in the opposite corner of the room. He could hear little voices coming from under a dirty quilt, which lifted slightly to expose several pairs of dark glimmering eyes. Again he heard the sound of giggles. He couldn't tell exactly how many children were there, but he knew right away there were more than just two.

The storm must have picked up force, for he could hear gusts of wind sweeping up against the house, then fading away. The paper flaps insulating the window frames fluttered wildly in the wind, and the snow drove itself little by little into the room. Minsu was suddenly struck by the desire to leave this house and find a cave or a hovel to sleep in rather than spend the night here. Yet at this time of night there was no way of knowing where to find such a cave, and it was impossible to simply turn around and leave without good cause. He sat there apprehensively, in a state of extreme unease, fearing that more than one person in this room might die over the course of the night.

A dinner tray was brought in for him. Feeling hungry Minsu scooped up a good spoonful of the main dish only to find that it was gruel, not rice. It was made of millet, boiled down with dried radish leaves. Though Minsu had always lived as a servant, he had never in his entire life eaten anything like this before. The smell of millet hulls, in particular, made it hard to stomach, but he did his best to slurp it down.

Just then a few children jumped up, one after the other, out of the corner of the room.

"Mommy, I want some food!"

"I want some too, Mommy!"

The man of the house glared at them threateningly.

"I should beat the brains out of you little brats!" he said, and turned back to Minsu.

"Please finish your meal. Those kids will cry for more even after they've just eaten."

Minsu's fingers trembled ever so slightly. He lost the courage to use his spoon any longer. He placed it down, and drew himself away from the tray.

"But . . . but why won't you eat? I suppose it's not good enough."

The man scratched his head and pushed the tray to the side. All four boys and girls swept out of the corner and grappled with each other over the dishes on the tray. In the scuffle that ensued none of them managed to eat any food.

The man jumped to his feet, picked up a long pipe and began striking the children. At a loss as to what was happening, Minsu grabbed hold of the man.

"What are you doing? They're just kids. Come on now, put it down. Put it down."

One of the children, in the meantime, had attached his lips to the edge of the tray and began sucking off the gruel that had spilled down its side. Ashamed that a stranger was witnessing this horrible scene, the man's wife grabbed the child and held him to her breast. Pretending to wipe away the snivel from the child's nose, she then dabbed the bow on her blouse into the corners of her eyes.

9

Perhaps in consideration of the stranger who was trying to hold him back, the man put down his hand and sat, now winded.

"Oh, who knows why we have so many kids. A sin in a previous lifetime, I guess. It must have been something terrible for us to end up like this."

Though he had just beaten his children in a fit of rage, the man felt so unjustly treated by the world he could barely hold back his tears. Distraught that he could neither feed nor clothe his hungry kids, he regretted the fact that he'd beaten the poor things too.

Moments earlier they'd been screaming and shedding tears, but now they whispered and giggled beneath their dirty quilt as though nothing had ever happened.

Minsu slept not a wink that night, as thoughts of all sorts churned through his mind. While he told himself this was another man's dilemma, he worried that something terrible like this might happen to his own family too. One after another these thoughts raced through his mind, as though driven by the wind that whipped the paper flaps sealing the windows.

Having remained awake all through the night, Minsu got up before the red of dawn had broken. Perhaps because he'd spent the night in the cold room, his body felt heavy, and he seemed to have caught a cold.

"You must be freezing."

The man of the house rose and sat directly across from Minsu.

"Well . . ." Minsu stuck a cigarette into his mouth and started to smoke, unable to offer a more direct reply. He pushed the pack of cigarettes in front of his host. The man bowed his head humbly, accepted one, and put it in his mouth. As Minsu took a deep drag on his cigarette, he heard the sounds of whispers in the corner. He lifted his head and looked in their direction.

From out of that pitch-black corner came the constant sound of whispering voices. Just about now Sŏnbi was probably getting up out of bed and whispering something to her own mother, maybe asking where her daddy had gone, he imagined. Minsu then saw Sŏnbi's face flash before him in the corner of the room.

"Mommy, I'm hungry!"

Minsu was shocked by how similar the voice was to Sŏnbi's. Unconsciously he flung his cigarette onto the floor. He shrugged off the idea that the voice might be Sŏnbi's, and yet for some reason this voice still pierced his heart, unbearably so.

Minsu felt horrible. He wanted nothing more than to get out of this place. When he stood up to go, he pulled out a one-wŏn note from his pocket without thinking.

"Get your kids something to eat!" he said, pressing the note into the palm of the man's hand.

20

The man was bewildered. But when he realized that this was money he was holding in his hand, he felt like collapsing onto the floor and breaking into tears. Minsu realized that his own legs were trembling. Then he pictured the furious expression he was likely to see on Tŏkho's face, and shuddered. He pulled himself away from the poor man, who had by now grabbed hold of him, and made his way out.

The snow had swirled into drifts on either side of him, becoming mountains of snow in some places. Minsu walked briskly along, his shoes crunching softly. He saw bird footprints here and there on the surface of the white snow, which to him looked like flower petals.

But Minsu felt sick to his stomach. He had no idea what he would tell Tŏkho. Considering all his options, should he just lie and say he'd only collected two wŏn from the other debtors? That way he could repay it later without anyone finding out . . . But then again, it was better tell the truth than a lie. The master of the household was a human being, after all, and if he knew the whole story, could he actually blame him? Certainly not . . .

After struggling for some time, Minsu found neither of the two options reassuring. He regretted that there was no one around he could ask for advice. In the end, he decided that he would tell a lie, if only to put his nerves to rest. But this had little of the intended effect. Why, he reproached himself, should a grown man worry about a single wŏn?

Having wracked his brain with these foolish thoughts, Minsu arrived at the outskirts of his village. He should have been delighted to be home, but he couldn't bring himself to go straight in. Only after standing for a while, staring distractedly at the entrance to the village, did he finally enter.

Having made it to Tŏkho's house, Minsu brushed off his shoes in front of the men's quarters and hoping the master wasn't at home, quietly pushed open the door. When he caught a whiff of Tŏkho's favorite cigarettes in the cloud of smoke that swept out the door, he hesitated.

"You must be cold. Come on in and warm up by the fire."

Tŏkho had craned his head around to look at Minsu. Each of the old men, sitting in a circle, offered him a short greeting. Minsu had no choice but to go inside. Sidestepping the charcoal brazier, he came in and took a seat.

10

Tŏkho pulled out the abacus from the top of his stationary chest.

"So did he cough up anything this time? That idiot in Pangch'ukkol?"

Tŏkho hated the man so much that he refused to call him by name. Minsu's face colored, and he hesitated for a second before speaking.

"No, he didn't."

"What? Well, don't tell me you just let him off, did you? Without twisting his arm or anything?"

"He didn't have the means to . . ."

Minsu couldn't finish his sentence, and simply hung his head. What came to his mind was an image of that little child sucking gruel from the dinner tray as though he were suckling at his mother's breast. The sight of that dark room now flashed in front of his eyes. When Minsu hesitated to speak, however, Tŏkho lost his temper.

"How dare someone without the means to pay borrow someone else's money!" he suddenly screamed.

Minsu started and moved back slightly in his seat. He was afraid that Tŏkho's hand was about to lash out at him.

"What about the others?"

"I . . . I got something from them."

The tight lines in Tŏkho's brow loosened a little.

"Okay, how much did you get out of them?"

"About three wŏn . . ."

Minsu was shocked by his own words. 'I collected two wŏn' was what he had planned to say—what had brought him to say three? Minsu right then and there decided he would tell Tŏkho the truth. The ringing in his ears was frightening.

"So you only got interest out of them . . . Well, that idiot in Pangch'ukkol is going to be a headache! He's trying to get by without paying his debts, is he? Just give me what you have."

Minsu took the money from his wallet and pushed it over to Tŏkho. His hand was visibly shaking. Tŏkho pulled the bills toward him and counted them.

"This is only two wŏn . . ."

Tŏkho looked over at him with a questioning eye. Minsu slowly lifted his head. The look in his eyes seemed to be begging for forgiveness— like the innocent plea of a young child.

22

"The man's kids were . . . they were starving, so I just . . . I gave them the rest."

Minsu's eyes were brimming with tears.

"You what?"

Instantly Tŏkho screwed up his eyes, and flung the abacus at Minsu. It hit him right between the eyes and fell to the ground with a rattle.

"Are you crazy! Your goddamn generosity has no place in my house. Now get the hell out! I make the decisions around here, so you give away your own damn money, not mine!

"Don't be so hard on him," said the other men, sitting around in their own circle.

"Well, it'd be one thing if he was hungry and had to buy something for himself to eat, or if he needed the money to get his job done. But the idiot didn't even collect a dime for his travel, and now this is the crap that I have to deal with. Don't I have a right to get angry? Now you, get out!"

Tŏkho jumped to his feet and kicked Minsu with all his might. If not for the others, he would have beaten him to his heart's content, but he was too worried about his reputation, so he held back his anger and sat down again.

"It's not a question of just a single wŏn. What right does this idiot have to give away even a penny of my money, especially to a man trying to rob me of his entire debt!

His teeth were now grinding with a vengeance, and he suddenly sprang on top of Minsu with the look of murder in his eyes. Then he quickly left the room. The others sitting in the circle scattered out in different directions. Shortly afterwards, Minsu regained consciousness and found the room completely empty. His vision was somewhat cloudy now, and when he put his hand to his brow, he felt something different about it.

Though Minsu had been beaten and insulted by the master of the house, for some reason he was neither resentful nor offended. On the contrary, he felt quite calm and composed, as though a heavy burden had been lifted off his shoulders.

He got right up and made his way home.

When he opened the brush gate, Sŏnbi and her mother ran out of the house to greet him. Sŏnbi threw her arms around him, and as Minsu held her tightly in his arms, his eyes filled unexpectedly with tears, blurring the path before him. The picture of those four little children again flashed into his mind. *I wonder if they got anything to eat today?* he thought, stepping into his own house.

Sŏnbi's mother was staring at the sight of father and daughter.

"What happened to your forehead?"

"Why? What's the matter with it?"

Minsu put his hand to his brow and rubbed it again. Then he lay down on the floor. Sŏnbi's mother took out a blanket and draped it over him. *Did he have some kind of run-in with troublemakers? Or was he just tired from his trip?* she wondered.

"Can I fix you some supper?"

"Well . . . maybe some rice porridge . . . Make me some, would you?"

Sŏnbi's mother now knew for sure that her husband was not well, for he had asked for porridge. She was about to ask him if he was in any pain when Minsu closed his eyes tightly and rolled onto his side.

11

The next day Minsu was terribly sick and unable to get out of bed. Sŏnbi's mother did everything she could to care for him, but nothing seemed to help.

Several days later, Sŏnbi's mother came in from the yard to speak to Minsu. The rims of her eyes were red and swollen.

"Is it true that the master of the big house hit you with his abacus?"

"Who told you that?"

"Just about everyone who saw it happen, that's who."

"I don't want to hear it! Don't pay attention to such rumors. And even if the master did hit me, do you really think he meant to hurt me? We're like a father and son to each other . . . "

"So he did hit you then."

"I said I don't want to hear about it, didn't I?"

Minsu groaned and turned over onto his side, but then his eyes flashed open and he looked over at his wife, as though he'd just thought of something.

"If by any chance I end up dying, I don't want you to take those rumors seriously."

Minsu knew that his afflictions were far from ordinary. But not in his wildest dreams had he ever imagined Tŏkho had caused them. As soon

24

as the word "die" fell from her husband's lips, Sŏnbi's mother felt dizzy, and she couldn't bring herself to mention the subject again.

Within only a few days' time, Minsu passed away. He would never know how Sŏnbi threw her arms around his body, sobbing with all her heart.

As she reflected on these past events, Sŏnbi's mother soon had tears running down her cheeks. She wiped them away and once again looked up at her roof—that dingy roof without a master. How many thousands of times her husband's strong hands had worked their magic upon it!

At the sound of the brush gate opening, Sŏnbi's mother assumed that her daughter had returned, and she quickly sat down. She removed the traces of tears from her face, and started plaiting her straw again. Then she thought she heard someone at the door. Maybe it's not Sŏnbi, perhaps someone else from the village has dropped by, she thought, tilting her head to listen for a clue.

"Anybody here?"

As soon as Sŏnbi's mother heard the voice, she knew whom it belonged to.

"My goodness, what brings you here?" She got up immediately and opened the back door. Sinch'ŏn Taek was standing there in the doorway, looking somewhat out of sorts. Her tired, puffy eyes were lit up by only a trace of a smile.

"Are you busy?" She ended her sentence with a deep sigh.

"No, please, come in."

Sinch'ŏn Taek entered the room and took a seat. She stared out blankly at the backyard, as though distracted by something on her mind.

"I bet my mom is also . . ."

She couldn't bring herself to finish the thought. Sŏnbi's mother understood what she wanted to say, though, and she felt sorry for the young woman.

"Are you feeling all right, dear?"

"Well, I'm afraid I'm going to have to move back home for good tomorrow . . ."

Tears were now streaming down her cheeks. Sŏnbi's mother was at a loss as to what to say and simply sat there silently for a while before speaking.

"Come now, what makes you say such a thing?"

"Well, I'm not going to be able to live in that house much longer. I mean, with him on my case all the time about giving birth to a son, how long do you think I'll last without giving him what he wants?"

Each time this young woman of hardly twenty years mentioned not having a child, Sŏnbi's mother looked over at her as though she was being rather silly. At the same time, though, she couldn't help feeling sorry for her.

"Well, what did he say to you?"

"You heard that I missed my period last month, didn't you? Well, I just got it again this morning!"

"You did? That happens once in a while, you know."

"Oh, why does the damn thing have to cause me so much grief?"

Ever since Sinch'ŏn Taek had missed her last period, Tŏkho had been badgering the villagers with orders for special foods and herbal tonics to give her.

When Tŏkho worshipped her like Heaven, Sinch'ŏn Taek was somehow easy to hate, but today the girl was sitting there simply a ball of nerves, and Sŏnbi's mother found herself both sorry for the young woman as well as amused at the situation.

"You'll have a baby sooner or later, dear. You've still got plenty of time, you know."

"Well, that's what I say. It's not like I'm forty years old, or even thirty. I don't know why he's making such a big fuss."

Sinch'ŏn Taek let out a deep sigh.

"I guess I'll have to go back home tomorrow. He keeps telling me I have to leave anyway."

"Oh, the master is just saying that. He doesn't really mean it."

Sinch'ŏn Taek shook her head and lowering her voice said, "He's been visiting Kannan's house recently, you know."

Sŏnbi's mother flashed a look of surprise at her guest.

12

A period of some three years passed by.

Sŏnbi's mother had lain in bed now for several days with chest trouble, and instead of going to work at the big house, Sŏnbi kept a vigil at her mother's bedside.

As always, they could not afford an oil lamp, so they burned wild sesame oil, poured into a small saucer just to the side of the bed. The flame from the saucer spewed out a long, black stream of smoke and flickered fiercely in the drafts that swept in through cracks around the door.

Her mother seemed to have fallen asleep, so Sŏnbi moved closer to the flame. Her rosy cheeks glowed all the more in the light of the oil. She stared vacantly into the flame, then slowly stood up and walked into the next room.

A short time later she returned with her sewing kit in hand, sat down facing the light and set herself to work.

At the sound of her mother groaning, Sŏnbi put down her sewing and turned to face her.

"Does it hurt again, Mom?"

Her mother's sunken eyes opened, but just barely.

"Bring me some water."

"You know you're not supposed to drink much water."

Sŏnbi came to her mother's side and looked down upon her. Maybe it was because she'd been sick for so long, but her mother seemed to give off a smell.

"Just get me some!" she cried, a bit louder.

Sŏnbi pleaded with her mother to the point of tears. But she wouldn't listen, and after crying out a few more times, she lifted her head up to get out of bed on her own. Sŏnbi knew she'd eventually have to give in, so she went into the kitchen to boil some water and brought a cup out to her mother.

"How could I drink that, you little rat!" said her mother, seeing the steam rising out of the cup. "Get me some cold water!"

"Oh, Mom, please . . ."

She helped her mother up and held the cup to her mouth. The woman shook her head a couple of times, then finally took a few sips of the hot water before lying back down again.

"Sŏnbi," she called out a few minutes later. Sŏnbi put down her sewing and again came to her mother's side.

"I saw your father in my dreams last night. But I wasn't excited to see him or even angry. It was just like things always were back when he was alive . . . He had you on his back, and he was heading off somewhere, so I followed after him and asked him where he was going. But he just kept on walking without saying anything to me . . . What do you think it all means?"

Sŏnbi now saw her father's face flash into her mind. But it wasn't clear, and she could just barely make out his features, as though his face were shrouded in mist. She looked at her mother. It seemed as though the woman was, at that very moment, staring at the ghost of her husband. A terrifying thought crossed Sŏnbi's mind, and she felt goosebumps all over.

"Mom!"

Sŏnbi placed her hand on her mother. Then she sat up close and stroked her face. Her mother's eyes rolled upward and stared at the ceiling. Those frightening eyes then turned onto her daughter.

"What's the matter, mom?"

Staring up at her daughter, Sŏnbi's mother began to sob with short gasps of air. Her lips began to tremble.

"Sŏnbi, we've got to find someone to . . . to take care of you . . ."

Her mother was speaking clearly, which comforted Sŏnbi. But it was a scary thing to watch anyone dying, thought Sŏnbi, especially when it was your own parent.

Just then, Sŏnbi heard the sound of the brush gate opening, and she quickly looked over to the front door. As the door opened she saw Tŏkho step into the room. Alarmed, Sŏnbi rose to her feet.

"She's still sick, is she? Well now, that's too bad."

Tŏkho spoke with concern in his voice, standing just inside the door and looking over at Sŏnbi's mother. When Sŏnbi's mother realized it was Tŏkho, she made an effort to sit up.

"Lie back down. Lie down," Tŏkho said. "Did she have anything to eat today?"

He looked over at Sŏnbi, who lifted her head slightly, but then hung it again.

"She hasn't been able to eat anything."

"Now, that won't do, will it? We should have some honey over at the house. You come on over and get some, mix it up with water and give it to her, you hear? She won't get any better if she doesn't eat."

Tŏkho lit his pipe, stuck it into his mouth, then looked as though he were about to sit down.

"What do you call that? How are you supposed to live here with that for a lamp?"

28

Tŏkho took out his wallet, pulled out a five-wŏn note, and tossed it in front of Sŏnbi. Sŏnbi was shocked. Then, once again, the front door rattled open.

13

They looked toward the door in surprise. It was Tŏkho's younger wife, Kannan, who had joined the family after Tŏkho had driven Sinch'ŏn Taek out of his house. After opening the door, Kannan hesitated, unable to bring herself to come inside. Tŏkho was glaring at her.

"What are you doing here? How dare you barge into someone's home like that . . . like some sort of commoner! Where the hell did you learn to call on people like that?"

Witnessing this spectacle, Sŏnbi and her mother did not know what to say to relieve their own embarrassment. After staring at the two for some time, Sŏnbi's mother finally broke the silence.

"Please come inside."

"What does she need to come inside for? Get out of here, you little bitch. Who ever taught you to barge in on people like that? I said, get out!"

His hand clenched into a fist, Tŏkho glared at the young woman.

"Oh, no. Please don't be upset with her," said Sŏnbi, standing up in the confusion of the moment.

Kannan's face turned bright red and she ran outside. Tŏkho slammed the door shut and came back into the room. He noticed the five-wŏn bill still on the floor.

"The nerve of that little bitch . . . Now, here, just take this and put it away somewhere. And you be sure to get a new lamp tomorrow and call the doctor. You hear?"

Sŏnbi's mother poked her daughter sharply in the side. Only then did Sŏnbi reply,

"Yes, Sir."

Sŏnbi still found it hard to pick up the money. And yet, she couldn't just give it back to him. As she hesitated, her mother picked up the money and thrust it into her hand. Sŏnbi accepted it reluctantly and shoved it beneath the bedding.

Tŏkho, standing there awkwardly, turned to leave.

"Don't forget to come by tomorrow for the honey."

"She won't," replied her mother. She poked her daughter in the side again and gestured for her to follow Tŏkho out the door.

Sŏnbi slowly got up and followed Tŏkho out to the gate.

"Goodbye, Sir."

"Stop by the house tomorrow, okay?"

"Yes, Sir."

Sŏnbi gently closed the gate behind Tŏkho and went back inside. She felt her heart racing for fear that Kannan might for some reason barge in again. She came to her mother's side and sat down.

"Mom, why do you suppose Kannan came by?"

Her mother had been trying to figure this out as well.

"Well, I . . . Oh, no, it's coming back again."

Her face contorted and she fell into a fit of coughing. As Sŏnbi rubbed her mother's back, she wondered what could have brought Kannan over so suddenly. Neither of them ever visits us here, so what could they have been thinking? Was it because mom was sick? Or was it something else? No matter how she thought about it, it was downright suspicious that both of them just happened to stop by.

Kannan had once been Sŏnbi's very best friend. But ever since she'd become Tŏkho's younger wife, the two had grown apart, and whenever it was unavoidable that they cross paths, they simply greeted each other with a faint smile. One day Sŏnbi had found herself suddenly working as a servant to her best friend, and while she was never bitter because of it, it had made things quite awkward between them.

After moaning for some time, her mother quieted down again. Sŏnbi covered her with the quilt and went over to the light. When she picked up her sewing, though, she couldn't concentrate on her work, and made little progress. She neatly folded her sewing and stared vacantly into the flame.

"Buy an oil lamp and get some light for this room . . ."

She murmured this to herself, picturing Tŏkho's face as he'd handed her the five-wŏn bill. Never before had he ever shown them such kindness! Sŏnbi hadn't the slightest idea how to interpret it, but a sense of unease unlike anything she'd ever felt before, weighed heavily on her chest.

She turned to her mother.

"Mom!" she called. But there was no reply.

She heard the faint sound of snoring. Her mother slept like this whenever her chest pain subsided. Sŏnbi couldn't grasp what had caused her to call out for her mother so suddenly. She stared at her mother's pale face, and then thought of the five-wŏn bill she had earlier slipped under the bedding. Unwittingly, she let out a deep sigh.

14

Sŏnbi felt a chill go through her body and she finally got up. She hadn't slept all night long, and now had a splitting headache. The pain her mother was suffering had been on her mind as well, but the way both Tŏkho and Kannan had appeared on their doorstep last night was also worrying enough to keep her from sleeping.

"Mom, shall I heat up some water and wash your hands and feet?"

"Please."

Her mother had barely uttered the word before she turned onto her side with another groan.

"Is the pain back again?" said Sŏnbi, coming to her side.

Her mother simply moaned in reply. Sŏnbi pulled the blankets over her mother's chest, then went outside.

The light of day hadn't yet broken. Sŏnbi was still lost in thoughts of the previous night as she quietly pulled open the kitchen door. The sour smell of fermenting vegetables hit her. "Oh, the *kimchi** is over-pickled," she muttered, as she swung both the front and back doors to the kitchen wide open.

She had filled a pot with water and was just lighting a fire beneath it when she heard somebody give the brush gate a shake. Kannan's face flashed into her mind. She kept perfectly still and listened carefully. Who else could it be this early in the morning?

Finally she heard the gate slowly creak open.

"Who's there?"

Sŏnbi stepped out into the kitchen doorway and looked outside. She jerked back in surprise and took a few steps backward, then ran back into the inner room in sheer terror. Her mother, quite alarmed as well, turned to look at her.

"What's going on?"

*A list of all italicized words and place names is located at the back of the book.

"A man just came in through the brush gate," said Sŏnbi, having come to her mother's side and set her eyes on the front door.

At this her mother attempted to sit upright, fearing a thief. But she quickly fell down.

"Who's there? Who is it?" she cried as loud as she could.

"It's just me, ma'am." The man stood hesitantly just outside the front door.

"Well, who is 'me'? And what are you doing here at the crack of dawn?"

She couldn't recognize him by the sound of his voice alone. Slowly, he pushed the door open. The two of them stared at him intently, trying to hide their fear. Though it was still too dark to see clearly, his silhouette and his height finally told them that it was Ch'ŏtchae.

But this untimely visitor was only cause for further alarm. What had that good-for-nothing come to do to them at this time of night, they wondered, their hearts racing faster than ever.

"So what are you doing here?"

"I heard that you were sick, ma'am, so I just brought over some sumac roots for you to make medicine with."

His words gradually faded into a whisper. The mother and daughter were somewhat relieved by what he had to say, but now they were even more confused.

"Well, thank you for going to such trouble . . . ," said Sŏnbi's mother, noticing the bundle of sumac he carried into the room with him. He placed the bundle down on the floor, then immediately turned to leave.

"Go home safely," Sŏnbi's mother called to him.

She waited for the sound of his footsteps to disappear into the distance.

"What does that boy think he's doing?" she said under her breath as she glanced at Sŏnbi. Though it was just a vague feeling, it hit her that maybe all of this had to do with Sŏnbi. She now felt even more pressed to make a decision about Sŏnbi's future as soon as possible.

The room filled with sunlight. The sumac roots poked through holes in the horribly tattered cloth in which the freshly unearthed roots had been bundled. Sŏnbi was still so terrified that she hadn't moved an inch. She even recalled how he'd once stolen her sourstem when they were younger.

"Sŏnbi, go and hide those somewhere. Someone might see them . . . What is that vagrant up to, anyway?"

The more Sŏnbi's mother thought about it the stranger it all seemed. Then all of a sudden she was seized with fear. Mother and son had been terribly ostracized by the village, but Ch'ŏtchae had made a name for himself as well by getting drunk and picking fights.

Sŏnbi, for her part, felt a little hurt by her mother's words, though she didn't really know why. She was overcome by an indescribable sadness when she looked at the bundle of sumac, a sadness that just wouldn't go away. For some reason, she simply couldn't pull herself away from these feelings. Only after glancing at her mother lying in bed did she manage to pick up the bundle of sumac and go into the spare room. As she stepped up to the door she thought, Did Ch'ŏtchae really stay up all night long digging these roots? She pictured Ch'ŏtchae's face in her mind's eye, just as it had appeared earlier that morning in the doorway.

Why in the world had he brought these over? A pink flush then rose to her cheeks, as her whole body was gripped by a fear. Without thinking she flung the bundle of sumac roots to the floor and ran out of the room as though something were chasing her.

15

Several days later, Sŏnbi's mother passed away. Thanks to Tŏkho's good graces, Sŏnbi managed to hold a funeral service. She then moved into Tŏkho's house for good. It was decided that she would stay in the room opposite the inner room, a room Okchŏm (Tŏkho's daughter) used to stay in.

Tŏkho and his wife treated Sŏnbi more kindly now that her mother had died, because they felt sorry for her. Besides, when it came to doing chores around the house, they would have been hard-pressed to find anyone more capable than Sŏnbi. With Sŏnbi now at her beck and call, Okchŏm's mother left all the housework to her.

Okchŏm's mother came out of the inner room with a long pipe stuck between her lips and found Sŏnbi on her knees, washing down the breezeway floor with a rag. Taking the pipe from her mouth, she said,

"Let Granny do that. You go and work on Okchŏm's clothes." Turning to the kitchen she called, "Granny. Come do the floors."

Sŏnbi put her rag back into the basin and went to the kitchen. She washed her hands and returned to the breezeway. Okchŏm's mother then came from the inner room carrying everything Sŏnbi needed for measuring and cutting out her daughter's clothes.

"Now, Sŏnbi, from what I hear, it's the fashion in Seoul nowadays to wear everything well-fitted, so I want you to make these quite tight."

Sŏnbi took the material and sat down in front of the sewing machine. She made a few adjustments to the machine, then set herself to work. She spun the wheel of the machine for a while, then suddenly brought it to a stop. Through the corner of her eye she caught a glimpse of Granny, who had worn herself out scrubbing the floor. She was now sitting there out of breath, her eyes glazed over. Sŏnbi felt sorry for Granny whenever she saw her like this.

"Don't tell me it's all that hard just to wipe the floor!"

At Okchŏm's mother's shriek, Granny practically jumped out of her skin and quickly went back to her scrubbing. Okchŏm's mother glared at the old woman as she scrubbed. The older ones are lazy, the younger ones don't listen—maybe I should just get my hands on a kid, she wondered.

Just then, Tŏkho came in. Okchŏm's mother barely glanced at him. He had practically moved into the house where his concubine was living.

"Well now, look who's found his way back home!"

Tŏkho's face tightened, his eyes glaring at her.

"You're the one causing all this trouble around here. And believe me, I'm sure as hell not here to see the likes of you."

Glancing over at Sŏnbi, who was working at the sewing machine with her back to him, Tŏkho stepped into the breezeway.

"I just got a letter from Okchŏm. She says she's sick . . . It's no wonder things like this happen to us with all the evil tricks you're up to."

He took the letter out of his pocket and tossed it to the floor. Okchŏm's mother became very upset. She picked up the letter and stared at it.

"Read it to me word for word. I can't understand these cursive letters. What does she say is wrong with her?"

Tŏkho took back the letter from his wife and read it out loud. Soon tears were rolling down her cheeks.

"Well, what should we do? You know, I've been having nightmares recently and I'm sure this is why. Do you think I should go see her?"

"And just what use would you be there? I'm the one who's got to go. Now hurry up and get my things ready."

In no time at all the the couple's anger toward each other had subsided. Okchŏm's mother went into the inner room.

"Sŏnbi," she cried, "stop what you're doing and start working on this. Granny, heat up some charcoal for the iron."

Sŏnbi neatly folded the clothes she'd been working on and went into the inner room.

"Sew a collar onto this right away," the woman barked. "When's the next car leaving?" She looked to her husband, who was peering into the room.

"Car? What car? I've got to ride a bicycle into town, then hop on a train."

As Sŏnbi stitched on the collar, she thought of Okchŏm's big, round eyes. Though Sŏnbi didn't know what was wrong with Okchŏm, she knew how lucky Okchŏm was to have a mother and father at home who worried so much about her.

She felt sorry for herself and lonely, for she had no one in the world who cared about her, even when she was sick.

"When I go to Seoul, I want you to have Sŏnbi sleep at the other house."

"Wait, who's going where? Why do you want Sŏnbi to . . . ?"

Okchŏm's mother stopped mid-sentence, her face growing long.

"Here we go again. I'm trying to get ready to go, and all she wants to do is cause more trouble." Tŏkho dropped his chin into the palm of his hand with a slap.

Sŏnbi glanced at him anxiously. Tŏkho looked over at Sŏnbi, then recrossed his legs.

"Where the hell is this woman's common sense?"

Okchŏm's mother was about to say something, but she held her tongue.

Just then Blackie, the dog, scampered into the courtyard, barking at someone behind him.

16

The middle gate swung open and in walked Okchŏm.

"Mother!"

Surprised to hear her daughter's voice, Okchŏm's mother rushed outside. She threw her arms around her daughter's neck and burst into

35

tears. A stranger in a Western-style suit, who had followed Okchŏm inside, stood there awkwardly staring at the mother and daughter.

"What's all this about?" said Tŏkho from the breezeway. "When did you leave? And why didn't you send us a telegram ? You said you were sick ..."

Okchŏm ran over and grabbed her father's hand.

"Father, this is the son of one of my teachers at school. He was on his way to Monggŭmp'o beach when we met on the train and I convinced him to stop by our house first."

Who's that in the suit? was the thought that had crossed Tŏkho's mind upon seeing the young man, who had made him very uneasy. He was now quite relieved to hear that he was the son of his daughter's teacher.

Okchŏm turned to the well-dressed young man. "This is my father," she said with a sweet smile.

The man quickly lifted his head, removed his hat, and came forward. He bowed to Tŏkho.

"Glad you could stop by. Come on inside," said Tŏkho.

Tŏkho started into the house, followed by the others. Okchŏm's mother fixed her gaze on the man in the suit who walked in ahead of Okchŏm. If only she had a son like him, she thought.

"My baby, didn't you say you were sick? Your father was just about to go visit you," she said, stepping up into the breezeway.

Okchŏm felt her cheeks going red. "Oh, Mother! Why do you still call me your 'baby'?"

All of them laughed at this. Okchŏm looked back and forth between her father and the man.

"Daddy, I've decided to go to Monggŭmp'o beach, too."

Tŏkho carefully examined the expression on his daughter's face.

"Well, are you feeling up to it? As long as you're not sick, you can go anywhere as far as I'm concerned."

Okchŏm smiled gleefully and then looked over at her visitor. But then she remembered something.

"Mother, didn't you say that Sŏnbi moved in to my room?"

"Yes, she did ..."

"Well, where am I supposed to go now?" she pouted.

Tŏkho looked at Okchŏm. At times like this, he thought, she was the spitting image of her mother.

36

"Now, don't you worry about it, dear. We'll just have Sŏnbi stay in here."

Tŏkho smiled, and looked at the young man.

"Still acts like a child, that one, doesn't she? Hah, ha!"

The man in the suit smiled back. After just a few minutes, he understood how preciously Okchŏm was treated in this family.

"Sŏnbi! Get lunch ready."

At her mother's words Okchŏm jumped to her feet.

"Is Sŏnbi really here? Right now?"

Rushing across the breezeway, Okchŏm ran into Sŏnbi coming out of her workroom.

"Sŏnbi! How have you been?"

Sŏnbi was about to take Okchŏm's hand when she caught a strong whiff of perfume, and suddenly pulled back.

As she did so, she could feel the warmth rush into her cheeks.

"Oh, Sŏnbi, you're so pretty now! How did you ever get to be so . . ."

Okchŏm unconsciously glanced over her shoulder. When she saw that all eyes in the inner room were fixed in their direction, she felt something forcing her eyes to twitch—the closest thing she'd ever felt to real jealousy. Now her own cheeks were burning.

Okchŏm spun around. Sŏnbi, her head down, went back into the kitchen, where Granny was busily preparing vegetables for a batch of *kimchi*.

"What is that man doing in there?" asked Granny, who found it offensive that an unmarried woman was traveling around with a man of no family relation.

"I have no idea," she said, recalling that Okchŏm had introduced the man in the suit to her father. "Anyway, she wants us to cook some rice."

"Cook more rice? We've got plenty leftover . . . She must want it for that man in there."

As she washed one of the pots, Sŏnbi thought about Okchŏm's powdered face and her pretty Western clothes. She looked at the charcoal glowing in the oven.

"Sŏnbi, I want you to fetch two chickens." Okchŏm's mother peered into the kitchen.

"Yes, ma'am."

Her message delivered, the woman went back inside. Then, at the sound of something fluttering above her, Sŏnbi lifted her head.

37

A single swallow swooped around the kitchen ceiling. Then out it went, like a black arrow soaring into that blue sky. Sŏnbi let out a faint sigh. It was as though she was looking out at that sky for the very first time.

"Did you hear that? She said to get *two* chickens!" Granny looked over at Sŏnbi as she lit a fire in the stove. Her smile was so wide that crow's feet appeared at the corners of her eyes. Whenever they killed a chicken, she loved to suck on the leftover chicken bones from which the meat had been removed.

Bwock! Bwock! cried the chickens, startling Sŏnbi. She wiped her wet hands on her apron and ran out to the back gate. The chickens were squawking and walking in circles atop their nests as she approached the coop, but as soon as they noticed Sŏnbi, they began flapping their wings noisily to jump to the ground. The smell of manure hit Sŏnbi in the face. Chicken feathers floated lightly in the air.

Sŏnbi stood there for a moment, coughing, and once the chickens had moved out of the way, she peered into their nests. The eggs the chickens had laid only moments earlier seemed to be smiling sweetly at her. Breaking into a smile at the sight of them, Sŏnbi picked up the eggs from the nests. They still felt warm.

"This makes forty," she said to herself, and made her way back to the kitchen.

Yu Sŏbang came inside clutching two young hens, blood still dripping from their necks. He looked over at Sŏnbi with a smile.

"Did they lay any more eggs?"

"Yes, they did."

Sŏnbi was so excited to show off the warm eggs to somebody, anybody, that she thrust her hands right out in front of her.

"You sure have a thing for eggs," said Granny, dropping the chickens into boiling water. "Counting these, Granny, I've got forty of them now."

"Well good for you, dear! But what's the use of saving them up like that?" she added softly.

Sŏnbi was a little hurt by her words. But only for a moment. When she looked down at the eggs again, they seemed prettier than ever.

Sŏnbi quietly opened the door to the pantry and went inside. The smell of mildew greeted her. She took down the egg basket, placed it atop a jar, and peeked inside. The chock-full basket still held the same of number eggs as it had before. She carefully placed each new egg inside, and just as she repeated the words 'this makes forty', a beam of orange sunlight, streaking in through the crack in the doorsill, lit up her hand. After one last good look inside the basket, Sŏnbi came back out to the kitchen. She sat down next to Granny, who was plucking the feathers out of the chickens.

They finally finished preparing the lunch and had set their own bowls down on the stovetop to eat when Tŏkho came in.

"Sŏnbi, go eat in the inner room."

Sŏnbi stood up. "No, thank you."

"Now, do as you're told. Come inside and eat with Okchŏm."

Tŏkho was being so impatient that Sŏnbi placed her spoon down on her tray as though she were finished. Tŏkho realized that it was useless to insist.

"Have you always eaten in the kitchen?"

With this, he headed back inside, where he must have said something, for the shrill voice of Okchŏm's mother then drifted outside.

"I have to put up with that stubborn girl night and day. She won't do anything unless you insist on it. I'm telling you, she's tougher than cowhide."

Sŏnbi's cheeks were burning. She felt the juices she'd just sucked off the chicken bones working themselves back up her throat.

After finishing the dishes, Sŏnbi was about to cross over to her room, when she ran into Okchŏm's mother standing in the breezeway.

"Now that Okchŏm is back at home, you'll have to sleep with Granny, or else in here with me."

Okchŏm popped out of her room.

"Come and clean out this room. What is all this stuff in here anyway? You've got more bundles of junk than a Chinaman. Hah, ha . . ."

Okchŏm turned to look at the man in the suit as she laughed. Sŏnbi was so embarrassed that she blushed to the very tips of her ears. She went into the room and gathered all her bundles together. As she took in what Okchŏm had just said to her, she tried to decide just where she would move her things.

Moving into the inner room meant having to sleep with Okchŏm's mother—she didn't want to do that—but moving in with Granny meant sharing a tiny little space. She couldn't decide what to do, and sat there lost in thought. Then she remembered the house in the lower village, where she and her mother had once lived. Though it was only a straw-roofed hut, it was still their very own home! She felt the urge to go see it now.

'I wonder who's living there?' she thought.

Sŏnbi looked down again at her bundles again. Slowly she rose to her feet, and with both hands lifted up her things.

18

"Man, is it hot! Come on and sing something, will ya?"

So short and squat that they all called him Little Buddha, the young man had turned to a tall man behind him. He dug his hoe into the ground, pulled out a foxtail, and tossed it to the side.

As the young men exchanged small talk, they called each other by their nicknames.

"A song, a song!"

"Come on, Sourstem, just sing something! I can't stand it any longer."

Little Buddha slapped his tall friend Sourstem on the back. Next to him, Ch'ŏtchae was working up a good sweat pulling out weeds.

"Come on, let's hear a song!" he echoed, turning around.

Little Buddha shot a glance in his direction.

"What does an oaf like you want to hear singing for?"

Without a few drinks inside him, Ch'ŏtchae hardly ever spoke a word to anyone. But once he was drunk he would jabber on and on, all night long, in words no one could really make out.

Ch'ŏtchae looked over at Little Buddha and grinned at him. He had the habit of smiling like this instead of actually answering.

From the mountain in front of them then came the sound, Cuckoo! Cuckoo! Sourstem looked over at the hillside.

"Hey, the cuckoos are the only ones singing!"

With this, he began his song, the blood vessels along the side of his neck slightly bulging.

> All the dirt and all the stones
> One by one I pick them out
> To eat myself and to give to my love
> I plant rice for the fall

40

He drew out the last note long and slow. Then the farmer nicknamed Earthworm softly closed his eyes.

> That thorn in my side
> The rich landowner
> To fill his metal storehouse
> Did I plant for the fall

The rising, twisting melody at times dropped in tone and then faded away.

"Now that's more like it!" shouted Little Buddha, striking his hoe into the ground. But then an overwhelming feeling of sadness pressed on their hearts.

"Hey, what are you waiting for? It's your turn again!" Yu Sŏbang looked at Sourstem with a smile.

"You old raccoon dog," said Sourstem. "How about you buy me a drink if I sing?"

"You got it."

Ch'ŏtchae was more thirsty than ever at this mention of alcohol. His mouth started to water as though he could see a bowl of milky-white brew right there before his eyes.

"No, I quit. My voice is worth more than a cup of booze."

"Oh, come on. Let's just do it."

Several of the men cried out at the same time. Yu Sŏbang then took off his straw hat and began fanning himself with it.

"It's hot as hell out here. Just sing something, will you? If you don't want brew, I'll buy you some hard stuff."

"Don't go getting a big head, Sourstem, just 'cause you can sing." Little Buddha knocked Sourstem's hat off his head with a tap of his hand.

"Hey, stop it . . . Whose place are you going to weed tomorrow, anyway?"

"I'm going over to help in Samch'i Village, why?"

"Those fields are packed with rocks. They must be hell to weed."

"Yeah, and the tenant pays five sacks of rice for them, too."

"Well, he must not pay the land taxes, right? With the rent so high . . ."

"He pays everything, the taxes, too."

"Out of his own pocket? You've got to be kidding! He's going to starve working those fields."

Sourstem cast a sidelong glance at Yu Sŏbang. Since the man worked for Tŏkho, the rest of them always kept their distance from him. Little Buddha spit on the ground.

"I don't know what the hell he thinks he's up to lately," he replied under his breath.

He wrapped his hand around a millet plant, so as not to damage it with his hoe, and he chopped into the ground, loosening the soil around it. The wind just then picked up, and the blades of the millet plants swayed softly in the breeze.

A calf lowed somewhere off in the distant. Sourstem lifted his own chin into the air:

> The grains of millet I pay to him
> Are round as chestnuts, round as dates
> And they roll around, roll around
> On the lips of my love

Earthworm cleared his throat and took a firm grip onto his hoe:

> The landlord lends me millet
> That is nothing more than chaff
> Which scrapes the grudge in my heart
> Each time I swallow

Each of them let out a deep sigh.

19

"Alright listen, if we're going to sing, I want something uplifting. Enough of these sad songs!" Little Buddha, flushed with anger, grabbed his hoe and flung it to the side. Like a whirlwind, a memory had swept through his mind—the memory of borrowing grain from Tŏkho on outrageous terms.

Tŏkho's barnyard that spring day had been crowded with tenant farmers who had come for loans of millet.

42

After they'd all waited for some time, Tŏkho finally came out with a long pipe between his lips.

"Why so many of you?"

This is what Tŏkho always said when he handed out his loan shark grain.

Tŏkho scanned the crowd standing in a circle around him. Each of the farmers who happened to catch Tŏkho's eye felt his heart stop and quickly bowed his head, afraid of being the unlucky one sent home empty-handed.

The lines set in Tŏkho's face tightened. In the crowd were people who hadn't even paid back their grain from the previous year.

"Humph! So what happened to everything you grew last year, huh? And you! Don't tell me you don't have anything left either?"

Tŏkho stared at Sourstem. The young man scratched his head. "Well, yes . . ."

"I wonder why . . . Looks to me like none of you boys know how to economize when it comes to food. If you keep on borrowing in the spring, things will be tough for you all come fall. Am I wrong?"

The farmers listened with their heads hung low.

Tŏkho was ready, pen in hand, to write down the names of each farmer into his notebook and note exactly how many bushels and scoops of grain they took away.

They all turned their heads toward the creaking sound of the granary door, which Yu Sŏbang was opening. Several of the men ran over to help him drag out sacks of millet. With a long swishing sound, they poured the millet onto straw mats spread out on the ground. Oh, that familiar sound of flowing grain! And all that chaff that flew up into white clouds of dust!

Driven by an unconscious urge, they huddled around the millet, then scooped up handfuls of the hulled grain to examine it closely, and placed a few grains in their mouths to taste.

The millet they had harvested and paid to Tŏkho the previous fall had a mellow flavor, like well-ripened chestnuts or dates, and they could actually roll the individual grains around on their tongues. But this millet, wherever it came from, had a coarse texture, as though it had been half mixed with chaff—it felt like they were chewing on the empty husks of grain.

The farmers had been thrilled to know they'd be able to receive grain, even on such outrageous terms. But now they were being cheated, and they knew there was no place they could make an appeal. The injustice of it all came to them in an overwhelming rush of feeling.

Yu Sŏbang looked at the farmers, who were exchanging desperate glances. "Well, come on, grab your bowls and make a single line."

Only then did the farmers pull themselves together and line up single file to collect their grain.

That sound of millet flowing from the scoop into their sacks! Had it been a stone crashing onto their chests, could it have been any less painful?

His mind having wandered this far, Little Buddha now let out a deep sigh and wiped the sweat from his brow. He looked absentmindedly at the millet stems, which he had cared for with as much love as he would his own children. He felt the urge now to simply walk away—wherever his legs would take him—and to leave his hoe right there where he had tossed it.

"Come on. Let's have another song!" Yu Sŏbang tried to break the silence. But Little Buddha remembered that it had been Yu Sŏbang himself who had doled out that millet half mixed with chaff.

"Hey . . ." Little Buddha started to shout at Yu Sŏbang, but couldn't think of anything to say. He stood there staring blankly at the man.

They weeded the row assigned to them, then turned back to start another. This one was overrun by more arid thistle than the other. The ground between the thistle was dotted white with shepherd's purse flowers. Sourstem jumped to his feet and looked up at the sun to estimate their progress.

"I wonder if we can get all this weeded before sunset," he mumbled.

"Are you crazy? There's no way we can finish by sunset." Little Buddha looked up as he spoke to Sourstem.

"Come on, let's hear another song."

Ch'ŏtchae looked over at them. Squatting on the ground, Sourstem began singing a field song:

> I'll follow you, my dear, I'll follow you
> I'll follow you, my love

Though I drag my lame leg behind me
I'll follow you, my love

"Now that's more like it!" Earthworm cried.
"Hey, guys," Little Buddha jumped to his feet. "Who's that?"

20

They all looked up at the same time. Coming right toward them was a man in a suit and a girl wearing high-heeled shoes. Burning with curiosity, they sprang to their feet.

"Come on, boys, that's Okchŏm, Master's daughter," said Yu Sŏbang.

"No way! That's Okchŏm? I heard she went to study in Seoul. What's she doing back here?"

"She said she wasn't feeling so good."

"So who's that in the suit?"

"Beats me!" Yu Sŏbang replied after a while.

"Looks like she went off to Seoul and caught a man for herself."

With this, Little Buddha plopped himself down on the embankment at the side of the road.

"Shit! Some men have all the luck. Pretty girls, money, you name it. The rest of us are stuck lonely and broke until the day we die."

Little Buddha took some dried motherwort out of his pocket. He placed it into a piece of newsprint, rolled it up, and after sealing it with spit began to smoke it. He watched as Okchŏm and the man in the suit gradually approached them.

The two of them glanced at the farmers as they passed by. Okchŏm's face was now turned toward the man. Whatever it was they were talking about, they both seemed to be enjoying themselves.

"Boy, she's something else, isn't she?" said Little Buddha, tossing away his cigarette butt once the two had walked off into the distance. He grabbed his hoe and started weeding again.

Shortly afterwards Earthworm gave Little Buddha a playful whack.

"Sounds like you're hankering to find a bride."

"You bet I am. Got anyone in mind for me?"

Earthworm, remembering something, called, "Hey, Yu Sŏbang. Sŏnbi's living over at Tŏkho's, right?"

"Yeah. Why?"

"They thinking about getting her married?"

"Well, I guess they are!"

Sourstem winked at Little Buddha. "Yu Sŏbang has no idea. How's he supposed to know anything?" he said, while Yu Sŏbang pretended not to listen.

Ch'ŏtchae, for his part, flashed his eyes wide open when he heard what they were talking about, but heaved a deep sigh. Little Buddha, more interested than ever, looked back at Earthworm.

"Hey, set something up for me, how about it?"

"Don't look at me. You're going to have to ask Tŏkho about that."

"That's what I mean, stupid. I want you to talk to Tŏkho on my behalf."

"And you think he'll listen to me?"

"Sŏnbi's pretty, you know, but she's got a good heart too . . . I'm telling you, she's the best."

Yu Sŏbang pictured Sŏnbi in his mind as he thought about what Sourstem had just said. Ch'ŏtchae too, if it hadn't been for the others, would have drilled Yu Sŏbang with questions about Sŏnbi.

The men kept weeding in the fields as they continued their small talk, and when the sun finally set over the horizon, they all returned to the village proper.

Ch'ŏtchae ate dinner at home, but went right outside again. For some reason it was too frustrating to sit inside—he simply couldn't bear it. He strolled around the village aimlessly. He pulled out a motherwort cigarette he had bummed off Little Buddha and lit it up. He took a deep drag on it, but choked on the smoke, which had none of the fragrant flavor of real tobacco. He flung the thing far away from him.

"How can anyone call that a cigarette!" he grumbled, and looked up to find himself behind the fence surrounding Tŏkho's house. He'd made a habit recently of taking a walk around the house every night. If he was lucky, he might someday see Sŏnbi, he thought. But so far he'd never once seen her near this house. Even so, he always walked here after dinner, hoping that tonight might be the night.

The stars hung here and there in the jet-black sky. The wind picked up and carried the faint scent of mugwort mosquito incense toward him. He let his thoughts drift, gazing at nothing in particular, and resting his hands firmly on his hips.

46

From Tŏkho's house came the faint sound of people talking, though he couldn't make out the words or the voices. Still, he could hear the sound of a man and woman laughing as clearly as he saw the stars right there above him.

After standing like this for a while, lost in thought, he remembered the motherwort cigarette he'd thrown to the ground. He searched his pockets, but found nothing. Smacking his lips a few times, he plopped himself down in the grassy field. The ground felt cold, helping to cool off the burning inside him. Just then he heard the sound of footsteps coming his way, and his eyes opened like a cat's in the dark.

21

The approaching footsteps stopped short, and he could hear the rustling sound of someone standing up closely against the reed fence. The way she caught her breath gave him the assurance that this was a woman.

He grew more curious, and his heart began to race: Could this be Sŏnbi? He inched backward slowly, so as not to let her know he was there.

The sound of the footsteps moved even closer toward him, then stopped. Whoever it was heaved a deep sigh, and stood still for a while as though she were lost in thought. Ch'ŏtchae was finally able to make out clearly the height and shape of her body in the darkness, and his hunch that this girl was in fact Sŏnbi gradually deepened. When the thought struck him that he was almost face to face with his beloved Sŏnbi—with only a few footsteps separating them—he took several steps forward. But having heard him move, she ran off in fright. Ch'ŏtchae chased after her. He would finish what he'd already started.

Knowing that she was no match for her pursuer, however, the girl slipped inside one of the houses in the village. Ch'ŏtchae had no choice but to hide beside a woodpile and suffer an agonizing wait for her to come back outside. After some time had passed, the girl still hadn't emerged. He started doubting himself: Maybe it wasn't Sŏnbi after all. But then who else was it? Who could have been standing outside, peeking into Tŏkho's house at this time of night? He closed his eyes and thought about it for a while, but no one in particular came to mind. He wanted so badly to believe it was Sŏnbi. He'd stay up all night if only he could meet her and share even one or two of the feelings that he'd kept locked in his heart over the years.

What would he say to Sŏnbi now if he met her? he asked himself. He couldn't seem to find a reply. Though his heart seemed ready to explode with everything he wanted to tell her, now that he tried to put it into words, he drew a complete blank. How about: Will you live with me? No, that wouldn't work. What about: Do you know who I am? "No, no," he said, shaking his head and cracking a smile. As he came up with different things to say, he never once took his eyes off the door.

He heard more footsteps coming toward him, and it seemed as though someone was passing in front of the house. He held his breath and squatted to the ground. Out of the blue, just as the footsteps came to a stop, he heard the sound of squirting and a stream of liquid shot down onto his face. Only as he moved out of the way, did he realize what it was—urine. Instantly, he jumped to his feet and came forward.

"Hey, you idiot. Where the hell do you think you're taking a piss?"

At the unexpected sound of someone's voice, the stranger jumped back in surprise, pulled up his pants, and backed out of the way.

"Who's that?"

Ch'ŏtchae knew exactly who it was from the sound of his voice.

"Watch where you take a piss, will you!"

Only now did Kaettong figure out it was Ch'ŏtchae.

"Well, what the hell were you standing there for?"

Ch'ŏtchae had nothing to say for himself. He fumbled for the right words. Kaettong moved toward him.

"I was just at your house."

"What for?"

"I wanted to see if you'd help weed our fields tomorrow."

"Well, I already promised Myŏnggu I'd help him."

"Myŏnggu? Damn it. I really need one more guy to help me . . ."

Just then the door rattled open, and out came a hand-held lantern. The two of them stared at it in silence.

"Be careful. It's dark out there," said Kaettong's mother.

"I will," came a young woman's reply.

Ch'ŏtchae wondered if this might be Sŏnbi's voice. If it hadn't been for Kaettong, he'd have chased right after the girl. But that option being out of the question now, he hesitated as to what he should do. The lantern was playing hide and seek with his eyes, flickering in and out of sight, as though it was laughing at him, ridiculing him. Ch'ŏtchae took a step forward, his heart in his throat. Just then Kaettong asked,

"Ma, who was that?"

"Goodness . . . What are you doing out here?"

Kaettong's mother came in their direction.

"That was Kannan, wasn't it? What's she doing over here at this time of night?"

"Kannan?" shouted Ch'ŏtchae suddenly in surprise. Kaettong's mother stopped in her tracks.

"Hey, who's that?"

"It's just me."

". . . Oh, Ch'ŏtchae?"

"Ma, why did Kannan come over to our house?"

"Good question . . . Maybe Tŏkho sent her over."

Ch'ŏtchae, for his part, was still staring out blankly at the hand lantern disappearing into the distance. Then he trudged off once again, wiping away more of the urine from his temple.

22

Ch'ŏtchae walked around aimlessly, and then, with one last spin around Tŏkho's house, finally made his way home.

He didn't want to go back inside though, and after walking circles in the front yard for a while, he plopped down beside the woodpile. The scent of rotting wood hit him, and he thought about how Kaettong had just pissed on him. Then he felt an indescribable rush of the anger pent up inside of him.

Leaning against the woodpile, he asked himself why he'd never even once been able to meet that damn girl. Is she sick, or something? he wondered, as a huge, bright star shot through the sky above him, dragging a long tail before disappearing into the darkness. As he stared vacantly into the spot where the star had disappeared, the black mole on Sŏnbi's brow entered his mind. That shiny black mole! Standing out on her perfect, glowing face. It was just like that shooting star, vanishing without a trace. He sighed deeply and shut his eyes tight. The tighter he squeezed, the more clearly he could see that black mole. Damn that girl! he said, jumping to his feet. Then he heard yet another set of footsteps coming toward him. This finally set off his temper.

"Who's that!" he shouted crossly.

"Is that you, Ch'ŏtchae? I've been looking high and low for you. And you were here the whole time? What are you doing over here?"

Fighting for breath, Yi Sŏbang came to Ch'ŏtchae's side, took his hand, and led him into the house. Ch'ŏtchae tried to suppress his anger, but his nostrils were still flaring.

"Ch'ŏtchae!" Yi Sŏbang moved closer to the boy's side. Ch'ŏtchae lay on the floor not wanting to be bothered. Yi Sŏbang placed his hand on Ch'ŏtchae's forehead.

"Something's hounding you, my boy, isn't it?"

Ch'ŏtchae pictured Sŏnbi in his mind's eye and tried to shake off Yi Sŏbang's hand. He rolled onto his side, refusing the man's gesture. After some time, Yi Sŏbang spoke again.

"You asleep?"

"No."

"Tell me why you've been up and about at night."

"Because I can't fall asleep."

"Well, why can't you fall asleep?"

He wanted to say something, but his lips remained tightly sealed.

"Come on Ch'ŏtchae, you don't have to hide anything from me. Just tell me what's getting at you, and I'll do my best to help."

Yi Sŏbang suspected that Ch'ŏtchae was losing sleep over a girl, but he didn't know for sure who she was. He hoped he could find out who, so that he could try to make things happen. If he let things take their natural course, Ch'ŏtchae might get sick before long, or even worse, end up causing a major incident.

Ch'ŏtchae had been quiet for some time now. Yi Sŏbang moved up close to him and lay down by his side.

"You've got a girl on your mind, don't you, Ch'ŏtchae?"

At the word "girl" Ch'ŏtchae's face flushed and Sŏnbi's delicate figure floated before his eyes. Ch'ŏtchae rolled to his side again.

"Good night, Yi Sŏbang."

Knowing that the boy wasn't ready to talk, Yi Sŏbang decided to bring up the subject again on another day, and went to sleep.

Ch'ŏtchae, however, did not sleep a wink. His mind ran in this and that direction all night long. As dawn broke the next morning, he finally sat up in bed, at the sound of a door in the inner room slowly opening. Shit! Another bastard spent the night here, thought Ch'ŏtchae. He

50

resented to no end what his mother was still doing—despite the fact she now had a full-grown son.

"Have a safe walk back home."

"Okay."

"When can you come again?"

"We'll see."

The man whispering to his mother was Yu Sŏbang, the man who worked for Tŏkho. And yet, Ch'ŏtchae was actually glad to hear his voice. He jumped to his feet. As he opened the door to the room, Yi Sŏbang stopped him.

"What are you doing up so early?"

Yi Sŏbang had gotten out of bed and grabbed the seat of Ch'ŏtchae's pants. He'd been afraid that Ch'ŏtchae might run out of the room and do something reckless.

By this time Ch'ŏtchae's mother had softly shut the gate behind her and was coming back inside.

"Mom!"

Normally Ch'ŏtchae would have still been asleep at this hour, so his voice startled his mother, who stopped short. Afraid he might spring at her in a rage, she took a few steps back unsteadily.

Yi Sŏbang did not know how to ease the tension between mother and son, but he stood there trying to think of something. Ch'ŏtchae, meanwhile, glared at his mother through the door, but without saying a single word slammed it shut and collapsed onto the floor. Only now could Yi Sŏbang sit down too.

23

Okchŏm had followed Sinch'ŏl to Monggŭmp'o for a vacation on the beach, then brought him back home for a proper visit. And although Sinch'ŏl had been planning to catch the morning train bound for Seoul today, Okchŏm's powers of persuasion continued to pay off—at least in her mind—for she'd once again managed to keep Sinch'ŏl from leaving. But it was less on account of Okchŏm's charms than in response to Tŏkho's adamant protestations that Sinch'ŏl had agreed to delay his departure. Truth be told, there was also something else about this household that had, for reasons beyond his control, made it difficult for Sinch'ŏl to leave.

It had not been a simple matter of staying as a guest in someone's house for a single day or two—indeed, he had been there for over a month already. And it was only because of his guilty conscience that he had originally decided to go back to Seoul. But Okchŏm was beaming now, and her eyes soaked in Sinch'ŏl's masculine physique.

"Shall we walk to the melon hut?"

"Well . . . Maybe it's not such a good idea for us to go alone."

"Well, then," replied Okchŏm, "who would you like to come with us?"

Okchŏm's powerful gaze seemed to penetrate right through him; he averted his eyes ever so slightly.

"Your father or mother. Either would be fine."

"Are you serious, Sinch'ŏl?"

"Well, won't it be a little boring for us to go off alone into the countryside—it's the middle of nowhere!"

"You know, you're absolutely right. Shall I ask mother to join us?"

"I'll let you decide."

Okchŏm sprang to her feet with a giggle and crossed to the inner room. Sitting in front of his desk, Sinch'ŏl looked at his face reflected in the small standing mirror placed upon it, and then glanced out the window absentmindedly. There in his line of vision appeared Sŏnbi, leaving the kitchen with a laundry basket balanced on her head. Sinch'ŏl instantly sat erect and fixed his eyes on her left cheek as he watched her pass by. He heard her stepping over the threshold of the middle gate, and realized she must be going off to do laundry—a strange light now flickering in his eye.

He had been in this house for close to two months already, but he had only been able to catch glimpses of Sŏnbi from a distance, and he'd never once had the chance to sit down with her and have a conversation! Such was the extent to which she had piqued his curiosity. When he watched her carry in his white shirts and underwear, freshly laundered and pressed, he was taken by how meticulous and precise she'd been with her work. When he touched his well-folded clothes, he thought to himself, Oh, if only I had a wife like her . . .

Never mind that she was so beautiful, with that black mole on her brow! Everything about her left an indelible impression on his mind. Now, if only he had the chance to talk to her, he said to himself. All he had to do was make his way to the riverside, and there surely, he'd be able to meet her. The hard part was coming up with a good excuse with which to shake off Okchŏm.

Okchŏm came back to his room.

"Mother's going to come with us."

"Good."

Though he was quick to offer this reply, Sinch'ŏl was now loath to go anywhere.

"Come on, get up, before it gets too hot."

Sinch'ŏl pondered something for a moment.

"Why don't we take your father along as well?"

"Father? What in Heaven's name for?"

She glanced over at him and smiled. He smiled back.

"Granted they're no spring chickens, but shouldn't the old couple go out for a stroll, too, every once and a while?" he chuckled.

Okchŏm laughed along with him. Surely it would make a good picture for her and Sinch'ŏl to walk side by side in front of her parents.

"Yes, let's take him along with us then . . . But I don't think Father has come up from the lower house yet."

Okchŏm pranced over to the men's quarters. As he watched her go, Sinch'ŏl wondered whether Sŏnbi was doing the laundry alone today. Okchŏm soon returned.

"Father's not even here . . ."

At this, Sinch'ŏl jumped to his feet. He grabbed his hat off the hook on the wall and placed it on his head.

"I'll get your father. You two go ahead. It's the same melon hut we walked to last time, right?"

A flicker of displeasure crossed Okchŏm's eyes, but then she burst out laughing.

"Oh, stop it, Sinch'ŏl. Forget about Father."

"No, you two go along. I'll find your father and meet you there."

Sinch'ŏl made his way out of the house. He could feel the hot sun beating down on his body. As he stepped through the front gate and paused for a moment, he thought: Okay, so what next?

24

Sinch'ŏl had managed to dash out of the house in his desperate attempt to lose Okchŏm, but once he'd made his way outside, he still faced the problem of pulling off a chance meeting with Sŏnbi.

He looked at the grove of trees in the distance surrounding Wŏnso Pond. Then he turned toward the lower village, where Tŏkho's concubine lived. Finally, he shifted his gaze to the fields straight in front of him, where the melon hut was located.

But then Okchŏm and her mother came out of the house.

"You haven't left yet?"

Okchŏm wore a powder blue dress with a straw hat fit snugly on her head. Okchŏm's mother stared at Sinch'ŏl and her daughter, her lips hiding a smile. Though there had been no formal discussion of it yet, in her eyes, the two were a future couple.

"Come with me to your father's place?" Sinch'ŏl asked Okchŏm.

"What? I told you I'd never go there. I don't ever want to set my eyes on that whore."

Okchŏm spun around and walked away. Sinch'ŏl had deliberately asked the question in order to solicit precisely this response.

"Well, why not? Doesn't she count as your mother, too?"

"*Ara ma!* Well, I never!" cried Okchŏm in Japanese, walking away with her mother's hand clasped in her own. "Hurry up and get Father . . . We'll be waiting for you."

Now Sinch'ŏl was hardly able to contain his excitement. Everything had gone far more smoothly than he ever could have imagined. He waited for his heartbeat to return to its regular rhythm, then slowly set off behind Okchŏm.

Okchŏm was just short of the entrance to the village when she looked back his way. She made some sort of gesture with her hands and then disappeared behind the buckwheat fields. Sinch'ŏl sighed with relief. Now for the hard part! he thought, setting off at a clip, his eyes fixed on Wŏnso Pond.

The closer he got to the grove of trees beside the pond, the shorter of breath he grew. He was afraid of the worst—that Okchŏm might come up from behind him—and he kept looking behind him.

He heard the sound of trickling water and stopped for a moment. Then, weaving his way through the willows, he quietly made his way into the grove. The long, draping branches felt cool as they grazed his shoulders. He hid in the cover of the trees, looking around this way and that to see if anyone else was there.

He could hear the sound of the laundry club, pounding wet clothes. It made the quiet grove of trees even more tranquil. His view of the laundry club was obscured by the willows, but the mere sound of someone pounding was enough to convince him that Sŏnbi was there. He gradually made his way toward her. Her right cheek appeared like a circle before him. Sinch'ŏl froze in place and looked once more over his shoulder. But what would he say to Sŏnbi if he went up to her? Whenever he came up with something to say to her, on second thought, it seemed he had nothing. Oh, what should I do? Again, he wavered. His feet felt like lead, his heart was racing.

He'd often gone with friends to cafés and the like. This was the first time he'd ever had trouble approaching a woman.

The pounding suddenly stopped and he could hear the sound of splashing water—she was probably rinsing out the clothes now. He leaned up against the trunk of a willow tree, thinking, Oh, just go back! What the hell are you doing? What use is there in talking to her anyway? He wanted to turn away, but here he was, still pressed against this tree. He shut his eyes tightly. He thought of Okchŏm waiting for him at the melon hut. But Okchŏm's image gradually faded away, and now it was Sŏnbi's face that he saw so clearly. "What's gotten into me? How long have I known this girl?" With this on his lips, he spun around. He stared down at some quartz shimmering beneath the flowing water. Father still thinks I'm restoring my health at Monggŭmp'o Beach, he suddenly remembered, jerking his head in the other direction. He grabbed a willow branch hanging down in front of him and snapped it in half. He stripped it of its leaves with a single swipe that left his hand stinging. Scattering the leaves into the flowing water, he slowly walked back to the village.

As he approached the melon hut, he stopped. In order to get rid of Okchŏm, he'd told her he was going to pick up her father, he remembered. Okchŏm climbed down from the melon hut.

"You're alone?"

He hesitated.

"Well, you see . . . on the way over there I . . . I changed my mind, and decided to come by myself."

His face went a little red. Okchŏm flashed her eyes brightly.

"Well, come on. Let's climb up inside. I picked out the ripest melons."

25

Sinch'ŏl had only taken a few steps towards the hut before he noticed the melons, each the size of a baby's head, growing beneath all the vines. He walked to the side of the patch to touch one, then removed his hat and began fanning himself.

"Just look at these. This is why I love the countryside!"

Okchŏm spun around, stood a moment, and walked over to him.

"It's hot out here. Let's go up inside."

Okchŏm had small beads of sweat forming beneath her nose. Sinch'ŏl wanted to catch his breath before climbing into the melon hut, so he plopped to the ground at the side of the field. Okchŏm's mother, meanwhile, had craned her neck to see what was going on.

"Why are you sitting there, of all places?" Okchŏm said with a scowl.

Sinch'ŏl shielded his face from the sun with his hat and wiped the sweat from his brow. He took a deep breath of air. Okchŏm stared at his broad shoulders. She was convinced that if she were in his position, she would never have sat facing away from him. It was unbearable that the two of them weren't sitting face to face—even for this brief instant. She felt ignored.

Sinch'ŏl jumped to his feet and took several brisk strides away from her. After searching in the grass for a moment, he lifted up a cluster of strawberries, leaves still attached. He held them up with a smile on his face as he walked back to Okchŏm.

"Oh, where did you find them? They're such a pretty color!"

Okchŏm snatched them out of Sinch'ŏl's hand and studied them, her head cocked to the side.

"*Kore anata no haato*? Is this your heart?" she asked in Japanese, staring up at Sinch'ŏl with a faint coloring on her cheeks. Sinch'ŏl looked back and forth between the strawberries and Okchŏm's face. He felt a strange urge grow inside of him.

"Come, let's go up now."

Okchŏm walked ahead, and Sinch'ŏl followed her up the ladder. Okchŏm's mother looked between the two affectionately.

56

"What's the matter? Did your father say he didn't want to come?"

"Who'd want to go and see that whore!" Okchŏm answered, as she tried to select a melon.

She glanced over at Sinch'ŏl, then turned to her mother, who still seemed a little disappointed. "Well, it is awfully hot today, isn't it?" Okchŏm's mother said, brushing off her hurt feelings with a smile.

"Did the owner say this was a sweet one, mother?"

Okchŏm held up one of the melons.

"Yes, go ahead and slice it."

Okchŏm cut it in half with a knife. The flesh was green, and gave off the strong smell of honey.

"Oh, look at this. I bet it's delicious."

Holding it up for them both to see, Okchŏm peeled off the skin and gave a piece to Sinch'ŏl.

"Why don't we give this to your mother?" he said, taking it from her.

"Oh, just eat it."

Glancing at him out of the corner of her eye, she tossed the knife to the floor. Then, picking up the strawberries she had placed beside her, she smiled. To her, they seemed like tokens of Sinch'ŏl's love. She stared at the strawberries from different angles, then attached them to her hat.

"Look. Isn't this pretty?"

Okchŏm's mother had dozed off for a moment, but started up at the sound of her daughter's voice.

"My goodness! Where did the strawberries come from?"

"Mother, didn't you know I had them?" she laughed, then added, "It looks like you're falling asleep again . . ."

"Let's go back, then."

"Already? Why don't you go ahead."

Her mother rose slowly. It seemed difficult for her to stay any longer.

"Enjoy yourself, young man. I'm going back now."

"Oh, but why not go back with us?"

Sinch'ŏl followed Okchŏm's mother to the base of the hut and bowed to her politely. Okchŏm looked down on them from atop the platform.

"*Anata wa baka shōjiki wa ne.* Don't be so earnest," she said with a chuckle.

57

Okchŏm's mother turned around to look at Sinch'ŏl once again, and thought what a fine son-in-law he'd make. When Sinch'ŏl climbed back into the hut, he found Okchŏm wearing her hat, posing with the cluster of strawberries.

"What do you think?"

"Very nice . . . But let's just eat them. I want to see how they taste."

Okchŏm took off her hat and picked off the strawberries. She placed one in Sinch'ŏl's hand and popped the other inside her mouth. As Okchŏm's lips took on the color of the berry's red juices, Sinch'ŏl thought about what she'd just said to him about the strawberries and his heart. Then he felt a keen sense of loss as the image of Sŏnbi doing laundry appeared before his eyes. It was possible that one of those willow leaves he'd scattered on the pond had eventually touched Sŏnbi's fingers, he imagined, but surely she would have brushed it indifferently aside!

26

"A penny for your thoughts?" said Okchŏm, inching closer to Sinch'ŏl.

Sinch'ŏl pointed to the fluffy cumulus clouds hanging high above the stalks of sorghum.

"Look over there. Isn't that beautiful?"

Okchŏm looked up to where he was pointing.

"So you want to become a poet now?"

"A poet?"

What Okchŏm had said quite innocently seemed to prick at Sinch'ŏl's very core. He had become prey to his feelings recently and he knew that this would only bring trouble.

It was precisely because he'd become far too sensitive that he had taken a leave of absence from school and come here to the countryside. He had left town saying he was off to strengthen his body and mind. But thanks to this girl, Okchŏm, whom he unexpectedly found himself spending time with, any hope for self-improvement had vanished into thin air. And now, day after day, he had a new cause for anguish! The situation seemed near impossible for him to keep under control.

When he'd first met this girl on the train, he'd found himself intrigued by her, but within the course of a few days he knew for certain that he wouldn't want to spend very much time with her—even if she might be enjoyable to have around for a while. And yet for some reason he didn't want to leave this house, or even this village. In fact that's why he had stayed only a few days at Monggŭmp'o beach before returning.

Okchŏm stared at the fluffy clouds for a while, before stealthily shifting her line of vision onto Sinch'ŏl. Oh, those eyes gazing out onto the clouds! And that nose of steel that came down between them! Okchŏm knew this was a mark of his intelligence.

At this point, her mother and even her father seemed to approve of Sinch'ŏl as a potential son-in-law—or rather, they seemed to acknowledge the tacit agreement they assumed she and Sinch'ŏl had already made between themselves. The fact was, though, that she and Sinch'ŏl had made no such agreement, nor had either of them even suggested such intentions. This made Okchŏm nervous. While Sinch'ŏl continued to feign complete innocence, Okchŏm, unwilling to appear too forward, had been trying to gently guage his feelings.

"Please say something, Sinch'ŏl."

Sinch'ŏl turned and looked at her. He was on the point of speaking, but then broke into a smile.

"Come on. You were about to say something, weren't you? So tell me . . . Say it."

She was practically begging him like a child. Sinch'ŏl pushed himself back.

"Okchŏm, where do you see yourself living in the future? In a city like Seoul, or in a farming village like this one, for example?"

At this unexpected question, Okchŏm tilted her head to the side and thought for a while.

"Why are you asking me that?"

"Well, since we've got nothing special to talk about, I thought it might be an interesting topic of conversation."

"Where would you like to live, Sinch'ŏl?"

"Me? Let's see . . . Well, I asked you first, so I think you should answer before me."

"I think I'd like to live," Okchŏm paused, "wherever you want to live."

These last few words she said under her breath. The color ran to the very tips of her ears, and she turned her face away. Watching this, it suddenly hit Sinch'ŏl: Could this girl actually be in love with me? He remembered again what she'd asked him earlier: 'Is this your heart?'

"Well, that's nice of you to say, Okchŏm. I think we should live in the same place then. We could find a quiet farming village like this, and plant our own melons and millet and beans. Wouldn't that be great?"

Sinch'ŏl was pretending not to have understood what she'd meant. Okchŏm smiled.

"So you like it here in the countryside?"

"Sure I do. I like the countryside a lot. I'd love to be able to farm the land and raise different kinds of livestock."

"Oh, stop it!"

Okchŏm looked at him as though he were joking. Sinch'ŏl stared right back at her, looking dead serious.

"You're really going to get out in the fields and pull weeds?"

"Sure. Sounds like a great job to me."

"Don't be absurd, Sinch'ŏl."

"Why do you say that?" he replied, his brow rising.

"How could you spend your life working in the fields? You'd be better off..."

She cut herself off mid-sentence. It was now Sinch'ŏl who smiled.

"It sounds to me, Okchŏm, that you don't really like the idea of living in the countryside."

"Well, I...."

Okchŏm glared at Sinch'ŏl resentfully. Then she began chewing at her fingernails. Why couldn't Sinch'ŏl understand how much she was suffering inside? she asked herself, suddenly overcome with the desire to pounce on top of him and rip at his clothes. She quickly lifted her head.

27

Sinch'ŏl was still staring at the sky. Like a ball of cotton just released from its seed, one of the blindingly white clouds had grown into the shape of a mountain range, and enveloped the towering peak of Mount Pult'a.

Okchŏm looked at Sinch'ŏl. She wanted to say something to him, but that expression on his face she so resented—he was just staring into that sky, completely oblivious to her existence—that face held her under such a powerful spell that she ended up swallowing her words.

"Well, we might as well go home."

Sinch'ŏl turned his head.

"Okay, let's go then," he said, jumping to his feet.

Okchŏm's words had slipped off her tongue. All she'd really meant to do was continue the conversation; the last thing she wanted was to leave so soon. She needed time to probe Sinch'ŏl's feelings further, and had even entertained the faint hope of finding a resolution to her problems right then and there. And yet there was Sinch'ŏl, without any regrets, brushing off of his pants, lowering that sturdy body of his onto the ladder, and climbing down the rungs, one unsteady step after the other.

What Okchŏm wanted more than anything was to kick him in the pants and knock him to the ground.

Sinch'ŏl reached the bottom, brushed off his clothes and turned around.

"Come on down."

Okchŏm now felt a flood of tears surging inside her, and only by biting down firmly on her lip was she able to keep them at bay.

"Just go back by yourself!"

"But Okchŏm, didn't you say you wanted to go?"

There was a sparkle of a smile in Sinch'ŏl's eyes as he spoke. Seeing him smile made Okchŏm even angrier, but at the same time, she couldn't help herself—she smiled back at him, and climbed down the ladder.

Only now did the owner of the hut slowly make his way back through the melon patch from where he'd been keeping himself out of sight. They paid him for the melons they'd eaten, then started on the main path.

After only a few steps, Sinch'ŏl turned to Okchŏm.

"Listen. Why don't we go back to the village separately?"

"Why?" Okchŏm asked, her eyes growing red.

"Because it's embarrassing."

"What's embarrassing?"

"You know, the kids trailing behind us, the dogs barking. Ha, ha."

Okchŏm laughed at this unexpected answer, but her heartstrings were by now stretched so unbearably taut that what she really wanted to do was hang her head and cry.

As they walked along the sorghum field, Sinch'ŏl asked,

"What are we going to do? Are you going to go first? Or do you want me to?"

61

Okchŏm sighed. "Oh, I don't care, Sinch'ŏl. I don't see what you're so afraid of."

Without thinking, Okchŏm ripped a leaf from a sorghum plant and stuck it in her mouth. Sinch'ŏl noticed the long shadows of sorghum stems playing on her fashionable dress.

"I'm serious. What kind of human beings could possibly be more frightening than peasants? You go ahead."

Okchŏm said nothing and just stood there pouting for a moment. Then she twirled around, tossing to the side the sorghum leaf she'd been holding.

"Be sure to follow right behind me."

She spoke to him without turning back and headed off, walking through the sorghum field, climbing over the embankment and then gradually disappearing into the distance. Sinch'ŏl stared at her as she walked away, then he collapsed onto a patch of grass. He thought of the grove of trees at Wŏnso Pond. Sŏnbi had most likely made her way home by now . . .

Whenever the sun set like this, he recalled with fondness the sunset he'd seen at Monggŭmp'o beach. He remembered it as though it was a famous work of art: there he was standing with his chest bare, facing the brilliant sun as it slowly descended over the horizon, burning a giant pillar of flames through the vast Yellow Sea.

He also remembered the crashing sound of waves endlessly beating against the rocks . . . And he could almost hear the voices of the fishermen calling out, "Ŏi-ya, ŏi-ya" as they rowed their boats over the softly rolling waves.

Sinch'ŏl smiled. As he gazed out at the sunset in the distance, he thought about Okchŏm's impatience with him earlier. By feigning ignorance, he had managed to get through the worst of it. The more Okchŏm reacted to him in this way, the more his own feelings toward her turned cold as ice, and strangely, the more fun he had watching her squirm. He was pondering the conversation at the melon hut when he again heard the sound of someone pounding laundry in the grove of trees near Wŏnso Pond. He painted a picture of Sŏnbi's pure, lovely figure in his mind's eye. Indeed, only at the place of work, he mused, could one discover the truth and beauty of human beings!

Suddenly, something whacked him in the face, and he looked up in surprise.

62

28

A single locust, flapping its green wings wildly, buzzed off toward a grove of trees in the distance.

Sinch'ŏl jumped to his feet, gently stroking the side of his face where the insect had struck him. Tomorrow he should go to Monggŭmp'o again, he thought, and spend a few more days there before heading back to Seoul.

As he reached the outskirts of the village, he saw Yu Sŏbang approaching him.

"They say to go inside."

Sinch'ŏl nodded, then went into the house. Okchŏm was standing in the breezeway. She greeted Sinch'ŏl with a smile.

"It took you so long to come back."

He had been out of her sight for only a short while, but once again Okchŏm felt herself overcome by an emotion completely new to her, something that seemed to sweep her toward that solid body of his.

"Would you like to wash up?"

Sinch'ŏl glanced toward the kitchen and shook his head. Okchŏm headed into the inner room.

"Come inside then."

She pulled out a pink towel and tossed it into Sinch'ŏl's lap as he sat down. He caught the scent of perfume in the air. Sinch'ŏl placed the towel at his side and stared into the backyard. There was a load of white laundry hanging to dry on the reed fence. It looked like a blanket of freshly fallen snow. His own white shirt stood out among the other clothes.

"Who does the laundry here?" he asked.

"Sŏn . . ." began Okchŏm. "Granny does it. Why?"

She stared at him.

"You've never done laundry, Okchŏm?"

She hesitated for a moment before replying.

"No, I've never done it."

"Why should she care about laundry," chimed in her mother from the backyard. "You don't think she does any housework around here, do you?" she chuckled.

Okchŏm's mother seemed to adore her, and certainly was proud of the fact that her daughter never worked. All Sinch'ŏl could do was smile. For some reason his smile made Okchŏm uneasy.

Behind the sauce jars in the backyard the white balloon flowers hung their heads modestly. Behind them loofa vines climbed the fence, their tendrils beautifully extended and dotted with yellow flowers.

"What kind of flowers are those?" Sinch'ŏl pointed to the white flowers.

"Those?" Okchŏm replied. "They're called white balloon flowers. You can make medicine out of them, you know. That's why Yu Sŏbang planted them here."

"He planted those loofas too?"

"No, that girl Sŏnbi planted all those."

It was her mother who replied this time. Okchŏm felt uncomfortable even saying the name Sŏnbi in front of Sinch'ŏl, who, for his part, was now so endeared to these flowers that he would have jumped outside to pick one of them and caress his face with it, had Okchŏm not been sitting there.

Just then, from behind the fence, they heard the sound of children singing.

> I won't hand it over—oh, but yes I will
> How about I catch a fly and offer it to you.

They listened silently to the tune. The singing gradually approached the reed fence, then suddenly came to a stop. A dragonfly net rose to the top of one of the fence posts, and then the newly caught dragonfly flapped its wings. "Yay!" From the other side of the reeds came the sound of several children shouting gleefully.

> I won't hand it over—oh, but yes I will
> How about I catch a fly and offer it to you.

The song then disappeared into the distance.

As the singing came to an end, it struck Sinch'ŏl that his own childhood was now over. He let out a gentle sigh.

"I remember doing things like that, too, when I was young," he said.

Okchŏm stared at Sinch'ŏl with a twinkle in her eyes.

That night, after they had stayed up late enjoying themselves, Sinch'ŏl wasn't able to sleep when he finally lay down in bed. He tossed and turned, felt aches and pains all over, and was sweating profusely.

He couldn't bear it any longer, so he got up out of bed, and quietly slid open the door to peer outside.

The shadow of the eaves was crisply stenciled into the courtyard. Sensing that the moon must be bright, he tried peeking out from under the eaves to catch a better glimpse of the sky. But the moon had already ascended beyond the roofline, and he couldn't get a good view of it. He threw on some clothes and went outside.

When he checked on the inner quarters, everything was quiet. All he found was a pair of Okchŏm's mother's shoes placed at the entrance to the breezeway, white rubber shoes that glowed in the moonlight. Sinch'ŏl turned and started walking to the outhouse.

29

When he arrived at the outhouse, he froze. The paper door to Granny's room was aglow from the light of a lantern. Wasn't she asleep yet? At this time of night? He felt drawn by a faint hope of some kind and made his way over to the door, constantly looking over his shoulder to make sure that no one was there. He searched frantically for a crack in the door, but found nothing even the size of a pinhole.

He put his ear to the door. Which one of them was still awake? Could Granny and Sŏnbi both still be up? Or maybe it was just Sŏnbi? But then again, maybe it was just Granny? Oh, if he could only figure out which one it was!

Had anyone seen him? he panicked, turning back to the outhouse. But he thought he heard someone talking, and stood still again for a while.

He didn't catch any voices, but he did hear the faint sound of someone rummaging through a pile of clothes. He went inside the outhouse, wracking his brain over how he could find out who was awake in Granny's room. For some reason he couldn't shake off the feeling that it was Sŏnbi who was still up working.

Sŏnbi—why did this name have such a soft, sweet ring to his ears? And that humble expression in those eyes of hers, which were always cast downward. And her face that seemed shrouded in mist. What he really wanted to do was throw open that door and march right inside. But that was simply out of the question. What am I doing here? Why

65

did I even come out outside? he thought. He regretted not having just dealt with the heat in his room.

He quietly opened the outhouse door and peered outside. The paper door was still aglow. But just then a shadow flickered over the doorframe, as though someone had stood up, and the door quietly slid open. Sinch'ŏl felt faint. There was Sŏnbi, walking straight towards him! He didn't know what to do, but he sprang to his feet. After calming himself, he stepped out of the outhouse. Sŏnbi was walking towards him, but froze at the sound of his footsteps, and looked up. Determined not to let this opportunity go by, Sinch'ŏl called to her as she turned back to her room.

"Hey, wait a minute. Wait a minute."

Sŏnbi had almost reached the door to her room when she stopped, hesitantly.

"Um, could you get me a small bowl of cold water?" he asked.

In the confusion of the moment, this was all he could think of, but it would do. Briefly, it seemed as though Sŏnbi was considering his request, but then she opened her door and stepped inside. Her affront registered throughout his entire body, and he felt like collapsing onto the ground. Why hadn't he just kept quiet inside the outhouse until he could jump out and grab hold of her? he asked himself.

"Grandma. Grandma," Sŏnbi was waking up the old woman. Sinch'ŏl held his breath in order to better hear her. Waking Granny was no easy task, it seemed, for all she did was grunt in reply.

"Grandma... The man from Seoul . . ."

Sinch'ŏl only caught a few of Sŏnbi's words. Perhaps Granny had woken, though, for now he could hear a rougher voice speaking.

"Just go and get it. How am I supposed to see anything in the dark?"

Sŏnbi murmured something to her once again.

"Oh, who cares, child. Just do it."

Sinch'ŏl had lost heart as soon as he'd heard that Granny was awake, but now that it seemed that Sŏnbi might appear in front of him with a bowl of water, his heart pounded uncontrollably. Another shadow flickered between the door casing, the door slid open and Sŏnbi came out. There she was, her head down, moving toward the kitchen. He thought it rather ridiculous that he was standing in front of the outhouse, so he followed her.

As the dark inner quarters appeared before him, he peered inside to

66

see if anyone might have awoken. What if those glowing rubber shoes had transformed into a person! What if he heard the doors to the inner quarters open! Or what if Okchŏm herself were to come outside! His heart was now racing faster than ever.

Having quietly opened the kitchen door, Sŏnbi appeared, carrying his bowl of water. Oh, the sight of her bathed in the pure white light of the moon! She looked many times lovelier than did the Sŏnbi of the daylight. While she'd disappeared into the kitchen, Sinch'ŏl had come up with a new plan of action, but now that he saw her coming toward him, his plan escaped him and he panicked. He took the bowl of water from her and put it to his lips. He was terribly thirsty, but for some reason his throat refused to comply. He swallowed the wrong way, and by the time he stopped coughing and tried to hand the bowl back to her, she'd already vanished. He looked behind him. The hem of Sŏnbi's skirt was disappearing around the corner towards the outhouse.

30

He stared into the darkness. Could Sŏnbi really dislike me so very much? he wondered. Then he realized how foolish and downright vulgar he was acting. He wanted to throw the bowl to the ground and smash it into a million pieces. But as he looked into the bowl with angry eyes, he saw the moon that had earlier hidden itself from his view. It had fallen into the water, and quivered there ever so slightly. He could feel the anger inside him gradually subsiding. The water now seemed to reflect something in his heart. But this, too, was yet another of his fleeting thoughts. For now he laughed at how foolishly he was behaving, standing there analyzing this bowl! A sadness swept through his body, a feeling that his heart was somehow barren. With the water bowl still in his hand, he went back to his room.

He heard someone walking across the breezeway, and his door slowly slid open. A woman walked into the room. He looked at her in surprise.

"Hey, why aren't you asleep?"

He caught the scent of face cream in the air along with the powerful scent of a young woman's flesh. He felt strangely excited by Okchŏm in an altogether new way.

"What are you doing up and about?"

Sinch'ŏl managed to keep calm with his reply, but all sorts of emotions now swept through him, together with the fear that she could very well have seen everything that had just transpired. On any other day, Okchŏm might have come up to Sinch'ŏl's side and whispered something into his ear, but now she just stood there awkwardly.

"Well, either sit down or go on back to bed."

Sinch'ŏl surmised that Okchŏm had indeed witnessed everything. Perhaps Sŏnbi had left him without taking back the bowl precisely because she had seen Okchŏm. He could have killed himself for being so stupid.

Okchŏm stood thinking for a moment, then sat down next to Sinch'ŏl.

"Sŏnbi is pretty, isn't she?"

The unexpected question was like a raised fist thrust before him in the darkness. Sinch'ŏl had been caught off guard, and he hesitated.

"Yeah, she is," he finally replied, looking at Okchŏm.

Okchŏm hung her head, then snapped it back up again. "I should officially introduce you then."

"Okay."

Okchŏm sprung to her feet.

"I'll go get her."

At this, Sinch'ŏl lost his composure. He grabbed Okchŏm's nightgown and pulled her toward him. Then, in an effort to preserve his dignity he spoke to her in a tone of reconciliation.

"Now, Okchŏm, don't be so childish . . . You have tomorrow and the next day to introduce us. Why ever would you want to do it at this time of night?"

Okchŏm grabbed the hand with which Sinch'ŏl was clutching her nightgown, and started to sob. All the passion she'd held inside until this moment seemed to find an outlet in her tears. Sinch'ŏl put his arms around her without thinking, and held her tightly around the waist. But the image of the moon quivering in his bowl of water flashed before his eyes, and he slowly saw Sŏnbi appear before him, glowing in the pure white light of the moon. He slipped his hands away from Okchŏm and tried to sit back, but a flame had been kindled inside of him by Okchŏm's sumptuous flesh, which was separated from his own by nothing but that thin nightgown. He shut his eyes tightly.

"Okchŏm, go back to bed now."

68

Sinch'ŏl's voice cracked and the words didn't come out clearly. Okchŏm shook her body from side to side and squeezed even closer against him. Her whole body burned like fire now, and Sinch'ŏl was at the end of his wits. He heard a voice in his ear, the merciless sound of his own reason falling to pieces. And yet he realized it was impossible for him lift a single finger from this woman's body.

Just then the sound of someone clearing her voice in the inner room vibrated through the door. Sinch'ŏl pushed himself away from Okchŏm.

"Come on, you have to go back now. It sounds like you're mother's awake," he said.

Only then did Okchŏm slowly straighten. She looked at Sinch'ŏl. "Don't turn on the light! I'll go."

But the light was already shining. Sinch'ŏl looked over his shoulder and smiled to himself. He felt something close to joy at having crossed a line he should never have breached. But again he saw a vision of Sŏnbi, flashing a smile on that pretty face of hers.

Sinch'ŏl went to Okchŏm's side and stroked her disheveled hair. The sense of exhilaration he now felt practically forced him to do so. Okchŏm blushed to the tips of her ears, but she couldn't bring herself to look Sinch'ŏl in the face.

"Alright now, Okchŏm, go back to bed, okay?"

Okchŏm grabbed the hand with which Sinch'ŏl was smoothing her hair and clenched her teeth around it. Her whole body was trembling now, and she started to lick his hand with the tip of her tongue. Sinch'ŏl blushed, and pulled away his hand.

"Okchŏm, go back inside."

"No! I don't want to!"

Again they heard the sound of someone coughing.

31

The next morning Okchŏm awoke with a start to find her father beside her, smoothing down her uncombed hair.

"Father?"

She instantly thought of the previous night and of Sinch'ŏl's hands. She sensed that the air in her room was thick with a hope that she couldn't quite explain.

"Why are you sleeping so late?"

"Oh, I stayed up too late last night."

The thought of how Sinch'ŏl had held her tightly the previous night brought color to her cheeks. She wanted desperately to share with her father what had happened, but she was too embarrassed to speak of it.

"Daddy . . . would you buy me something?"

Tŏkho smiled.

"What now?"

"Well, how about a piano?"

"A piano? What's that?"

He'd never heard the word before. Okchŏm laughed.

"Oh, Father! Haven't you seen the pump organ they use to teach children to sing over at the school?"

"I suppose so."

"Well, it looks like that."

"So you want me to buy a Western-style organ? What the heck for?"

"To play, of course, Father . . ."

"Well, you can forget that! You've already got the chance to study. What do you need something like that for?"

"Oh, but Daddy, I simply must have one. Won't you buy one for me, please . . . ?"

"Hmm . . . Well, how much are they?"

"Do you promise to buy one?"

"Just tell me how much."

"Only if you promise to buy me one."

Perhaps Tŏkho realized that he would eventually give in if Okchŏm started to plead.

"All right, I'll get you one."

"Well, I heard that a decent one costs at least a thousand."

"A thousand wŏn?"

Tŏkho's eyes opened wide. He was speechless. Okchŏm grabbed her father's hand and squeezed it tightly.

"Oh, Father, are you really that surprised? I'm going to get all your money anyway, won't I? You aren't going to leave it to anyone else, are you?"

She smiled at him with a twinkle in her eye.

"Well, no, I suppose not. But mind you, even if you're going to inherit

70

my money, what sense does it make for me to go out and buy this foolish thing if you're not going to use it?"

"But no, Father, no, I will. If you go to Seoul, you'll see that every family with a respectable home has one. You've just never been in one before."

"What use will this thing have anyway? I'd be the first person to get one if it did something like mint silver or gold, but what's the point of spending money on something that does absolutely nothing for you? Do you have any idea how much interest a thousand wŏn will make in a year? Well, do you?"

"Oh, Daddy, if you don't get me one, I'm sure I'll fall ill, I want one so badly ..."

"You're something else, girl," he chuckled. "You need one so badly that you're going to be sick? Well, I'll think about it."

When Okchŏm saw that he didn't outright refuse her request, she had a hunch that he'd give in. Tŏkho, however, had something else on his mind.

"Now, this boy Sinch'ŏl. Where did he say he goes to school?"

"Kyŏngsŏng Imperial University! He said he's going to graduate next year."

"Hmm. And you'd say his family is well off?"

"Well, his father is a teacher, so I suppose they have a monthly income. I don't know, they might even have some land in the country as well."

Okchŏm blushed.

"Alright, Father, please go now. I've got to get up."

"You see, I could tell he was the son of a gentlemen, brought up in a proper family. Hell, those manners of his are perfect."

"Well, I guess so ..."

Okchŏm painted a picture of Sinch'ŏl in her mind and felt a twinge of embarrassment thinking about the next time she would see him. This made her heart race even faster. Looking satisfied with himself, Tŏkho smiled and left her room. Okchŏm rose and dressed. She picked up her nightgown and held it tightly against her. The thought that Sinch'ŏl had held that nightgown in his arms last night sent a tingle down her spine. She folded her bedding and put it away. She opened her door just a crack and saw that the door to the side room where Sinch'ŏl slept was wide open, though she couldn't see Sinch'ŏl. It looked as if he had gone out for another walk. He had a habit of going out before the crack of dawn. Okchŏm quietly crossed to his room. It had been cleanly swept and the books on his desk had been carefully arranged. There was a pair of Sinch'ŏl's dirty socks rolled in a ball under the desk. As Okchŏm stood there staring at them, reflecting on the events of the previous night, she wondered, Does Sinch'ŏl really love me?

32

As she sat and pondered this question, she recalled the scene she had witnessed: Sŏnbi and Sinch'ŏl standing face to face with a bowl of water between them. A wave of jealous feelings now swept uncontrollably through Okchŏm. Could Sinch'ŏl be in love with Sŏnbi? But what could he love about her? No, no, I must have this wrong, she thought. How could a person like Sinch'ŏl fall for somebody's servant? And especially for a hick like that who's never been to school and doesn't know anything. She might be pretty, but what else is there? Once Okchŏm had thought things through in this way, she felt somewhat reassured. Yet something still lingered in her mind, a cause for unease and discomfort. She made up her mind to ask Sŏnbi what had happened the night before, and hurried to the kitchen.

Sŏnbi was shuttling around the room clearing up the dishes.

"Hey, you, Sŏnbi! Come out here for a minute."

Sŏnbi followed Okchŏm to the backyard. The loofa vines climbing the marsh reed fence had just set forth their first yellow blossoms of the season. Sŏnbi glanced at them delightedly, then went over to Okchŏm.

"Why did you leave your room last night?" Okchŏm asked.

Sŏnbi didn't at first seem to understand.

"Me, when?"

"Don't try to hide anything from me, Sŏnbi. Weren't you up last night getting water for the guest from Seoul?"

Only then did Sŏnbi understand what she meant.

"Oh, yes! I was on my way to the outhouse last night when I saw the guest from Seoul come out of it. He asked me for a bowl of cold water, so I went and got one for him. Why do you want to know?"

"Hmm . . ." Okchŏm nodded her head as she looked at Sŏnbi. "Go back to work then," she said, turning back to go inside.

Sŏnbi returned the kitchen, wondering what was going on. Maybe the guest from Seoul had said something to Okchŏm? Maybe there'd been a fly in the water bowl, or maybe a pine needle had fallen into it and he'd complained. Sŏnbi was so worked up she could hardly enjoy her breakfast.

After clearing her breakfast tray, Sŏnbi picked up the laundry Granny had earlier boiled in lye. As she stood there hanging it out to dry on the marsh reed fence, she looked toward the inner room. Okchŏm was working on her embroidery, and for some reason there she was, calling Sŏnbi over with a wave of her hand. Sŏnbi was worried Okchŏm might ask her more questions, and her heart started pounding. She kept looking into the house to see if the guest from Seoul was inside, but she didn't see the man who always seemed to be with Okchŏm. He must have left this morning, she concluded, and after hanging out the rest of the laundry, she went into the room.

"Sŏnbi, come and learn how to embroider."

The truth was that whenever Sŏnbi saw Okchŏm work on her embroidery she wished she could try for herself sometime.

"Well, I've never done it before."

"All you have to do is this."

It was a picture of what seemed to be a pair of white cranes resting beneath a pine tree. Sŏnbi watched Okchŏm carefully.

"Did you learn this at school, too?"

"Of course I did. Not only this design, but all sorts of other ones as well."

Sŏnbi stared at the colorful silk threads in Okchŏm's embroidery. Oh, if only I could sew like that, too, she thought, even just once. Gradually, she saw the crane's wings taking form.

"Isn't this picture nice? Our teacher came up with the motif all by herself. Don't you find it so . . . aesthetic?"

Whatever Okchŏm was saying, Sŏnbi hardly understood a word of it. It seemed like Okchŏm was bragging about how wonderful her picture was. At least that's what Sŏnbi thought.

"Embroidery isn't very hard, you know. Everyone selects one's favorite animal or landscape and then sketches it onto a piece of paper. Then all one has to do is simply stitch it up like this with thread . . . and there you have it: embroidery."

Okchŏm rattled on answering unasked questions, for she knew that Sŏnbi envied her ability to embroider, and even more, she wanted to make sure that Sinch'ŏl, who was talking with her mother in the side room, was well aware that she was sewing. Though it was only an instinct, she had the feeling that Sinch'ŏl would be pleased to know she was hard at work.

Sŏnbi listened attentively to Okchŏm's words, going over in her mind what Okchŏm had just said: embroidery was simply a matter of sketching something one liked and then stitching it up with thread . . .

"So, Sŏnbi, what sort of design would you like to embroider? If you tell me, I'll sketch it up for you. And give you some thread, too."

So excited was Sŏnbi by Okchŏm's kindness that her heart was racing. Oh, how I want some of that pretty thread! she thought, almost dizzy from her own delight. She put her head down to think about it. Mount Pult'a? Wŏnso Pond? Several images came to mind, before she found the right one. She lifted her head, ready to say it, but the words weren't coming out. Staring at Sŏnbi's cheeks, Okchŏm thought of what had happened the night before.

"Quick! Out with it."

"Well, I'm not really sure . . ."

"Oh, come on. I said I'd give you some thread if you told me."

"Well . . . a chicken laying her eggs is what . . ."

"Oh, how embarrassing! Really, Sŏnbi, how could you!"

Okchŏm cried these words out loud, while Sŏnbi's face went bright red.

33

In no time at all, the hot month of August had passed.

Okchŏm and Sinch'ŏl had just finished their preparations for their trip to Seoul. They would be leaving the next morning.

Okchŏm's mother looked at Sŏnbi, who was working beside them, folding clothes and placing them into a wicker trunk.

"Sŏnbi, see that 'picnic pasket' or whatever it's called. Well, go fill it up with eggs."

Sŏnbi felt a lump in her throat. If it hadn't been for Okchŏm, she'd have collected close to 100 eggs by now, but ever since Okchŏm had come home, not a single day had passed when Okchŏm didn't eat all the eggs the chickens laid. It wouldn't have been so bad if Okchŏm had gone and collected them with her own hands, but she'd developed the habit of asking Sŏnbi to get them for her. Whenever Sŏnbi was asked to get the eggs, a sense of loss she couldn't quite explain weighed heavily on her heart.

Sŏnbi slowly rose and went into the pantry. She took down her egg basket from atop the jar. Before Okchŏm had come home, she used to treat this basket as something so very important and precious to her, but today she didn't even want to set her eyes on it. Those cute little eggs she'd so painstakingly collected—all she wanted to do with them now was smash them one by one onto the floor. She could feel her nostrils flaring with this sudden impulse. She's been eating up the eggs every day now, thought Sŏnbi as she passed through the threshold of the pantry. You'd think that'd be enough for her. But, no! Now she wants all the rest of them as well. The nerve of her! But just then—just as she stepped up into the breezeway—Sŏnbi stumbled. Two eggs rolled out of the basket and cracked.

"Watch out for those eggs!" cried Okchŏm. She ran up to Sŏnbi and snatched the basket away from her.

"Just what do you think you're doing! Carrying something like this around without paying any attention. You might be good at housework, but you are a perfect fool when it comes to this sort of thing. Simply unbelievable!"

Okchŏm made sure she shouted loud enough for Sinch'ŏl to hear. She was thrilled to be able to find fault with Sŏnbi within his earshot. Okchŏm's mother came in shortly thereafter carrying some clothes. She stood face to face with her daughter and Sŏnbi.

"And just what am I supposed to do with you? You came an inch away from breaking them all. A girl your age should be walking slowly, not racing around however she pleases . . ."

Mercilessly attacked by both mother and daughter, Sŏnbi felt the color rush into her face. She realized that all the sorrow she had tried hard to keep inside was about to pour out of her. She stood still, trying to keep back the flood of tears, when Okchŏm's mother started berating her again.

"There's not a single thing I can get done around here without having to worry about whether you'll do it properly. The minute I look the other way, there you are neglecting your work again. Tell me what a girl close to twenty years of age is doing behaving like that. Now, get back into that kitchen, find something to do with yourself, and tell Granny to get the hell in here!"

The woman's scream was so shrill that it sent vibrations through the entire breezeway. Sŏnbi went back into the kitchen. Granny stood in front of her, wide-eyed.

"What happened, dear? What's the matter?"

Sŏnbi held onto a shelf in the cabinet and started to sob. She was mortified to have been insulted by the woman and her daughter, and even more upset that every single egg she'd collected that spring had now been taken from her.

As the tears streamed down her cheeks, all she could think about were the eggs—dozens and dozens of those, lovely, oval-shaped eggs.

"Granny, get in here!"

As soon as Okchŏm's mother yelled for her, Granny ran, wiping away the traces of tears from her face. Granny had the habit of crying whenever Sŏnbi cried.

"That girl broke the eggs," said Okchŏm's mother as Granny came into the room.

"No!" Granny was shocked. She remembered how Sŏnbi had always carried her eggs around so lovingly.

"How many did she break?"

"How many? Well . . ." the woman mumbled, unwilling to admit that Sŏnbi had actually only broken a few. "If it hadn't been for Okchŏm, they'd all be broken. Okchŏm had the sense to take them right away from her. I'll tell you, it's a good thing my daughter knows something about running a household."

It was shameless how she heaped this praise on Okchŏm. Granny sat there with her head hung, sorting out Okchŏm's clothes. Well, I guess you're always going to think your own children are perfect, she concluded. Okchŏm came back into the room.

"Mom, I don't want these things!" she said, as she looked at the long, cotton drawers her mother had put in the trunk. "Who'd ever wear anything so rough against the skin?"

"Well, what are you going to wear then?"

"I'll buy my own underwear. These . . . these I'll just give to Granny."

Okchŏm flung the underpants over at Granny, who jumped back in surprise.

34

Okchŏm's mother snatched back the underpants and put them inside the wardrobe.

"If you won't wear them, I will."

Coming across a pair of cotton underwear had been such a stroke of good fortune for Granny that the lines in her face had begun to twitch uncontrollably. But such was her disappointment at losing them now that her heart felt pierced by the stinginess displayed by Okchŏm's mother. The overpowering smell of the moth balls helped to stifle her breathing. She turned her head to the side and sneezed a couple of times; her eyes began to tear.

"Mom, Sinch'ŏl is going to pack the eggs in the picnic basket. He wants me to get him some straw or something to put underneath them."

"Oh, heavens! I am so relieved. He must have noticed how frantic we've been. What a thoughtful young man! Don't you agree, Granny? Heaven knows that girls aren't usually so careful, but you certainly don't expect such consideration from a man. Now, Okchŏm, you'd better follow his example!"

Okchŏm was so happy that she hardly knew what to do with herself.

"Granny, get me some cotton out of the closet."

Whatever does this girl want with cotton all of a sudden? wondered Granny, as she opened the door to the closet and took out a bundle of cotton. She started picking through it.

"What kind did. . . ?"

"No, no, not that! We're going all the way to Seoul. How is that old stuff supposed to look? Give me the new cotton underneath that."

Only now did Granny understand that the cotton was to be used for cushioning the eggs. She took out some of the fluffy new cotton from the bottom of the bundle and handed it to Okchŏm. Whatever it was that drove her to such urgency, Okchŏm practically ripped the cotton out of Granny's hands and stormed out of the room, her feet pounding against the wooden floor. As Granny watched her rush off, she thought of the cotton balls she had harvested last autumn.

They said it was only a half-acre plot, but the cotton field down in front of the village sure seemed much bigger. Granny, Sŏnbi and Yu

77

Sŏbang had spent day after day there picking cotton until the sun went down. They were all so enchanted by the beautiful fluffy balls that they never got bored of the picking. One ball of cotton after the next, Sŏnbi and Granny went on picking until their skirts were simply bulging! But oh, how they had pricked their fingers and stubbed their toes on those plants in order to pick the cotton! And how they had endured such agonizing pain in their necks in order to balance it all on their heads! Here these people were too stingy to give her anything better than worn-out old padding for her winter jacket, and yet those eggs bound for Seoul were to be cushioned with fluffy, new cotton. By the time Granny's train of thought had meandered this far, her eyes were red and swollen, and she sneezed once again.

"You know, Granny, 'Even dogs don't catch colds in June.' What's the matter with you?"

No, we're no better than dogs, are we! These words were on the very tip of Granny's tongue, but she managed to hold them back. As she continued to shuffle through the clothes, she could still feel on her fingers the clean texture of that new cotton she'd just touched. Oh, heavens, we're going to have to collect even more of it this fall! And carry it all the way back up here again . . . The old woman sighed deeply.

"So, Granny, did you know that our guest staying over in the side room goes to university? It's the best one in all of Korea. Next spring he's going to graduate and make a huge monthly salary . . . Now, what was it he's going to do again?"

She tilted her head to the side pensively.

"Oh, dear, it's slipped my mind! Well, anyway, as I was saying, there's certainly nothing to be ashamed of in choosing him as Okchŏm's match. I tell you, I am so relieved, I could die tomorrow . . ."

Okchŏm's mother went on excitedly, but it seemed as if she was talking to herself. In any case, Granny didn't catch a single word she said. No matter how long she stayed in this house, all she got out of it was more and more work, thought Granny. It didn't even look like they'd have the decency to give her a set of proper clothes. Maybe she'd be better off quitting come fall. But if she left this house, what could a woman like herself do, without any children of her own to depend on? Oh, help me, I'd be better off dead . . .

"Granny, when do you think we should hold Okchŏm's wedding?"

Granny didn't quite catch what the woman was saying. She simply looked at Okchŏm's mother, lost in her own thoughts.

"I'm talking about Okchŏm's wedding ceremony."

"Oh, yes, yes," the old woman finally replied, looking back down at her work.

"When do you think would be the best time?"

"Well, I . . ."

"People usually hold their ceremonies in the fall, you know, and I really wish we could too. But I have absolutely no idea what the two of them have in mind! Now, mind you, these days the children arrange all the details by themselves. So all we old folks have to do is, well, 'Sit back,' as they say, 'and enjoy the fruits of another's labor.'"

If Okchŏm's mother thought about anything at all in recent days, it was her daughter's wedding. Granny, on the other hand, had just realized something: if they were fixing to hold a wedding this year, she didn't stand a chance of getting any new cotton.

35

The next morning Sinch'ŏl rose before dawn, and with a towel and a bar of soap in hand, he headed outside. Yu Sŏbang had already drawn the water from the well and was feeding the chickens. Sinch'ŏl could hear the sound of twigs being snapped in half in the kitchen. He went through the middle gate and quickly peeked into the kitchen, but it was still so dark outside that he couldn't see exactly who was in there. All that caught his eye through the smoke was a flame burning in the fireplace. Suddenly he felt like crying. It dawned on him that he might leave without ever having had the chance to sit down face to face with Sŏnbi, after whom he had longed all this time. He walked out the main gate and then hesitated. And why? Why did he hesitate? He wasn't even sure of that. He paced back and forth for some time, then made his way to the other side of the fence.

He had the faint hope of catching one more glimpse of Sŏnbi's face through the slits in the reed fence, though he knew this was unlikely to happen. He stood there lost in his thoughts, staring up at the sky as dawn gradually broke. Once he left this place it wouldn't be easy to make his way back. In the meantime, he thought, Sŏnbi will end up going off somewhere to get married. She'll have a son and then a daughter and work on a farm, and then sooner or later she'll have a wrinkle or two on that lovely face of hers! These 'sentimental' thoughts tugged powerfully at Sinch'ŏl's heart. But as he looked off at the distant horizon, it became more and more clear to him that his longing for Sŏnbi would forever remain a secret, one buried deep in his heart. He let out a sigh and then set out toward Wŏnso Pond. Every morning he had come down to the pond to wash up, exercise, and whistle a tune, hoping he might by chance meet Sŏnbi there. And yet, ever since that day when he'd scattered those willow leaves onto the water and watched Sŏnbi from afar, he'd never even once spotted her at Wŏnso Pond.

Several times he had seen Granny there, but for some reason he never managed to come across Sŏnbi. Perhaps if he were actually to come face to face with this maiden named Sŏnbi once again, she might not even be very special . . .

As he came up to Wŏnso Pond, the blue water seemed to greet him in its own wordless way. It was as though the sound of the trickling water was offering him its deepest regrets at their imminent separation.

Looking around him through the grove of willows, with drops of dew hanging from their leaves, Sinch'ŏl felt again as if he were experiencing the harmony of nature. A pair of wild geese appeared on the surface of the blue water, with long graceful necks, and beautiful white silhouettes. What luck to see a pair of wild geese right there before his eyes! And what feelings of tenderness and innocence they evoked inside him . . .

This was Yongyŏn village in the morning mists! And today would be his last glimpse of it. If only he could meet Sŏnbi just one more time, and ask her about her aspirations in life . . . As his gaze settled on Okchŏm's family's house, he imagined Sŏnbi's pitiful, lovely figure, just as he had seen it yesterday when both mother and daughter had attacked her so viciously. Poor Sŏnbi had to spend day after day in Okchŏm's house— that den of wolves—prey to every sort of contempt! He now felt as though he had an obligation to rescue her from her situation. I wonder if she even knows how to read Korean? he thought. If only there were some way to bring her to Seoul . . .

He set his mind into gear. If he really wanted to bring Sŏnbi to Seoul, it would only be a matter of coaxing Okchŏm into it. But he couldn't in his wildest dreams go as far as marrying Okchŏm in order to do so. She was so oblivious! And that look in her eyes, that way she laid on that charm—anyone could plainly see that it all came from watching American movie stars on the big screen! That one-of-a-kind look on her face that might have bewitched any man passing by on the street—oh, how it made Sinch'ŏl tire of her even more.

He'd been raised in the big city and known nothing but its cosmopolitan comforts, so he couldn't quite figure out why this type of woman didn't appeal to him. His classmates even mocked him for it, going to the extent of diagnosing him with an abnormal personality disorder. And yet, after coming out to the countryside and unexpectedly coming across this girl Sŏnbi, he was surprised by the way the frigid side of his personality had been cleanly swept away.

He thought long and hard about how he might be able to bring Sŏnbi to Seoul. If only she knew how to read, he would have jotted down a few words to this effect and passed them on to her. But Sinch'ŏl had the feeling that she didn't even know the alphabet.

When he took out his pocket watch to see what time it was, he felt something claw at his heart.

Pressed for time, he went straight down to the base of the slope to wash up. As he scooped up a handful of water, he looked at the pond. There were the geese again, circling around and around over that blue water! It slipped his mind that he was in a hurry, and he splashed water toward the geese a few times. After a moment he came to his senses, finished washing up, and made his way back into the village. As he passed around the reed fence behind Tŏkho's house, he suddenly froze. There was a hand reaching up over the fence.

36

When Sinch'ŏl looked up to where the hand stretched, he noticed a single summer squash, half-hidden by one of the leaves. The hand snapped the dew-drenched squash off the vine and slowly lowered it behind the reeds. Sinch'ŏl took one step closer to the fence. Whose hand is that? he wondered, just as it disappeared from sight. That hand! It had thick knuckles and cracked nails . . . he had no idea whom it could have belonged to.

Sinch'ŏl quickly walked over to the reed fence and grabbed onto it, trying to look through it to find out whose hand it was. All he could see was the tail of a skirt that had already turned at the woodpile and was disappearing into the kitchen. Who could it have been? Granny! That's it! How could Sŏnbi's hands look anything like that? No matter how hard she works, she still has her youth . . . It couldn't have been Sŏnbi's! It just couldn't have! He shook his head emphatically. From the kitchen he could hear the sound of someone washing dishes and of someone chopping, and then he heard Okchŏm laugh—this medley of sounds swept toward him all at the same time.

The image of thin, slender fingers came to his mind. Yes, these are Sŏnbi's hands! he thought. The unpleasant thoughts he had suffered on account of that one ugly hand were clearing up of their own accord. Yes, that was someone else's hand. How could Sŏnbi's hands look anything like that? Especially someone as pretty as Sŏnbi! That one ugly hand had caused him to make a gross mistake about Sŏnbi's hands—hands that he had no doubt taken unconscious note of . . . Sinch'ŏl's analysis of the matter complete, he now longed for Sŏnbi even more strongly, and he wanted to postpone his departure, even by just a little.

"Yu Sŏbang, go on over to the mountainside and tell our guest from Seoul to come back." Sinch'ŏl was walking into the courtyard just as Okchŏm's mother was saying this.

"Oh, there you are. Come inside and have something to eat before you leave."

Okchŏm stood in the breezeway waiting to greet him, freshly primped and powdered as she always was in the morning. Sinch'ŏl stepped up into the breezeway, conscious of the strong scent of her powder in the air. Tŏkho came from the inner room where he had been sitting.

"Well, be sure you visit us again soon, you hear."

Ever since Sinch'ŏl had asked Tŏkho not to be so polite with him, Tŏkho had always addressed him in these familiar terms.

"Well . . . I'm afraid I've put your family to a great deal of trouble by staying here."

"Oh, don't be ridiculous."

Staring at Sinch'ŏl's wide, handsome eyes, the thought struck Tŏkho that he might want to use this opportunity to make a few decisions, even in very general terms, about Sinch'ŏl's marriage to Okchŏm. But since the two of them seemed to have a tacit understanding between themselves, he kept this to himself, thinking it would be best to wait until they brought up the subject. Besides, he knew that educated kids had their own ideas, even when it came to getting married, so he decided to stay out of it for now.

The meal trays were brought in. Tŏkho craned his neck to take a good look at them.

"Not much there by way of side dishes, but try to enjoy it anyway . . . Oh, and you, kiddo, don't you go eating any of that chicken broth, you hear me? You know you're not supposed to eat meat while you're taking that medicine."

Okchŏm shot a glance at her father.

"Daddy! I'm not taking any of that horrible medicine. How is anyone supposed to drink anything so bitter?"

"Oh, come girl! I'm telling you to take it, because it'll do you some good . . . You're as stubborn as a mule!" Then he turned to Sinch'ŏl. "Try to talk some sense into her, young man. The girl is fully grown all right. But she's spoiled rotten and won't listen to a thing you say . . ."

Tŏkho looked back and forth between Sinch'ŏl and Okchŏm affectionately. While he didn't show it, Sinch'ŏl was now alarmed. He knew that these were no ordinary words on Tŏkho's part and he could feel the color rising into his own face. Okchŏm picked up her spoon and looked down at her meal. Her eyebrows seemed too heavily penciled.

"Now, do please help yourself," said Okchŏm's mother, coming in from the kitchen. Sinch'ŏl collected himself and looked up at her.

"Yes, I will. Thank you."

"Hey! Heat up another bowl of soup!" she called.

Soon Sŏnbi appeared with a bowl of soup in her hands, standing sideways at the kitchen door that led through the breezeway. Oh, that glowing face, flushed pink by the steam billowing from the soup!

And standing out so boldly on her brow, that black mole was surely a sign of her self-composure. Sinch'ŏl could feel Okchŏm's dagger-like eyes glaring upon him as he took the bowl of soup. Oh, no, this is the very last bowl of soup Sŏnbi will ever prepare for me! he thought, his hands slightly trembling. All the passion he'd held back these past few months, he now felt gushing towards the steaming bowl.

With the coming of fall, Tŏkho's trips into town became more frequent. One sometimes found him dressed quite smartly, even in Western suits, which he never used to wear before. Just as he started to visit town more frequently, he sent Kannan off somewhere. Rumors began to spread among the villagers: he'd gotten a *kisaeng* for himself, or else he'd found a young virgin mistress. Naturally, Okchŏm's mother was furious, and instead of staying at home all alone, she also went into town more frequently, often on the heels of her husband.

On this particular night, it had already been five days since Okchŏm and Sinch'ŏl had gone off and no one had received a single word from town. Sŏnbi and Granny were feeling rather lonesome, left to themselves in the huge house. At night at least Yu Sŏbang would come to stay in the men's quarters after work. But since he was always so tired from working all day long, he was asleep as soon as his head hit his pillow. As a result, neither Granny nor Sŏnbi was able to go to bed with her mind at ease—they were too afraid to even turn out the light in their room.

Tonight the two were picking clean the cotton balls they had gathered that afternoon, talking affectionately with each other just as a mother and daughter might do. The sound of the *tubu tchige* bubbling away on a charcoal brazier in the corner had gradually died down, and now it had completely stopped cooking. Sŏnbi turned to look at the brazier.

"I guess Mother isn't coming back today."

"Well, she won't be coming home this late, that's for sure. It must be going on midnight."

Granny looked up at the clock hanging on the wall. Sŏnbi peered up at it too.

"It's half past eleven," said Sŏnbi.

"No matter how long I look at that thing, I can't ever figure it out," said Granny, still staring up at the clock. "What's that big hand and little hand supposed to mean again?"

When asked to be that precise, Sŏnbi didn't exactly know, either. She simply smiled and said, "They just show you what time it is, that's all."

Granny nodded. She was picking out the dried pepper stems caught in a ball of cotton. When she finished, she placed the cotton ball into her basket.

"Well, I reckon we've got another bumper crop of peppers this year. We should have planted all peppers in that field instead of the cotton."

"But where would we plant the cotton?"

"Down yonder, in the valley. The peppers are growing good in the field we used this year. But cotton doesn't take to soil that's too rich, you know. Best to have a bit of sand mixed in with the soil."

Sŏnbi picked up a ball of cotton and showed it to Granny.

"Yeah, but just look at this. These cotton balls are huge. Just a few of them would be enough to pad a whole jacket! They're plenty big, if you ask me."

Glowing beneath the brilliant light of the lamp, that single ball of cotton set Sŏnbi's heart aflutter. It came to her that something like this would be just the thing to sketch out and make into a work of embroidery. But then she hung her head when she recalled Okchŏm's scornful laughter—it was like the sound of silk tearing. She felt a surge of hateful feelings toward Okchŏm rush into her.

Granny started speaking again softly.

"It'd be mighty fine of them this year to give us some of this here cotton for our jackets . . ."

"It sure would."

Granny opened her saggy eyes, and went back to the task of picking out the specks of dirt from her ball of cotton. She sighed. Sŏnbi thought of the old, dirty cotton lining Granny's jacket, which would be little protection this year against the wind. She didn't know how many years that same cotton had been in her jacket, but by now it had certainly lost all of its give and had nothing of the delicate texture it once had. Even if she tried pulling it apart to fluff it up a bit, the fibers themselves would probably rip in half . . . Sŏnbi looked at Granny once more. The old woman's eyes were red and swollen.

"Oh, Granny, they'll give us some cotton this year for sure! Last year they had to sell it all. That's why we didn't get any. They're not going to sell it again this year."

"Well, you can just forget about that, kiddo. Don't you know what they did with the cotton this summer? They used it all up to cushion those eggs Okchŏm took with her to Seoul."

At Granny's mention of the eggs, Sŏnbi remembered how she had tripped while carrying the egg basket, and she unconsciously let out a deep sigh. This led her to think of the unexpected guest they'd had from Seoul. They must be a happy couple! she thought. She imagined that Okchŏm and her guest from Seoul would someday get married and have a wonderful life together. When she thought of her own future, however, things looked more and more bleak. Then the image of Ch'ŏtchae's face flashed before her eyes.

She never used to think of Ch'ŏtchae like this, and since the harvest season had begun, she'd been far too busy to think about anything at all. But recently when she lay down to bed at night, she'd been finding it difficult to fall asleep, and no matter which direction her mind chose to wander, her thoughts invariably drifted back to Ch'ŏtchae.

Just then, the middle gate creaked open and she and Granny looked at each other in alarm.

38

At the sound of footsteps plodding down the hallway Granny called out, "Yu Sŏbang, is that you?"

The door soon opened, and both Yu Sŏbang and Tŏkho entered the room. As soon as they saw Tŏkho, the two women jumped to their feet in surprise.

"We never expected you back so late at night."

Tŏkho was staggering, so Yu Sŏbang took him by the hand and sat him down in the warmest spot on the floor. A smell of liquor filled the air. Tŏkho looked at Sŏnbi and Granny with a dazed expression, then sprawled out onto the floor. Sŏnbi quickly took out a pillow and handed it to Yu Sŏbang.

"Sŏnbi, massage my legs for me, would you?"

Tŏkho's speech was slurred. Sŏnbi shuddered and found it difficult to go to Tŏkho's side. Granny sharply signaled for Sŏnbi to do as she'd been told.

"The Missus won't be coming home this evening?"

"Okchŏm's ma? Oh . . . Oh, hell, am I drunk! Ptew. . . ptew . . ."

Tŏkho spit up into his spittoon, his arms and legs convulsing each time. The others just stared at him with their mouths agape, worried he might lash out at them for doing something wrong. Each time Tŏkho coughed, their eyes widened as they tried to read the expression on his face.

"Can I cook you some rice?" offered Granny after a few minutes. Tŏkho looked at Granny and Sŏnbi with a dazed look in his eyes.

"No, but Sŏnbi, I want you to pat down my legs a bit."

Sŏnbi's face colored and she looked over at Granny. Yu Sŏbang and Granny both looked back at her, beckoning her to do as she was told.

"Come on, girl ... Give me a massage ... My legs hurt, my legs!

Tŏkho kicked his feet up and down banging them against the floor. Granny poked Sŏnbi in the ribs and motioned her over to Tŏkho with her eyes. Sŏnbi had no choice but to go to Tŏkho's side. Grabbing his legs, she began chopping down on them with the sides of her palms. It seemed he had spilled liquor on his suit pants, for the smell of alcohol was thick in the air. Sŏnbi's brow furrowed slightly.

"Oh, that's it. What a good daughter I have!"

Tŏkho craned his head to look at Sŏnbi, then sprawled back down on the floor.

"Oh hell, am I drunk. Drunk, drunk, drunk! You go on off to bed," said Tŏkho, looking over at Yu Sŏbang.

Yu Sŏbang was so exhausted that he'd barely been able to keep his eyes open, but since he was sitting in front of Tŏkho, he was trying his best to stay awake by biting down on his tongue. As soon as Tŏkho told him he could leave, he stood to go.

"Granny, make sure my breakfast is ready early tomorrow morning."

"Yes, Sir," replied Granny, caught somewhat off-guard. She hung her head to avert her eyes from Tŏkho's line of vision.

"Go on off to bed. Otherwise, how are you supposed to make me an early breakfast?"

"Yes, Sir."

"Well," began Tŏkho, "tomorrow I'm off to the county office, yes, I am. Not that I could turn them down anyway. . . I bet they make me county deputy, or maybe even township mayor. Hah, ha ..."

Tŏkho mumbled on like this, laughing to himself, as though no one else were in the room. Granny and Sŏnbi glanced at each other. They were happy to hear that the Master might be appointed mayor. Though they had always found it difficult to trust Tŏkho, his new status made him seem far more trustworthy.

"Sŏnbi, take out my bedding, and then go to bed with Granny."

Sŏnbi let out a faint sigh of relief. Her whole body felt unburdened now, as though she had just been relieved of a heavy load. She promptly laid out Tŏkho's bedding and headed out of the room, but turned around again to turn down the lamp before leaving with Granny.

"I wonder if the Master will really be mayor of the township?" said Granny, who had by now crossed over to the side room. Sŏnbi smiled and spread out the bedding.

"Well, looks like the Master's got some talent. Mayor of the township, now that's something! Who else do we have like that in Yongyŏn?"

Sŏnbi listened carefully to Granny as she folded her hands behind her pillow and stretched out her legs. She instantly felt relief from the exhaustion that had built up inside her over the course of the day. She sighed gently, wishing that she too could have a father like Tŏkho, just like Okchŏm. If only my own mother and father were still alive! she thought. But then she remembered what Granny Sŏbun, who lived in the house just in front of them, had once told her: "Rumor has it in the village that Tŏkho killed your father with one hell of a beating." Ever since she had learned this, the old woman's words had haunted Sŏnbi whenever she had the spare time to let her mind wander. And yet she felt that what the old woman had said couldn't possibly be true. Especially considering the way that Tŏkho now treated her . . . Sŏnbi firmly refused to accept what she had been told, and she turned onto her side so that she wouldn't think about it any longer. She picked up a ball of cotton lying at her bedside and pressed it against her cheek.

"Sŏnbi!" It was Tŏkho's voice, calling out to her.

39

Sŏnbi quickly lifted up her head.

"Sŏnbi!"

Hearing the call a second time, Sŏnbi shook Granny awake.

"Grandma. Grandma."

Granny let out a groan, then turned over toward Sŏnbi.

"What's the matter?"

"The Master is calling."

"For me?"

"No, he's calling for me."

"Well then, go and see what he wants."

"But I want you to get up too, Grandma. Let's go together."

"Good grief, what's the matter now? He must want you to do something." Granny was half-asleep, and the last thing she wanted to do now was get out of bed. But Sŏnbi did everything she could to get Granny up, then led her into the breezeway.

"Did you call for me?"

"Sŏnbi? Is that you?"

"Yes, it is."

"Go get me some water."

Granny went back into the side room while Sŏnbi went into the kitchen to fetch the water. When Sŏnbi came back into the breezeway, Granny was gone. She hesitated for a moment before opening the door to Tŏkho's room. Cautiously, she made her way inside.

The air was heavy with the stench of liquor, and all she could make out was Tŏkho's head in the dim light of the flame. Sŏnbi quickly turned up the wick of the lantern, then went to Tŏkho's bedside. Perhaps the effect of the alcohol had started to wear off, for the look in Tŏkho's eye seemed more focused.

"Look here, when someone goes to bed drunk, you're supposed to leave water at the bedside."

Covering himself up with his blanket, Tŏkho sat up and took the bowl of water from Sŏnbi as he spoke. Sŏnbi felt a lump form in her throat. Afraid that Tŏkho might give her a scolding, she stood still, looking down at her feet.

"Oh, I forgot to tell you! We got a letter from Okchŏm telling us to send you down to Seoul! She wants to send you to school."

Sŏnbi was stunned by this unexpected news. Suddenly she felt as though the room was spinning around her.

"What do you think? Do you want to go to Seoul? I'm an old man without a son, so I might as well put you both through school. Hell, what else do I have to live for?"

Whenever Tŏkho got drunk, he always complained about the fact that he had no sons. Tŏkho stared blankly at Sŏnbi for a moment, then sighed deeply.

"Think about it, okay? You and Okchŏm are no different in my book. Though I can't say how you feel about me . . ."

Sŏnbi was so touched by Tŏkho's words that she actually felt as though her dead mother and father had come back to life again. Tears began welling up in her eyes. She wracked her brain, trying to think of something to express even one fraction of what she was feeling. But her heart raced so fast that she couldn't come up with anything to say.

Tŏkho finished drinking his water and handed the empty bowl to Sŏnbi.

"Well, it's awfully late, so you go on off to bed now. Give it some thought and give me your answer tomorrow or the day after . . . I'll do whatever you want me to do for you . . . Okay?" Tŏkho watched her face turn an even deeper shade of pink, overcome as she was with emotion. It seemed like Tŏkho was ready to do whatever Sŏnbi wanted him to do. She took the bowl from him, with her face cast slightly downwards as a show of respect and went back to the side room. There she collapsed on top of the sack of cotton. 'Oh, Okchŏm!' She had never in her life called out Okchŏm's name like this. The room was pitch-dark and, except for the sound of Granny snoring, perfectly silent. She imagined Okchŏm's face. That expression in her eyes and lips that once seemed so cold and distant! That nasty tongue of hers that she used to wag at will! Even these, Sŏnbi now thought upon with fondness. Could this be true? Sŏnbi wondered. He did say she wanted me to go to school, and that he would send me to Seoul. But did he mean it? Or was he just saying that because he'd been drinking? Question after question came into Sŏnbi's mind. She got up, turned on the light and began picking clean more of the cotton.

One ball after another, Sŏnbi gathered the white cotton into her skirt, her thoughts piling in her mind just like the cotton balls in her lap. She had no idea what to think. What do I do? If it's true, can I really go to Seoul? she wondered. That way I could go to school with Okchŏm and even learn how to do embroidery! Just then, Sŏnbi pictured in her mind's eye all those colorful skeins of silk thread, which she'd always looked at so longingly. She was holding one of the cotton balls tightly in her hand now, and as she stared into the light of the flame, she lost herself again in her thoughts: Do I go to Seoul? But then who'd pick the cotton? And who'd do the spinning? she wondered, looking over at Granny, who was sleeping beside her so soundly. Then unexpectedly, Ch'ŏtchae's face again appeared before her. She turned her head, thinking: I wonder if he'll live here forever?

40

Once the sun had set and dusk had fallen, the threshing at Kaettong's house was finally over. Oh, the sight of that pile of newly threshed rice glowing in the darkness! Standing in a circle around it, the farmers were drunk with excitement.

Yu Sŏbang and Tŏkho made their appearance. Yu Sŏbang went inside to light a lamp, which he brought back outside with him. Earthworm picked up a dry measure, approached a pile, and, running his hands through the newly threshed grain, filled a half-bushel with the dry measure.

"Here ... we ... have ... one ... half ... bushel." Earthworm lingered on the soft notes, his melody twisting and turning on each word in the tune. Soon thereafter came the sound of grain flowing into a straw sack—a soft swoosh! Something about this made them feel a warmth in their chests. They pressed against each other, unconsciously, and leaned on their friends' shoulders to get a better look.

"Hey, man, I'm going to fall over!" several of them cried, breaking out into laughter.

One sack, two sacks, three sacks of rice were tied up like this, one after another. Each of them looked back and forth with curiosity between the filled sacks and the pile of rice: how many sacks would it amount to?

Earthworm filled up his last half-bushel scoop and poured the grain into the sack.

"Fifteen ... sacks ... and ... five ... half ... bushels ..."

He drew out each note with great feeling, as though he were singing a plaintive ballad.

"Fifteen sacks and five half-bushels! Well done!" they all said in unison, having stood there in anxious anticipation.

Earthworm brushed off his clothes with a few pats of his hand, then rose to his feet. He slapped Kaettong on the shoulder. "Hey, man, I guess the drinks are on you!" he said. "I bet none of us brings in this much."

"Oh, come on," laughed Kaettong, as he glanced over at Tŏkho. He couldn't quite make out the expression on Tŏkho's face, but he could see him standing quietly there, and he knew that Tŏkho was satisfied. When the harvest was bad, Tŏkho always started complaining, and it was impossible for him to stay still—he would pace back and forth, shouting abuse at all of them: they hadn't worked the fields well enough, or else they'd eaten part of the crop on the sly.

Yu Sŏbang wheeled over a cart and loaded a few sacks of rice on it, each with a loud thud. The others picked up more of the sacks and lifted them onto the cart.

"Boy, is this heavy! How can one sack of rice weigh so much?"

They mentioned this on purpose for Tŏkho to hear. But Tŏkho just stood there in the darkness, puffing away at his cigarette.

"Kaettong! We're going to settle up your accounts right here! Even if you'll need some of it later . . . got it? Now, how much was it you borrowed?"

Tŏkho wanted to hear what Kaettong would say to this. But Kaettong's heart had been in his throat all along. He feared that Tŏkho might bring up the topic of his debts, and now Tŏkho's mention of them seemed to sap him of all of his remaining strength. Tŏkho looked expectantly at Kaettong, who couldn't even bring himself to speak, and it suddenly dawned on him: the boy wasn't even fixing to repay his loans! If he didn't manage to get his sacks of rice here and now, he might never get back what was due to him.

"It was last January I gave you fifteen wŏn, wasn't it? That makes ten months counting this one, so you figure in the interest . . . and it comes to twenty wŏn. You owe me four sacks first off just for that. Even so, I'll end up losing a good three or four wŏn. But then we've got the cost of fertilizer and seed to settle up here too, so . . ."

He looked at Yu Sŏbang.

"Just bring seven sacks over. Now, you'll still owe me ten wŏn, mind you. But I know you've got to live on something, so I'll let you take at least one sack home—half for your share, and half as a bonus from us. Think of it as thanks for all your good work this year." Tŏkho chuckled.

As soon as Tŏkho had finished talking, Yu Sŏbang lifted each sack of rice onto his back with a grunt and loaded them into his cart. The others, after their long day's work, suddenly felt a tide of exhaustion sweep over them. Each of them collapsed into a pile of straw. Then Ch'ŏtchae thought of old man P'unghŏn.

His crops had been seized by creditors before they were even harvested, and the frantic man had been running circles around the village, stopping each person he met.

"How can they get away with this? Before I even harvest my rice . . ."

The man had been too choked up to continue. Ch'ŏtchae, wondering what he was talking about, followed him down to his paddies. At the corner of the field stood a small wooden sign with something written on it.

41

P'unghŏn pointed to the wooden stake.

"Some man wearing a suit—he called himself a 'bailiff' or something—stuck that sign there and told me I couldn't harvest my crops..." said P'unghŏn, looking out over the yellowing ears of grain.

Ch'ŏtchae came up beside him. "How much did you borrow? And from who?"

"Well, from Tŏkho. I only asked him to be a little patient, so why did he have to do this? The postman brought me this just the other day, but, you know, I didn't know what to make of it, so I just set it aside. I mean ...I never dreamt it'd come to this."

P'unghŏn had pulled out from his pocket an envelope worn down at the edges. Of course, there was no way that Ch'ŏtchae could understand a word of it. He held the envelope, turning it this way and that, and returned it to P'unghŏn.

"Well, what does it say?" P'unghŏn asked, leaning forward and looking intently at Ch'ŏtchae. Ch'ŏtchae simply scratched his head: "How am I supposed to know?"

"What should I do?"

"Did you talk to Tŏkho about it?"

"You think I haven't tried? I practically begged him all night long. But it wasn't any use. What do you figure I should do? You think you could talk to him for me?"

Oh, that pleading look in P'unghŏn's eyes! Ch'ŏtchae simply had to turn away from him. He wanted more than anything to head straight to Tŏkho's place and throw a few good punches. But knowing full well that it would do no good, Ch'ŏtchae let out a helpless sigh and stared blankly into the distance. All those ears of rice! They'd be reaped in less than ten days now. The rice was so mature that the stems hung their heads to the ground.

"Just look at it! A mighty fine crop if you ask me."

P'unghŏn pointed to the ears of rice, then ran over to the paddy to sweep his hands through them. Then as he glared out at Mount Pult'a, lost in his thoughts, his salt-and-pepper beard shook frightfully. Ch'ŏtchae couldn't think of anything to say to comfort the man. He could feel how even the air surrounding them seemed as heavy as lead. P'unghŏn squatted in the corner of his paddy and set himself, out of habit, to fixing part of the embankment that had begun to erode. Ch'ŏtchae just watched him.

"So these paddies belong to someone in town?"

"They sure do. The gentleman's name is Han Ch'isu . . ."

He let out a long sigh.

"But I don't get it. Nothing like this has ever happen before . . . No matter how hard I try, I just can't make sense of it! I'll have to go into town tomorrow and have a talk with this Mr. Han Ch'isu."

"I think you'd better."

Ch'ŏtchae couldn't make sense of it either. P'unghŏn jumped to his feet again.

"You know, I might as well just go and see him now," he said, turning toward the road into town. He rushed off without even once turning around. Ch'ŏtchae watched the man walk off into the distance and around the mountain bend, and only then did he go back into the village.

After having not seen P'unghŏn for several days, Ch'ŏtchae asked someone what had happened to him, and learned that he'd already moved away. He heard that P'unghŏn had taken off with his wife and kids, and nothing besides a few gourds in tow.

The sound of a cart rolling by roused Ch'ŏtchae from these memories. But sure enough, the man who'd driven out P'unghŏn—both friend and father figure to Ch'ŏtchae—had been Tŏkho. Now Ch'ŏtchae knew for certain that Tŏkho was trying to drive out Kaettong and himself as well.

"What! When did I ever say I wouldn't repay my loans?"

Kaettong's voice seemed to ring through the thick air. He'd spent a whole year working on these crops . . . If he'd at least been able to place all the rice in front of his own house before they took it away, well, he might have felt a little bit better. Then there was the current market price of the rice they were using to calculate—they said five wŏn per sack, but it might easily go up to six or even eight wŏn in no time at all. It had been simply too much to bear for Kaettong to have his crops seized on such unfair terms.

Just as soon as Ch'ŏtchae heard Kaettong say these words, he dashed forward without really knowing what he was doing. He knocked Yu Sŏbang to the ground with a single blow.

"Hey, what's going on here? You rascals! Get back over here!"

Though it wasn't their fight either, the others felt Kaettong's anger too, and they rushed forward following Ch'ŏtchae's lead. They pulled off the rice sacks loaded onto the cart, then they searched for Tŏkho. But he had already run off and they couldn't find him.

"Let him just try to take this rice away from me!" shouted Kaettong.

A lamp shone in the distance as it made its way closer to them. They knew now what was happening: the police were on their way! Quickly they scattered in all directions.

They could hear dogs barking here and there in the distance. Then came the sound of footsteps, and more footsteps . . .

42

The next day at dawn, Kaettong's mother went to Tŏkho's. Nothing had changed: the main gate was still locked. How many times had she already come to this door since last night! There had been nothing else she could do but go back home, but each time, a new worry crossed her mind, and she'd found herself yet again standing in front of this gate. She wondered if anyone was awake, and kept peeking through the cracks in the doorframe. But not even a stray dog caught her eye. Pacing back and forth, she practiced out loud what she was going to say to Tŏkho when she met him. Even though she'd spent all night thinking about it, every time she made her way up to his house, she was at a loss for words.

She heard the sound of footsteps approaching from inside, so she stepped back a ways, keeping her eyes set on the door. There was a rattling sound, and then the door squeaked open. Yu Sŏbang limped outside, but then he stopped short upon seeing Kaettong's mother.

"What do you want?"

With the happenings of last night fresh in his mind, Yu Sŏbang's temper was still flaring.

Kaettong's mother hung her head.

"I'm awfully sorry for what happened. Please forgive the boys, won't you? They just lost their heads, that's all. Won't you please help us out?"

"Lost their heads? Shit! They knew exactly what they were doing. Just look at me. I'm a cripple now!"

He turned back into the house with a snort. Kaettong's mother went in after him.

"Is the mayor awake yet?"

"What do you want him for?" Yu Sŏbang asked.

"Won't you please help us out just this once? Oh, please . . . I'm begging you."

Kaettong's mother was in tears now.

"Nothing I can do," said Yu Sŏbang. "Those imbeciles . . . That ungrateful, double-dealing bunch of them. The bastards!"

Yu Sŏbang went inside. Kaettong's mother hesitated for a minute. She heard Tŏkho's voice coming from inside.

"Well, who is it?"

"Kaettong's mother," answered Yu Sŏbang.

"Kaettong's mother? What does she want?"

"I'm not sure."

Kaettong's mother stood outside the door for a moment before bringing herself to speak.

"Mr. Mayor. Please forgive them this once. The boys just lost their senses . . ."

It seemed that Tŏkho had not yet gotten up out of bed.

"Is that you, Kaettong's mother? Well, come on inside. It's too cold for old folks to be out in this weather. What are you standing out there for?"

This unexpectedly warm welcome from Tŏkho sent the woman's head spinning. Only then did Yu Sŏbang add, "Go on in, then."

When Kaettong's mother opened the door, she found Tŏkho lying in bed. She froze.

"Come in," insisted Tŏkho.

Kaettong's mother entered the room but kept her eyes on the floor.

"Won't you please help us out, Sir, just this once? Consider the fix we're in now."

Tŏkho cleared his throat, got up off the floor, and covered himself with the bedding as he sat up.

"Well, I'll tell you, watching those imbeciles carry on like that got me worked up enough that I didn't want to forgive them. And I have half a mind to make them suffer, suffer real good . . . But since I'm in charge of the township now, and especially considering how hard it would be for all you folks back at home, I don't think I can really do that now, can I?"

Kaettong's mother was so relieved by his words that she felt like crying. The very idea that Kaettong and his friends had turned a blind eye to this gentleman's kindness made her furious at the whole lot of them.

"So you'll help us out then? For my sake, if nothing else . . ."

"Well, it just so happens today is a holiday and I'm not going into the office, so I guess I could head on over to the police station to get them released. These past ten years it's been me they've got to thank for giving them work, you know. Now, that's called biting the hand that feeds you, is what I say. I've got no sons myself, you know, so I love those boys like they were my own. Why, just yesterday I let them have a free bag of rice. And this is the thanks I get? For the third year in a row?"

"They aren't deserving of your kindness, sir. Let them all rot in Hell, for all I care, every single one of them. But please have mercy on us old folks, oh please, Sir . . ."

"All right. You go on back home. I'll head out in a little while."

Kaettong's mother bowed deeply and then went outside. Tŏkho lay back down on the floor, thinking. He wanted all of them to suffer a bit longer and get a taste of the law of the land. But since the days were gradually getting colder and the rest of the rice still had to be threshed before it started snowing again, he really had no other choice but to arrange for their release. And besides, there were rumors floating around that the new rice policies were coming into effect this fall. The price of rice would be sure to rise if these rumors turned out to be true. Then it dawned on him that he'd better clear up accounts with them while the price of rice was still low. And with this, he jumped out of bed.

43

When Tŏkho arrived that morning the young men who had spent the night in the police station were finally released, but only after receiving a stout warning by the chief of police and promising never to cause such trouble again. They weren't even allowed to eat a proper breakfast on the way back from the station; instead, they were sent straight to the threshing ground. Once they had gathered the sheaves of rice they'd left out to dry, they swept up the remaining grain, then began whirling around the thresher in the corner. As they set themselves to work, every bone in their bodies ached. Each time they moved an arm or leg it felt sore. The pain was so bad they couldn't bend down or turn their heads as they pleased. Couldn't we have gotten a day off to recover . . . ? Each one of them had this same thought on his mind, as if they'd actually talked it over.

Tŏkho showed up, smoking a cigarette and flourishing a cane. He was elegantly dressed in silk pants and a silk shirt, with a serge waistcoat worn over them. As soon as the young men saw Tŏkho, their hearts sank and their heads hung of their own accord. They were anxious, indeed quite shaken, by the thought that he might give them another tongue-lashing.

"All right boys, keep up the good work, you hear? Eat hard, work hard—now that's the kind of man this township needs, I say. Hah, ha . . . you boys don't quite understand, do you? On account of what happened yesterday. But I know it was a just misunderstanding. And besides, now that I'm in charge of the township . . . well, it's my responsibility to step in here and do what I can to make things easier for you."

Tŏkho cleared his throat loudly and continued. The young men were standing with their heads hung and their hands folded politely in front of them.

"Whatever may have happened yesterday, I want you boys to understand something. I collect this rice for your sake, not mine. Just try to sell your rice yourselves and to pay back your loans in cash. You'll end up being late with your payments, you won't get a decent price for your rice, and you won't be able to sell it at just the right time to get the best return. That's where I come into the picture—even though I end up losing money, mind you . . . And just why do I lose money? Well, it's as plain as day that the price of rice is dropping, as you all should know can happen. Now, I want to know why on earth you can't get this into your heads? You know, I think of you boys as my own sons, but none of you seem to realize it. Just think about what happened yesterday—if it was anyone else besides me, do you really think they'd have let you go free? When I went down in person and pleaded with the chief of police to release you, I wasn't just thinking about you boys, I was thinking about your families as well. Why can't I get you to realize this? Now, I understand anyone can make a mistake, mind you, but you better be damn well certain this never happens again!"

With a grin on his face, Tŏkho looked around at the men gathered around him. He could see how moved they were by his words. They looked as limp as blades of grass hit by a frost, and he knew that it was the power of the police station that had done it to them. There's nothing like the whip, it dawned on him, for bringing imbeciles like these into line.

After Tŏkho left, the men breathed a bit easier. But they couldn't agree with everything Tŏkho had said. Setting themselves back to work, they lined up five separate threshers, side to side, and assigned three men to each one. One positioned himself in the middle to keep the mechanism spinning. The other two carried the sheaves of rice to either side of the machine, where they untied them and passed them on to the man spinning the thresher, or else one of them climbed up on top of the stack of sheaves and fed them down, while the other tied up the threshed straw and carried it away.

"Hey, come on! Move it, will you?" Little Buddha shouted to Ch'ŏtchae. Then he snatched an ear of rice from him.

"That idiot! It's all his fault that we got the shit kicked out of us yesterday." Little Buddha said to Sourstem. Sourstem continued to feed rice into the machine as he spun it.

"Well, that's what happens when a beggar starts thinking too hard. I mean, what rights do you have when you live from hand to mouth? Someone tells you to die, man, and you'd better fall down and play dead."

Overhearing them talk like this, Ch'ŏtchae tried to hold back the anger flaring inside him. He could feel his insides twisting, and his face went deep red.

Though they had all acted in unison on this threshing ground, it was now Ch'ŏtchae, and Ch'ŏtchae alone, who in the course of a single day had become the target of everyone's resentment. More than the abuse he received from Tŏkho, more than the beating he had gotten from the police last night, it was the animosity of his friends that almost moved Ch'ŏtchae to tears. He found himself overcome by the loneliness of a man walking by himself on a dark road at night. He stared absentmindedly at the freshly harvested rice in front of him. There had once been a time when he'd looked at stacked rice like this with such joy in his heart . . . Just then, a policeman approached from the distance.

44

Ch'ŏtchae panicked. It seemed as though the policeman had somehow read his mind and was coming to catch him. He crouched down and fumbled through the rice stalks for a while. Only when he heard the sound of the man's sword grow distant did he feel relieved enough to look around. The policeman's sword, still clanging with each step he took, flashed in the sunlight. He had just met Tŏkho, and they were coming back in this direction. Ch'ŏtchae was again struck by the fear that had seized him moments earlier. But the two men passed right by, casting only a whiff of cigarette smoke in his direction. They were talking with interest about something or other, then broke out into laughter.

"Hey, you pedal for a while," Little Buddha called to Ch'ŏtchae as he stepped away from the thresher. Ch'ŏtchae quickly came over. Cranking the pedal of the thresher with a single foot, he fed into the thresher each of the bundles of rice that Little Buddha handed him. He happened to look up, and there were Tŏkho and the policeman, sitting in the township office and looking right down on him through the glass window. No wonder Little Buddha moved away from the thresher, he realized. He couldn't bear facing them! Ch'ŏtchae quickly hung his head, convinced that the two men were staring straight at him and discussing whether or not to take him to the station.

Grains of rice flying out of the machine lightly pelted his face as they dropped to the ground. He found the current of air created by the revolving wheel of the thresher annoying—it made him shiver. Yet this was the very same breeze he had once thought so refreshing . . .

"Hey, I want a smoke!" said Little Buddha.

Ch'ŏtchae, too, felt a craving for a cigarette, and he looked at Little Buddha. Everyone stopped working for a second or two and exchanged glances—as though they had actually agreed to stop at the same time. They could see in each other's eyes how much they all wanted to smoke, but they were so afraid of being singled out by the gaze of the men in the township office that not one of them dared to take a break. Each sighed deeply and hung his head, and watched the falling grains of rice steadily pile up on the ground. Here they were dying for a single puff on a cigarette, and all that grain they'd worked so hard to grow was bound straight for Tŏkho's metal storehouse. The thought stirred inside them the same emotions that had led them to smash his cart the day before.

Look at that pile of rice covering the entire threshing ground! Look at those tiny little beards, like the yellow feathers of a baby chick, sticking out of each grain and pointing up to the sky! To them, each and every grain looked so beautiful, so brilliant. But now this rice was on its way into Tŏkho's storehouse before they had the satisfaction of touching it.

At home, the children would say, "Daddy, do we get to eat white rice today?"

They would cling to their Daddies when they came home today and whisper these words in their ears. But what could the men say to their children now! You'll get white rice come fall!—is what they'd promised all summer long. But now that autumn was here what could they say? When the men looked down at the rice with these thoughts on their minds, the grains seemed like tiny arrows stabbing at their hearts.

Their thoughts drifted back to what had happened yesterday, and they all turned to look at Ch'ŏtchae. But then they noticed Tŏkho and the policeman walking toward them. Once again, their hearts began pounding, and they forgot what had just been on their minds. Tŏkho went into his house with the policeman, and they all heaved a deep sigh of relief. Their thoughts drifted away again, and they stared out at Mount Pult'a. That mountain would be covered in snow again before long... What in the world, they all wondered, will we have to eat then?

Mount Pult'a on a clear, crisp fall day. That deep blue sky racing above it. Ch'ŏtchae gazed silently into the sky, and he suddenly remembered the words of the chief of police who had rounded them up last night: "Looks like I'm going to have to teach you all something about the law."

"The law . . . the law," muttered Ch'ŏtchae. "There are laws that will get you killed if you break them—isn't that what he said?"

Ch'ŏtchae didn't know exactly what the law was, but he did know that people had traditionally held it to be sacred and unbreakable, and he himself still thought of it in these terms; but as he tried going over everything that had happened yesterday, a real sense of confusion about the law filled his mind. It was like a tangled knot of thread he couldn't manage to unravel.

"How was fighting against Tŏkho yesterday breaking the law? The law . . . the law . . ."

He muttered the words several times under his breath. The more he tried thinking about it, the more frustrated he became. He couldn't quite untangle this knot of confusion.

Then Little Buddha turned around to him.

"What in hell's name is he mumbling about now?"

Ch'ŏtchae, too, had been surprised by the sound of his own voice, and he quickly hung his head.

45

It was early winter, just after the harvest. The county magistrate had come in from town and sent word to have all the farmers gather to hear him give a talk. It was the county magistrate, after all, so they all assumed that they had no choice but to drop whatever they happened to be busy working on. They were afraid that if they didn't, they might have to pay a fine, so every one of them turned up.

The farmers managed to squeeze inside the township office, which must have been a good eighty square yards in size. On the platform sat the county magistrate, and Tŏkho as mayor of the township, and next to them sat the township clerks. The farmers all stared wide-eyed at the fat man in the suit who had just been appointed county magistrate. First Tŏkho came forward and very simply introduced the county magistrate to the farmers. Then the magistrate came forward, and after clearing his throat a few times, began to speak.

"Now, let me see . . . The township office has, no doubt, already told you of the purpose of my visit today. I'm here in order to take a look around the county in my capacity as new county magistrate, but also to do my best to reach out to all of you in a sincere way.

"In this land of ours called Chosŏn, ah . . . farmers make up over eighty percent of the population. The truth is that the destiny of our great nation has always depended on the fortunes of our farmers. Has it not been said since ages past that farming is the very foundation of the world beneath the heavens?"

Never before had they heard such praise for farmers like themselves come from the lips of such an important official. Nothing could have described how moved they were by his speech.

"Now, it goes without saying that we all need to work diligently when it comes to farming, but ah . . . let me also emphasize that there are several methods to go about doing this. The traditional farmer was under the impression that his duty was to weed the fields quietly, but this was where he went wrong. The farmer must now ask himself: How can I make my paddies yield the most grain? How can I make a small paddy yield as much grain as a big one? In other words, he must go

102

about his work with a firm grasp on the best methods of farming. So . . .
for example, ah . . . let's say we have a certain job we need to get done.
If we want to find the best man for the job, we have to think about the
particular talents of each of our workers, don't we? Well, the same principle applies to farming as well. How much grain you end up harvesting
depends on whether you've planted the right sort of crop in the right
sort of field. If you plant millet or upland rice in a field that's best suited
for sorghum or beans, you can't very well expect to have a good harvest.
So what I'm saying is that before you plant your crops you've got to
figure out which fields are best for which crops. And, ah . . . Oh, then
of course there's the matter of compost. The best thing you can do for
your fields is to prepare as much compost as possible and work it into
the fields come spring. Now, if you all worked just a little bit harder . . .
ah, well, what I mean is that you need take advantage of your break
time. Cut down a bit of grass and pile it up from time to time, so that
after a while you'll have a good heap of matured compost. By spring,
I'll tell you, it'll be mighty fine fertilizer. Why take the trouble of going
into town to buy chemical fertilizer and lugging it all the way back here
when you can make it for yourself in your own backyard?"

That he had gone to the trouble of figuring out the precise logistics
of farming made them all feel an incredible sense of gratitude toward
the man. They looked around the room at each other, their mouths
practically agape.

"Ah . . . and you also should wear dyed clothing. One of the reasons
why the people of Chosŏn are so poor is that we've always worn white
clothes. Please get yourself some properly dyed clothes as soon as possible. When you wear white clothes, you've got to keep washing them,
which, first of all, is a waste of time, and second of all, wears them out
too quickly. And . . . don't wear rubber shoes, either. Make use of your
free time to weave straw sandals. Now, one last thing. Please economize when it comes to spending money on ceremonies, marriages, and
funerals. Mind you, if you follow this advice, I'm sure you'll all be rich
men one day. What do you think about that?" he chuckled.

The farmers all laughed as well. It really seemed as though, if they
only did what the county magistrate told them to do, they'd soon be
living the good life—maybe starting as early as the next year.

"Oh, yes, and one more thing . . . I just want to emphasize, finally,
how much effort we've invested in making the township an institution

that works to help you all enjoy a richer, healthier life here in the village. So it's wrong for anyone to dismiss the importance of the township office in any way. The land taxes, the household taxes and the various other fees that the township collects from you are used expressly in an effort to create a better life for you. And that's why it's so imperative that you pay all your taxes down to the last dime. Well, I have many more things to say that will have to wait until next time, but let me leave you with the simple request that you please follow the guidance of the township office."

With these words the county magistrate stepped back to his chair and took a seat. Tŏkho then came forward with a grin plastered on his face.

"Well, now that we've had the great pleasure of listening to the wisdom of our county magistrate, I think it is perhaps appropriate for all of us from the township to offer his honor a proper sign of our respect, as a pledge of our commitment to heed his advice. So all rise please."

The farmers stood up in unison, and after bowing deeply several times they went their separate ways.

Ch'ŏtchae made his way out of the township office along with the others. He took a few steps forward, but then stopped short. But whose land will I work next year? he wondered. The others glanced back at him mockingly, and headed off together in the opposite direction.

46

Ch'ŏtchae had lost tenant rights to his fields. The magistrate said that the township office was supposed to help all the farmers enjoy a better life . . . Does that mean I'm no longer one of the farmers? he wondered. I mean, Tŏkho is mayor of the township, and yet isn't he the one who took away my land? And all because I broke some so-called law by smashing a wagon . . . the law . . . the law . . . Hell, I'll probably be breaking the law if I don't do what the magistrate said today either. But if I don't have a field to sow, what use is there in me making compost? The law . . . The more Ch'ŏtchae thought about it, the more his doubts about it seemed to creep under his skin. He told himself he wouldn't think about it anymore, but this tangled knot of questions kept coming back to haunt him! He couldn't bring them under control. Ch'ŏtchae still tried hard to abide by this 'sacred and unbreakable' thing called the

104

law, but for some reason as the days went by, he'd become increasingly caught up in it.

Having made his way home, Ch'ŏtchae stood beside the woodpile lost in thought.

"What do I do now?" he said softly, sensing the growing darkness of the path that lay ahead of him, just as keenly as he felt the chill of the winter day against his skin.

At the rustling sound of someone twisting straw he snapped out of his thoughts and quickly looked at his house. They'd all been making rope before he'd gone to the township office, so he headed inside, wondering if Yi Sŏbang had stayed home today instead of going out to beg. When he opened the door, he couldn't tell immediately who was sitting inside. He could only hear the sound of somebody twisting rope in the darkness.

"Back so soon? What did they call you in for?"

Having taken his seat in the room, only now did Ch'ŏtchae realize that it was his mother twisting the rope. He scratched his head before speaking.

"The county magistrate gave a speech they wanted us to hear."

His mother pushed aside the rope, her illusions now shattered. When the clerk from the township office had stopped by and summoned Ch'ŏtchae, she had clung to the faint hope that maybe they'd given Ch'ŏtchae back his fields. But her son's words dashed these hopes for good.

Ch'ŏtchae could feel her disappointment as though she had placed it in the palm of his hand. Indeed, the entire room seemed filled with an indescribable sense of grief. Ch'ŏtchae was unwilling to look at his mother, so he turned away from her and started to twist together a piece of rope. Under normal circumstances he would have had plenty of uses for this rope, and indeed, he kept working away at it as though he would still use it. If he had just sat there doing nothing, all the questions and all the grief building up in his heart would have nearly killed him! He was so sick and tired of everything that all he wanted was to keep himself busy.

"Why the hell did you have to go off and do that? Look at what's happened to us after all that nonsense of yours. Like it or not, Ch'ŏtchae, when you're poor like us, you've got to do what the rich man says to do . . . I hope you're happy now, because starting today, we're out of food.

You just can't wait to send me to an early grave, can you . . . ? With a paddy to farm, we might have been able to get some rice for the time being, granted at extra interest. But just who do you think is going to give us free handouts of rice now?"

"Would you shut up for a minute?" cried Ch'ŏtchae suddenly.

"Oh, the nerve of you! You've yanked me around by my hair ever since you were a little brat, and here we are going hungry, all because you still can't control your goddamn temper! Well, maybe you'll finally learn your lesson when you go hungry, you fool!"

"Oh, so you did everything right, and I'm the one who messed it all up?"

"Ha! Who do you think brought food to your table when you were a little kid? You just wait and see, you little idiot! Do you think I did something wrong because I liked doing it? I was starving, and I did what I did because I had no choice! Just wait and see!"

His mother's words sank into Ch'ŏtchae, and he felt his heartstrings pulled more taut than he could bear. "I was starving and I did what I did because I had no choice," she'd said, "Just wait and see!" The words his mother had flung at him felt like a barrage of arrows piercing every inch of his heart. She did it because she had no choice! But what did she mean by that? Once again, that knot of confusion was trying to take over his mind! He tossed aside the straw he was twisting and jumped to his feet. He slid the door open with a clatter and ran outside.

Little drops of frozen rain had begun falling from the sky. In one corner of the yard, where the woodpile had been stacked, the sound of it falling was especially clear. The sight of the sleet that had accumulated there seemed to wring his heart even tighter. Hell, maybe I'll collect some wood and sell it for a bushel or two of rice . . . But fat chance those idiots in the forest patrol will let me chop down any trees . . . The law? Ch'ŏtchae stamped his foot into the ground.

47

He considered going to a friend's house. But he remembered how the whole lot of them had laughed at him in front of the township office, so instead he strapped on his wooden pack and set off alone.

The frozen rain that hit his burning face sent pleasant chills through his body.

He stared out at the misty fields in front of him and sighed. He knew that all his hopes and dreams had revolved around these very fields. But now that he'd lost them, what sort of dreams could he have anymore! The only path in life open to him seemed as dark as night.

Before, he used to come to work with a hoe hoisted high over his shoulder. He used to let his mind drift to the far corners of the earth.

Make a living working hard in the fields, sell what's left over and save up enough on the side to buy a field with the cash. Then marry Sŏnbi, have a few sons and daughters, and live happily ever after. How many times had this scene played out in his mind! But now he could only snicker at the foolish castles he'd built in the air. He could plainly see how that glimmer in his eyes, which had once burned with such desire, was giving way to scorn and resentment.

Soon he'd made his way to Wŏnso Pond. He couldn't help seeing a resemblance to his own lot in life in the haggard grove of leafless willow trees. Yet after staring at the trees for some time, he managed to imagine something strong inside them, a vital energy waiting to sprout forth in the spring. Leaning against a willow tree, he gazed at Wŏnso Pond and thought of its legend.

"When they broke the law, they were either killed or severely beaten." He didn't know when the story had taken place—hundreds, maybe thousands of years ago—but he sensed how much in common he had with those farmers in the olden days who'd found themselves in such dire straights.

The sound of footsteps came from behind him. Probably someone coming to fetch some water, he imagined, but he didn't feel like turning to see who it was. Whenever people saw him, he always felt they were making fun of him for having lost his fields, and he could feel the color rising into his face.

He sensed, listening to the footsteps, that they belonged to more than one person. Somewhat embarrassed to be standing there, he stepped away from the willow trees and saw two women approaching the path. He felt a surge of blood rush through his body; he was short of breath, and his heart started racing. He stood there frozen in place, and watched them.

The two women were carrying heavy loads of laundry on their heads, and one of them was Sŏnbi! Beneath that white towel draped down over her ears was a face so lovely that it seemed to glow like a chestnut out of its shell. He could just make it out, obscured as it was by the falling snow. And yet, he no longer sensed the tenderness that had once so touched him. That glowing complexion of hers seemed only to intensify what he now saw as an icy scorn.

The women put down their buckets of laundry, placed the clothes on some stones, and began pounding on them with their laundry clubs. The pounding of the clubs sounded to him like a voice saying, "You idiot, you lost your fields, didn't you? You lost your fields, didn't you?" For a moment, he wasn't sure what he should do. Sŏnbi then put down her laundry club, started to rinse out her clothes, and stole a brief glimpse of him. He quickly turned to face the opposite direction. He felt dizzy, and everything in front of him started to spin. He took a firm grip on his walking stick. What do I need a woman for anyway! he muttered under his breath. He walked slowly away from the pond.

The sound of the pounding gradually faded as he walked further along. His vision of Sŏnbi now seemed to turn into a cold block of ice. He stopped short. The lovely image of Sŏnbi that had fixed itself in his mind was changing—of that much, he was more and more certain.

He climbed up the hill and threw himself onto the ground. With his wooden pack still strapped to his back, he took in the view below him and allowed his thoughts to drift away. He remembered the time he had climbed this hill to get wood when he was younger; he'd found Sŏnbi here and had stolen some of her sourstem to snack on. The more he thought about the past, the more he realized he'd always had a special place for Sŏnbi in his heart. But still, he hadn't even once been able to talk to this girl whom he'd been in love with for so long, and he knew that he'd probably never have the chance to meet her. He picked up his walking stick and pounded it into the ground next to his foot. Then he jumped to his feet.

The frozen rain appeared to be falling heavier now. And through it all, how far away the village seemed! Already there were streams of dinner smoke climbing up out of several houses. The thought crossed his mind that maybe Yi Sŏbang had come back home.

48

Ch'ŏtchae went around to the side of the hill, cut some dried grass, and headed home with it. When he arrived at the entrance of the village the sound of rice pots rattling and the smell of herring on the grill drifted out of several houses, whetting his appetite terribly. Though he'd had a bit of rice the night before, all he'd eaten this morning was gruel hardly fit for a cow. The very thought of it sent a chill even deeper into his body. But as he neared home, he pictured Yi Sŏbang with his dirty old sack chock full of rice. This sent him dashing ahead as quickly as his feet could take him.

When he reached his house, he threw down his A-frame and raced inside to see if Yi Sŏbang's shoes had been left outside the door. But on the floor of the hallway, swept as it was by that frigid wind, there was but one pair of straw sandals—his mother's. He came to a sudden stop. Yi Sŏbang isn't home yet? he wondered, as he opened the door. His mother had been lying on the warmest part of the floor, but she now bolted upright.

"Yi Sŏbang, is that you?"

Ch'ŏtchae's head began to swim, for he now knew for sure that Yi Sŏbang hadn't returned. And as soon as his mother saw that he wasn't Yi Sŏbang, she lay back down on the floor. The room seemed to echo with the muffled sound of her moaning.

He slammed the door to the room shut and turned to face outside. Why isn't Yi Sŏbang back by now? he wondered, staring out into the growing darkness. The path over which Yi Sŏbang would have carried home his heavy sack of rice was covered with a deep layer of falling snow. Not even a stray dog scampered along it. He left his house and set off with long determined strides on the newly built road into town.

After walking for some time, his head hunched against the cold, Ch'ŏtchae paused for a minute to scan the horizon. Yi Sŏbang was nowhere in sight. Maybe he'd catch a glimpse of him around the next bend in the mountain road, Ch'ŏtchae thought. But once he turned the bend, all he found was more and more snow—snowflakes falling everywhere, like a swarm of bees—not even the silhouette of a man who might resemble Yi Sŏbang. By now it was pitch-black, and even Ch'ŏtchae couldn't make out which direction was which. What if something happened to Yi Sŏbang? What if he froze to death on the side of the road? Maybe he hurt himself and found shelter in a water mill? One after another, these fears plagued him as the night wore on.

The howling winds that had picked up earlier that evening hadn't yet subsided. The large, wet flakes of snow lashed him mercilessly in the face. Ch'ŏtchae stopped and stood up straight for a moment to clear his thoughts. There was no way Yi Sŏbang would come home tonight—he knew this much—so he finally turned around and headed back home alone.

Ch'ŏtchae and his mother stayed up throughout the night waiting, convinced that come morning, Yi Sŏbang would be home for sure. Yet when morning came, he still wasn't there. Ch'ŏtchae's mother was almost certain that something terrible had happened to him.

"Ch'ŏtchae!" She turned to her son. "Yi Sŏbang must have gotten in an accident. Go into town and see what you can find out."

Last night, Ch'ŏtchae hadn't found it difficult to put up with his hunger, so it hadn't been an obstacle to his going in search of Yi Sŏbang. But this morning he was so famished that he could hardly move. He looked over at his mother.

"How I am supposed to go on an empty stomach? Can't you ask someone for some food?"

His mother looked at him, lying there exhausted, and she felt her heart tear in two. She picked up a gourd bowl and went outside, hoping to get a spoonful or two of cooked rice from someone. Ch'ŏtchae watched his mother leave the house, then shut his eyes. He began seeing visions of bowls and bowls filled with rice. It was too much for him to bear. His eyes flashed wide open. Directly in his line of vision, he noticed the jar in which they'd stored their rice until just a few days before. He jumped to his feet and went to look inside it. It was hollow, completely empty. The jar had been chock full in the fall. How could so much rice disappear so quickly? he wondered.

Tŏkho had given him this rice when he took away his fields, saying that he was doing him a favor. He had subtracted from his final settlement only his loans and the cost of the high-interest grain that Ch'ŏtchae had owed him. He had waived the cost of fertilizer and the rice that Ch'ŏtchae had borrowed to eat on occasion. At the time Ch'ŏtchae had thought that all this rice would last for months, but they had eaten it day after day ever since then, and now less than two months later, not a trace remained. Hoping to find a few grains by chance stuck to the side of the jar, he carried it to the door and examined it closely, twisting it around. When he saw there wasn't a single grain to be found, he let out a deep sigh. He laid his head on the side of the jar and glanced at the door.

Tears slowly rolled down his face. But then he heard footsteps outside, and he jumped to his feet.

49

The door slid open and his mother came in.

"Oh, I thought you were Yi Sŏbang..."

"A poor man's born with hungry belly," said his mother, putting down the gourd bowl and pushing it toward him. Ch'ŏtchae quickly looked inside it and saw it held some acorns and some rice. To the wolf in his stomach, even his mother looked edible at this point. He snatched up the bowl and dug into the food with his bare hands. To amuse oneself by lifting a spoon or a pair of chopsticks was the sport of a man who knew no hunger, and as far as Ch'ŏtchae was concerned, he needed nothing of the sort.

"Hey, hey, slow down, will you!"

Ch'ŏtchae's mother had planned on taking a few mouthfuls herself, but with her son gobbling down the food like that, she wasn't able to taste a single acorn. On the one hand, it was heartbreaking to watch him eat like this, but on the other hand, she was terribly hurt that he was being so inconsiderate.

"There's nothing else?"

There was a wild look in Ch'ŏtchae's eyes, and clearly the only thing in his mind was that maybe his mother hadn't handed over all the food she'd collected. The mother glared at her son.

"The nerve of you! Gobbling it all down yourself... What more do you want?"

She couldn't help but get this off her chest, for she felt her heart was being pierced by a needle. Why hadn't she just eaten some of it on the way back here! From Ch'ŏtchae's perspective, however, she'd hardly given him anything worth eating, and here she was talking as if he'd eaten his fill, which made him furious.

"And just how much do you actually think you gave me!" he shot back at her.

A fire now seemed to be flickering in his eyes. His mother was at a complete loss for words, and refused to look at him. She turned to face the wall and lay down on the floor. Staring at his mother's silhouette,

Ch'ŏtchae imagined what a feast he'd have, if only his mother had been edible . . .

"Where did you get the rice from?"

For the life of him he had to find out where that food had come from so he could get some more. The pangs in his stomach were simply unbearable. His mother lay there as still as a picture and refused to answer him. Ch'ŏtchae wanted to give her a kick, but he held himself back and stared up at the ceiling, engrossed in his thoughts. Where could he go to get some more food? Maybe he could go to Kaettong's? When Ch'ŏtchae rose to his feet to go outside, a long belch worked its way out of his throat, to his own surprise. Suddenly his mother pounded her fist on the floor.

"You see, you selfish pig! You stuffed yourself so full you burped!"

She knew that if only he had shared a few spoonfuls, her feelings wouldn't have been hurt. Ch'ŏtchae ran to her side and gave her a shove in the backside with his foot.

"How much rice do you actually think you gave me? A whole basketful? A whole bowlful? Well, how much then, huh?"

His mother was furious, and she jumped to her feet.

"You selfish little bastard! You just burped, didn't you! You eat up all our food and then have the nerve to burp right in front of me. You don't give a rat's ass if I die, do you? So long as you can go and stuff your own face . . . Here I go out to get us something to eat and you gobble the whole thing down all by yourself. Well, the nerve of you! And how dare you treat your own mother like that? Oh, you wait, you just wait, Ch'ŏtchae, because let me tell you, Heaven is watching you! Ahh . . . Ahh . . ."

The woman began weeping out loud. Ch'ŏtchae, loath to watch her cry, quickly left the room.

In the blanket of snow covering the yard the traces of footsteps were still clearly visible. He stared vacantly upon them, wondering if Yi Sŏbang might come back today, and then shifted his gaze to the horizon.

His mother was still inside wailing, but Ch'ŏtchae was far more worried that Yi Sŏbang might never come home. He stepped out the front gate, figuring he might as well try to get a handout from somebody. When he walked through Kaettong's front gate, Kaettong's mother opened her front door and peered out at him. There was a time when she would have welcomed him inside her home, but today she offered him no such invitation.

"What are you doing here?" asked the woman with a mean look in her eye.

"Is Kaettong here?"

"He went to work over at the mayor's place . . . Why?"

"I just wanted to see him," said Ch'ŏtchae, for he couldn't come up with anything else to say.

He left Kaettong's house and wandered around for a while, trying to figure out whose house he could go to next, but then he stopped short.

Puffing away on their cigarettes, Tŏkho and a man in a suit were headed straight towards him. Ch'ŏtchae ducked his head and turned into an alley close by. The two men, engrossed in their conversation, passed right by him. Tŏkho gave his cane a twirl. When Ch'ŏtchae caught sight of the other man's face, all the blood in his body rushed to his head, and a shiver shot down his spine.

50

Late, very late that night, Ch'ŏtchae came back home.

"Mom!" he called out excitedly. His mother had gotten out of bed, mistaking him for Yi Sŏbang, but when she saw it was Ch'ŏtchae, she lay back down without a word in reply. Ch'ŏtchae put something into his mother's hand. She sprang upright, catching the smell of rice in the air, and realized that in her hand was a bag of rice.

"Come out and light a fire!" she said, heading straight to the kitchen.

Ch'ŏtchae followed his mother. He began making a fire in the fireplace while his mother cleaned the rice with a sieve. She happened to glance over and see the lower half of her son's body, which was lit up by the fire. For a moment she was stunned, but she quickly turned away, as though she'd been looking at something she shouldn't have seen. His clothes had been torn to sheds. Ch'ŏtchae, for his part, was overjoyed to hear the sound of rice being cleaned. And as he stared at what in the dim light he could just make out to be white rice under water, his mouth began to water. After swallowing several times he went to the water jar and took a drink with the ladle.

Just as they had finished cooking the rice and had brought it inside, they heard the front gate bang shut. Ch'ŏtchae threw open the back door and slipped outside. His mother quickly hid the rice bowl and remained completely still to see if she could hear who it was.

"You sleeping? Ch'ŏtchae! You asleep?"

At the sound of the voice, Ch'ŏtchae's mother dashed to the door.

"Open the door, will you?" Yi Sŏbang cried.

Ch'ŏtchae's mother heard the gasping of someone short of breath. She stepped into the dirt-floored hallway, but her hands were shaking so much she could hardly bring herself to open the door. Maybe someone was just pretending to be Yi Sŏbang, she wondered.

"Open up . . . for crying out loud . . . Aach . . ."

"Is that really you, Yi Sŏbang?" she asked, her mouth at the crack of the door.

Yi Sŏbang must have been upset now, for he knocked his head against the door in reply.

"Oh, heavens, it really is you! Well, come in, come in."

Only then did Ch'ŏtchae's mother open the door in relief. Yi Sŏbang slowly crawled inside.

"What happened to your walking stick?"

"Aach . . ."

Yi Sŏbang could only moan in reply as he climbed up into the inner room and collapsed onto the floor. He made the frightful groans of a very sick man. Ch'ŏtchae's mother took out the bowl of rice she had just hidden. Only after eating the whole bowl was she able to regain her senses and try to help Yi Sŏbang.

"Are you hurt, Yi Sŏbang?"

The man didn't reply. Apprehensively, Ch'ŏtchae's mother slid to his side to put her hand on his forehead.

"I wish I could turn a light on," said the woman softly. "But we don't have any oil . . ."

Yi Sŏbang let out another groan, and then turned onto his side.

"Where's Ch'ŏtchae . . . where's Ch'ŏtchae . . . ?"

Now that she'd heard him speak, her apprehension subsided.

"Where does it hurt, Yi Sŏbang? What's the matter?"

"I caught a cold."

"A cold? So that's why you didn't come home?"

The back door gently slid open.

"You're back, Yi Sŏbang?" asked Ch'ŏtchae.

114

"Yes, I . . ." The man seemed to melt into tears, and could say no more. Ch'ŏtchae was relieved and came inside.

"Mom, give me some of that rice!"

His mother placed a bowl into his hands.

"There's rice in my bag!" said Yi Sŏbang, wiping away his tears.

Ch'ŏtchae's mother went back to the kitchen and threw another log into the fire.

The next day they finally awoke. The sunlight was shining brightly through the paper door. Ch'ŏtchae craned his neck to look at Yi Sŏbang. Though the man had never been much more than skin and bones, he now looked like a living skeleton to Ch'ŏtchae.

"Yi Sŏbang!"

"What?"

The man opened his eyes with a start. He didn't appear to be in so much pain today, perhaps because he'd had a warm bed to sleep in.

"Why were you gone for so long?" snapped Ch'ŏtchae. He looked at Yi Sŏbang as though he harbored a grudge against him.

51

"I was so sick, I almost died . . . I knew well enough that you'd all be waiting for me, but hell, I couldn't even move. And then those bastards stole my walking stick . . ."

As he let out a deep sigh and shifted his gaze to Ch'ŏtchae, the look in the old man's eyes told of the grudge he held against the world. Ch'ŏtchae could feel his heart tearing to pieces. He thought of everything that had happened to him while Yi Sŏbang was away. Though it had only been a few days in total, to Ch'ŏtchae it had felt like a lifetime.

Ch'ŏtchae's mother carried in a brazier, into which she had placed some burning wood. They could all feel the room growing nice and warm. Yi Sŏbang glanced at his beggar's bag.

"Why don't you toast some rice cakes for Ch'ŏtchae?"

The very sound of the words 'rice cakes' whetted Ch'ŏtchae's appetite something terrible, so he jumped up and sat down next to the fire. His mother took out the cakes one by one from the dirty bag. Ch'ŏtchae snatched one away and began to snap off bits of it to chew on.

"Wait till they're toasted!"

Ch'ŏtchae's mother placed some of the cakes onto the fire.

Just watching the two of them sitting there, Yi Sŏbang felt relieved of a heavy burden. As he had crawled home last night through the snow, with the bag of rice cakes hanging around his neck, he'd felt as though head might fall off, and was on the point of throwing that bag away on more than one occasion. But each time he thought about how Ch'ŏtchae and his mother were going hungry at home—waiting desperately for those very rice cakes!—he felt more and more determined to carry them home, even if it meant risking his own life. Oh, the very sight of them sitting there! Mother and son, with their rice cakes placed inside the brazier, now peering into the fire at the soft, warm cakes they'd soon be eating! Yi Sŏbang felt he would have no regrets were he to die right then and there. In fact, he could think of no better way to die than to see the two of them with food in front of them. It was simply too hard for the old man to go on begging any longer.

As these thoughts ran through his mind, Yi Sŏbang unconsciously reached for his walking stick.

"Oh, those bastards! Why the hell would anyone go and take somebody's walking stick?"

"Who took it from you?"

"Well, I was laying in a millhouse, you see, when a bunch of kids came running in and then just up and took off with it. The damn lot of them!"

"Why'd you let the bastards get away with it?" asked Ch'ŏtchae, glaring at Yi Sŏbang. "You should've killed them!"

Ch'ŏtchae's mother stared at him sharply.

"It's high time you quit running off your mouth like that. What sort of nonsense is that anyway—killing people for no good reason at all!"

"So it's all right to let the idiots go free?"

"Yeah, well, who says *you* get to decide what's right and what's wrong? And, besides, some nerve you have . . ."

Mother and son were suddenly reminded of what had happened the night before, and Ch'ŏtchae quickly hung his head. After staring into the brazier for a while, he looked up again and asked, "Yi Sŏbang, do you know what the law is?"

Yi Sŏbang was caught off guard by the question, and had no idea what Ch'ŏtchae meant by this.

"The law?"

Ch'ŏtchae knew that Yi Sŏbang hadn't understood, and he wanted

116

to explain what he meant, but he just sat staring into space, unsure of what to say.

"What do you mean by the law?" asked Yi Sŏbang again impatiently.

"Come on, you know, this thing they call the law."

"Huh? Speak some sense, boy! What do you mean?"

His mother stared at him, too. Ch'ŏtchae knit his brow and raised his voice slightly.

"If you don't know, let's just forget about it!"

He poked at the fire in the brazier, fished out a rice cake and then began chewing on a piece of it. Ch'ŏtchae's mother picked out one that was well done and gave it to Yi Sŏbang. When Yi Sŏbang took a bite of the warm cake, tears started to roll down his cheeks. Seeing this, Ch'ŏtchae's mother began to cry also. Ch'ŏtchae turned around to face the opposite direction.

"Why are you crying? I don't need to watch this, that's for sure," he grumbled.

Ch'ŏtchae stared vacantly at the door, which was glowing in the sunshine. The image of Sŏnbi doing laundry at Wŏnso Pond popped into his mind. And then everything that had just happened to him flashed before his eyes—what the county magistrate had said to them that day, how he had gone to beg for food at Kaettong's, and how, finally, he had run into Tŏkho on the path.

"What do you mean by the law?" asked Yi Sŏbang again.

Ch'ŏtchae spun to face him.

"Why don't you get it? They drag you to the police station, don't they, if you break the law?"

52

When Ch'ŏtchae started explaining what he meant by the law, it suddenly struck him quite viscerally that what he had done the night before was to break the law. Once again, that knot of confusion rose into his mind. He remembered what his mother had said to him earlier: "I was starving and I did what I did because I had no choice!" Indeed, he too had been starving, and he did what he did because he'd had no choice. However, what he'd done was against the law. He'd been starving and had gone off to find something to eat without even thinking

117

about what he was doing. But now that he'd eaten his fill of these soft cakes and this white rice, it finally dawned on him that he had, once again, broken the law.

Yi Sŏbang seemed to understand what Ch'ŏtchae was getting at, but to him, the issue needed no further explanation.

"Look, the law is the law, and that's all there is to it. We've always had it."

"That's all you can say?"

"Well, I guess so. It's just the law."

It had never crossed his mind that people might have actually created the law. Indeed, Yi Sŏbang seemed to think that the law had existed in the world well before people ever did. Hearing what Yi Sŏbang had to say about the matter, Ch'ŏtchae's sense of grief grew even more acute. Here was this inescapable, ironclad rule called the law! And yet why was it that he alone—or rather he, his mother, and Yi Sŏbang, this old man moaning in front of him—were the only ones forced to break it?

As he mulled this over, his heart began racing. Right about now, some family would discover that their rice was missing. And of course they'd go off to the police station and report the theft . . . A policeman might already have headed out to investigate. There might even be someone standing right outside our front gate, thought Ch'ŏtchae, stealing a glance toward the door.

Each time the wind blew, he feared it might be a policeman coming. Each time Yi Sŏbang rolled onto his side, he thought someone might be opening the door, about to walk in. He kept glancing at the door in alarm.

And yet, despite the anxiety that plagued him, Ch'ŏtchae couldn't stop stealing. He made a habit of going out each night to find food. And while his mother and Yi Sŏbang were in no position to tell him not to, they too, were increasingly on edge as the days went by.

One night just after Ch'ŏtchae had come home, Yi Sŏbang sat down beside him.

"Ch'ŏtchae! You've got to get out of here now."

"Why?" said Ch'ŏtchae, his nostrils flaring.

"What do you mean why? You've just got to leave. This isn't the only place people can make a living . . . I hear they've got these places in Seoul and P'yŏngyang they call factories, where poor folk like us can go to work and make money—earn a decent living. You should go find one."

118

A policeman had dropped by the house that afternoon, and Yi Sŏbang had become even more afraid for Ch'ŏtchae's welfare. He was worried that Ch'ŏtchae might be arrested—maybe even tonight.

"You know . . . I'm just a cripple, Ch'ŏtchae, so I can't go anywhere. But if I had a set of strong legs like yours, do you really think that I'd stay cooped up here in the middle of nowhere?"

When Ch'ŏtchae thought about it, Yi Sŏbang seemed to make sense.

"So you're sure that these . . . these things exist? These . . . factories?"

"Well, how am I supposed to know for sure? But that's what my friends from Seoul and Pyŏngyang say! They worked in factories when they were young, then quit when they got older and came back home to beg for a living."

"Well, I guess I'll just have to find out for myself!"

The prospect of working for money at a factory seemed like the dawn of a new day to Ch'ŏtchae, a ray of sunshine brightening the dark future he'd always pictured for himself. He didn't want to stay in that village for a moment longer. He jumped right to his feet.

"All right, Yi Sŏbang, I guess I'm off to Pyŏngyang, or maybe Seoul."

Yi Sŏbang had only mentioned the factories because he'd been afraid the police might surprise Ch'ŏtchae and take him into custody. But now that Ch'ŏtchae was saying he was ready to take off, Yi Sŏbang felt the world spinning around him.

"What? You can't go off just like that."

"Sure I can! The only reason I'm still here is that I never knew any better," answered Ch'ŏtchae, heading straight out the door. "You take care, Yi Sŏbang. I promise to come back with lots of money . . . Just don't tell mom anything, okay?"

Yi Sŏbang followed after him, walking with the aid of the new stick Ch'ŏtchae had made for him.

"You know, Ch'ŏtchae, now that I think about it, I'm not so sure now if those things called factories actually exist. Why don't you just wait and ask around in town first? You can't just head out like this . . ."

But Ch'ŏtchae was running off without a word in reply. Yi Sŏbang somehow found the strength to chase after him. Once Ch'ŏtchae was gone, he might never see the boy again! He just wanted hold his hand one last time, so he scrambled as best he could out the village gate. But Ch'ŏtchae had long since vanished from his sight. Out from behind the hill in the distance, the crescent of a moon slipped into the sky.

53

On the morning of December 25th, giant flakes of snow silently filled the skies over Yongyŏn village, burying all its houses, both high and humble, with snowflakes the shape of peony flowers.

Before long the bell started to sound: cling-clang, cling-clang. Its peal pierced through the white snow, drifting far, far off into the distance.

"Heavens, the bell is already ringing."

Changing into her soft and silky Sunday best, Okchŏm's mother glanced down at Sŏnbi, who was helping her into the clothes, with a look that told the girl to work faster. After helping her into her skirt, Sŏnbi picked up her blouse. Okchŏm's mother quickly took off the blouse she'd been wearing, revealing the half moon of her plump shoulders.

"Oh, how wonderful you are, my daughter! You've warmed them up for me."

The clothes had been laid out on the hottest corner of the heated floor, so her back was now toasty warm. The door opened, and Tŏkho came inside.

"Aren't you ready yet?"

Tŏkho took a seat in the warm corner of the room and lit up a cigarette.

"I think maybe I'll skip work today."

"Well, yes, what's wrong with not going to the office on such a happy occasion?"

Okchŏm's mother looked at Tŏkho, beaming with joy. Ever since they'd gotten rid of Kannan, the two hardly fought at all now.

"I'll have to make an offering today," she said. "Could you give me some money?"

"Another offering? What for?"

"Today's collection is for the destitute . . . You know, for all the beggars. We're making an offering in order to rescue the poor creatures. Give me something, okay? Generous donors get their names posted up on the wall. You don't even have to be a believer to make an offering, either. Some people who come just to watch make offerings, too, when they feel like it. You should go over to the church yourself and offer five wŏn . . ."

"What money do I have?" snapped Tŏkho.

120

"Well, you could do it for my sake. They all call me 'Mrs. Mayor, Mrs. Mayor,' you know."

"And you know perfectly well that I'm not made of money."

"Oh, just be a dear and give me something today, wouldn't you? Two wŏn from me and five wŏn from you? That's seven wŏn altogether." She could already envision her name written up there on the wall of the chapel, alongside her husband's.

Tŏkho tossed his cigarette butt into the ashtray.

"Things aren't exactly easy right now. We keep spending and spending, but we hardly bring in a thing . . ."

As he mumbled something else under his breath, Tŏkho fished out his wallet from inside the pocket of his waistcoat. Okchŏm's mother held out her hand with insistence.

"Money doesn't grow on trees, you know."

He handed her a ten-wŏn note. The nerves around her mouth started to twitch, which they had a habit of doing whenever she was pleased.

"Okay, let's go Granny," the woman called out, stuffing the bill into her pocket. Granny came into the room.

"Oh, heavens, you're not going to wear that, are you? How humiliating!" cried Okchŏm's mother, her eyes fixed on Granny's dirty jacket.

Granny was at a loss for words.

"Go on now. Put something different on! What is that thing, anyway? Surely you've got a cotton one."

Sŏnbi jumped to her feet, went off to Granny's room, and brought back her cotton jacket. Granny hadn't wanted to wear out this new one, which she'd made that fall. After changing into the new clothes Sŏnbi brought her, Granny picked up the cushion that Okchŏm's mother would sit on, as well as the woman's Bible bag and the pouch into which she would place her shoes. Okchŏm's mother looked at Tŏkho.

"Tell me you'll stop by this evening?"

She stood there staring at him, as though she wasn't going to leave until he replied. Tŏkho smiled.

"We'll see how things go . . . Oh, hell, you know the last thing I want to do it go to church and watch all those people praying . . . What is that all about anyway, everyone closing their eyes . . ." He chuckled.

Hardly surprised by her husband's remarks, Okchŏm's mother spun and left the room. Oh, if only I could go too, thought Sŏnbi as she gathered up the clothes Okchŏm's mother had taken off and carefully folded them.

"So have you thought about what I said to you the other day?" asked Tŏkho, watching her from the side.

Sŏnbi looked at Tŏkho in surprise, and then hung her head in silence. It had been so long since Tŏkho had brought up the subject she'd assumed that he'd simply been drunk when he first mentioned it.

Sŏnbi breathed not a word in reply.

54

"Now, Sŏnbi, I've been meaning to ask you about this for some time, but I've been so busy at the office that it completely slipped my mind. Hah, ha. You can't very well start in the middle of winter, though, can you? So let's make it this spring. How about it?"

His words were incredibly tender. Sŏnbi was so overcome with emotion that she blushed all the way to the ears.

"Nowadays, a girl can't marry into a decent family if she doesn't know how to read. And you know, I think of you a member of the family, Sŏnbi, so I don't see why I shouldn't help make your dreams come true . . . Especially someone like me without a son of his own. Hah, ha . . ."

Whenever Tŏkho opened his mouth, he always ended by saying that he had no heir—though it was more an unconscious addition than an intentional one.

"Well, what do you have to say about it?"

Tŏkho slid to Sŏnbi's side and stroked her hair. Sŏnbi bent back a little in her seat.

"Don't you want to go off to study?"

He craned his neck to peer into her eyes. But this was too much for Sŏnbi, and she gently rose to her feet.

"Why won't you answer me? Heh, heh . . . You're like a daughter to me, Sŏnbi . . . Why shy away from me? Sit back down! And answer me, will you?"

Sŏnbi had risen to her feet in confusion. She didn't want to sit back down again, but at the same time, she didn't dare just leave. She stood there at a loss as to what she should do.

Tŏkho looked at his watch, then jumped to his feet.

"Well, I guess I'll just have to ask you about it some other time . . . But you have to give me a straight answer, Sŏnbi . . . There's no reason for you to be so reserved—we're all family here . . . I don't understand why you're acting like this."

Tŏkho patted Sŏnbi's warm cheek lightly with his hand. Sŏnbi flinched and took a step backward.

"Hah, ha . . . I guess you're old enough now not to want to mix company," said Tŏkho. He opened the door and went outside.

When she finally heard his footsteps tread through the middle gate, she sighed in relief and rubbed her face with both her hands. She could still feel the spot where Tŏkho's hand had touched her cheek. Does he really mean to send me to school? she wondered, collapsing onto the floor. And what in the world would she say if he asked her again? How about, 'I'm going to Seoul!' No, no, that won't do! 'Please let me go to school!' That's more like it . . . 'Oh, Father, please let me go to school.' Now, that's what she should say! And as these words rolled off her tongue, Sŏnbi truly believed she'd soon be going off to study in Seoul. It had been almost as long as she could remember since she'd actually said the word 'Father,' and while there was still something strange about it, she really did feel as though she'd met her father once again after a long separation. These emotions pulsing through her made her heart pound all the more.

Why didn't Father talk about this when Okchŏm's mother was around? she asked herself. Then it struck her that she should probably be saying 'Mother' and not 'Okchŏm's mother.' And yet, Okchŏm's mother was the one person she couldn't, with all her heart, address in that way. Whenever she said the word 'Mother' she remembered her own mother, and she always fell into a state of indescribable sadness.

Sŏnbi decided that Tŏkho hadn't mentioned this subject in front of Okchŏm's mother because he knew full well that she would have certainly opposed the idea, and she now felt grateful to Tŏkho for not doing so. Yet she knew that in the end it couldn't all happen behind the woman's back. He'd probably tell her after he'd already sent Sŏnbi to Seoul, or else the day before she was about to leave, or so Sŏnbi imagined. She could just picture the expression of utter shock on the woman's face, and those angry eyebrows slanting in disapproval. But, it won't matter anyway. Father's been planning to send me off to school this whole time, she reminded herself, shifting her gaze toward the door.

It now dawned on Sŏnbi that she'd survived for so long in this household only thanks to the protection that Tŏkho had been kind enough to give her. And there was no question about it—she'd have to let Tŏkho take care of her in the future as well . . . Or rather, she firmly believed that he would always be there for her in the future. And this was the reason why whenever Sŏnbi stayed up late at night worrying about one thing or another, she could always put her mind at rest and fall to sleep with the comforting thought that the master of the household would do whatever was in her best interests.

From the time she'd been a small child, her mother had always referred to Tŏkho as Master of the household, and she, too, had come to refer to him as 'Master.' And yet this morning for the very first time, she had decided to call him 'Father'! She had made up her mind, and from now on, 'Father' was how she would address him.

"Oh, Father, please send me to school!" Sŏnbi repeated these words once again. She was so overwhelmed with emotion that her eyes glistened with tears.

The middle gate creaked open.

55

Sŏnbi quickly wiped away her tears and looked out the glass window. Yu Sŏbang was coming in with the pair of straw shoes he had made for her. She opened the door and went outside.

With a broad smile on his face, Yu Sŏbang made his way to the breezeway.

"Here, try them on!"

Sŏnbi took the shoes from him, the hint of her delight betrayed only in the arch of her eyebrows.

Yu Sŏbang had asked her to measure her foot yesterday, and she had done so using a piece of string.

"Come, try them on. If they don't fit, I'll make another pair for you."

"You don't have to do that . . ."

Sŏnbi glanced at Yu Sŏbang, but she made no move to try on the shoes.

"Come on, kid. I said try them on . . ."

For his own peace of mind, Yu Sŏbang wanted to see for himself that the shoes he'd worked so hard to make actually fit her. Sŏnbi finally agreed to try on the shoes and bent down to put them on, but the instant she looked at her feet, her face went red.

"I'll try them on later," she said, dashing back into the house. Inside, she bent to look at her socks again. What is that, blood? Where did that come from? Oh, this is so embarrassing . . . And so strange! At the tip of her sock was a round red spot—she touched it and examined it carefully. It was nothing but a drop of dried liquid from some *kimchi*. Only now was she able to breathe easily again. But what if Yu Sŏbang had thought it was blood? she wondered, peering through the pane of glass. With the same broad smile on his face, Yu Sŏbang was watching Blackie scamper this way and that through the snow. Perhaps the dog understood Yu Sŏbang's smile, or perhaps he was just excited by the falling snow, for he plowed his nose through the snow and dug his paws into it, jumping this way and that, and rolling about.

At each stunt, Yu Sŏbang urged him on under his breath.

"That's it! Hah, ha," he laughed. "Go, go!"

As far as Yu Sŏbang was concerned, that dog was his one and only friend. Sŏnbi felt the same way. The dog was attached to Yu Sŏbang, Sŏnbi, and Granny. Perhaps because they were the ones who fed him.

After watching the dog for a while, Yu Sŏbang peered through the glass window.

"So they fit?"

"Yes." Sŏnbi looked at the shoes placed beside her before answering.

Yu Sŏbang seemed satisfied with her answer, and headed back outside toward the middle gate. Blackie, still coated white with snow, followed him. Sŏnbi's gaze shifted down to her straw shoes. She tried them on, and they fit perfectly. "Oh, how beautifully he wove them!" She stared at her feet. Yu Sŏbang had woven these shoes especially for her, and she was terribly grateful to him for them. And when she imagined who might weave shoes like these for her in the future, the first person who came to mind was Ch'ŏtchae. But didn't they say he ran off somewhere? He did something bad and ran off, didn't he? What in the world was wrong with him? But with a mother like that, how could anyone turn out okay? Despite her misgivings, Sŏnbi felt sorry about his leaving. If only she'd been able to see him one last time before he'd left—it was this lingering sense of loss that stayed with her for some time as she gazed down at those newly woven shoes. But, I'm going off to school, so none of this even matters . . .

That evening, Tŏkho's whole household went to the chapel. The children were supposed to put on a special show, so everyone—even Yu Sŏbang and Tŏkho—had gone to see it.

As Sŏnbi sat in that enormous room all alone, winnowing the rest of the cotton she had started that afternoon, her mind wandered in many directions. From out of the cotton gin flowed white clouds of round, plump cotton. They passed through the gin, one after the other, just like the myriad of thoughts that seemed to flow through her mind.

Only hours earlier Sŏnbi had looked forward to going to the chapel that night, too. But after her unexpected conversation with Tŏkho, she was more than content to just sit there, entertaining thoughts of her studies in Seoul. So when Okchŏm's mother told Granny to watch the house and asked Sŏnbi to come along to the chapel, she had declined and let Granny go instead.

Each time Sŏnbi thought of studying at a school, the first thing that came to her mind was learning how to embroider. This was the only kind of studying she'd ever seen with her own eyes. She assumed that students had to dress up in fancy western clothes and use powder and face cream and lipstick—just like Okchŏm did. And she imagined that being a student meant walking around with boys as if it were nothing, eating lunch with them and studying alongside them without ever getting embarrassed. It was with this mixture of embarrassment and distress on the one hand, and pure joy on the other, that these thoughts churned through Sŏnbi's mind to the rhythm of the cotton gin. But then the door slowly slid open.

56

A cold wind swept inside and Sŏnbi shivered. She jumped to her feet in surprise.

"Who's that?" she cried in the confusion of the moment. But when she turned around, it was of all people Tŏkho. She was ashamed to have been so alarmed, and her face went red.

"Did I scare you?"

Tŏkho brushed off the snow that had fallen on him and took a seat in the warm corner of the room. Then he started stroking his beard.

"There wasn't a thing worth seeing. So many damn peasants there, it was more like torture than entertainment."

Tŏkho had taken the liberty of striking up a conversation with Sŏnbi, but Sŏnbi picked up the cotton gin and stood up to go.

"What's the matter? Why are you getting up?"

"I'm just going to gin the cotton in the side room."

"Oh, just do it here . . . Come on, girl, don't go now. I've got something to talk to you about."

Sŏnbi put down the cotton gin and sat down again, thinking that he probably wanted to ask her whether she wanted to study in Seoul.

"Put that gin away and sit over here."

Sŏnbi would have felt too exposed without holding the cotton gin in front of her, so she kept her hands firmly clasped onto it. Tŏkho got up and sat closer to her.

"So do you really want to study?"

Sŏnbi felt awkward for some reason and she couldn't give him an immediate reply.

"Come, child, why won't you answer me? When an elder asks you a question, you've got to be quick with an answer." He chuckled. "Boy, are you something!"

Sŏnbi cracked a smile, then hid her face from him. She was both embarrassed and deeply moved, and she could feel her heart racing at a frightful speed.

"So you don't want to go?"

Tŏkho moved closer to her inch by inch, whether conscious of it or not.

"I want to study . . . " replied Sŏnbi, still looking at the cotton gin.

She had finally spoken, but had left off the 'Father' that she'd been planning on using since that afternoon. She considered saying it again, and glanced over at Tŏkho. Tŏkho smiled.

"So you want to study . . ."

The blushing face of this girl half hidden behind the frame of the cotton gin! Tŏkho could feel the lust surge unbearably inside him. He sprang to Sŏnbi's side.

"Stay still! No one's going to hurt you."

He quickly grabbed her hand, just as she jumped up in alarm. Tŏkho's hand was as hot as fire. The scent of alcohol and the powerful odor of a strong middle-aged man were almost suffocating. Sŏnbi didn't know what to do, and started to tremble.

"Please let go of me!"

She tried to shake off Tŏkho as he slowly pulled her closer, but she also had to fight back the wave of tears that were building up inside of her. And then, just as she thought she might finally break free from him, that fatty yellow flesh on Tŏkho's face, like an over-grown squash, pressed up against her cheek.

"Oh, Sŏnbi! Just do what I tell you, and I'll give you anything your heart desires, much more than the chance to go to school! You understand, my girl?"

Sŏnbi whipped her face away from his.

"Oh, Father! Please stop it!"

"Aha, hah, ha . . . Father! You said Father! Oh, you sweet little thing, you. Now then, why be afraid of your own father? Come, my girl . . . "

He whispered this into her ear and squeezed Sŏnbi so tightly that she now felt sick to her stomach.

"Father, I think maybe you've had too much to drink."

"I know, my girl, I'm dead drunk."

Tŏkho was breathing heavily. And as his lips moved ever closer toward her mouth, he started slobbering all over her. She had no idea why Tŏkho was doing this to her. She struggled to break free from his arms, kicking like crazy. She was squirming like a freshly caught fish, as Tŏkho saw it, but once he'd savored that flesh of hers, he knew she'd taste just fine raw. He kicked the cotton gin to the side and dropped to the floor, Sŏnbi still in his arms. He grabbed the waist of her skirt and pulled it down.

"Father, Father, oh, I'm sorry! I'm sorry!" she cried out, finally breaking into tears. Once again, she tried to shove him away.

"Not going to stay still, are you? Well, if you won't do as you're told, then just get the hell out of this house! Get out! Right now!"

Glaring at her with his fierce, blood-shot eyes, Tŏkho was so terrifying that Sŏnbi was convinced he was on the point of murdering her. This was the same Tŏkho she had so trusted, so depended on! The same Tŏkho she had entrusted with her future in place of her own dead mother and father . . . Could she ever have imagined—even in her wildest dreams—that in the course of an hour he could transform into this monster! Sŏnbi turned her head to the side and closed her eyes, so she wouldn't have to watch him.

57

Returning home late at night, Sinch'ŏl opened the main gate very qui-etly and entered the yard. Approaching the door of his room, he stopped short when he heard someone speaking in a hushed voice.

" . . . No, I'm all right . . . It's just that it seems like Sinch'ŏl has found a girlfriend."

The voice belonged to Okchŏm.

"Oh, come now, that boy? A girlfriend?"

This was his stepmother making excuses for him. When he heard his father clear his throat, however, he glanced briefly at the inner room, removed his shoes, and opened the door to his own room, where Okchŏm and his stepmother were sitting. Judging from the expressions on their faces, they'd been taken by surprise. The sight of them con-firmed to Sinch'ŏl how much Okchŏm resembled his stepmother.

"My goodness, I didn't hear you come in."

With a broad smile on his face, Sinch'ŏl looked at Okchŏm. He hung his overcoat on the wall.

"So you've come over to visit . . ."

"Where on earth have you been, Sinch'ŏl? I'll bet . . ."

Stopping mid-sentence, Okchŏm smiled sweetly. His stepmother smiled as well.

"Okchŏm dropped by earlier this evening and has been waiting for you ever since."

"I see. Well, you'll have to forgive me."

Sinch'ŏl took a seat in the chilly room.

"This floor is freezing."

His stepmother slid a cushion over to him, which he pulled to him-self and sat on. Her round eyes seemed to roll from one side of her fair-skinned face to the other as she looked back and forth between Sinch'ŏl and Okchŏm. Her trademark snaggletooth jutted out from between her lips.

Okchŏm noticed that the tip of Sinch'ŏl's nose was red.

"I got a letter from home the other day," she said.

"A letter?"

Sinch'ŏl instantly thought of Sŏnbi. His curiosity was now piqued. Had they sent Okchŏm a letter saying they'd be sending Sŏnbi to Seoul?

"Does your father say he's well?"

"Yes, he does . . . And as far as Sŏnbi goes, he says they're going to send her here in the spring."

"Well, good," replied Sinch'ŏl, though he felt somewhat disappointed. "It'll be easier for her to enroll in classes then."

His stepmother rose to her feet.

"Well, I'm going to my room. Enjoy yourself, dear."

Okchŏm promptly stood up as well, to say goodnight.

"Yes, good night then."

When Sinch'ŏl's stepmother finally made her way into the yard, Okchŏm breathed a sigh of relief. She gazed into the lamplight, lost in her thoughts. She could hear the sound of a taxicab whizzing by in the distance. The honking of its horn rang in her ears like the sound of a vibrating wire.

"Where have you been going off to all the time? There's a girlfriend in the picture now, isn't there, Sinch'ŏl?"

She stared him square in the face. Sinch'ŏl brushed some of the dust from his trousers, then tried to blow it away.

"Uh . . . are you talking about me?"

"You are so easily distracted! You won't even listen to me when I'm talking to you. Are you thinking about someone else?"

"Me? Who should I be thinking about?"

He tilted his head to the side as though he were pondering her question.

"Sinch'ŏl! Does what I say mean anything at all to you? Why do you always treat me like this?"

Her eyes were now as bright as glass beads, and had begun to well up with tears. She thought about how she had walked circles around this neighborhood night after night in the hope of running across Sinch'ŏl. Had she gone to all that trouble just to hear this sort of insincerity? She regretted everything now, and jumped to her feet.

"I'm going!"

"You are?" replied Sinch'ŏl, as he watched her stand up. Then he smiled. "You're not going home all alone, are you?"

"Well, why not? Do you think I'm not up to it?"

She put on her gloves and wrapped on her scarf. She could feel the warmth of her breath in her scarf and a faint dampness against her cheeks. She realized she was on the verge of tears.

130

"Now, Okchŏm, why don't you just sit back down for a while. Then I'll walk you back home."

Once Okchŏm had stood up to go, he had thought the empty room rather lonely.

"Do you mean it?"

With this offer to walk her home, much of the resentment lodged in Okchŏm's heart seemed to melt away of its own accord.

"Of course I do."

Then something occurred to her.

"You know, your father might scold me for being in here," she said, glancing over at the door and then back at Sinch'ŏl. "Let's go back to my place. I'll order something for you to eat when we get there." With a tilt of her head, she looked at him like a child begging for something.

Sinch'ŏl jumped to his feet. He threw on his overcoat and they went outside.

58

They set off on foot, walking side by side. There were no buses or taxicabs to be seen on the street, nothing but the dim light from the streetlamps standing guard at the alleyways. They walked along slowly, casting long shadows on the ground. The biting wind of a winter's night swept icily up the edges of their clothes. It was finally Okchŏm who broke the silence, as she looked up at a streetlamp.

"I wonder how many times I've walked this street," said Okchŏm softly, "all alone . . ."

She looked out at Paksŏk Heights, which rose in the distance. She let out a gentle sigh.

"Hey . . . I was wondering how old Sŏnbi is now," said Sinch'ŏl.

"I guess she's about eighteen. Why do you want to know that?"

"I just thought I should know."

"Why should you know that?"

Okchŏm stared up at Sinch'ŏl. Was Sinch'ŏl asking these questions, she wondered, because he couldn't get the girl out of his mind?

"Come, Sinch'ŏl, I want to know why you need to know?"

"I . . . well, if she's going to come to Seoul in the spring . . . you've got to know how old she is in order to enroll her in a school, don't you?"

"Oh, I see . . . I don't know why I was so . . . Hah, ha," chuckled Okchŏm.

Sinch'ŏl laughed, too.

"Well, she's too old to go to a primary school. So I guess you'll have to enroll her in some sort of private academy."

"Yes, I suppose we will . . . But as far as studying goes, you know, I'm not really sure that she's up to it. I think you're right about having her come up and work as my maid for a while. That way we can show her around the city a bit, and when we find a nice family for her, we can get her married . . . It'd be shame to waste those good looks of hers in some village in the middle of nowhere."

Okchŏm pictured Sŏnbi in her mind's eye. Indeed, the only virtue she had to waste was a pretty face, considered Okchŏm.

"Now, tell me," she asked. That cousin of yours you mentioned the other day, is he really going to marry some country girl?"

"Yes, he is! He doesn't have much of an education, you know, so for a wife he decided to choose a real bumpkin."

"I suppose he'd have to. If two people aren't equals, they certainly aren't going to live long, happy lives. In any case . . . I guess that settles it then. Once we bring the child to Seoul, we'll have to send her to school for a few months so she can learn how to read the Korean alphabet, and then we can arrange for her to get married."

"Yes, well, we can worry about that part later . . . But in marriage, you never know what'll happen until you actually get a chance to meet each other. I mean, all that really matters is that you like each other, isn't it? Hah, ha."

"Well, naturally!" she said with a chuckle. "Of course, you must be fond of each other."

As they walked along, Okchŏm moved closer to Sinch'ŏl's side. If only she could find some way of bringing a quick conclusion to their own plans to get married . . . Perhaps I should just ask him about it tonight? she thought.

Before long, they had come to the crest of Paksŏk Heights. The wind blowing through the dark forest that surrounded the University Hospital carried with it the faint scent of disinfectant. But down there, beneath those romantic stars, the bare trees of Ch'anggyŏng Park and the surrounding wall that snaked around it brought to mind the enduring history of the five-century long Yi Dynasty.

"See, this is the part I hate most about walking home alone."

"Hate? Well, I suppose you shouldn't go out so often then."

"Oh, Sinch'ŏl!" she said in exasperation, then grabbed onto his overcoat. In a secluded place like this, she thought, it would have been nice if he'd at least offered the warmth of his hand in hers. No matter how she thought about it, Sinch'ŏl truly seemed like a person without any feelings. She even wondered if maybe he had some sort of physical defect. Before long, they had arrived at Okchŏm's boarding house, where Sinch'ŏl came to a full stop.

"Well, I guess you'd better go on in now."

"Come on inside with me."

Okchŏm stepped in front of him to block his escape. She seemed exceedingly desperate for something to happen.

"Oh, come on, Okchŏm, it's late . . . I've got to go back home and get some sleep. How am I supposed to make it to school tomorrow?"

"Oh, just for a few minutes . . ."

Okchŏm was practically clinging to Sinch'ŏl now. Sinch'ŏl didn't object exactly, but nor did he think it a particularly good idea. He remembered the debate they'd had today in his reading group about relations with women.

"I'll come again tomorrow."

"Come again tomorrow? I've had enough of your false promises! Come inside right now."

Okchŏm grabbed hold of Sinch'ŏl's hand and pulled on it. Should I go inside? Sinch'ŏl wavered. Or maybe not?

59

Sinch'ŏl finally went through the gate, against his better judgment. Well, as long as I don't make any foolish mistakes, he said to himself, everything will be fine! Inside Okchŏm's room, there were books piled here and there on her desk, and the floor was littered with apple peels. Judging from the rolled-up futon that had been shoved into the corner, it seemed as though she'd come over to his house right after climbing out of bed. Okchŏm went around the room picking up the apple peels and found a cushion for Sinch'ŏl to sit on.

"It's awfully messy in here, isn't it?" she laughed nervously.

If only she'd known Sinch'ŏl would be coming over, she would have made a point of cleaning up the place—this sense of regret, and the fear that Sinch'ŏl would think her lazy, both struck her at the same time. There was nothing that she could do about it now. Her face felt hot just thinking about it.

Sinch'ŏl pulled over the cushion, took a seat, and watched Okchŏm as she tidied the room. He noticed the whitish dust that had collected on the rim of the electric lamp, the cosmetics carelessly left around the room, and the socks that had been pushed into the corners.

"Would you like to read this letter?"

Okchŏm picked up a blue envelope from the stationary chest on her desk and handed it to Sinch'ŏl, with the purpose of diverting his attention from everything else he might see in the room. Sinch'ŏl pulled the letter from the envelope, and after reading it through a couple times handed it back to Okchŏm. She was sittting right in front of him, in the middle of peeling a pear. He knew at first glance that she must have paid at least four or five chŏn for it. Her pointy fingers seemed somewhat pinkish in contrast to the pear she was peeling. Just then, he suddenly remembered that ugly hand, that hand that he'd seen disappear behind the reed fence, holding a summer squash! Whose hand had that been? he wondered again. Okchŏm cut the pear in pieces, stabbed one slice of it with the end of her knife, and handed it to Sinch'ŏl. She also took out a box of chocolates from her desk drawer and placed it down in front of him.

"Have some of these, too . . . Can I get you anything else to eat? I can wake up the owner and send him out for something."

She cocked her head and stared at Sinch'ŏl with eyes that seemed to overflow with affection for him.

"No, this is great. I couldn't ask for more."

"But . . . maybe you'd prefer something warm . . ."

"Oh, please stop. I'm very happy with this."

"Well, shall I have the brazier brought in? It's awfully cold in here, isn't it?"

"Don't worry about me, Okchŏm. I'm fine."

Sinch'ŏl ate his slice of pear and then unwrapped a piece of chocolate. Okchŏm crunched away on her pear, staring at him bright-eyed.

"You know, your mother is such a nice person."

"Yes . . . I suppose she is."

Okchŏm smiled and asked again, "I bet you have a girlfriend some-where, don't you, Sinch'ŏl?"

"Well, that's the first I've heard of it."

"But your mother said that you did."

"My mother? I have no idea what you're talking about."

Okchŏm laughed.

"Sinch'ŏl, why do you always seem so tired of me?"

"Me, tired of you? I don't quite know what you mean . . ." He laughed.

Sinch'ŏl thought it rather silly that Okchŏm was trying to probe his feelings. Oh, why don't I just go home to bed instead of wasting time like this, he thought to himself. He wiped his mouth with his handker-chief and stood up to leave.

"Thank you for the snacks, Okchŏm."

Okchŏm stared up at him in surprise.

"You're not going yet, are you?" She grabbed the hem of his over-coat and pulled it toward her. One way or another she was going to find some sort of closure—even Sinch'ŏl saw the determination in her eyes.

"I'll come by again tomorrow. If I don't go home now, I won't make it into school tomorrow."

"Oh, just stay a little longer . . . Another half an hour . . . No, how about just twenty more minutes?"

"I said I'd come back tomorrow."

"I don't want you to go. Tomorrow is tomorrow."

Sinch'ŏl found this all rather awkward, and he hesitated, at which point Okchŏm stood up and backed him into the corner.

"I won't let you go home tonight!" She was breathing excitedly, and her cheeks were flushed. The sight of this was so amusing to Sinch'ŏl that he couldn't stop himself from laughing. This girl's about ready to pounce on me! he thought.

"Why are you laughing? You think I'm a joke, don't you, Sinch'ŏl? Well, I already know that! So just tell me why you're playing all these games with me."

As she said this, Okchŏm thought back to the time in the country-side when he'd held her so tightly around her waist. Sinch'ŏl, for his part, stared back at her, perplexed.

60

Several days later, when Sinch'ŏl came home after school, he found his father sitting at the dinner table, looking rather pleased.

"Still at the library this late at night?" his father asked him.

Since he had instructed Sinch'ŏl quite some time ago to begin studying for the bar examination, his father had assumed that Sinch'ŏl was working hard in preparation for it.

"Yes, I was," replied Sinch'ŏl as he sat his younger brother Yŏngch'ŏl onto his lap.

"Gimme some caramels?" said Yŏngch'ŏl, staring up from Sinch'ŏl's lap.

Sinch'ŏl then showed the boy his empty pockets.

"I forgot to buy them today," he said. "I'll get you some tomorrow, okay? I promise."

"You better not be lying again. You already promised to get me some."

His mother looked affectionately at Yŏngch'ŏl.

"That boy sits around all day long, talking about nothing else. The little rascal. . . ."

"I'll buy you some tomorrow, okay? Cross my heart," said Sinch'ŏl.

Yŏngch'ŏl's raven-black eyes lit up.

Just then the maid carried in a brazier, which Sinch'ŏl's stepmother moved in front of him. The soft hair on either side of his cheeks rose in the heat.

"Now, come over here, Yŏngch'ŏl, and finish eating."

The boy came to his mother and sat in her lap, but then his father chimed in, and beckoned him with a wave of his hand.

"Yŏngch'ŏl, come over here."

"Wait . . . Let me first give him some rice with this soup. . . ."

His mother bent her head around to see if the boy was eating properly and then smiled sweetly at him—her pointy snaggletooth sticking out all the while. Sinch'ŏl noticed that his father had been waiting for him and hadn't eaten a single mouthful, so he quickly sat down in front of the dinner table. The pungent scent of seasoning greeted his nose.

"Next time don't forget to buy my caramels . . ."

Yŏngch'ŏl looked at Sinch'ŏl again, his cheeks puffed out in a pout.

"That's right. He forgot them today, but he'll get you some tomorrow. Now, be a good boy and eat your food," said Sinch'ŏl's father.

All you can think of is caramels, isn't it, sweetie? Now, eat this up for mummy."

They all smiled at the boy. Sinch'ŏl finished his meal and stood to go.

"Wait," said his father, taking a sip of scorched rice tea. "Sit back down for a minute."

Sinch'ŏl assumed his father had something to say to him, and he looked to his stepmother for a clue. She returned his glance with a smile. His father had his dinner table taken away.

"I think it's about time you got married . . ." said his father, looking straight into Sinch'ŏl's eyes. Sinch'ŏl could feel his heart sinking, and he winced self-consciously with a mild sense of shame. He hung his head as he listened.

"You're already twenty-five years old . . . and in a couple of days, you'll have a degree in your hands . . . This is just the right time for you to find a wife . . . Tell me, have you got your eyes on anyone in particular?"

Sinch'ŏl wondered if a prospective family had made themselves known to his father.

"I haven't given much thought to getting married," he replied.

What had immediately come to his mind, however, was the image of Sŏnbi carrying a bowl of soup to him. He could see Yongyŏn village right there in front of his eyes.

His father's face glowed with satisfaction. He recalled something that he had heard from his wife a few days earlier. "Oh, Okchŏm has fallen for Sinch'ŏl all right," she'd said with much relish, "but I do think it's a case of unrequited love." The man was delighted to know that his son was so focused on his studies.

"Well, then . . ."

His father seemed to have something else on his mind.

"What do you think about this girl Okchŏm, who's always stopping here?"

Sinch'ŏl thought of the night several days earlier when he'd dashed out of Okchŏm's room.

His father lit up a cigarette.

"Now, having grown up as an only child, she may well be somewhat accustomed to having things her own way . . . but the girl is a fine person, as far as I can tell. What do you think?"

As his father was making this extraordinary case for his marrying Okchŏm, Sinch'ŏl stared sadly into the brazier beside him, considering what his father was trying to do to him. All the faith and trust he had placed in his father now seemed to transform before his eyes into that heap of dirty coal piled up at the brazier's edge. He couldn't bear sitting there any longer. He looked up at the man, and spoke.

"Father . . . I am not yet ready to get married."

61

Sinch'ŏl jumped to his feet. But his father looked all the more commanding.

"You sit right back down . . . Are you aware of the fact that Okchŏm's father has come to town?"

Sinch'ŏl froze. "No, I wasn't. When did he get here?"

"He came down on the train today. He went out of his way to pay us a visit, but unfortunately he couldn't stay long. So I want you to go over and see him. He was kind enough to let you spend the whole summer at his house last year, and now that he's in town, you are to give him the courtesy of a visit."

The knowledge that Tŏkho and his father had already been conferring in private was cause for even greater alarm. But at the same time, maybe Tŏkho had brought Sŏnbi with him. With this thought his heart started racing.

"Fine, I'll go see him," he replied promptly, then left the room.

Yŏngch'ŏl opened up the door again and poked his head outside. "Don't forget my caramels, okay?" The light was shining at just such an angle that the boy's head cast a round shadow on the floor of the breezeway.

"Yes, okay," said Sinch'ŏl, putting on his shoes.

"Make sure to pick up something to take with you," called his father.

If he had known for sure that Sŏnbi was in town, he would have eagerly gone out of his way to buy something special to take with him. But as he wasn't sure that she'd come along, he didn't have the slightest interest in taking a gift. He put his hand in his pocket, felt for his wallet, and went outside.

From down the street a ways there was a bus barreling straight toward him with its red and blue lights flashing. He could see the familiar face of the bus girl inside. Maybe I'll take the bus, he thought, taking a few steps toward it, but then he changed his mind. No, I'm just going to take my time, he said to himself as he turned his back and started walking.

From this direction a taxicab and a bus came racing toward him neck and neck. Sinch'ŏl caught a powerful whiff of gasoline and stepped to the side of the road. Maybe Okchŏm, Sŏnbi, and Tŏkho were all riding inside? Maybe they're coming to find me? Each time he caught sight of a young woman sitting inside a bus, the same thoughts came to him. As he slowly walked along, he painted a picture of these two girls, Sŏnbi and Okchŏm, in his mind's eye. Then he began mulling over what his father had said. Was it a good idea to get married now? Or wasn't it? It was purely in a theoretical vein that he asked himself these questions. Up until now he had never given consideration to anything like marriage.

But the closer he came to Okchŏm's boarding house, the more these unresolved questions belabored his mind; his head was spinning. And what would happen if Sŏnbi had actually come to Seoul? He had managed to coax Okchŏm into bringing Sŏnbi to Seoul only through a variety of unusual measures, and now that it seemed Sŏnbi had made it to town, there were other issues that would need resolving, which promised to place him in a very awkward situation.

"Hey, is that you Sinch'ŏl!"

The slap on this shoulder had startled him and he turned to look. It was Inho, a fellow classmate. He was wearing one of those mortarboards, pressed tightly down on his head, as well as tortoise shell glasses. There was a cigarette hanging out of his mouth, as usual.

"Where you headed?"

"Me? Oh, just off to see someone . . ."

"Well, who? Looks to me like you're off to meet your . . . *lover*."

His eyeglasses glinted in the streetlight.

"Well, whatever you say . . ."

With a smile stretched across his face, Sinch'ŏl set off once again. Inho followed.

"Hey, there's a real beauty over at Café Dahlia now—fresh from the countryside. Any interest in going?"

"A real beauty?" mumbled Sinch'ŏl. "From the countryside?"

He painted a picture of Sŏnbi's face in his mind's eye. But then he caught a strong whiff of cigarette smoke in the air and turned his face in the opposite direction. Sinch'ŏl could tell from the smell that his cigarettes were *Shikishimas*.

"Where you headed? Just tell me."

"Oh, my father sent me out on an errand."

Although he was only trying to get rid of Inho by saying so, he really felt as though this was nothing more than an errand he was running on his father's behalf. All he really cared about was whether he'd see Sŏnbi.

"An errand? Oh, come on! What kind of man runs around for his father these days? You're hopeless . . . Mr. Virtuosity!" He burst out laughing.

"Mr. Virtuosity?" chuckled Sinch'ŏl.

Sinch'ŏl's sinuses were stinging from the *Shikishima* smoke. He happened to spot a *yakiguri* vender passing by on the other side of the road.

"Well, I'll see you later."

Inho offered his hand to Sinch'ŏl and then flicked away his *Shikishima*, having smoked barely half of it. In the middle of the street its red embers glowed brilliantly.

62

He's going off to some raunchy café again, isn't he? thought Sinch'ŏl, as he watched Inho dash off to catch the streetcar to Yongsan. 'A beauty from the countryside,' he mumbled.

After arriving at Okchŏm's boarding house, he couldn't immediately bring himself to enter the building, so he took a minute to see if he could hear movement inside. After trying to calm his racing heart, he cleared his throat. At the sound of his cough someone in Okchŏm's room came to the door.

"Yes, who's there?"

Okchŏm opened the door just a crack and was now peered outside.

"It's just me," said Sinch'ŏl, stepping up to the door.

"Oh, Sinch'ŏl! Did you run into Father on the way here? He just went over to your house."

"He did? Well, no, I didn't see him."

"Well, you must have passed right by each other on the street . . . Please, come inside."

140

At the thought that Sŏnbi might actually be sitting inside that room, Sinch'ŏl felt his face burning. He slipped off his shoes and quickly peeked into the room. He saw no one else inside.

"Well, aren't you coming in?"

Now that he'd found only Okchŏm in the room, he wanted to turn around and walk away. He even felt a grudge against Okchŏm, who was smiling there so sweetly at him.

Sinch'ŏl dragged his feet into the room unwillingly. He caught the faint scent of medicine in the air. Then he noticed the bedding laid out in the warm corner of the room, from which Okchŏm seemed to have just arisen. Okchŏm went over and looked at her face in the mirror.

"I haven't even freshened up yet. Oh, I look just a wreck!"

She smoothed down her hair and then grimaced at herself in the mirror. Sinch'ŏl saw in Okchŏm's distorted face the same scowl with which her mother had always scolded Sŏnbi. There's no sign that they've even brought her here, thought Sinch'ŏl, quickly taking in everything around him.

"You know, Sinch'ŏl, I've been sick this entire time."

"What's wrong with you?"

Okchŏm blushed.

"Ever since the other night . . ."

Both of them recalled what had happened that night. Sinch'ŏl smiled at first, but then it dawned on him: his father and Tŏkho were probably at this very moment discussing the issue of their marriage.

"Has your father come to town all by himself? He should have brought your mother along with him." Sinch'ŏl could see quite clearly that Sŏnbi hadn't come with Tŏkho, but he still couldn't resist probing further.

"Well, I actually asked Mother to come, but Father came by himself."

Sinch'ŏl felt almost dizzy with disappointment as he stood in the bright light of the electric lamp.

"You know, Sinch'ŏl, I really thought you'd never come. I thought I'd die without ever seeing you again . . ."

Okchŏm hung her head and started to sob. Sinch'ŏl felt terrible watching the tears stream down her flushed cheeks.

If only he too could break down in tears, so that he could get everything out of his system . . . Could he actually be in love with Sŏnbi? He could still hear his father asking him if there was any girl he liked in particular.

Okchŏm jumped up as though she'd just remembered something. She opened a basket and took out, one after another, an apple, a pear, a persimmon, some chestnuts and some rice cakes.

"Please have something to eat. Father just took some to your house as well. He brought all of these with him . . ."

A faint smile broke over her tear-drenched face. Sinch'ŏl stared back at her blankly.

"It looks like we're having a party here."

"A party? Oh, this is nothing."

As she looked at Sinch'ŏl and spoke these words to him, Okchŏm just barely managed to restrain herself from telling him that they should get married right away, and have the most fabulous wedding banquet they could ever imagine.

"Take whatever you'd like . . . Just pick something. How's this one? Or this one? Or how about one of these?"

Okchŏm extended her arm and touched each of the fruits she offered him. But Sinch'ŏl didn't feel like eating. He felt out of sorts, like he'd lost something that had always belonged to him, like he'd been deeply betrayed.

"Well, will you have one of these then?"

She took down the same box of chocolates they had eaten from several days earlier. She very meticulously removed the foil from one of them.

"Now open wide. I'll pop it into your mouth from here."

The color rising in her cheeks, Okchŏm looked at Sinch'ŏl, who grimaced slightly, then forced a smile.

63

"Please just give it to me."

Sinch'ŏl quickly stuck out his hand. Okchŏm gave him a hurt look, and glancing down at the piece of chocolate, blushed up to her ears. Sinch'ŏl reached over for the box of chocolates and picked out a piece for himself. He was just unwrapping it when they heard the sound of footsteps.

"Oh, that's probably Father," said Okchŏm softly.

The door opened and Tŏkho came inside. Sinch'ŏl scrambled to his feet and bowed his head politely to the man.

"I see, so this is where you've been . . . I was just at your house . . . how's school going?"

Tŏkho took off his overcoat and laid it down. He took a quick look at Okchŏm, then shifted his gaze to Sinch'ŏl, at whom he smiled so wide that crow's feet appeared at the corners of his eyes.

"I'll tell you, my boy, this girl said she was so sick, I had to drop everything I was working on and come right down . . . Now, you, you get back into that bed."

Just a while ago Tŏkho had been under the impression that Okchŏm was practically on her deathbed, but now he saw her sitting there as if nothing in the world was wrong with her. Tŏkho was relieved that his daughter's illness was not serious, and now that he saw she was alright, he was anxious to come to a quick decision as far her marriage to Sinch'ŏl was concerned.

"I hear that you're going to graduate pretty soon."

"Yes, I am."

"So . . . Oh, this is nothing fancy, but please have something to eat . . . Now, tell me, there's some sort of examination you take after graduating?"

Sinch'ŏl guessed that Tŏkho had been talking to his father.

"Well . . . nothing's quite certain yet."

"I see . . . well, I wish only the best for you . . . I'm actually pressed for time, so I'll have to take the train back home tomorrow. I had to drop everything in the office to come here, you see, so I'm a bit worried about work now . . ."

Sinch'ŏl recalled something that Okchŏm had mentioned the other day, that her father was now mayor of the township. It was no wonder, he realized, that the man was wearing such an expensive suit.

"Tell me what you want to do, Okchŏm. It doesn't seem to me like you're very sick. Do you want to come back home with me? Or can you manage to get some sort of treatment here? Just make a decision."

Okchŏm thought about it for a moment, her eyes shifting.

"Well, how would you like to come to the countryside for a while?" she asked, looking at Sinch'ŏl.

Sinch'ŏl immediately thought of Sŏnbi and was quite tempted to take her up on this offer, despite his better judgment. But he remembered what his mission in life was, and realized that if he went along with them at this point, there would be no way out of this marriage.

"How could I possibly take you up on such an offer? I put you all to so much trouble last summer, after running into Okchŏm on the way to Monggŭmp'o Beach . . ."

Tŏkho hung onto each and every word Sinch'ŏl said, and was given no little concern by what he heard. Last summer he and his wife hadn't doubted in the slightest that Sinch'ŏl and his daughter had an understanding between themselves to marry, and that was why they'd allowed the two of them to lounge around in the same room unsupervised. But now that Sinch'ŏl spoke to him this way, he sensed that Sinch'ŏl was trying to make excuses in order to pull out of the arrangement. Yet, he'd been certain after his conversation with Sinch'ŏl's father that the marriage was a foregone conclusion. That conversation was a comfort to him now.

"Well, maybe this is a bad time for you to come, but when you graduate this spring and it gets a bit warmer outside . . . by then this girl of ours will have recovered . . . and you'll have to come up for a visit together . . . Ever since last summer my wife keeps saying she misses you more than she does this girl."

"Well, that's awfully kind of you to say . . ."

Sinch'ŏl bowed his head, cast his eyes to the ground and placed his hands politely on his knees. Oh, that masculine, dignified face, thought Okchŏm, and those hands! If it weren't for her father being there, she'd have instantly clasped them into her own, so great was the excitement in her breast. Tŏkho stared at Sinch'ŏl for a moment, and it seemed to him that there was something about the boy that was just a little too good for Okchŏm. But what a fine son-in-law he'd make! thought Tŏkho, his eyes still fixed on him.

According to what Okchŏm had told him, Sinch'ŏl did indeed love her, but he was simply too well-mannered and far too shy to actually express his love outwardly. And yet, the way Sinch'ŏl was sitting face to face with him like this, Tŏkho certainly didn't get that impression. Or maybe Sinch'ŏl simply looked down on Okchŏm, and this had kept him silent for so long. The only other possibility was that the two already had a physical relationship and the boy was now tired of her. In any

144

case, it was the one or the other, Tŏkho was sure of it. He was more worried than ever now, and was determined this time to see the issue of their marriage officially settled.

"While you're in Seoul, you should make some time to enjoy yourself before you head home again," said Sinch'ŏl looking up at Tŏkho.

"Well, I tell you, I'd like nothing more than to spend a few days talking with your father . . . but the way things are right now . . . well, there's a matter of business to take care of in the township, and without me there, things are pretty hopeless."

Sinch'ŏl thought of what Inho had said to him on his way over here. "You're hopeless, Mr. Virtuosity!" Sinch'ŏl rose to his feet. "I look forward to seeing you again soon."

64

Having eaten a bowl of *kake udon* in the cafeteria, Sinch'ŏl made his way back to the library. Looking around him, he realized that there were fewer students there than before he'd left for dinner. Maybe I should just get the hell out of here, he thought, fishing his watch out of his pocket. It was ten past six . . . Instead of leaving, he pulled out his chair and sat down, only to realize once again how sore his backside was. He'd been sitting here all day long without even getting up to attend lectures. He stood up again and then sat back down, correcting his posture. Then he took out the book he'd put away in his bag and flipped it open.

As he looked through the pages, his head started pounding with everything that had belabored his mind throughout the day. When he'd left for school that morning, his father had said to him, 'Be sure to come home early today,' and now Sinch'ŏl could almost feel those words stabbing into his chest. His father wanted to hear his final decision today, there was no doubt about it. He and Tŏkho had had a frank discussion the night before and it seemed to Sinch'ŏl that today would be the day of reckoning. He knew they were going to gang up on him and force him to give them an answer.

What the hell am I going I do? he said under his breath, laying his head down on his arm. His father didn't even have to say it— it was already perfectly clear to Sinch'ŏl that he was moving things along quickly because Okchŏm was the only daughter of a rich man.

Money . . . Money! His father had gone mad, it seemed, and was jump-ing at the chance to ruin his life. All, for the sake of money.

Sinch'ŏl closed his eyes tightly. He saw an image of Okchŏm, fol-lowed by one of Sŏnbi. He couldn't bring himself to say that he loved Sŏnbi. In fact, his heart told him that he shouldn't marry her, though he didn't really understand that feeling. Why couldn't he get Sŏnbi out of his mind? The main reason he liked her was that he found her attrac-tive—and she was such an honest hard worker! That was all there was to it. He thought about her all the time simply because he'd spent nearly two months with her in the same household, even though he'd never once had the chance to sit down and speak with her.

If Sŏnbi had given him the same sort of persistent attention that Okchŏm always did, he might very well have treated Sŏnbi the same way he treated Okchŏm.

He realized something else: While he'd had the chance to meet a good number of women, there wasn't a single one of them he could honestly say he liked. If he was forced to pick one of them, it would have to be Sŏnbi.

From the moment he'd met Okchŏm, he had never really thought of her as anything more than someone to keep him company while on vacation, a girl with whom he could kill some spare time. And Father was now telling him to marry someone like that? A scornful smile crossed his lips. He felt he was losing all the trust he'd once placed in his father. The man made only a meager salary and had lived a hard-pressed life; now with this pool of money within arm's length, he seemed ready to grab it without considering any of the consequences.

When I get home tonight, Father is going to chew me out for being late. Then he's going to bring up the marriage again . . . But what am I supposed to do, when I don't even like her? I wonder if Tŏkho has gone back home yet or if he's still here in Seoul? Sinch'ŏl dreaded the very idea of having to sit face to face with Tŏkho again. Then again, maybe he could sit down with him before he left Seoul and somehow persuade him to send Sŏnbi down in the spring . . . But this, he real-ized, would be impossible to accomplish without first consenting to marry Okchŏm . . . Well, if it doesn't happen, I'll just have to give up on the whole idea . . . He wasn't the type of person who was going to go crazy over a girl, but he did at least want the chance to meet her. He just wanted to hear her voice.

146

Indeed the worst thing about his refusing to marry Okchŏm was that it would put a stop to any future he might have with Sŏnbi. His failure was in not getting them to send Sŏnbi to Seoul before all these issues arose, as he originally had intended. This winter, or perhaps in the coming spring, they might very well end up sending her off to get married somewhere . . . He closed his book and stared out blankly into the electric bulb. The glowing bulb? Or the black mole? . . . Just then he heard somebody mumbling behind him. It was his friend Pyŏngsik, holding a copy of *The Compendium of the Six Laws* against his chest. He had his eyes closed tightly in concentration and was trying to memorize something: Article no. 131 . . . Article no. 131 . . . Article no. 131 . . . Article no. 131, he said over and over. His face showed the signs of the first stage of consumption, and in the glare of the electric lights his forehead seemed to protrude even further than usual. Sinch'ŏl smiled scornfully despite himself. They must all be dreaming of becoming judges or prosecutors, he thought, going on the way they do like that. He couldn't stand being in the library for a minute longer.

65

Once he was outside, Sinch'ŏl felt a few snowflakes fall against his face. He looked up and watched them falling in the glow of the streetlamps. They seemed like mayflies swarming around electric lights on a summer's day. By the time he reached the front gate, he heard the closing bell ring in the library. Already nine o'clock? He quickly turned around. That towering black building, piercing the dark sky, was the very best college in all of Chosŏn! He bolted upright: it seemed as though he was staring at a giant question mark looming dizzily before his eyes, asking him what in the world he had spent almost every single day of the last three years learning inside there.

Hearing the voices of all the students leaving the library, Sinch'ŏl turned and started walking. When he arrived back home, he heard his father clearing his throat in another room and felt an unaccustomed rush of emotion.

"Is that you, Sinch'ŏl?"

His father's voice seemed so strident as he opened the door to his room that the hairs on the back of his neck stood up straight in attention.

"Yes, it is."

"Didn't I tell you to come home early today?"

Sinch'ŏl quietly went inside his room, placed his bag on top of his desk, took the books from inside it, and then inserted each into its place on the bookshelf. His mind was racing, and he wouldn't have been able to calm himself down without carefully putting his things away. He neatly arranged everything on his desk again, and after wiping the surface off with a rag, he leaned up against the wall, all ears; what was Father going to say to him next?

Then he heard someone walking across the floor, and his stepmother slid open his door.

"Come in and have your supper."

"I already ate."

"Where?"

"Somebody . . . a friend invited me out . . ."

After sensing something was wrong with him, his stepmother stepped into the room.

"Now, tell me why you didn't come home early today."

"Why should I have?"

His stepmother came to sit by his side, smiling.

"Your father and Okchŏm's father were waiting for you, you know. I think they wanted to make your marriage to Okchŏm official. Well, how about it? He's rich, isn't he?"

Sinch'ŏl was so distracted that he stared at the woman without hearing a word she was saying.

"Oh, come now, let's settle this tonight . . . You should be happy, dear! You'll never find anyone who's absolutely perfect, you know. And your father really approves of the match . . . Why are you being difficult?"

"What have I said against it?" asked Sinch'ŏl.

"Oh, well, goodness . . . It's all settled then. Let's go over to the inner room. Okchŏm's father might stop by again soon . . ."

"You mean he hasn't left Seoul yet?"

"How is he supposed to go home without settling things? He was planning to take the train tonight, but did you ever show up? He waited all day long for you."

Sinch'ŏl couldn't help but smile.

"Sinch'ŏl!" his father was calling him.

"Don't make your father more impatient," his stepmother added. "Just give him a straight answer, will you?"

148

When Sinch'ŏl entered the room, his father took off his glasses before speaking.

"Now, let's get him something to eat."

He glanced over at his wife, signaling her to set up a dinner table for him.

"He said he already ate . . . A friend of his invited him."

"I see . . ."

As he looked at Sinch'ŏl, who had now cast his eyes downward, his father pondered over something for a while.

"You don't by any chance have an objection to marrying Okchŏm, do you?"

Sinch'ŏl looked up.

"I'm not going to marry her!"

At such an unexpectedly straightforward reply, the look on his father's face instantly soured.

"And why not?"

"I have no particular reason," replied Sinch'ŏl curtly, hanging his head once again.

His father moved up closer to him.

"You have no reason not to marry her? Well, is there some other girl you'd rather marry?"

That instant Sinch'ŏl pictured Sŏnbi standing off in the distance. But the vision began to fade away just as soon as he had it.

"No, there isn't."

"Then, settle it now!" shouted his father. "And stop all this nonsense!"

66

Judging from Sinch'ŏl's previous behavior, his father assumed that while the two didn't see eye to eye on the marriage, Sinch'ŏl was likely to give in, and it was precisely for this reason that he had decided to lay down the law.

It was a great surprise to Sinch'ŏl, however, to hear his father take this stance. He had never thought his father so reckless as to push him into something of such grave importance to his own future without giving due consideration to the opinions of the very person whom it most affected. He had assumed that after his father had applied a little pressure, surely he would back down when he expressed objections.

149

"Okchŏm's father is coming by again shortly, so you are to stop this nonsense and give your willing consent to this marriage . . . You won't come across another prospect like this ever again . . . What you have done is lost yourself in a world of idle dreams, but let me tell you right now that the real world is a far different place. There was a time when I'd lost my head in the clouds as well—until they led me straight into prison . . . And that's why everything has gone so badly for us. Do you know how miserable our lives would be, if I lost my job at a time like this? As long as you graduate this spring and pass the bar, you shouldn't have to worry . . . But even so, without the proper support, it'll be hard for you to climb the ladder of success. Do you understand what I'm saying to you, my boy? All you have to do is agree to this marriage and the future is yours, full of promise. You've got to understand, Sinch'ŏl, that I'm only doing what I think is best for you."

His father had lowered his voice by now and was trying to speak to him from his heart. It wasn't that Sinch'ŏl didn't know from the very beginning how his father would present his argument, but now that he was sitting face to face with him, listening to him speak in such intimate terms, Sinch'ŏl realized that there was precious little hope that his father would reconsider. He had probably concluded that Sinch'ŏl would be his only heir. Of course there was Yŏngch'ŏl, but he was still a child, and always sick, so it was doubtful whether he would survive to see adulthood. Even so, Sinch'ŏl hadn't the slightest intention of simply putting his life into his father's hands by taking the law exam, marrying into money and then carrying on the family name. He didn't like the potential bride. As far as he was concerned, there was absolutely no room for negotiation.

"So what you're telling me, Father, is that I should marry for the money whether I like the bride or not?"

Sinch'ŏl looked his father square in the face. The man was appalled that his son had addressed him in such blunt terms.

"Humph! You don't like her? Then tell me this: why did you stay at Okchŏm's house for almost three months? And why have you been going out with her almost every day since then?"

Sinch'ŏl averted his eyes from his father's fierce scowl.

"An unmarried man staying at a young lady's house? And not for just one or two days, but for two or three months! Tell me who would call that normal? Now, go on, say something for yourself."

Sinch'ŏl was at a loss for an answer and said nothing.

"Or are you just one of these sex addicts? And now that you've had your fun, you're just tired of the girl . . ."

Even Sinch'ŏl was unable to hold himself back after this remark.

"Father! Now you have simply gone too far. As long as two people regard each other as friends, why shouldn't they be able to go out together and enjoy each other's company? Your feudal preconceptions lead you to look at a man and a woman who spend time together and automatically assume that there's something going on between them . . . It makes no sense . . . And as far as last summer is concerned, it was only in respect of your position as Okchŏm's teacher that I accepted their polite invitations to extend my stay, after which things have simply evolved into this mess . . . I never once thought of Okchŏm as someone I could possibly marry."

"Enough! I don't want to hear another word of this. Call me feudal or whatever you want to, but once a man and a woman start going out together in public, there's no turning back. If you call off this marriage at this point, Sinch'ŏl, I will be utterly disgraced. And another thing . . . what are you doing with all those damn books on that desk of yours? Your own father pinches pennies and can't even buy a pack of cigarettes for himself, and here you are, with no thanks to me, buying these useless books and coming home to talk back to me, calling me a bloody feudalist or whatever—and you say I'm the one with preconceived ideas? Where the hell do you get off treating me like that? And to think, you actually have a university education . . ."

Sinch'ŏl's father saw that all the hopes he'd held for his son were now dashed. He felt an uncontrollable rage surge through him, right to the top of his head.

"Why don't you just stick to what you need for your exams . . . ? You fool! Instead of buying all those useless books . . ."

"Those books are my textbooks, I'll have you know, Father . . . And you, I might remind you, are the one who told me to take the bar. I've held my tongue for far too long, but you know what? The truth is that I don't really give a damn about this exam!"

"Oh, so that's the truth, is it! Hah, ha . . . you little bastard! How dare you speak this sort of rubbish to me. Get out of my sight!

He sprang at Sinch'ŏl and slapped him across the face, then grabbed him by the shirt and shoved him out the door.

"You and I have nothing to do with each other. You have no right to be part of this family! Now get out of here! Get out of my sight!"

67

Sinch'ŏl's stepmother grabbed her husband.

"Stop this! How can you do this?"

"I am no father of yours and you are certainly no son of mine!" Sinch'ŏl's father shouted after him.

Sinch'ŏl ran to his room, and stuffed several books and some clothes into his bag. His stepmother came running out of the inner room.

"Are you out of your mind? What in the world has gotten into you, child? Your father gives you a little scolding, and this is how you react?"

She grabbed Sinch'ŏl's overcoat and dropped to the floor. His father then threw open the door to the inner room and pulled his wife back inside.

"Get out of here! Or are you too much of a coward? Now get going! Go!"

Awoken by the sound of the banging door, Yŏngch'ŏl came out of his room, crying. Sinch'ŏl's father had never imagined that Sinch'ŏl would take things to such extreme, and actually leave. When the man saw Sinch'ŏl going out the door, bag in tow, as he'd been ordered, he suddenly felt dizzy, and his body started to tremble like the leaves of a poplar tree.

Sinch'ŏl heard Yŏngch'ŏl crying as he stepped out the front gate. The snow was falling heavier now than it had been earlier. In no time at all his clothes were white with snow. When he reached Paksŏk Heights, he heard someone's footsteps behind him, and he quickly turned around, thinking perhaps they belonged to his stepmother. But it turned out to be some other middle-aged woman he didn't know. Sinch'ŏl felt an unbearable loneliness, and thinking of his own dead mother, he was brought to the verge of tears.

Where should I go? he wondered, as he slowly walked alone. But no matter how long he considered it, he could think of nowhere. Mulling over various possibilities, he finally made his way to the Chongno district. Chongno, however, made him feel even more lonesome. There were people walking here and there, but no one seemed to be roaming the streets, as he was, without anywhere to go. They all hurried along, swinging their arms and legs to the loud sound of the jazz flowing from all the cafés.

When he made it to Pagoda Park, he stopped. "Maybe I should go over to *his* place," he said to himself, recalling how he had met a friend several days earlier right here in Pagoda Park. Passing in front of the Chosŏn Theater, he eventually found himself at the Anguk-dong intersection. And then, with a rush of feeling, he felt himself arriving at a rather grim conclusion. He'd never again step foot into his own house . . . He'd been hoping that his stepmother might be following somewhere behind him, but now that he'd made it as far as Anguk-dong, he had to abandon that hope altogether.

Even if his stepmother had followed after him and tried to bring him home, Sinch'ŏl probably wouldn't have gone back with her; he'd already made up his mind to leave. Still, he'd kept thinking that maybe, just maybe, she was somewhere behind him.

He was passing by the front of Posŏng College when someone stretched out a hand at him and called out his name.

"Hey, look who's here."

Startled, Sinch'ŏl took a good look at the man and realized that it was the very person he'd just set out to look for.

"My friend! I was just on my way to see you."

"See me?"

The man stared at Sinch'ŏl dubiously. His complexion was pale and his eyelids were particularly thin. He had a slender figure and was quite short. But with a solid chest and hair tossed back like the prickly spikes of a chestnut burr, anyone could see he was no one to mess around with. He sometimes seemed friendly and sometimes cold. He took a moment to give Sinch'ŏl the once-over.

"What's that for? You're carrying a suitcase around in the middle of the night?"

Sinch'ŏl hesitated before answering, "Pamsongi! I've left home for good!"

"Left for good?"

Pamsongi imagined he hadn't quite caught what Sinch'ŏl was saying, and he looked searchingly at him.

"What? So I'm not allowed to leave home?" Sinch'ŏl replied, after a while.

"No, it's just that . . . I'm not sure what you mean . . . You mean, you're never going back?"

"No, I'm not . . ."

Sinch'ŏl smiled sadly. His friend stared back at him, wide-eyed.

"So, were you headed somewhere?" asked Sinch'ŏl a moment later.

"Me? I was just on my way to bum some food off somebody," he laughed, brushing the snow from his shoulders.

"Well then, come along with me."

68

After they each ate a bowl of *udon*, they bought some bread and went back to Pamsongi's house.

"Hey, I've got bread. And a guest," called out his friend, smiling, as he opened the door. Sitting there face to face, with an electric bulb of no more than six watts between them, the two men had taken their shirts off and were in the middle of hunting for lice. They threw their shirts back on and looked up wide-eyed at Sinch'ŏl. Then they picked up the bread Pamsongi tossed to them, broke off a few pieces, and started eating.

Sinch'ŏl caught a whiff of something rancid as he entered the room and took a seat on the floor. Do they ever turn the heat on in this place? he wondered, as he sat on what felt like a solid block of ice.

His friend introduced him.

"Our new friend's name is Yu Sinch'ŏl."

The two men chewing on their bread greeted him with quick smiles. There seemed to be something akin to disdain in the expressions on their faces.

"Well, it's just been the three of us here, cooking for ourselves, but now I guess we have you to share our suffering," Pamsongi chuckled.

His wild hair shook as he laughed. He looked at the two men hunched over in the cold, dressed in nothing but filthy underwear.

"Today we're not going hungry, my boys. The unexpected has happened! Our new friend has come in search of me." He laughed again.

"We've still got tomorrow's breakfast to worry about," said one of the men, with a round face. He was called Kiho. The other was Ilp'o.

"Tomorrow is tomorrow. Why worry about it now? They say a man can always get by when he has to."

154

Pamsongi turned to look at Sinch'ŏl, who was almost in a daze as he looked back at all three of them: What had he gotten himself into, to agree to spend the night in a cave like this? There wasn't a single mattress in the room, and it horrified him to think he'd have to sleep in a place that literally chilled him to the bone. He had a gut feeling that his bag and his coat, in fact everything but his own flesh and blood, was going to be pawned the next morning. He could feel his head spinning. And then it suddenly dawned on him that reality was far more terrifying than anything he'd imagined at home . . . or rather, imagined from the comfort of his own desk! The more he envisioned this reality drawing in upon him, the darker and darker his surroundings seemed.

Sinch'ŏl got through the night but without a wink of sleep. The next morning he dumped out all the money in his wallet and handed it over to Pamsongi, who went out to buy rice and firewood. While one of them picked clean the rice, another started the fire. This sped things along, and the rice was cooked before long.

"We've got a proper meal today, my boys!"

There was gray ash all over Pamsongi's face and hair. Sinch'ŏl smiled at his friend. He saw how his new friends were perfectly content with their lives. Hell, I can put up with this! he suddenly thought, determined to stick it out as well.

After eating their meal, each of them tried to get someone else to do the dishes, and in the end they each picked up their own bowl and piled it in a corner of the kitchen.

"Hey, I guess she's not going out today."

Ilp'o winked at them and then looked over at the front door.

"Doesn't she work the night shift now?" chimed in Kiho. "I don't think she gets out till 1:00 today . . . Why don't we go over and introduce ourselves later?"

Sinch'ŏl's friend looked over to him and said in a whisper, "You know what they're talking about? Over there, in the side room, there's this beauty who works in a spinning mill . . . These guys can't stop talking about getting a date with her."

"Oh, yeah? And you don't want a date with her? Truth is your body's burning up for her at *one hundred percent* capacity."

They shared a good laugh over this one.

But the next day, Sinch'ŏl's friend suddenly decided that it wouldn't be a good idea for them all to live together, so after talking things over, he decided he would be the one to move to a different location. He stopped by occasionally, but only if it was necessary that they see each other.

Sinch'ŏl gradually grew accustomed to living away from home. He cooked his own meals and washed his own clothes. And as soon as he finished eating, he'd set himself to lice hunting, or busy himself darning his socks. Since Sinch'ŏl was so meticulous with everything he did, the others gave him the role of managing the household.

Ilp'o and Kiho had already spent time in prison, so all they did now was snicker amongst themselves on the sidelines, rather than take an active role in what was going on. They whiled away their time, day after day, making a laughing stock of other people. And whenever the topic of women came up, they became particularly excited.

"Hey, Sinch'ŏl! I was crossing the bridge out front last night, and all of a sudden, there I was face to face with that beauty . . . It was like . . ."

The beauty he spoke of was the factory girl who lived next door.

69

Okchŏm had stopped pounding away at the keys of her piano, and lost in her thoughts, stared at the moonlight streaming in through the window. She turned around and looked at Sŏnbi.

"Sŏnbi. Didn't Sinch'ŏl say anything to you that night?"

Trimming the ends of the cucumbers she had picked that afternoon, Sŏnbi looked blankly at Okchŏm from the doorway, a cucumber still grasped in her hand. What in the world is she talking about? she wondered. Okchŏm quickly lost her temper.

"Sometimes you seem to have completely lost your mind. What's wrong with you, anyway?"

Okchŏm had hardly given Sŏnbi the time to think about the question before she started cutting into her. "Did Sinch'ŏl say something to me that night?" Sŏnbi repeated under her breath. What could he have said to me? she wondered, unable to piece together what Okchŏm was talking about.

It wasn't just what Okchŏm was saying to her—she'd felt like this for quite some time now. And she had no idea why. Glancing down at this bucket chock-full of cucumbers it seemed to her like her own head was chock-full as well—with all sorts of anxiety and stress and feelings that

156

she found difficult to understand. Maybe she had in fact lost her mind, just like Okchŏm said. In any case, some part of her, something clear, something bright—she wasn't quite sure what—was gone. She cut off the stem of the cucumber with her knife and let out a gentle sigh.

"So you still don't remember anything?"

"No, I don't," replied Sŏnbi, lifting her head after some time.

"How can anyone be so stupid! I'm talking about the guest we had who came up from Seoul last summer..."

"Well, what about him?"

"Lord, how in the world did you turn into such an idiot? Just forget it and go back to making your damn pickles! Talking to you is like teaching scriptures to a cow!"

Okchŏm spun back around in her chair. She started playing the piano again and singing a sad song to accompany the music. Lost in her thoughts, Sŏnbi stared at Okchŏm and listened to her sing. It seemed like Okchŏm's song was ridiculing her, sneering at everything about her. Glowing there in the moonlight, which streamed through the window like a rainbow, Okchŏm's beautiful fingers seemed to be jumping lightly over the keys as though they were little white fish.

"Hey, Sŏnbi! Turn on a lamp in that room," shouted Okchŏm's mother, coming in from outside. Sŏnbi jumped to her feet in surprise. At the sound of the woman's voice, Sŏnbi's heart always began to race in fear of what words might come next. Would it be just another scolding? Or would it be something far worse, like, You dirty bitch! Get the hell out of my house! It was impossible for Sŏnbi to set her mind at ease.

"No, leave it alone . . . I like it like this, Mother. The moonlight is enough to see by . . . And besides, what do I need a light on for anyway? I just feel like I want to die . . ."

Okchŏm looked at her mother, who was peering into the room. Her mother was alarmed by what Okchŏm had said about wanting to die.

"Just what are you saying? How can anyone with the education you have say anything so foolish? I don't ever want to hear you say that again!"

Okchŏm's mother had plenty more to say to her daughter, but she left it with this, for her throat was tightening with sorrow.

"And what are you still trimming those cucumbers for? Take them out of here, light the lamp in the inner room and spread out the bedding. And then do the same thing in here! For crying out loud! You get slower by the day. I don't know why we didn't just keep Granny here . . ."

When Okchŏm had come back home after graduating that spring, Sŏnbi had again been kicked out of Okchŏm's room and into Granny's. That was why Tŏkho made Granny leave.

"Oh, Mom! I . . . well . . . I saw Granny over in Onjŏng . . . And she was crying and everything. I feel so bad for her . . ."

"I know, dear, but that stubborn father of yours was determined to get rid of her. I felt sorry for her too . . . And I tried my best to keep her here."

Okchŏm's mother glanced at Sŏnbi, who had just picked up her bucket of cucumbers and was heading into the kitchen. The flames of jealousy deep inside her had been kindled some time ago, but she felt them now as a hot tingling in her breast.

"That was all her fault, too, damn it," thought Okchŏm's mother.

What other possible reason could he have had for getting rid of Granny just as Sŏnbi was moving into Granny's room? There's just something fishy about the way he handled that, thought Okchŏm's mother. She did her best not to reveal these thoughts to her daughter.

Okchŏm, meanwhile, had draped herself over the keyboard.

"It's all so strange . . ." she said, her arms pulled tightly against her breasts. Okchŏm's mother approached her excitedly.

"So you think it's strange, too?"

70

Okchŏm stared at her mother in surprise.

"What could that old fox be up to? Something suspicious alright," said her mother.

"Oh, good heavens, Mother, is that what you're talking about? What could you possibly be suspicious of?" Okchŏm laughed.

Okchŏm's mother felt an incredible anger surge up inside her.

"And just what do you think is so funny!"

"What's the matter, Mother? Why are you so angry?"

The woman was so embarrassed that she had to turn away from her daughter.

She could hear the sound of Sŏnbi striking matches in the inner room, which then lit up brilliantly. She went inside and glared at Sŏnbi, who was spreading out the bedding.

"Now, spread that evenly!" she shouted.

Sŏnbi's heart was already racing uncontrollably. Her hands now started to tremble, and she was unable to look up at Okchŏm's mother. After spreading out the bedding, she came straight into the breezeway, where Okchŏm was still sitting at the piano, her head slumped over the keys. Sŏnbi couldn't tell if she was thinking about something or sleeping. The only thing she remembered was that Okchŏm had just told her she did not want the lamp lit in this room, so she sat down beside the doorway to see if she could figure out what Okchŏm wanted next. Want me to turn on a lamp? is what Sŏnbi wanted to ask her, but she was too afraid that Okchŏm would make fun of her again and say something she couldn't understand, so she just sat there, staring blankly into the darkness.

"Maybe I should just go to Seoul tomorrow?"

With this, Okchŏm suddenly stood up from the bench, and as she backed away from the piano bench, she said, "Oh, turn on the damn light! What are you doing just sitting there? You idiot! Look, something just spilled all over the place!"

Okchŏm had knocked over her bowl of water. Sŏnbi quickly ran over and lit the lamp.

"If you had bothered to turn on the lamp instead of just sitting there like that, this never would have happened. Damn it, Sŏnbi, I've just about had it with you! Get this cleaned up, fast!"

Okchŏm quickly crossed to the inner room. Mother and daughter were now talking about something or other.

After wiping up the room with a rag, Sŏnbi picked up the empty brass bowl and brought it into Granny's room. As she was walking into the room she realized, Oh no, I meant to bring this bowl into the kitchen . . . But as she made an about-face and stepped out the door, she reconsidered. Oh, I'll just bring it back tomorrow, she thought, dropping down onto the floor.

Without even turning on her light, Sŏnbi sat in her room, completely motionless. They had given her such a hard time all day long, and she was now so beside herself that she hardly had the energy to think. As she stared vacantly at the moonlight streaming in through the window, she gradually felt a stronger desire to follow that moonlight and leave this house forever. "What do I do?" she sighed.

She had stared out the window night after night and had made up her mind to run away on several occasions. When she was on the point of picking up her things to leave, however, it always came down to one thing: there was no place to go.

Sŏnbi found herself stroking the empty brass bowl. Maybe I should just find the courage to finally make a break for it? I'll even take this brass bowl with me . . . she thought. Then that scowl on Okchŏm's mother's face flashed before her eyes. She shuddered and pushed the bowl away. Yet for some reason, she'd feel sorry to leave this bowl behind. It was in fact the only thing about this house that she'd miss. Sŏnbi saw before her eyes the whole array of dishes that filled the cupboard: brass bowls and porcelain bowls, soup bowls, platters and plates of all types. All the dishes she handled day after day with such care: dishes with flower patterns and animals carved in relief, dishes round and square, big and small! They were the only things in this household for which Sŏnbi had any affection.

She pulled the brass bowl over to her once again and held it closely against her chest. She looked out the window lost in thought. And right then and there, she decided to leave her room. She slowly rose to her feet and picked up her bundle of things. Then she stopped once again. . . . But where do I go? And what if I run into someone out there even scarier than Tŏkho? With these fears, Sŏnbi gently set down her bundle and gave up on the idea for the time being. But no matter how much she thought about it, she knew deep down inside that she wouldn't be able to stay in this house for very much longer.

I've got to find someplace to hide before Tŏkho comes in again, thought Sŏnbi, and with this in mind she went outside to investigate whether Tŏkho was in the men's quarters. There was no lamp turned on inside the building, and all that lit the doorframe was a ray of moonlight.

Sŏnbi let out a gentle sigh and went back into her room.

71

In her room, Sŏnbi picked up her bundle of things several times, only to be seized by the fear that Tŏkho might be standing at the front gate, or held back by the thought that she might run into him on her way outside. So each time, she laid the bundle back down on the floor.

160

After wavering like this for some time, she decided to go outside just to test what it would be like to walk through the village at night. Coming through the middle gate, she saw a light glowing in Yu Sŏbang's room. She stopped short, but then made a mad dash through the front gate as though someone were actually chasing her.

Once outside the front gate, she took a quick look in each direction. Not a soul in sight. But she was still afraid that someone might see her, so she kept close to the reed fence and crept forward little by little. She didn't see anyone who might grab onto her and shout: Hey, girl! Just where do you think you're going? But all the same, to head out of the house like this was in itself terrifying. She tried her best to escape anyone's notice.

After walking some distance, she stopped in her tracks. Ahead of her was the newly paved road that led into town, gleaming in the light of the moon. Whenever she had looked at this road, it had always struck her that it wouldn't be much longer before she herself would have to make her way down it, terribly sad and all alone. And whenever she actually stepped onto the road, determined to leave, it was those dark pine groves in the distance and the way the road disappeared into them that she feared: they seemed to be hiding some man far more frightening than Tŏkho, a man who was waiting for her with glaring eyes. She felt goose bumps all over her body and turned around to look in the other direction. There, in full view, was Yongyŏn village! And, with its cluster of buildings set behind a tin-roofed storehouse, there was Tŏkho's private estate, practically calling out for attention! The idea of going back inside that house made Sŏnbi feel like something was scraping against her heart—she didn't even have the words to describe the pain. She turned around again, facing the road that led through the forest, and took several steps forward . . . Oh, what do I do? What do I do? she asked herself, staring up at the moon, which had slipped into the far corner of the sky.

She then thought about Kannan. Before Sŏnbi had been raped by Tŏkho, she had always thought of Kannan as a common whore. But once he'd come after her, too, she began to see Kannan in her dreams, and for some reason they would be hugging each other and crying in each other's arms. Whenever she found herself hesitating like this over whether or not to run away, thoughts of Kannan always came to mind. What did they say she was doing now? Making good money somewhere . . . If only

161

I knew how to write a letter, I'd send her one now, thought Sŏnbi, her footsteps taking her in the direction of Kannan's old house before she even knew where she was heading. Many a time had she come this far on a moonlit night, hoping to learn news of Kannan. Yet she'd never been able to bring herself to enter the family's house. After pacing back and forth in front of their reed fence, she'd think: I'll find out some day, and besides, what if Kannan's mother gets suspicious of me? It was always this sense of anxiety that turned her back around again. Whenever this happened, she could barely restrain herself from crying out "Oh, Kannan," her throat tight with emotion, as she thought about how she had played with Kannan as a child. Why hadn't she been able to understand Kannan's feeling when she'd still lived in the village? Why had she been so unwilling to give Kannan even a single word of comfort?

Lost in these thoughts, she stood in front of Kannan's house. She set her mind on going straight inside to find out whatever news she could about Kannan.

First she attempted to see if anyone else from the village might be visiting. She then listened carefully to hear if Kannan's father was home. Everything inside seemed absolutely still. All she could see was the dim light of an oil lamp shining through the doorframe, and all she could hear was the faint sound of someone coughing. Were they already asleep? Maybe she'd just have to come back tomorrow, she thought, turning away. But then she reconsidered: Oh, hell, I'll just go inside, she told herself, forcing her reluctant feet to shift direction.

At the sound of her footsteps, someone called from inside.

"Who's there?"

It was Kannan's mother. Sŏnbi froze, unsure what to do, and it wasn't until the door actually opened that she finally felt compelled to step forward.

"It's me ..."

Kannan's mother came outside to take a better look at Sŏnbi.

"Oh, I had no idea who ... Well, what are you doing here?"

Kannan's mother clasped Sŏnbi's hands into her own and led her inside. Why in the world has this child come here? she wondered. Maybe that no-good Tŏkho heard Kannan was making good money in Seoul and sent Sŏnbi to find out where she is? Then something else hit her—maybe what happened to my Kannan has happened to this poor child, too ... She stared into Sŏnbi's face searching for a clue.

162

72

"How long has it been since I last saw you? That must have been back when your mother passed away . . . But you sure are mighty pretty now."

With these words, Kannan's mother hoped to cheer up the downcast girl she saw sitting before her. She waited for something, anything, to come from Sŏnbi's lips.

Sŏnbi, for her part, hadn't the peace of mind to utter a single word. She'd managed to enter the house all right, but she was terrified that Tŏkho or Okchŏm's mother might have followed her, and might be standing this very moment on the other side of the door. As soon as she stepped out of the house, they would probably chase after her, shouting, "Why did you come here, you little bitch!" All Sŏnbi could do was sit nervously, glancing at the door. Kannan's mother could tell that there was something upsetting Sŏnbi. She recalled how before her own daughter had run off to Seoul, she had stayed up all night long, roaming around outside, before finally coming in to tell her, "Mom, it looks like Tŏkho has his eyes on Sŏnbi! And wants to get rid of me for good . . ."

Kannan had said this with a deep sigh. They were words her mother could still hear ringing in her ears. The more time passed with Sŏnbi sitting there silently, the deeper the woman's suspicion grew that this girl was being kicked out of Tŏkho's house just like Kannan. On the one hand she thought: Why, you little bitch, it serves you right for causing my Kannan so much pain! But on the other, when she saw how forlorn Sŏnbi looked, she almost felt as though her own Kannan was sitting right in front of her, as though she was staring right now into the eyes of her own child.

After some time, Sŏnbi broke the silence.

"Mother, where is Kannan now?"

"Why? Why does he need to know that?"

Jumping to the assumption that Tŏkho had sent her to ask about her daughter, Kannan's mother fired back this retort. Sŏnbi, for her part, didn't have the courage to rephrase her question. She sat there silently, twisting the bow of her blouse around her finger.

"What does he want by knowing where Kannan went? Ruining my girl's life wasn't good enough for him, huh? What else could he wring out of her?"

Kannan's mother went on like this without really knowing what she was saying. And all the while Sŏnbi's cheeks were burning with shame, no different than if she'd been slapped right across the face. Oh, I knew I shouldn't have come, she thought with regret. But at the same time, it became more apparent than ever to Sŏnbi that her own life had also been ruined by Tŏkho, and she felt an uncontrollable rush of anger pulsing through her body. At least Kannan had parents who looked out for her whereas she had no family whatsoever to stand up to people in her defense.

"Oh, Mother!" she cried.

Kannan's mother lifted her head. She stared at Sŏnbi piercingly: What in the world would this girl say next?

Sŏnbi had called out to Kannan's mother in a state of utter confusion, but now she had nothing to say. This woman in front of her wasn't the same mother she had just called, but then again, somehow it still felt like she was.

After a minute or two staring blankly into the darkness, Sŏnbi shifted her gaze to the flame of the lamp, flickering in the draft from the crack in the door. Tears streamed down her cheeks. And though they hadn't exchanged a single word about it, Kannan's mother knew then that Sŏnbi had met the same fate as her daughter Kannan. Oh, the poor thing! How could he be so cruel! she thought, conjuring up an image of Tŏkho in her mind. I hope I live to see the day that bastard is struck by lightning . . . How can God be so indifferent!

"Oh, Sŏnbi!" she cried. "Why do you look so sad?"

Her voice was cracking, and she hid her face to dab away her tears with the hem of her skirt. Seeing Kannan's mother crying like this, it was almost impossible for Sŏnbi to hold back the wave of tears that was engulfing her. But she bit her lip, and between her sobs, managed a few words.

"Mother, wh . . . wh . . . where did Kannan go?"

"Do you want to go there too, dear?"

"Uh-huh . . . "

Kannan's mother rose to her feet. She opened up a little drawer, pulled out an envelope, and sat back down in front of Sŏnbi.

"Now, where in Seoul is she again? I hear the name all the time, but I can't for the life of me remember. Here, look at this. Her address is supposed to be written down here . . . That bastard! How are we ever going to get revenge on him? If your mother was still alive, what would the dear thing have done? Oh, Sŏnbi, it just breaks my heart to think how . . ." Kannan's mother beat her hand against her chest.

With the envelope clenched in her hand, Sŏnbi realized that Kannan's mother had guessed what had happened between her and Tŏkho. Her whole body began shaking uncontrollably with hatred toward him, but also with deep shame. She looked carefully at the envelope in her trembling hand, but the light was far too dim for her to see it clearly. Still, there was no way that she could have made out those Chinese characters, having barely even learned the Korean alphabet.* She rose to her feet, the envelope clenched tightly in her hand.

73

Watching Sŏnbi stand to go, Kannan's mother said, "Now that you've seen the envelope, give it back to me."

Only after hesitating for a moment did Sŏnbi reply, "Please let me have it, Mother."

"I can't do that! Just think what would happen if Tŏkho ever got his hands on it?"

"You don't really think I'd let that happen . . . do you?"

"Well, then, you keep it hidden well, and be sure to bring it back to me. Just please promise me you won't let that bastard even lay his eyes on it."

Following Sŏnbi outside, Kannan's mother repeated her plea several times. Sŏnbi stuck the envelope into her bosom, but at the thought of Tŏkho's hands fondling her breasts, she pulled it out again. She didn't have a single place she could hide the envelope. When she thought about how that ugly old man had deprived her of even these secret places, she felt like dying.

After saying goodbye to Kannan's mother, Sŏnbi again crept her way along the shadows of the reed fences until she made it back to Tŏkho's house. What do I do with this envelope? she wondered. She eventually stuck it into her sock, then quietly opened the main gate. Now even Yu Sŏbang's door was pitch-black. The shadow of the eaves stood out

*The Korean language was often written during the colonial period with a combination of Korean letters and Chinese characters.

clearly on the ground. There was no sign of change in the men's quarters either. Then, with a leap of her heart, something struck her: Maybe Tŏkho snuck into my room while I was gone. As she approached the middle gate, she hesitated, but the place was dead quiet so she softly closed the gate, went through the inner quarters, and opened the door to her room. And what darkness greeted her from inside! She hesitated for an instant, thinking that maybe Tŏkho had gotten drunk and was lying right in front of her. Suddenly she felt an intense desire to turn around and run far away, run anywhere. But she reminded herself of the secret she had hidden away inside the folds of her sock.

Once she'd ascertained no one else was inside, Sŏnbi entered her room. She was determined not to open the door for him tonight, and pulled it firmly closed, then locked it. She collapsed on the floor without even spreading out the bedding. So many thoughts flashed through her mind once she lay down that it seemed like she was watching a slide show. She couldn't help thinking that Tŏkho was right outside her door, just about to pull it open.

Shortly afterwards, the door rattled. Oh no, he's here again . . . she thought, and closed her eyes tightly. Her heart kept racing frightfully. The door rattled again even louder. Tŏkho clearly knew from experience that Sŏnbi wouldn't be sleeping. And while it was true that she'd only make Tŏkho angry by not opening the door for him, she decided to ignore him. What more could he do to her, she thought, besides chase her out of the house? The door began rattling again with more and more persistence. Then Sŏnbi heard the sound of the door paper ripping, and then the latch of the door clinking open. Sŏnbi stayed on the floor, pretending to be asleep. Tŏkho seemed to be out of breath. He came up to Sŏnbi and gave her a shove in the backside with his foot.

"Damn it, girl, why didn't you open the door? You little bitch. Just because I like you . . . don't you go thinking you can get stubborn with me! You better watch it!"

Only then did Sŏnbi slowly sit up, pretending that she'd just awoken.

"You didn't hear me trying to open the door?"

"I didn't hear anything."

"You little vixen."

Pulled into Tŏkho's arms, Sŏnbi caught a whiff of that distinctive smell Tŏkho always gave off. After being held close to him for a long time, she would stop noticing it, but whenever he first grabbed her like this, she was always conscious of his strong odor. She turned her face away from him. Then she tried to squirm out of his embrace and sit up straight again. But Tŏkho only pulled her closer.

"Getting tired of me, huh? Well, maybe I'll just have to get me another girl. How about that? Come on, do what you're told."

Tŏkho was breathing heavily as he put his mouth to her ear and whispered to Sŏnbi. The words tickled her ear, and she tried to pull away from him again.

"I bet you've got another man on the side, don't you? What else could it be? A girl like you is supposed to stay up at night so she can let her man inside. You've got to greet me proper, put on some of that charm of yours to put me in the right mood, damn it . . . You can't just fall asleep like that whenever the hell you feel like it, you sneaky little bitch! I treat you too well, that's it. No wonder you've lost all your goddamn manners . . . Now tell me, did you get your period this month?"

All Sŏnbi could think about right then was that Okchŏm's mother might be standing right outside her door, and her tiny heart was beating a mile a minute. She hardly caught a single word of what Tŏkho was saying, which is what always happened whenever Tŏkho came into her room.

74

"Answer me, girl."

Tŏkho was stroking Sŏnbi's stomach. She didn't want to answer, but neither did she want him to keep on talking like this.

"No, I haven't had it yet . . ."

"Well, I guess I got lucky this time. You be sure to tell me if you're craving something, you hear? None of this shy business of yours . . . Do you feel like eating anything?"

As Tŏkho said this to Sŏnbi, he put his lips up to her face and slowly started to lick her all over. Sŏnbi felt sick to her stomach, but she managed to control it and sat up straight again.

"How about a rack of ribs?"

"Oh, please stop saying that."

"Hey, that's no way to talk. You've got my boy inside here to think of now."

Tŏkho took Sŏnbi into his arms again and sent a shudder down her spine by licking around her ears. Then he took some money out of his wallet and handed it over to her.

"You take this and buy whatever you want with it. And if you feel a craving for anything, you tell me. Got it?"

Sŏnbi clenched the money in her hand and thought of the envelope stuck inside her sock. She didn't know how much money it was, but she made up her mind that she'd use it to find Kannan.

"Okay, now please go back. Mother might come out."

"Oh, who cares if she does? You're number one in my book now. Now that you've got my boy inside you here, don't you worry about that bitch any more. In a couple of months she'll figure things out for herself and we'll just kick her the hell out of here . . . Then I'll make you my legal wife. How about that?"

"Please, please lower your voice. Somebody will hear you."

"Makes no difference. I'm telling you, you come first in this house from now on. Oh, yes, now listen up! When you get pregnant, I hear you start craving things that taste sour. You have any cravings like that?"

Sŏnbi felt even more disgusted by Tŏkho now that he was getting worked up by the thought of his baby. But she began to wonder if indeed, as Tŏkho assumed, missing her period really meant that she could be pregnant. Tŏkho had, after all, already dirtied her body, why shouldn't she just bear him a son and take over the reins of power in this family? This thought, Sŏnbi realized, was taking root deeper and deeper in some corner of her mind whenever she sat like this face to face with Tŏkho. And now she felt so sick to her stomach that she started to heave.

Taken by surprise, Tŏkho cupped his hands below her mouth. Sŏnbi already had a splitting headache, and now as she caught yet another whiff of Tŏkho's odor from the hands thrust out in front of her face, she turned her head away from him.

"Hell, you must be pregnant! Since when have you been so sick to your stomach?"

Sŏnbi pushed away from him.

"Oh, please, go back inside. My whole body aches . . . Just for tonight, please."

"Your whole body? Well, there's no doubt about it then. You've got to be pregnant! You've lost your appetite, right? How would you like me to buy you some fruit?"

168

"No, no. Now, please, just go back now. Please."

All Sŏnbi could think about was that Okchŏm's mother could be right outside her room, listening to everything the two of them were saying.

"All right, I'll go. But you better take care of that boy of mine. I'll get you some beef ribs tomorrow, and you be sure to eat a lot of them! Got it? You pretty little thing, you. You have my boy inside you, don't you!"

Tŏkho gave Sŏnbi another tight hug, and then went back outside. Sŏnbi sighed and tried her hardest to figure out how much money she was holding in her hand. Only then did she hear the main gate squeaking open and the plodding sound of Tŏkho stepping through the middle gate. On nights when Tŏkho visited Sŏnbi's room, he always tiptoed away from her room back to the main gate. Then he made a point of clearing his throat as he closed the middle gate with a clatter. But now Sŏnbi clearly heard the sound of footsteps on a wooden floor as they made their way into the inner room, where Okchŏm's mother slept. As she let out yet another sigh, Sŏnbi felt something close to jealousy. She listened as the door to the inner room opened and closed again, and only then did she remember the bill in her hand. She was dying to know how much it was worth, and felt around the base of the lamp for a match, which she finally managed to light. She couldn't quite tell what the bill was in the light of the single match, but it looked like one of those ten-wŏn bills she'd always seen in Okchŏm's wallet. As she watched the glowing tip of the match gradually fade, she began thinking: If I add this to what mom gave when she died, that'll be ten wŏn plus five wŏn. How much is that altogether? A hundred nyang plus fifty nyang makes . . . wouldn't that be a hundred and fifty nyang? And nowadays they call that fifteen wŏn, right? This was the first time in her life that Sŏnbi had even said the words fifteen wŏn. Maybe I can make it to Seoul with this? she thought, clenching the bill even more tightly in her hand. But then, whether conscious of it or not, Sŏnbi bent her ear in the direction of the inner room. An unpleasant thought had crossed her mind, and she was feeling an emotion she didn't quite understand.

75

It was evening, now well into summer. The sky had been overcast all day long, and Sŏnbi glanced up at it as she made her way out to the kitchen. It seemed certain that Okchŏm's mother had found out about what was going on, for she and Tŏkho had fought throughout the night. The woman hadn't eaten any breakfast, and for lunch someone had sent an errand boy from the township office with some noodles. She lay in bed like an invalid, her head wrapped in a towel. Sŏnbi hadn't slept a wink all night either, and all she'd been able to do today was sit quietly in the kitchen, worrying about what might happen next and staring out the door at a sky as dark and overcast as her own state of mind. She washed out some rice and put it into the pot, ready to be boiled, but then she didn't know what else to do with herself. She paced back and forth for a while and then went into the pantry to scoop up rice—until it dawned on her that she'd prepared some already. What's gotten into me, she wondered, leaning up against the cupboard and trying to calm herself down.

But her efforts were in vain. Okchŏm's mother had found out! She must know, Sŏnbi thought. But then again, she couldn't have found out! I wouldn't still be here if she actually knew about it. She would have kicked me out of the house last night . . . Sŏnbi then heard something crack, and she looked down in alarm. The gourd scoop filled with rice, which she'd been holding in her hand, had fallen against the kitchen slop pot placed just below it. Now both the scoop and the pot had cracked. The rice had spilled out of the gourd into the water, and now everything was gushing out of the broken pot. Sŏnbi frantically tried to gather the rice from the floor. She could hear the sound of angry footsteps approaching.

"That little bitch, what the hell has she screwed up this time!"

Her hair a tangled mess, Okchŏm's mother bolted through the breezeway and down into the kitchen. She then grabbed hold of Sŏnbi by the back of her hair.

"Oh, you bitch! If you don't like it here then just get the hell out—don't you dare start breaking our dishes! I'll rip you to pieces, you bitch . . . Now get out!"

It was as though Okchŏm's mother had been holding back until just this very moment. She started ripping out clumps of hair from Sŏnbi's scalp. Sŏnbi had no intention of fighting back, and it was with nothing but sheer horror written on her face that she allowed the woman to slap her around at will. Okchŏm entered the kitchen, her eyes wide in alarm.

170

"What's going on here . . . ? Oh, my . . . just look at her . . . Ah, hah, ha."

Okchŏm let out a peal of laughter and pointed to Sŏnbi's clothes, which had been thoroughly drenched by the spilled water and then soiled by the dirt floor. Having spent day after day in the same boring routine—eating, sleeping, and playing the piano—Okchŏm now watched this fight play out before her eyes with the excitement of someone desperate for anything new to happen. But it was also with a certain relish that she greeted this new development. Okchŏm had long suspected that Sinch'ŏl was more fond of Sŏnbi than he was of her, and her jealousy had led her to hate Sŏnbi. Now she felt the impulse to give Sŏnbi a good slap across the face. Okchŏm's mother, however, was still whacking Sŏnbi around the kitchen floor, pushing her face down to the floor and then pulling it up again, while Sŏnbi put up no more resistance than a lamb. At first, Sŏnbi's face had stung with each slap the woman delivered, but the longer she continued, the less conscious Sŏnbi was of the attack, and the less pain she felt with each blow. How she only wished she might die after this beating! For how could she bear all the humiliation and the pain? How else would she escape this terrifying family? And yet, now that she'd had a taste of their whip, she felt freed from some of the anguish in her breast.

Okchŏm's mother eventually ran out of steam. She stepped away from Sŏnbi and smoothed her hair back down into place.

"Now, get out of here, you bitch! And to think I raised you like my very own daughter . . . If you'd ever used that head on your shoulders, you might have at least thought about that. But instead you have the gall to . . . Oh, I knew all along what you two were up to, though I held my tongue. You little slut!"

"Oh, Mother. How embarrassing! You don't suppose that Father could have done anything like that, do you? But then again, I bet she's capable of anything. I caught her standing face to face with Sinch'ŏl one night. For all I know she and that idiot Sinch'ŏl have had some sort of affair. Oh, she looks like an innocent fool on the outside all right, but she's really just a double-dealing little . . ."

Not a moment had gone by when Okchŏm had been able to forget Sinch'ŏl, and she had grown to hate him even more because of this. She had allowed herself to play out every possible scenario in her mind, including one with Sŏnbi. Okchŏm jumped forward and slapped Sŏnbi

171

across her face, though it was already red as blood. Sŏnbi was driven back ever further into the corner of the kitchen. Now she really felt like she wanted to die.

Just then Tŏkho came in.

"Hey, what's going on here?"

"Well, I didn't want to say anything at first Father . . . but it looks as though Sinch'ŏl and that girl had some sort of relationship."

"What? With Sinch'ŏl?"

Tŏkho stared at her with wide-eyed suspicion.

76

"Are you sure?"

"I am positive. I distinctly remember seeing that girl and Sinch'ŏl late one night standing face to face with each other, chatting away about something in the moonlight. And just think about it. After we went back to Seoul, didn't Sinch'ŏl keep trying to get us to send her to Seoul? I didn't understand it back then, but it all makes perfect sense now. Something was going on between the two of them, but I just never put all the pieces together."

Okchŏm spun back around to face Sŏnbi.

"You and Sinch'ŏl had some sort of relationship, didn't you? Admit it, you whore, or I'll kill you!" threatened Okchŏm.

Tŏkho also glared at Sŏnbi with terrifying eyes. He'd been convinced that she was pregnant with his child, and had fed her every sort of delicacy imaginable. At the very thought of this, Tŏkho was beside himself with rage. As Sŏnbi looked up at Tŏkho, she felt tears coming to her burning eyes. Of all people, Tŏkho, at least, should have made an effort to understand her pain at being so grossly mistreated. Tŏkho took several steps toward Sŏnbi.

"Is it true you had a relationship with Sinch'ŏl? I went out of my way to take this girl in off the streets, and here I am, the innocent one, being made into the villain with all these false accusations . . . Now, look here, dear, if you don't believe me, just ask this girl for yourself. Do you really think some slut trying to get to Seoul, who's already hooked up with that boy Sinch'ŏl, is going to do what I tell her to do? Think about it. Being a little suspicious is one thing, but have some sense, will you? . . .

172

Now, tell me, did you have something to eat today? Did you eat any of the noodles the delivery boy brought from the office?"

Tŏkho felt awkward standing in front of Sŏnbi, so he took Okchŏm's mother by the hand and led her back into the house.

"Now, get the hell out of here. We don't want you in this house any longer," shouted Okchŏm, following her parents out of the kitchen.

Sŏnbi now knew for certain that she'd have to leave. Listening to all these outright lies—even from Tŏkho, whom she'd actually come to trust—proved to her that he planned to send her packing. Well, so be it! she said under her breath, as she made her way back into her room. The fury inside her now raged with such intensity that her whole body trembled. But not a single tear did she shed any longer. She collapsed on top of her bundle of things and waited for night to come.

And, oh, that night! With her bundle clutched to her side, she made her escape from Tŏkho's household. The night was as black as ink in all four directions. It wasn't raining, as she had feared it might earlier, but the wind was slowly gathering speed. Sŏnbi made her way up to the road that led into town. A gentle breeze blew warmly against her stinging face. Lightning flashed in the eastern sky, illuminating the mountains every so often. The sound of thunder rumbled in the distance with each flash. Once, Sŏnbi would have been terrified by a night like this, but nothing could have frightened her now. She was so firm in her determination, she was ready to take on anything, even death.

The sorghum and foxtail millet growing densely on both sides of the road swirled and swooshed at the whim of the wind. The sound of rustling leaves faded, then surged up again like a wave gathering strength on the ocean. And then, riding on those undulating waves, came the sound of a piano! Clink, clink, clunk! At first it sounded to Sŏnbi as though she were standing right next to the piano, but the next moment, the sounds were as faint as if she were hearing them in a dream. Whatever the case, the notes seemed to pierce into her very core. Fighting off the vision of Okchŏm sat at her piano, Sŏnbi placed her hands over her ears.

But just then she heard the sound of whimpering, and felt something in front of her block her way. Sŏnbi jumped back in alarm. She then realized it was Blackie, the puppy she always used to feed, and she scooped him up into her arms. All the rage that was sweeping through her body transformed into a flood of tears. Blackie's wagging tail thumped against her face and he started whimpering even louder. Then he started licking Sŏnbi's face.

"Oh, Blackie!"

Sŏnbi buried her face into the puppy's neck and dropped down onto the road. And right there, twinkling off in front of her, she saw the lights of the village. To her tear-drenched eyes they looked like pieces of thread from a skein of orange silk. How similar those lights were, she thought, to the lamp she had gazed upon at the moment of her mother's death.

"Oh, Mother!" she cried, turning toward the mountain where her mother had long been buried. What then flashed into her mind, however, was not her mother's face, but that bundle of sumac roots, and then Ch'ŏtchae's big, round eyes. The thought of what she'd done just before her mother's death now struck her with no less force than a bolt of lightning. The money that Tŏkho had given her she had carefully placed inside her bedding, but the sumac roots she'd received from Ch'ŏtchae she had tossed into a back corner...

"Oh, Blackie!" cried Sŏnbi again. "Do you want to come with me?"

A bolt of lightning flashed through the sky.

77

"Hey, hey! Don't you think you've slept long enough? Wake up already, sleepyhead!"

Sinch'ŏl awoke with a start. His friends were already awake and washed up, it seemed, for their foreheads were shining. Kiho stared down at him.

"We don't have a thing to cook for breakfast. Come on, you're going to have to get up and figure something out."

"Oh, leave me alone, will you. I'm just going to sleep for a little bit longer."

"Come on, get up. It's almost high noon out there. If we can't have breakfast, we're still going to have to find something for lunch or dinner... The longer the days get, the longer we've got to worry about going hungry! Hah, ha."

Sinch'ŏl sat upright. The sun shone brilliantly into the room.

"How can anyone live with these damn things biting you all the time... Shit!"

174

Sinch'ŏl tore off his undershirt and began picking off lice the size of grains of barley. Ilp'o sat beside the door with the discarded butt of a cigarette, one of the cigarettes he'd bought back when he had a bit of spare change. He lit the cigarette and took a long drag. The smoke streaming out of his nostrils snaked its way up into the air. By the way Ilp'o kept looking at the side room, Sinch'ŏl guessed that the pretty girl who lived there was at home today.

Ilp'o looked chubby, and had some real flesh on his bones. So whenever they ran out of food to eat or had no wood to light a fire, he never seemed very nervous about it. In the mornings, after waking up, he would always go over and sit by the door, just as he was doing now, all the while glancing at the side room. If he didn't have any cigarettes to smoke, he'd pick his nose or clean out the dirt between his toes, and he'd constantly sniff at his dirty fingers. Sinch'ŏl pretended not to notice any of this, and kept himself from even glancing over in his direction. Kiho, on the other hand, could never hold his tongue when he caught Ilp'o cleaning his toes and sniffing his fingers.

"Oh, Hell! Are you at it again? How can you be so disgusting! Does it really smell all that good?"

Ilp'o always pretended not to hear to what Kiho was saying, and went on picking and sniffing uninterrupted. Wiping his fingers on his socks was yet another of his dirty little habits.

Luckily today he had a cigarette to puff on, so he wasn't picking anything.

"You think you can find something for us today?"

Kiho looked at Ilp'o. Ilp'o, as usual, ignored Kiho and concentrated on his cigarette. Unless he was bad-mouthing someone or had something to say about the pretty girl next door, Ilp'o never got worked up about anything. And when Kiho asked him to fetch rice or wood, or when Kiho was doubled over laughing at him for picking his nose, Ilp'o always pretended not to hear. Now, he just smiled contently and puffed away on his cigarette. Sinch'ŏl finished picking off the lice from his undershirt, and he put it back on. Then he tried to set his mind into gear: what might he still have to bring to the pawn shop?

They had already pawned all his valuables, down to his very last book, so that now practically all that remained was the flesh on his bones. Sinch'ŏl considered going to Pamsongi again to ask for something. Pamsongi had recently found a job delivering newspapers and

175

now had some spare cash on hand, which was why Sinch'ŏl was always bumming five or ten chŏn off him to buy rice or bread.

Sinch'ŏl put on his suit before going outside. It was the one set of decent clothes any of them owned. The three of them had decided they would share it, for whenever one of them went out.

"Make sure you find something to bring back . . . And if it looks like you can't manage it, just do whatever you have to, even if it means going back home. If you're hungry enough, you're just going to have to eat some of that pride of yours. Hah, ha. Am I right?"

"That you are!" chimed in Ilp'o. Sinch'ŏl smiled as he went out the front gate. He pictured Ilp'o's chubby face and those wide eyes of his, constantly ogling the girl in the room next door. He found Ilp'o's arrogance quite detestable, but when he thought of how he picked at his feet and nose and sniffed his dirty fingers, he couldn't help but laugh. Sinch'ŏl had come to think of Ilp'o as the perfect picture of a fallen intellectual. Sinch'ŏl himself could well have been considered a member of the intellectual class, but he had recently developed an intense disgust for these so-called *intelli*. And something about the way Ilp'o kept sniffing at his smelly feet seemed to reek of the intellectual class in general.

With these thoughts on his mind Sinch'ŏl came upon a public swimming pool and a crowd of swimmers. Their red and blue caps, bobbing up and down, stood out against the surface of the water sparkling in the sunlight. Just last summer, Sinch'ŏl remembered, he and Okchŏm had run on the beach of the wide open Western Sea. Then a picture of Yongyŏn village drifted into his mind, followed by an image of Sŏnbi's lovely figure.

78

In no time at all Sinch'ŏl began to feel the warmth of the sun on his back and to hear a grumbling sound coming from his stomach. He slowly started down the hill in Samch'ŏng-dong. If he couldn't get anything out of Pamsongi, where else would he go? He'd already made the rounds so many times to bum money off his friends that it seemed shameless to ask them for anything more. It was still early in the day and he wasn't yet very hungry. But a few more hours of this and the pangs in his stomach would be enough to make him throw himself at the feet of any one of his friends.

He finally arrived at Pamsongi's house in Kwanch'ŏl-dong, but he was told that his friend had just gone out. Clicking his tongue, he turned around and went back outside. When he made it to Chongno, he stood lost in thought. A bus heading toward Tongsomun zoomed right by him, sending a cloud of white dust into the air. He missed his home. More than anything else, he missed the way little Yŏngch'ŏl used to stick out his hand and say, 'Gimme some caramels.' And even more than Yŏngch'ŏl, he missed the *tubu tchigae* always set out for him on the dinner table, made with tofu and meat, simmered in red pepper paste and seasoned with garlic . . . It was this on his mind and nothing else as he slowly dragged his feet forward. By now he wasn't just hungry, he was famished. Where the hell did Pamsongi go? Sinch'ŏl asked himself. He couldn't come up with a single place where his friend might have gone. He'd already delivered the morning paper, and the evening edition wouldn't be out until much later . . . So just where the devil could he have gone?

Sinch'ŏl circled through Chongno and headed toward Hwanggŭmjŏng. There seemed to be no end to the streetcars that whizzed by from this direction and that. Countless numbers of taxis and buses raced by him as well. Sinch'ŏl had inhaled so much dust that his throat was burning, and it took all the strength in him just to walk over the asphalt. Gradually the heat of the midday sun bore down on him harder and harder. Sinch'ŏl was still wearing his winter fedora. He was afraid someone might see him, afraid that maybe his father or stepmother might come out for the day and run into him. He lowered the brim of his hat to shield his face and he walked with his eyes fixed to the ground.

The shoes he'd once polished every day before school had now, for a lack of shoe cream, gone without a polish for who knew how long. They were covered in dust, and the leather at the very tips had peeled away in places. His feet seemed hotter and heavier now than back when his shoes had been properly cared for.

"Hey, man! How many you sell today?"

"Barely broke even today . . . How about you?"

"Yeah, me too."

Sinch'ŏl turned around. The two men were walking side by side, wooden A-frame packs strapped to their backs. Hey, maybe I should become an A-framer too, thought Sinch'ŏl. I could walk around selling anything I wanted. Maybe for now it would just be plain old Chi-

177

nese cabbage, he thought, but then I could switch to anything . . . Yet it hardly seemed plausible that Sinch'ŏl might one day strap an A-frame on his back and pound the pavement like those two men. But why not? Why the hell not? Sinch'ŏl had the vague feeling that his own inability to do anything like lug around an A-frame on his back was hardly different from that stubborn way Ilp'o was perfectly willing to sit there and go hungry.

I wish I could leave my work here to somebody else and get a full-time job somewhere off in the countryside, he thought. That way, it seemed, he could spend time working the land and learning about all sorts of things alongside the farmers. For all the world it seemed impossible for him to get a job like that here in Seoul. Too many people know my face here, and besides, my father and stepmother live here, and so many girls here know who I am, thought Sinch'ŏl. He could see the smirks on their faces now as he stared at the pavement.

He looked around and saw he was at the Mitsukoshi Department Store. Why not go inside? he thought, taking several steps toward it. But he hesitated: What if someone who knows me is shopping there? This always came to Sinch'ŏl's mind whenever he found himself in front of this building. And again, as he always did, he looked down at his shabby clothes.

The only people heading in and out of Mitsukoshi were properly groomed ladies and gentlemen. He hadn't yet seen a single person dressed as he was, in a shabby suit and felt hat. Everyone seemed to be wearing bright summer hats that gleamed in the sunlight. And everyone was dressed in cool summer clothes. But there was nowhere else where he could give his feet a needed rest. He could climb up to Namsan, but it was far too hot to head all the way up there. So for the time being, he thought, why don't I just go inside here for a little rest.

Sinch'ŏl took the elevator to the top floor of Mitsukoshi, sat in a chair and stared blankly into the fountain. The man and woman in the chairs beside him, who had ordered shaved ice with fruit, seemed to be enjoying themselves talking about something when they suddenly started laughing. To Sinch'ŏl it seemed as though they were laughing at his shabby appearance, so he glared in their direction for a while and finally turned his back to them. It took everything inside of him to keep from spinning back around and shouting, Oh, you people, you don't even know the slightest thing about what it means to live a life of honor!

79

Sipping on their shaved ice and giggling, the young couple had so sick-
ened Sinch'ŏl that he'd turned to face the opposite direction, but now
he could feel the couple's gaze aimed straight at his back and the nape
of his neck. The sun, too, shone down on him unbearably. He pulled
a handkerchief from his pocket and wiped his forehead. This was, of
course, the last of the handkerchiefs he still had with him. He had
brought four or five of them when he left home, but each of his friends
had taken one for himself, and this threadbare hanky was the only one
left over. The voice of the woman eating shaved ice next to him slowly
started to sound similar to Okchŏm's. Oh, was Okchŏm married yet?
And did she still think of him? These questions were beating down onto
him just like the fierce rays of the sun—yet he couldn't help but smirk
at the way he was being carried away by his feelings. For a while he was
able to simply laugh them away, but then he started to miss the time
he'd once spent with Okchŏm. In fact, he really did miss her! And what
a happy time that summer had been for him! At this, Sinch'ŏl jumped
out of his chair. Such thoughts were even more old-fashioned, more
disgusting, than Ilp'o's nose picking.

The streetcars sped by from this direction and that, and Sinch'ŏl stood
there, staring down on them as they passed by. His eyes were dazzled by
the rows of buses and taxis endlessly following behind each other. And
yet somehow the longer he stared down at all those streetcars and taxis
and buses from up high like this, the more they seemed to move further
and further away from him—he could somehow feel this in his very
soul. No matter how much he thought about it, he hadn't the faintest
memory of riding in that streetcar bound for the Han River, except for
when he'd ridden it with Okchŏm last summer. There was no mistaking
the fact that he'd of course taken that streetcar many times, but these
memories had become dim, and all that was still clearly engraved in his
mind were the times he had done so with Okchŏm.

Sinch'ŏl felt sick to his stomach. He knew that the girl eating shaved
ice had caused him to entertain these unpleasant—indeed, positively
sickening—thoughts. As he wandered on the rooftop, he pulled from
his pocket the newspaper that Pamsongi had given him last night. He
opened up the paper and turned straight to the political page. As he
scanned the prominent headlines, the pangs of hunger in his stomach

became unbearable, and he felt in the pounding of his head the beginning of a migraine.

Then he noticed from the corner of his eye that the couple who'd been sitting next to him were going inside to the flower exhibition. He collapsed back into one of the chairs. Judging from when the noon siren had gone off, he guessed that it was somewhere around two-thirty or three o'clock. A continuous stream of people were coming and going on the rooftop. But he was so famished that he could hardly focus his eyes on them. His mouth was bone dry and his stomach was growling. He closed his eyes and leaned back in his chair. If his mother had still been alive and he'd run away from home, thought Sinch'ŏl, she would surely have . . . No, she would never have even let him leave in the first place, never mind let him go hungry to the point where he could hardly move! He resented his father. And he needn't even waste the energy to think of his stepmother. He even resented poor little Yŏngch'ŏl, who was hardly old enough to understand what had happened. At the same time, he knew full well that it was cowardly for him to think this way.

If only he had five chŏn, he wouldn't be so hungry . . . Five chŏn! Only five chŏn! He could see the nickel coin before his eyes now. It was slightly smaller than the ten-chŏn coin, and thinner. He was going hungry because he didn't have one of these simple five-chŏn coins! With this thought on his mind, he quickly took a look behind him. If he was lucky, the couple might have left behind a five-chŏn coin after paying for their shaved ice. He peered over to their table, but he couldn't see anything there.

The young couple came out of the exposition hall, having bought a parrot.

"*Konnichi wa.* Hello there," said the girl, staring into the cage.

Both of them laughed. How many five-chŏn coins had they spent on that thing, Sinch'ŏl wondered, counting in his head all the coins they must have handed over to buy it. As he glanced at the two of them, it struck Sinch'ŏl that had he only married Okchŏm, he too would probably be shopping right now, buying things just like that parrot.

I wonder if Pamsongi is back yet, thought Sinch'ŏl, once the two had disappeared. I better go and find out. He could be out delivering the evening edition soon, he thought, quickly standing up to go. But the view was dizzying, and he felt like he was being spun around and around. He grabbed a chair to get his bearings, and for a moment just stood staring ahead. The thought entered his mind that he wouldn't hesitate, for even an instant, if someone came up and offered him five chŏn to jump. Perhaps it was precisely because he thought about it in these terms that he now saw the distance shorten, little by little, between the rooftop up here and the ground down there.

80

Sinch'ŏl took the elevator to the basement floor. As he got out of the elevator, he saw a woman he knew coming straight toward him and panicked. He dodged her by heading toward the restaurant. Pretending to look over the food in the display case, he waited anxiously for the woman to go upstairs, but she seemed to be intent on finding something, and he could see she was still walking around the store. Glistening on the other side of the glass in the display case were neatly arranged samples, curried rice, egg *donburi*, sushi, just waiting there to dry out uneaten. His hunger was so intense that he couldn't bear looking at them any longer—he turned around without thinking.

"Sinch'ŏl? Is that you?"

The woman walked right up to him. Sinch'ŏl removed his hat and clutched it with both hands behind his back. Then he pressed up against the display case so that she wouldn't see his tattered shoes.

"Oh, it's so nice to see you again," he answered.

"Now, tell me, why haven't you come over to visit?"

"Well . . . I . . . I've been ever so busy."

The fact that he was standing in front of a restaurant made him feel all the more humiliated. If only this woman would just get the hell out of here! he thought to himself, but it seemed as though she had no intention of budging.

"Well, I really must be going now," he said, slowly taking a few steps backward. The woman gave him the once-over, as though something about him wasn't quite right.

"Okay, well, good-bye then. And do stop by sometime."

"Yes . . . yes, I will."

Sinch'ŏl made his way through the Mitsukoshi doors as though he had been running for his life. As he let out a deep sigh of relief, he could feel the beads of sweat slowly dripping down his back. He was so itchy that it felt like he was being eaten alive by lice. But he was far too con-

181

scious of the people passing by him to do anything like give himself a good scratch. As he walked, the sweat kept pouring down him.

He made his way into Pon-jŏng. From both his left and right sides came a cacophony of sounds filling the streets—records blasting from storefronts, Japanese wooden clogs clanking against the asphalt, the hustle and bustle of people buying and selling in the shops. And the flood of people, swimming through the middle of it all like fish in water! All of them with chins held high and arms and legs swinging with such vigor.

Sinch'ŏl's shoulders were slouched over even further now, and his back was itching like crazy. Just then he caught the powerful scent of pomade in the air, and he noticed a young Japanese man walking toward him. He was dressed for the season in a cool *yukata*, and his hair was glistening with perfumed oil. His face was glowing as though he'd just come out of the bath. This suddenly made Sinch'ŏl conscious of an odor emanating from his own body. He felt as though he was dragging along on feet made of lead.

He passed through Yŏngnak-chŏng and crossed through Hwanggŭm-jŏng to the Sup'yo Bridge. As soon as he made it there, he stuck his hand underneath his shirt and then reached behind to scratch himself as he collected his thoughts. Well, he's probably gone back to the newspaper office by now, he thought. Maybe he'll be coming out soon to deliver the evening edition. Sinch'ŏl made his way quickly through Chinatown and finally came to Chongno. He was surprised by how empty it was. Though the streetcars were still speeding back and forth, there were hardly any people riding inside them; it all seemed so desolate. He went to Pamsongi's house, but no one was home, so he headed over to where his friend delivered papers. Soon he heard the sound of someone ringing a bell in the distance, and there was Pamsongi, coming straight toward him. Pamsongi's eyes lit up in surprise at the sight of Sinch'ŏl, but he gestured for him to come his way.

Sinch'ŏl followed him into an alleyway. Pamsongi took a quick look in each direction and spoke to him in a whisper.

"It's been decided that you're going to Inch'ŏn. Now make sure you get on a train tonight or tomorrow morning at the latest."

"Inch'ŏn? Fantastic! That means that I . . ."

Sinch'ŏl wiped the sweat off his brow. Then he smiled almost sadly. Pamsongi took out three one-wŏn bills from his wallet and handed them over to Sinch'ŏl.

182

"Use this for the train fare and for whatever other expenses you might have. When you get to Inch'ŏn, you'll probably have to go straight to the day-labor market . . . Let me give you this address in Inch'ŏn."

Pamsongi took out a scrap of paper and a pencil and wrote something down. After looking at it for a while, Sinch'ŏl nodded his head. His friend put the scrap of paper in his mouth and chewed on it, looking carefully down the alleyway.

"Okay, well . . . take care . . ."

Pamsongi hurried off with a bounce in his stride. Perhaps because he was now clutching three wŏn in his hand, Sinch'ŏl too felt somewhat lighter on his feet than before. As he came out of the alleyway, he made up his mind to stop somewhere for a bowl of *udon*. He remembered what Pamsongi had written down on the scrap of paper: Mr. Kim Ch'ŏlsu, No. 3 Oeri, Inch'ŏn. Sinch'ŏl repeated this once again to insure he wouldn't forget it.

81

Sinch'ŏl ate two five-chŏn bowls of *udon* in front of the Umigwan movie theater, and only then did he come back to life. He bought a small packet of rice and a few loaves of bread and made his way home. Lying on the floor with towels tied around their heads, Ilp'o and Kiho quickly sat up when they saw Sinch'ŏl come in. They each snatched a loaf of bread and started hungrily biting off large pieces.

"What happened? You bought bread, you got rice. Did you strike it rich today, or what?"

Only after finishing his loaf of bread could Kiho bring himself to ask the question.

They both noticed that Sinch'ŏl had walked in with a full stomach, and they were trying to figure out if he still had money left in his pocket.

"Give me a five-chŏn coin," said Ilp'o. "I've got to get a swig of *makkŏlli*. I don't see how anyone can live like this."

The rims of his eyes were red, and the hand he stuck out toward Sinch'ŏl was like that of an opium addict, bleached of all color.

"Oh, hell! We don't even have firewood and you want to waste our money on booze. Give me some money for firewood, Sinch'ŏl. I'll go get some wood so we can cook our rice."

Both of these guys had a hand thrust out toward him. For the alcohol, Sinch'ŏl doled out ten chŏn, and for the firewood, thirty. He slipped off his jacket and flung it across the room. Then he took off his fedora and threw it to the floor.

Ilp'o and Kiho found the strength to go outside, while Sinch'ŏl peeled off his sweat-soaked underwear and hung it out to dry. He was determined never to let himself sink into such despair again. Hadn't he known how everything would turn out in the end when his father kicked him out of the house? Hadn't he known well before that? How vulgar it had been of him to indulge in such nostalgia about the past, just because he'd gone through a bit of hardship!

He was determined to rid himself of this vulgarity once he got to Inch'ŏn by becoming a strong, true friend of the workers. Should he go down tonight by train? he wondered. Then he repeated the address to himself as he went back inside: Ch'ŏlsu! No. 3 Oeri. He saw that Kiho seemed to have bought some firewood as well as a few vegetables for side dishes.

"Hey, we almost died waiting for you today, you know . . . And I've had just about all I can take of Ilp'o. He actually sat there all day long picking at his toes!"

Kiho laughed as he imitated Ilp'o's toe picking. Sinch'ŏl smiled, too. Then he wondered what these friends of his were going to do once he left for Inch'ŏn. They'd be far better off by going back to the countryside, he thought, to give their wives some help on the farm. The more he tried to analyze their minds, the more amusing, even absurd, it seemed for them to want to stay here in this corner of Seoul, despite all their suffering.

Their only desire was to latch onto some sort of capitalist and start up a newspaper or journal with his financial assistance. In any case, they wanted to become leaders of the people and at least make their names well-known on the front lines of the movement. For them, it seemed, the only possible way to do this was to come to the center of it all and take charge of a publication. When they were hungry, as they were today, they didn't have a single word to say on the subject. But put a bit of food in their bellies and they quickly launched into a critique of what this newspaper or that journal was writing. Listening to them rattle on for a while was enough for anyone to think them first-rate polemicists.

184

The way Sinch'ŏl saw it, it was some sort of feudal heroism that fueled their ambitions and kept them blinded from a more clear-cut path of action; every time he looked at Ilp'o and Kiho, he was convinced that they would have to get rid of that old-fashioned, offensive petit-bourgeois mentality at the root of their thinking. And yet judging from what had happened to him today, it was clear that something similar had rooted itself deep inside his own mind.

The next morning Sinch'ŏl left the house, telling the others he'd be back soon. By the time he made it to Chongno and found a clock in one of the shops, it was almost time for his train to leave. He wondered whether he should jump on a streetcar or a bus. Just yesterday five chŏn had seemed like an enormous sum, but with a small fortune in his wallet now, he didn't feel like walking all the way to the station. Oh, to hell with it! I haven't been on one of these in months, he said to himself, catching up to the streetcar that had just passed him. He jumped onto it. The streetcar picked up speed and zoomed past the Hwasin Department Store on its way to Hwanggŭm-jŏng. Once there, a crowd of men in suits, no doubt heading toward Yongsan, filled the car to capacity. Sinch'ŏl felt uncomfortable sitting there, wedged into his narrow seat. Each time he caught the eye of one of them, he could feel his heart in his throat: What if somebody I know is in here . . . Finally, he simply turned his head around to face outside.

His eyes fixed on a rickshaw in front of the Chosŏn Bank that was heading straight toward him. The girl sitting inside it looked somewhat uncomfortable, as though she'd never ridden inside a rickshaw before. And as Sinch'ŏl took a closer look at the girl, he gasped and jumped out of his seat. He tried to push his way through the car full of people, but despite his best efforts, he just couldn't get through.

82

Rising one day at dawn, Sinch'ŏl put on the knee britches and light jacket that his friend Ch'ŏlsu had brought to him. Then he pulled on his leg gaiters, slipped on his work shoes, and went outside.

The streets of Inch'ŏn were still enveloped in the morning mists. Only a few electric lights flickered here and there. Sinch'ŏl went over again in his mind what his friend had explained to him in detail the night before, and then made his way out to the main road. Inch'ŏn at dawn—this was the only Inch'ŏn that belonged to the workers! Dressed in their leg gaiters, and with towels draped around their necks, the workers milled around him in search for a place to work for the day. In the faint glow of an electric light he saw women with lunchboxes in their hands and towels draped completely over their heads—there was a whole line of them that went on and on. Later he would learn that these women worked in the rice mill.

Sinch'ŏl first went to get breakfast in one of the places lined up along the road where they sold rice soup. The place looked just like the taverns they had in Seoul. It was already filled with workers, pouring steaming soup on top of their rice and slurping away at it. There were even people gulping down their bowls of soup while they were still standing. The bowls of boiling soup were being filled up in the corner and then carried over to the customers. Workers dashed in and out of the place.

Sinch'ŏl sat down on a makeshift wooden bench. One of the workers who couldn't wait to be served picked up a self-serve bowl and brought it to the soup pot, where he filled it up for himself. As Sinch'ŏl began to gulp down his own soup, he noticed through the corner of his eye that one of the workers sitting beside him, with whom he had walked in, had almost finished eating his entire meal. Sinch'ŏl looked at the man's full spoon with horror. How on earth can he digest his food when he eats like that? Sinch'ŏl took another look at the man and saw him put down his spoon and gulp a long draft of his *makkŏlli*. Wiping his mouth with his fist a couple of times, the man glanced over at Sinch'ŏl, jumped up out of his seat, and went outside. Sinch'ŏl couldn't eat all his food, so he stood up and left. The *makkŏlli* had left a bitter aftertaste in his mouth. He headed toward Ch'ŏnsŏk-chŏng. This was where they were building the new Taedong Spinning Mill, a construction project that he'd heard employed four to five hundred workers a day.

Sinch'ŏl walked the streets of Inch'ŏn as the day gradually dawned. He looked out onto the horizon beyond Yŏngjong Island at a sky that seemed close enough to touch—and he could almost feel the courage welling up inside him. Then, he thought of Sŏnbi, sitting so uncomfortably inside that rickshaw he'd chanced to see from the streetcar the other day. How foolish, how irresponsible he had been! And how weak-willed he'd been, jumping out of the streetcar like that—like some madman—and then wandering around in search of her rickshaw. The color

186

rose into his face at the very thought of it. But then he thought, I'm a worker now, damn it! Not one of those blasted intellectuals, all words and no action. And he certainly wasn't the kind of vulgar person who'd go chasing after women. It took all the courage Sinch'ŏl could muster to deny what he had indeed been quite capable of doing.

When he arrived in Ch'ŏnsŏk-chŏng, he found several hundred workers milling around a Japanese supervisor, dressed in a jacket with his company's logo on it. The workers were making quite a racket as they vied for their work tags. Sinch'ŏl worked his way into the crowd, and finally got a tag for himself. When he looked at this small piece of wood they called a work tag, he noticed the number sixty written on it.

"All right," shouted the supervisor. "Let's get this done, chop-chop!"

The workers with tags enthusiastically set themselves to work as the supervisor directed, while those without tags looked out at them enviously, then turned around to go, their heads hanging.

"Now get over here and move these things."

Sinch'ŏl joined the crowd of men who were being called over to the supervisor. They were to carry the sacks of cement to where the cement was being mixed with water. Each of the workers placed a yellow bag of cement onto his shoulder and dashed off. When Sinch'ŏl's turn came, he managed to balance the bag of cement that was lifted up onto his shoulder. But he heard something crack inside him. So heavy was the pressure on his chest that he could hardly breathe. Watching the other workers lift these bags onto their shoulders, he hadn't had the faintest idea that they would be this heavy. He'd assumed that each bag would be no heavier than a sack of flour. But now that he was carrying one on his own shoulders, it felt more like a sack of stones. Sinch'ŏl managed to keep the bag on his shoulder all right, but his legs were about to give out from under him.

"Hey, you! Pick up the speed!"

Sinch'ŏl managed to move forward at the sound of the foreman's thundering voice. He was gasping for breath, his chest was tight, and his collarbone, it seemed, was about to snap right in half. Mustering all the strength left inside him, Sinch'ŏl pressed his head up against the bag of cement, staggered forward for fifty paces or so, and then finally let the bag drop to the ground with a heavy thud.

83

Sinch'öl picked himself up off the ground, where he'd collapsed along with his bag of cement. He stood there watching the workers next to him mix the cement, adding water to the powder and stirring it with their shovels. What they were doing didn't seem very difficult at all. They mixed up each bag of cement in what seemed like the wink of an eye. He stared at them enviously and then turned back around, doubting his ability to carry another bag. But he had managed to get one of those tags, and surely he could put up with it for a day. It certainly wasn't going to kill him, he thought. Just do it! He set back to work again, walking on legs that felt as heavy as lead.

Next they were told to carry bricks. The workers doubled over a long piece of wire and piled two rows of bricks between the wires, with thirteen bricks in each row. The best workers managed to stack up fifteen or sixteen. They put a piece of burlap over their backs, then cut off another strip of burlap, attached it to the ends of the wire, and strapped the bricks onto themselves before standing up. But Sinch'öl came up with a better idea. He decided simply to carry the bricks with his hands, and managed to carry over two stacks of ten bricks in his bare arms. After carrying a few loads like this, though, his hands started to sting as if they'd been pricked by a thorn bush. And when he looked down at his hands, he saw that they were scraped and bleeding. He felt a shiver run up his spine as he turned back to stack up more bricks—there wasn't an inch on his body, it now seemed, that hadn't been scratched by them. Only then did he notice, to his horror, that each brick had tiny little spines that were stabbing him.

"Hey, you can't do that with your bare hands. They'll get all scratched up and you won't be able to do a thing with them. What, is this your first day on the job or something?"

When Sinch'öl looked up, he saw the worker who'd been sitting next to him eating his breakfast that morning. A smile twinkled in his eyes, the left one of which was double-lidded. The man came over to Sinch'öl and showed him how to put the burlap over his back.

"You've got to put on one of these before you carry the bricks. It'll be a heck of a lot easier than using your hands. Now, go ahead and try it this way."

Sinch'öl managed to stand up, but he staggered and toppled over. His legs started shaking like the leaves of a poplar tree. And soon every muscle in his body seemed to be twitching uncontrollably. Sinch'ŏl wanted to stick his stinging finger into his mouth and cry like a baby. He piled up the bricks that had scattered around him and lifted them back onto his back as he was told.

"No, no, this way. It's too hard to do it like that. You've got to make sure the burlap sticks to your back, and then lean over like this."

Double-lid showed Sinch'ŏl how he should stoop slightly over.

From behind them they heard someone call out: "Hey, you idiots, keep it moving!"

"Shit, they never let up," said Double-lid under his breath, lifting his own bricks onto his back and walking alongside Sinch'ŏl.

"You must have been ruined by the rice market too, huh?"

People who'd suffered losses after the price of rice collapsed had nowhere to turn in the cities, and many had ended up using up all their family's assets. They'd simply run out of food to eat and had no other choice but to come down to the labor market. Since they were doing work they'd never done before in their entire lives, it goes without saying that they weren't as skilled as the longtime workers, and Double-lid had seen many of them struggling to keep up.

Dripping with sweat, Sinch'ŏl was far too short of breath to answer his question. Several times he almost toppled over. Double-lid helped lift his bricks from behind. Sinch'ŏl felt like dumping the whole load on the ground and running away.

Sinch'ŏl worked from six in the morning until eight that night, with a forty-minute lunch break in midday. By the end of the day he felt sapped of every drop of strength left in his body. He followed Double-lid to the place where they received their wage vouchers. In front of a make-shift office built like a barrack, a crowd of workers was pushing their way forward to get their vouchers. In the office, someone called out different numbers. After waiting close to an hour, Sinch'ŏl finally received his little piece of paper, then ran to the office where they exchanged their vouchers for cash.

It wasn't until he actually had forty-six chŏn in his hand that he realized that his daily wage was supposed to be fifty. In the process of exchanging his money, he'd been duped out of the missing four chŏn by yet more people who were out to exploit him. With a heavy sigh, Sinch'ŏl looked out around him. The streets of Inch'ŏn were decked out in electric lights, and the city was swarming with all sorts of people, everyone from the rice soup peddlers collecting their credits to the wives of workers who'd come out in search of their husbands and the makings of a home-cooked meal.

Sinch'ŏl had lost track of Double-lid, and after searching for him for a while, decided to leave. As he looked out at all the electric lights twinkling in the darkness, something came to him—the extraction of surplus labor! How much more terrifying, how much more grave, he realized, was the extraction of labor he'd experienced today, than anything he'd ever read about, sitting at his desk, in Marx's *Capital*.

84

As soon as he got home, Sinch'ŏl collapsed into his bed. Then Ch'ŏlsu came in from the labor market.

"Hey, my friend, did you have a rough day?"

Sinch'ŏl looked at him.

"Oh, is that you? I'm afraid I'm a bit too sore to get up now."

"Don't worry about it. But, your nose is bleeding!"

"My nose?" Sinch'ŏl suddenly felt the blood trickling down. Ch'ŏlsu came in with some cold water and a washcloth. Sinch'ŏl made an effort to get up, but his body felt so heavy that he couldn't move a muscle. Then, just as had happened to him when he'd been carrying bricks earlier that day, he lost control of his muscles and his whole body started shaking violently. Sinch'ŏl had no choice but to leave himself to Ch'ŏlsu's care.

"Not cut out for labor, are you, my friend?"

Sinch'ŏl knew full well that his body was falling to pieces, but he still took Ch'ŏlsu's words as an insult. He closed his eyes tightly and groaned. The tighter he squeezed his eyes, though, the more vividly he recalled the terror of having to carry all those bricks. He started growing tense, and his shoulders felt heavy—it was just as if he was carrying the bricks again.

"Did you get something to eat?" Ch'ŏlsu asked.

"Yes. I had some rice soup."

"Well, I think you should give up the manual labor and just . . ."

Ch'ŏlsu stopped mid-sentence and looked down at Sinch'ŏl, who opened his eyes and looked back at him. Sinch'ŏl shifted his gaze over to the wall. At this, Ch'ŏlsu stood up.

190

"I haven't eaten yet, so I'm off to get some supper."

"Yes, and there's no need for you to come back here. You must be exhausted anyway, so please go to bed."

Sinch'ŏl knew for certain that Ch'ŏlsu had worked all day at the wharf, but he didn't show the slightest sign of being tired. Sinch'ŏl bid him good-bye and turned over on his side, facing the wall. Aaah! He couldn't help but moan in pain, so sore was every bone in his body.

The extraction of surplus labor! He kept repeating this to himself as he stared at the wall. It struck him again how much weight these words now carried. It was the weight of all the sweat and blood shed by the workers. It was the crystallization of their sweat and blood. And it had taken him until today to finally feel the true meaning of these words.

The self-styled polemicists and leaders of the people were oh so fond of talking about surplus labor, but without knowing the depth and gravity of the term, they could only use the words like jargon, as a means of showing off.

Now the extraction of surplus labor was for him a term encased in a ton of brick, pressing down on his chest unbearably. His eyes flew open. Am I hallucinating now? he wondered.

He tried not to think about it any longer, and made an effort to reminisce about the past in order to get everything else out of his mind. He painted a picture of Sŏnbi in his mind. She was riding in that rickshaw headed into the crowded streets of Seoul. Why would she have come to Seoul? Maybe she found a husband? But then surely somebody would have picked her up at the station when she arrived. Maybe some low-down scoundrel ended up seducing her? Fat chance Tŏkho had simply sent Sŏnbi off to school . . . But then maybe Okchŏm actually came through and found her a match somewhere in Seoul? Oh, Okchŏm, Okchŏm! For some reason it was now Okchŏm whom Sinch'ŏl was thinking of—Okchŏm's hands and her eyes.

Judging from how Sŏnbi had always been somewhere in the back of his mind, it would have been natural for him to long to be with her—especially since he had seen her pass right in front of him a few days earlier. But his once burning curiosity seemed to have fizzled away, and now all that was left were these lingering mysteries he still entertained about her. Instead, it was Okchŏm—those lively eyes, those hands, that face—that he now tried to imagine.

Could Okchŏm be married now? She was so devoted to me, he

reflected, and I was so ruthless! There were tears welling up in Sinch'ŏl's eyes, though he did not know why exactly.

Only now could he see how sweet her face had been when she'd unwrapped that piece of chocolate for him and blushed with the words, 'Open up wide.' Oh, if only he had a second chance, he'd . . . But Sinch'ŏl caught himself before finishing the thought. "Oh, you disgusting hypocrite!" he shouted out loud.

He heard the sound of a taxi honking its horn in the distance. The clock in the inner room struck ten. 'Dong! Dong!' He closed his eyes tightly in an effort to fall asleep. But all he saw were bricks, and more bricks.

85

A few days later Sinch'ŏl met Ch'ŏlsu and told him of his plans to go out to the labor market again. Ch'ŏlsu smiled.

"My friend, if you try that again you'll end up in bed for twice as long next time, maybe for a good week! Just give it up."

Sinch'ŏl's readiness to perform manual labor was admirable, but without a body toned to carry out that sort of labor, it seemed rather problematic to Ch'ŏlsu. Sinch'ŏl smiled back at his friend, but deep down he felt hurt. When Sinch'ŏl compared himself with Ch'ŏlsu, it didn't seem like Ch'ŏlsu was any bigger or stronger than he was, or in any way better than him. The way Sinch'ŏl saw it, he simply wasn't yet properly trained to carry out this type of labor, and once he'd made it over that hurdle, the work wouldn't be very difficult for him. And come on! If Ch'ŏlsu can do it, and if labor is what human beings do, why should I be any different? I'll do it. Even if it kills me! he thought. What was more painful to Sinch'ŏl than anything was the fact that he was sitting around all day long, eating food that his friends bought with the earnings from their own labor. But Ch'ŏlsu seemed to sense what was getting at Sinch'ŏl.

"All right then, well, why not give it one more try," Ch'ŏlsu said, with a smile. "Let's go out to the wharf together tomorrow morning. The pay is bad, I'm telling you, but the fact is that carrying bricks is the easiest job in town."

At Ch'ŏlsu's mention of bricks he shook his head emphatically.

"No way! No more bricks!"

He felt a chill run down his spine and a prickling sensation in his fingers. He'd prepared himself to do any sort of labor, no matter how hard

192

it was—even if his friend had said it was harder than carrying bricks. But he knew he could not handle the bricks. He never wanted to see another brick again.

That night the two of them stayed up late, as Ch'ŏlsu gave Sinch'ŏl a very detailed explanation of the kinds of work they did on the wharf. The next day at dawn Sinch'ŏl went there along with Ch'ŏlsu. By the time they passed in front of the customhouse, there were already several dozen workers gathered around a man in nickel-rimmed glasses, all vying for his attention, "Mr. Foreman! Mr. Foreman!" Ch'ŏlsu pushed his way through the crowd.

"Mr. Foreman! One over here, please."

Nickel-rims glanced at Ch'ŏlsu over his glasses and then stretched out a hand with a red band in it. Ch'ŏlsu immediately took the band and made his way back to Sinch'ŏl.

"This band is your work tag. Make sure you keep it tied around your wrist."

Looking down at the band Ch'ŏlsu was tying onto his arm for him, Sinch'ŏl could feel his heart thumping.

"Okay, I'm going to be unloading freight over at the station . . . You hang in there, okay?"

Ch'ŏlsu dashed off as soon as he'd finished speaking. Even though Ch'ŏlsu had given him a detailed explanation of the work the red-bands did, as he watched Ch'ŏlsu leave, it dawned on him that he didn't have a clue what he should be doing. He concentrated on what all the men with red bands were doing and tried to follow their every move without attracting any attention.

The harbor works in Inch'ŏn, in the very heartland of Chosŏn, were of such a grand sight and scale that nothing else like it existed in all of Korea. Huge ships weighing thousands of tons were lined up one after another, their broadsides banked up against the wharf. From their thick smokestacks black puffs of smoke billowed high up into the sky. Out on Wŏlmido, that dark island jutting out of the sea, stood a white light-house. Far beyond that lay the horizon.

The workers swept down onto the wharf in a massive crowd. In no time at all the harbor works were abuzz and swarming with what looked like several thousands of workers. More than half of them carried A-frames on their backs, but there were others, people pushing handcarts, people rushing into cargo holds with rice sacks on their shoulders, people carrying things in pairs with poles resting on their shoulders; young ones, old ones, even children, all brushing up against each other as they wove their way through the masses of people.

Nickel-rims stood up on the deck of one of the ships.

"All right, you morons! Now get over here and put up a ramp!"

At the sound of the man's thundering voice, the red-bands ran over toward him and started building the ramp. They laid several logs between the ship and the concrete wharf and then laid wide boards across them as they gradually worked their way up to the ship. Then one of the red-bands standing next to the base of the crane pulled a lever which sent a cable whirring down into the cargo hold of the ship. There was a Japanese man they called "the supervisor" standing on deck, watching the cable go down inside and making a continuous gesture with his hand. When he stopped moving his hand, the crane operator took it as a sign to stop the cable. A minute later the supervisor made another gesture, this time raising his hand into the air. The crane operator immediately pulled the lever. The crane began whirring again, but now there was a piece of freight as big as a house attached to the rising cable. When the workers crowded around the ship saw the size of the load, the hue and cry on the wharf grew even louder.

86

What must have been several thousand pounds of freight dangling from the crane was lowered onto the wharf with another whir of the crane. Pushing back against each other to make room for it, the workers then rushed up to the cargo and started to take down the separate pieces of the load, handing them off to the red-bands, who circled busily around, first grabbing the packages with their iron hooks and then lifting them up onto the porters' A-frames. Sinch'ŏl wanted to make use of the hooks that Ch'ŏlsu had given him, but he didn't know how. He had no other choice but to fasten his hooks onto the back of his pants and use his bare hands. A new red-band stood facing him with each load, as he lifted up package after package without a moment's rest.

The freight continued pouring out onto the wharf with each whir of the crane. Sinch'ŏl lost his breath, and his arms felt like they were about to fall off. He lifted all sorts of things—huge boxes, sheets of iron, cakes of soybeans.

"Alright, you idiots! Get that cargo unloaded fast!" thundered Nickel-rims, his eyeballs practically popping out of their sockets. Sinch'öl had at some point injured his fingers, and blood was streaming down his hand, but there was nothing he could do about it, so he wiped it off on his breeches and continued to stack the packages on the backs of the workers—they kept coming and coming.

"Hey, there! Your hands are going to kill you, if you don't use those hooks!" shouted a red-band in front of him. Sinch'öl unfastened his hooks and grabbed hold of the package, but the hooks slipped and he ended up whacking one of the porters in the head.

The porter immediately turned around to him.

"You idiot! What do you think you're doing? Hitting someone in the face like that! You almost poked my eye out, you moron. Pay attention!" The man glared at him ferociously.

Sinch'öl's eyes brimmed with the tears he'd been trying to hold back. Without a word in reply, he turned away and looked out onto the deep blue water. He felt like diving into that water and escaping from this place forever. The rough talk they used and the way they behaved—it was no different from the nails in the crates and the sheets of iron that mercilessly ripped his aching hands!

"Hey, come on! Load me up?"

His arms shaking uncontrollably, Sinch'öl tried to lift one of the big crates, but he kept having to put it down—he just couldn't lift it. In the end, he practically fell head first over it.

"Oh, come on . . . I've got a job to do here. If you're going to end up on the ground, just get out of here!"

The red-band standing in front of him would have preferred Sinch'öl to quit. Far from helping the man, Sinch'öl had become but another burden. He was barely able to collect his senses and stand up again. He wished he'd banged himself up a bit when he'd fallen, so that he might at least have an excuse to leave. But when he checked himself, he couldn't find a single scratch.

The dust coming off the cargo and the dirt swept up by the wind hung heavily in the air. Thousands of toiling workers milling around kept it from settling down to the ground. The fierce rays of the sun, it seemed, were frying people to a crisp, and Sinch'öl could practically feel his skin peeling off him. The air was choking him; his throat was dry; his mouth was filled with dust. Water, water, water! He needed water!

But there was no option of slipping away, for even a minute. Of all the people milling around him not a single one of them—not even the children—seemed so incompetent, so feeble as he.

He could hear the screech of a machine sawing wood at a lumber mill in the distance. On the next dock he saw mountains of coal piled up, as it was scooped out of a steamship docked just to the side.

"All right, boys, if you want to fight, just move it on over there," yelled the red-band standing in front of Sinch'ŏl.

Sinch'ŏl turned to look. Two men had been grappling over the same load, and the argument had finally come to blows. Soon the men had pushed the package to the side and began rolling around on the ground. In the meantime, someone else picked up the package they were fighting over and carried it off. The men rose and went to take back the package, bringing yet another into the fight. There were three of them, then four, going after each other.

When Sinch'ŏl realized that one of them was Double-lid, he felt like running over to stop him. But it was only a fleeting thought, for Sinch'ŏl knew that he had a hard enough time keeping himself out of harm's way. Anyway, in a place like this, a fight was just a fight. Hardly anyone even blinked an eye at the sight of them. When the men eventually tired themselves out, they brushed the dirt from their clothes and got up off the ground.

Well after the electric lights came on, the workers were still working. But eventually Sinch'ŏl and the other red-bands followed Nickel-rims to collect their day's wages. At the sound of somebody whistling, Sinch'ŏl looked behind him and saw Double-lid, A-frame and all, slowly making his way toward him. Even he looked completely exhausted.

87

"My friend!"

Sinch'ŏl called out to Double-lid as he passed by. Double-lid stopped and looked around in confusion.

"Hey, I was looking for you!" continued Sinch'ŏl.

Only then did Double-lid notice Sinch'ŏl.

"So you're back again, huh?"

"How much money did you make today?" Sinch'ŏl asked.

"Money? All I did was fight."

"Fight over what?"

"Nothing, I guess." Double-lid scratched his head.

"Swing by my place sometime, okay?"

"Where do you live?"

"You know the Catholic Chapel on the way up to Sa-jŏng?"

"The ca-tho-lic . . . what?"

Sinch'ŏl drew the sign of the cross in the air with his hand.

"You know, that building with this symbol sticking up on the roof."

"Oh, you mean the church. Okay."

"If you go past the church, there's a public toilet, right?"

"Yeah, yeah."

"Just up the hill is a place where they chop firewood for sale. And just beyond that is a small grass-roofed house.

"Okay."

"My room is in the back of that house."

"Got it. I'll stop by sometime."

"Be sure to, okay?"

"I will."

And without so much as word of good-bye, Double-lid was striding off again. Sinch'ŏl watched him walk away—a man like that would be first-rate if only he had a proper consciousness, he thought.

Nickel-rims slipped into an inn of some sort. The red-bands who were following him stopped and waited for him to come out. They turned around and saw Sinch'ŏl and started snickering amongst themselves. When Sinch'ŏl realized they were mocking how he had worked that day, he felt so humiliated and so indescribably alone that a moan almost escaped from him before he caught himself. He felt a heaviness bearing down upon him impossible to resist, so he dropped to the ground and sat with his back to the standing red-bands.

In front of him was a cement-sealed wall over which golden letters spelling out 'King Bar' in Japanese were lit up with electric bulbs. Tears welled up in his eyes. He looked down at his shabby appearance and the feeling of loneliness intensified, as though he'd been completely forsaken by the world. He'd come out to the labor market in a desperate effort to make friends with the workers, and here they all were making a laughing stock of him, unwilling to offer him even the slightest bit of sympathy.

No, no! I've got so many comrades behind me! he thought. It was simply the unique situation he found himself in that made him feel so lonely and isolated. Sinch'ŏl watched as a 'modern girl' and 'modern boy' came toward him. They were walking side by side with synchronized strides, almost as though they were dancing. He jumped to his feet and leaned against the wall.

The man and woman gave off the scent of a designer perfume as they passed by, and he was instantly reminded of Okchŏm. Then he remembered the time he and Okchŏm were on the beach looking at the setting sun, and especially the way her face and her clothes had looked just then, as though they were glowing in front of the dancing flames of a fire. In the confusion of the moment Sinch'ŏl heaved a deep sigh. He missed Okchŏm so much. Could she possibly be here in Wŏlmido on vacation? Was she still pining after him, the poor thing? Why had he done that to her!

Then a different thought struck him like a slap in the face: How did my mind get back in the gutter? He looked up and realized that he was still leaning against the wall all by himself. The pain that he'd managed to forget for a moment raced through his body unbearably. He sat back down. If it weren't for the others, he would have lain right down on the ground. He leaned against the wall with a moan, and thought: I wonder if there's anything interesting in the papers today?

As recently as when he'd been at school, his heart would race with anticipation each time he read the newspapers. He was convinced that the world was being shaken up before his eyes, that something big was sure to happen any day. But now a year had passed, and nothing at all seemed to have changed. It could be decades, maybe centuries, before the current state of affairs changed. These doubts took root in a corner of his mind.

Then Nickel-rims came outside.

88

The crowd of red-bands gathered around Nickel-rims and sat in a circle. They each exchanged the band tied around their wrists for ninety-five chŏn, their daily wage minus five chŏn for the cost of lunch.

Sinch'ŏl took his ninety-five chŏn and stood to go. The remaining red-bands glanced at him and started snickering again. Sinch'ŏl had worked all day alongside these men, and wanted at least to offer a pleasant good-bye. But when he saw them laughing at him like this, his lips automatically tightened. He took several unsteady steps through the crowd. He couldn't be sure of when exactly it had happened, or why, but he knew that an invisible wall had formed between him and the workers, one that had completely severed them from each other. He felt trapped in a position where he couldn't approach the people on either side of him.

He watched a worker lift onto his A-frame a load of pine wood and what seemed to be a five pound sack of rice, to which he added a few more groceries before setting off at a clip into the distance. The man was on his way back from the wharf as well, it seemed. Judging from what he had learned that day, Sinch'ŏl figured that after fighting to carry around packages for an entire day in that dust bowl, the man would have been lucky to take home even fifty or sixty chŏn. Working as a red-band, Sinch'ŏl seemed to get one of the highest wages offered on the wharf.

Sinch'ŏl bought a bowl of rice soup at a place on the side of the road and then headed home.

From that day forward, Sinch'ŏl gave up any ideas of going back to the labor market. He managed to survive one day at a time by relying on what Ch'ŏlsu gave him out of his earnings.

One day very late at night he heard a deep voice calling to him.

"You in here?"

Double-lid strode into his room. Sinch'ŏl quickly pushed behind him the letter he was writing to Pamsongi and stretched out his hand.

"Well, look who's here! Good to see you. I waited so long for you to stop by, I figured you'd forgotten all about me . . . Please, have a seat."

Sinch'ŏl, delighted to see Double-lid, shook his hand heartily. Double-lid smiled and took a seat where Sinch'ŏl had motioned for him to sit. He took a quick look around the room.

"Have you been sick?" asked Sinch'ŏl, staring into Double-lid's face and detecting a lack of color in his complexion.

"No."

Double-lid patted down his hair and hung his head slightly. His fine head of hair, which hadn't been cut in quite some time now, was coated with a white layer of dust. From beneath his jaw projected the hairs of his thick beard. Sinch'ŏl could tell that this was the body of a man simply exhausted from a day's work in the labor market, and he remembered struggling to lift those iron plates. Just the thought of it now made his legs tremble. Sinch'ŏl neatly stacked several of the books he used as a pillow and pushed them toward Double-lid.

"Why don't you lie down here for a while. You must be incredibly tired, my friend."

Double-lid glanced over at Sinch'ŏl and then drew back in his seat a bit.

"No, I'm not . . ."

"Oh, come on. Please just lie down."

Sinch'ŏl moved to Double-lid's side. He caught the smell of sweat and of something else rancid in the air. He grimaced unconsciously, then quickly forced a smile. He noticed that Double-lid's clothes were stained with patches of dried sweat. The closer Sinch'ŏl moved to his side, the more uncomfortable Double-lid seemed. He gradually drew back further from where he'd been sitting, scratching his head nervously.

"What's the matter? Why don't you lie down for a bit . . . You went to work today, didn't you?"

"Yes."

"Well, where did you go? To the wharf again?"

"No. You know how they're reclaiming the land in front of Wŏlmido? Well, I was over there today."

"How are the wages there?"

Double-lid looked up, but hesitated to say anything. Maybe he didn't understand the word 'wages,' thought Sinch'ŏl, convinced he'd have to learn the language of the workers as soon as possible.

"Uh . . . I mean, how much did you get paid?"

"Oh, yeah, yeah . . . If you work hard enough, you can make seventy to eighty chŏn. Otherwise, maybe forty or fifty."

"I see . . . Well, just sit back and relax, so we can have a nice chat. Please, make yourself a little more comfortable. You know, we've known each other for a long time and yet we don't even know each other's names . . . I'm Yu Sinch'ŏl. How about you?"

Sinch'ŏl looked Double-lid square in the face.

89

"Me? I'm Ch'ŏtchae."

"Ch'ŏtchae! Now, that's a fine name. And what about your hometown?"

Ch'ŏtchae wasn't sure if he should tell Sinch'ŏl the name of his hometown or not. In the end, he decided there was no need to mention it.

"I don't have a hometown," said Ch'ŏtchae, his eyes shifting down to the floor.

"No hometown," said Sinch'ŏl under his breath, oddly touched by what Ch'ŏtchae had said. Coming from someone like Ch'ŏtchae, the words were most likely sincere.

Talk of his hometown reminded Ch'ŏtchae of Yi Sŏbang and his mother. Were they dead by now? Or were they still hanging on, waiting for him to come back with the money he'd earned? The more he thought about them, the more these dormant feelings started to stir again inside of him. Back when he'd left home, he'd planned on coming back for Yi Sŏbang and his mother after making some money, but he'd never been able to make as much as he'd expected, and as time passed by, with him being so busy at work and all, his thoughts of Yi Sŏbang and his mother gradually faded from his mind.

"Why don't you just lie back for a while. You must have worked awfully hard today."

Sinch'ŏl stared for a while at Ch'ŏtchae's hands, comparing them with his own. He felt ashamed of himself, but he was also incredibly envious of Ch'ŏtchae, who seemed to have forearms made of cast iron. And at the same time, it seemed like everything he'd ever learned up until then had served no other purpose than to make him into a weakling—both in body and mind.

"The work isn't too hard for you, my friend?"

"Well, the morning's fine, but I do get a bit worn out come sunset."

"I can imagine. Have you been working as a laborer ever since you were young?"

"No. I started out weeding in the fields, before doing this . . ."

Sinch'ŏl was completely taken by Ch'ŏtchae's deep voice and unpretentious words. He didn't know why, but he felt more and more like he could really trust him.

"I don't know a thing about what goes on out there. Do you think

201

you could come over every now and then to teach me a thing or two about the work?"

"What's there to teach about work? You just do it, that's all." He let out a chuckle.

Ch'ŏtchae found it amusing that Sinch'ŏl was asking him to be the teacher. But he also remembered how hard Sinch'ŏl had struggled carrying bricks. Sinch'ŏl, meanwhile, felt even more attracted to Ch'ŏtchae when he saw him laugh.

"Well . . . I was just wondering, for example, how they calculate your pay when you carry those sacks of rice and stuff down on the wharf."

"Oh, that? It all depends on how heavy the load is. You get about five or six li for a sack of rice, four li for a cake of pressed soybeans, and then five li for just about anything else."

"So, you mean to tell me you've got to carry a hundred sacks of rice just to make fifty or sixty chŏn?"

Sinch'ŏl grimaced at the thought of carrying a hundred sacks of rice. But then he also thought of the thousands of laborers he'd actually seen slaving away on the dusty wharf. He let out a long sigh. His mission was now clearer to him than ever before.

"How much did you make the other day, my friend? The day I was out there."

"No idea. Don't remember."

"Oh, you know. The day you got into that fight. Weren't you guys fighting over the same package? "

"I don't remember."

"Well, I don't think you should fight any more. You'll only end up hurting each other in a fight, you know. I mean, a good fight you've got to fight to the bitter end, but what's the sense of fighting with your friends? You'll just end up hurting each other."

"Yeah, but what do you expect me to do when someone is trying to take away the load I'm supposed to be carrying? . . . Anyway, what are you doing manual labor for?"

"Me? Well, I've got to feed myself somehow . . ."

"Seems to me a fellow like you could easily get a job as a town clerk or policeman."

When Ch'ŏtchae had first come into the room, he had seen Sinch'ŏl writing, and judging from the clothes hanging up on the wall and the books placed under the lamp, Sinch'ŏl didn't seem like someone who normally did manual labor.

Sinch'ŏl tried not to smile.

"Does being a town clerk or a policeman appeal to you?"

"Sure it does."

"Well, I tell you, I wish I could become a laborer like you."

Ch'ŏtchae got a good laugh out of that. But then as the words 'town clerk' and 'policeman' sank into his mind, he thought back to the town clerks and policemen in his own hometown. For some reason he now felt a burning impulse to ask Sinch'ŏl a question.

"Hey . . . I was just thinking about the police, and . . ."

Ch'ŏtchae didn't finish his sentence. Sinch'ŏl looked at him, "Okay, what about the police?"

"Well . . . I mean, I just wanted to know how you avoid getting caught by the law. Can you teach me something about that?"

90

Kannan had come home late that night. She smiled as she watched Sŏnbi wake up from her nap.

"Bedbugs not biting?"

"They sure are! Where have you been?"

"I, ah . . . someone I know wanted to meet with me."

Kannan slipped out of her best set of clothes and hung them on the wall. She sat at Sŏnbi's side.

"Listen, Sŏnbi, have you heard of Inchŏn? Well, they've just built this huge spinning mill there, and it's got way more factory girls than the place I work now . . . I hear they're going to hire something like a thousand girls . . ."

Sŏnbi was wide-awake now, her eyes sparkling with unusual luster.

"Do you think maybe I could work there?"

"Sure you can . . . I'm planning to go there, too! We can go together, Sŏnbi. How about that?"

Kannan was all smiles. She adjusted her hair and reinserted a hairpin that was about to fall out. Sŏnbi, meanwhile, was lost in thought, and the color rose in her cheeks. An image of the spinning machines she'd heard about from Kannan flashed before her eyes.

"But I don't know if I can do it . . . They'll kick me out if I don't work good enough, won't they?"

Gazing into Sŏnbi's face, Kannan remembered how clueless she herself had been, and how frightened and embarrassed she was when she first came to Seoul.

"Why shouldn't you be able to do the work? You've just got to learn how, that's all . . . I know lots of new girls who came in knowing a lot less than you, but they were just fine once they got the hang of things. Don't you worry about it."

Sŏnbi sighed softly. Then she smiled.

"So listen, Sŏnbi! I decided to quit my job at the mill today . . ."

"Well, when do we leave then?"

"Right away, I guess . . . but I've got a few things to take care of first, which means we'll have to wait a couple of days."

Kannan thought for a moment about the secret mission T'aesu had just given her. Yu Sinch'ŏl . . . No. 5 Sa-jŏng in Inch'ŏn, she said to herself, setting the address to memory.

"Is this place called Inch'ŏn somewhere in Seoul?"

Kannan glanced at Sŏnbi and giggled.

"No, it's about twenty-five miles away by train, from what I hear."

Sŏnbi felt the color again rise in her cheeks. Kannan was always learning new things from other people and saying smart things that she didn't understand. It really seemed like Kannan knew just about everything. Sŏnbi wondered if she'd be like that someday.

Then they heard a roar of laughter come from the room across the way. They stopped talking and glanced at the door.

"Looks like they're not going hungry today if they're laughing up a storm like that . . ."

Sŏnbi got up and began spreading out the bedding.

"What do those people do for a living?"

Sŏnbi usually felt too uncomfortable to leave her door open, and often wondered what those men actually did for a living, cooped up in that room of theirs all day long. Whenever Kannan went off to the factory, Sŏnbi was sure to keep her door shut and locked.

"Well, they're unemployed . . . What are they supposed to do?"

What does 'unemployed' mean? wondered Sŏnbi, holding back her desire to ask Kannan yet another question.

204

"They're a good-looking bunch, don't you think? But no one in today's world is going to give them jobs, so what else can they do?"

Kannan stared blankly into the flame of the oil lamp. Yu Sinch'ŏl, No. 5 Sa-jŏng, she repeated, worried she might forget his name and address. Then very carefully she went over everything that T'aesu had told her. Sŏnbi thought it suspicious that Kannan retreated into her thoughts like this, whenever she came back late at night. It reminded her of what Tŏkho had done to her night after night when she'd lived in the countryside, which made her shudder. As she studied the expression on Kannan's face, she feared that Kannan was doing something she shouldn't be doing.

"Sŏnbi! It's been ages since you came to Seoul, but I've been too busy even to show you the sights. Want to walk to Namsan Park tomorrow?"

"Namsan Park? What do you do there?"

"You know how back home we have the ridge up over Wŏnso Pond? Well, it's a mountain just like that. Remember how we always used to climb up there and chew on sourstem? Oh . . . I wish I could go home and see my mother!"

What came to Sŏnbi's mind just then was that dirty hand of Ch'ŏtchae's that had poked her so sharply in the brow long ago. She wanted desperately to ask Kannan if by any chance she'd seen Ch'ŏtchae. But she suffered in silence, without letting Kannan know what was on her mind. Ch'ŏtchae might even be right here in Seoul, she thought. Then she hung her head.

91

The next day they took a spin through Ch'anggyŏng Park, then made their way up Namsan.

"That's what they call the Chosŏn Sin'gung."

Kannan pointed up to the Shrine of Korea. Sŏnbi simply nodded in reply—she didn't understand the words Kannan was using. Then, feeling somewhat woozy, she looked back down at the steep flight of steps they had just climbed.

"We're not going back down that way, are we?" asked Sŏnbi.

"Why?"

"Isn't there another way back down?"

Kannan caught on and smiled sweetly.

"Oh, Sŏnbi, you're such a country girl! Are you scared of falling down and breaking your neck? All right then, we'll take a different way back down."

Laughing, they passed by the front of the shrine, then walked down into a grove of pines, where they sat down side by side.

As they rustled in the wind, the trees slowly showered the two girls with pine needles that gently grazed the hems of their skirts. Sŏnbi, lost in thought, clenched some of the needles in her hand.

"I can't believe it's already fall. Time passes so quickly," said Kannan, glancing at the needles gripped in Sŏnbi's hand.

Sŏnbi looked at Kannan with a start and smiled. Kannan had taken the words right out of her mouth.

They looked at the view in front of them. There were red and white brick buildings soaring boastfully up into the sky, and off in the distance, at the base of Mount Pugak sat the White House, as though it were showing off the eternal nature of its might.* Between them, like so many tiny crabs driven this way and that, crept all the lowly houses.

At the sound of the streetcars and taxis zooming to and fro, they shifted their gaze down to Namdaemun, which loomed darkly, as though whispering to itself the secrets of yesteryear. This was the center of a spider web of electrical wires that spun outward, lighting up the signs on the storefronts to a dizzying effect.

"Do people actually live in all those houses?"

Kannan turned to Sŏnbi.

"Sure they do. What else do you think lives in them?" she giggled.

When she'd first run into Sŏnbi, quite out of the blue, Kannan had been taken aback by her beauty. But now that several months had passed Kannan could tell that Sŏnbi had actually been quite pale at the time. Even though she had few side dishes to eat with her rice, Sŏnbi had put on weight since coming to Seoul, and Kannan was glad to see it. It was about time to start teaching her, thought Kannan, and to bring her into the light of class consciousness.

---

*Kang here uses the word "White House" (Paegakkwan) as a roundabout reference to the Office of the Governor General, which was built on the grounds of Kyŏngbok Palace.

"Sŏnbi, don't you just hate Tŏkho?"

The color rushed into Sŏnbi's face. Kannan, it seemed, had guessed that something had gone on between her and Tŏkho, even though she hadn't until now said a word about it. It was for this reason that whenever Kannan even mentioned their hometown, Sŏnbi felt awkward, even afraid, and always seemed somewhat depressed.

"There's so much I want to tell you, Sŏnbi, now that I've got the time to talk. Things have been so hectic up until now that we haven't had the chance . . . For starters, what do you think of Tŏkho? Let's start with him."

Sŏnbi's ears were bright red now and she hung her head. The only sound she made was with the pine needles, which she crunched between her tightly pressed fingers. Kannan, judging from her own experience, sensed that Sŏnbi still was having trouble getting Tŏkho out of her mind. Before meeting T'aesu and benefiting from his guidance, Kannan herself had had a hard time forgetting Tŏkho. She used to see him in her dreams: Oh, Master, I missed my period! I know I must be pregnant. She would cry out loud and then wake up in tears. But that wasn't all! She remembered how jealous she'd been before coming to Seoul when Tŏkho's affections had shifted toward Sŏnbi. Once, she'd been out walking in the middle of the night, and was so petrified by a man she thought was chasing her that she actually ran right inside Kaettong's house. What an utter fool she had once been! And this was why she felt so sorry for Sŏnbi. Sŏnbi simply sat there silently, her head down, far too ashamed even to show her face. Tŏkho's scary, disgusting face had flashed into Sŏnbi's mind, and all she could do was pray that Kannan would soon change the subject.

Kannan, too, felt distressed at the thought of Tŏkho. She shifted her gaze from Sŏnbi onto the view down below. But then another thought struck her: How many Tŏkhos were out there in that bustling city?

Suddenly they were startled by a loud, unpleasant sound, and they turned around. Below the pine trees they could hear two sets of *geta*, one big and one small, clamorously making their way up the stone stairs. As they turned, they saw above the pine grove, crafted out of solid granite, the massive *torii* gateway looming against the sky.

207

92

Two days later Kannan and Sŏnbi went to Inch'ŏn, at first staying with a friend of Kannan's whom she had gotten to know in a factory. With the help of this friend, they found jobs in the Taedong Spinning Mill and easily got guarantees of identity at the police station. They also learned that the Taedong Spinning Mill didn't allow its employees to commute to work. It was a strict regulation that all female employees live in the dormitory. The three of them decided to enter the dormitory together the following day, and they wandered around Wŏlmido Island and Man'guk Park until the sun went down.

After eating a nice supper, they pushed aside their dinner table and chatted about this, that and the other. Then Kannan stood up.

"Insuk, I'm just going to make a quick trip over there."

"Where?" asked Insuk. You're not going to go look for that man again, are you?"

On their way to Man'guk Park, Kannan had mentioned that she had to pay a visit to the older brother of a friend who had asked her to check up on him. After walking through Sa-jŏng, Kannan had figured out where Sinch'ŏl was living, but she'd pretended to have lost her way and said she'd have to come back later that night to find him.

"You're going all alone? Do you actually think you'll find him without the right address?"

"Well . . . might as well give it one more try. At least I can say I tried my best, right? I've really messed this up, though, haven't I? What was that damn number again?"

"Oh, Kannan! What are you thinking? How do you expect to find the place when you don't even know the right street number? You'll never find him."

"Look, if I don't come right back, just assume I've found the place. And if I'm back soon, well, I'll just have to eat my words."

Kannan smiled, then went outside. After making sure the coast was clear, she headed towards Sa-jŏng.

Having arrived at No. 5, Kannan again looked to either side of her and went through the main gate. She looked around the place, wondering where Sinch'ŏl's room might be, but there didn't appear to be any rooms separate from the inner quarters. Assuming she'd entered the wrong house, she went back outside. Then she had a change of heart and went back to try again.

"Hello? Could I bother you for a moment?"

The door to the inner quarters opened and a woman peeked outside. Kannan hesitated.

"I'm sorry, but you wouldn't happen to have a boarder staying here?"

Before Kannan had finished speaking, the woman came out onto the breezeway.

"Yes, yes, please go on back this way and see if he's in."

She pointed to the small path leading behind the kitchen. Kannan entered the dark passageway and then stopped in front of a small door. Her heart started pounding and she was almost breathless. She could tell somebody was inside. A shadow flashed across the doorway and she heard the sound of somebody flipping the pages of a newspaper.

"Hello? Is anyone there?"

The door opened and a man appeared. She felt she'd met him several times before.

"Are you Yu Sinch'ŏl?"

Sinch'ŏl was surprised to see a young woman standing in front of his door at this time of night, addressing him by name. Then he remembered the message he'd received from Ch'ŏlsu.

"Yes, that's right. Please come inside . . ."

It wasn't until Kannan had entered the room that she realized that Sinch'ŏl was one of the struggling young men who cooked their own meals in the room opposite hers in Seoul. Sinch'ŏl, too, recognized Kannan as soon as he'd taken a good look at her.

"We used to run into each other all the time back in Seoul. You were in the room directly opposite from where we lived, weren't you?"

"That's right! This is actually quite funny, isn't it," she laughed.

"Hah, ha. A friend living right next door and I hadn't the slightest idea. Tell me, when did you get here?"

Sinch'ŏl hadn't known that Kannan would be arriving so soon. Back in Seoul, she'd been nothing more than a simple factory girl in his eyes, but now that he was sitting right in front of her, he saw her courage and strength of character. Powderless, her rosy cheeks glowed in the light of the lamp.

"I arrived by train yesterday. But you, my friend, must be having a difficult time here.

Kannan studied the look on Sinch'ŏl's face. She was waiting for him to say something.

"Well, it hasn't been all that difficult . . . Tell me, have you come to town on some sort of errand, or are you moving here for good?

Sure enough, Sinch'ŏl was unwilling to let down his guard until she spoke first. Kannan thought for a moment and then replied.

"I'm here to work in the spinning mill. Or, perhaps you already know that?"

93

After a good night's sleep, the three friends moved into the dormitory at the Taedong Spinning Mill. All three were to stay in the same freshly plastered room, about six-feet square. They took a tour of the dormitory, which must have been some six hundred feet square in total, and then they peeked into the factory. Even the spinning factory outside the T Gate in Seoul was nothing in comparison to this place. The dormitory and the factory building aside, the mill was outfitted with all sorts of machines that one never saw in Seoul. There were generators and reeling machines in different places in Seoul, but everything here was of an enormous size, far bigger than anything they had seen before.

The cauldrons used to boil the silk cocoons had been nothing more than washbasins back in Seoul, and each person had a single *waku* (reel) to work on, but here the cauldrons were long and rectangular in shape, and seemed ten times the size of the ones in Seoul. It was set up so that each person controlled ten or twenty *waku* in front of them. Sŏnbi didn't know the difference, because it was her first time inside a factory, but Kannan and Insuk could hardly believe their eyes.

That morning Kannan and Insuk took numbers 500 and 501 and headed into the factory, where they set themselves to work. Since it was Sŏnbi's very first time, she stayed beside Kannan's station and learned how to reel the silk off the cocoons.

The noise coming from the generator and the rotating *waku* was so ear-splitting that it was almost impossible to concentrate on the factory floor. Sŏnbi stood there idly watching Kannan reel her silk. Since Kannan had always done this sort of work, it came to her quite naturally.

First of all, one of the male workers brought over the pre-boiled cocoons, which were poured into the cauldrons of boiling water. Kannan stirred them with a small broom of sorts and pushed them down into the water. After a while the tips of the silk threads would stick to the broom. At first she pulled off all the bad threads and attached them to the nails sticking out of either side of the cauldron. Then she passed the broom through the water again to fish for more threads. This time they were transparent and had a slightly golden hue. Kannan grabbed the thread tips with her left hand, and with her right hand she separated each one and attached it to a porcelain needle. The threads began to slowly unravel as they glided up into the air.

At the factory in Seoul each person had one, or at most two, porcelain needles to thread—nowhere near the dozens of needles they were put in charge of here. Kannan attached threads to three of the needles. At first she worked with just these three until she got the hang of it, but then she gradually increased the number of needles she used. The southern wall of the factory was made entirely of glass, and even the ceiling was fit with glass windows. There were two rows of spinning machines, each facing the other, with a corridor between, the length of which the supervisors walked up and down. In Seoul there were only five supervisors, but here it seemed like there were thirty.

From here at station No. 500 the line still stretched into the distance, with hundreds more stations. Her face flushing in the heat, Sŏnbi watched as the thread tips were drawn up and out of the cauldron. Kannan's hands were already bright pink, scalded by the boiling water. Her fingers were white and swollen.

"Kannan! Let me do it for a while."

Sŏnbi spoke with her mouth to Kannan's ear. The sweat was dripping off of Kannan's face like droplets of rain. Kannan smiled and shook her head. She kept picking off threads and attaching them to the porcelain needles.

"Pretty good for a first-timer."

When Kannan turned, she saw one of the supervisors standing to the side of her. He then looked over at Sŏnbi.

"Now, pay good attention to how she does this. The sooner you get to work, the sooner you'll start making money."

Sŏnbi had already been terribly self-conscious of standing there doing absolutely nothing, but now she was at her wit's end after what this man had just said to her. The supervisor stared at Sŏnbi's lowered face out of the corner of his eye, and remained there in front of them.

The electric lights flashed on brightly. Taken by surprise, Sŏnbi looked up at the lamps, then stared out at all the machines and women workers stretching out before her eyes. Have I entered a different world now? she wondered, taking in the transformation of her surroundings.

"Hey, Sŏnbi. You give it a try!"

Kannan moved aside. When Sŏnbi grabbed one of the thread tips, her hand began to shake and her arms and legs started to tremble. She couldn't maneuver her hands the way she wanted to.

"Careful! One of the threads is broken!"

Kannan stepped firmly on a pedal and the machine shut down. Kannan fed the tip of the thread through the porcelain needle and then tied the thread back onto itself.

"When the thread breaks, you've got to tie it back together like this. Look, Sŏnbi! And if you want to shut down the machine, you press this pedal down here and it stops the spinning."

Just then the sound of a siren pierced the air. Sŏnbi looked to either side of her, wide-eyed, in alarm.

94

"Oh, Sŏnbi! When that siren rings, we get to go. It means the night shift is coming in to continue the work."

Before Kannan had even finished speaking, the women on the night shift started to pour out onto the factory floor. After shutting down her machine, Kannan pulled out her *waku* of spun silk. Before she left the factory, she took her place at the back of a line, where the women workers were queued up outside the appraisal office.

"Sŏnbi, you just go on ahead."

Sŏnbi waited outside the factory doors. The machines inside the factory continued to produce a terrible roar. When she saw Kannan coming, she walked up to her. The bell was ringing in the cafeteria.

"Hey, let's go! That sounds like a dinner bell or something . . ."

Since they were living in the factory dormatory, even Kannan was unsure of how everything worked. When they made it to the cafeteria, they found the place filled with hundreds of factory girls sitting down to dinner. The cafeteria was in the basement, directly below the dormitory. The rectangular shaped room was warm and humid with the steam of cooking rice. Four rows of long, wooden boards stretched from one side of the cafeteria all the way to the other, with wooden rice pots and empty bowls laid out neatly on the tables. Just seeing the rice whetted their appetites, so they picked up their spoons and dug into their food. The stuff was boiled rice all right, but it had no flavor. It tasted like reheated cold rice and it gave off a smell almost like gasoline. Kannan took another spoonful and examined it. She looked over at Sŏnbi and then at Insuk. They were all thinking the same thing.

"What's the matter with this rice?"

A group over in the corner was talking about the rice, too. If only the side dish had been tasty, the rice might have been edible, but what was supposed to be fermented baby shrimp seemed to have been only recently pickled, with a lump of salt still stuck in the middle of it. It gave off a fishy smell and was simply impossible to eat. They were all so hungry that their stomachs were grumbling, and yet their taste buds weren't tempted in the least. Each of them looked at the others, spoons still in hand. After trying a few more spoonfuls, most of the factory girls left the cafeteria in tears. A few of the girls who had been among the first to begin working at the factory and had become accustomed to the food spoke up.

"You just wait 'til you're really hungry! You'll be down here gobbling up this Annamese rice, believe me. Try not eating for a couple days and you'll see. Do you really think they're going to run out of this imported stuff? Ha!"

Granted, they had suffered from stomach trouble for the first few days, and had had diarrhea for a week or so. But eventually they'd had no other choice but to eat the rice. And now that they were accustomed to eating it, they no longer got sick or thought it smelled like gasoline. Nothing was worse than being hungry. And they knew that anyone who refused to eat the rice would change her mind when she got really hungry.

About an hour had passed since they had come upstairs from the cafeteria when the bell in the dormitory started ringing.

"What's that bell mean?" Kannan asked one of the girls who had stopped by.

"You don't know? That's the night school bell . . . Come on, let's get ready."

"You mean everyone has to go?"

"Well, of course. Isn't it good we've got a chance to study? Come on, girls, let's go."

She hurried off with short, quick steps. A smirk settled on Kannan's lips, and she looked back at Insuk and Sŏnbi. They were leaning up against the window, hungry and listless, as they stared outside.

"Kannan! I think the food here tasted so awful because we had such a good breakfast at home this morning."

"Probably . . . What did they call it again? Annamese rice?"

"I think so."

"Well, no wonder it smells like gasoline! How do they expect anyone to eat it?"

"Beats me, but if that's what they give us, there's not much we can do about it! Okay, let's quit the small talk and check out this night school! I wonder what they're going to teach us . . ."

Sŏnbi was hungry, but she pricked her ears at the mention of night school, and got up slowly. She recalled a scene from her past—when Tŏkho had robbed her of her virginity, after luring her with the promise of sending her to school. She barely managed to keep her legs from trembling enough to follow the others and take a seat in the lecture hall.

Up on the platform stood the same supervisor, with large, dark-rimmed glasses, who had given Kannan a compliment earlier in the day. He took furtive glances at the factory girls as they made their way into the hall. For this man with dark splotches around his eyes, these glasses were his sole attempt at personal grooming. Once all the girls had gathered, the supervisor told them they would go over the factory rules instead of studying because so many new girls had just arrived. He cleared his throat, quickly looked to either side of him, and began to speak.

95

"What sets our factory apart from other smaller ones is the special consideration we give to the future lives and everyday convenience of each of our employees. As you can see before your eyes, we've spared no expense in building this dormitory, in arranging for this night school, and in setting up a store that supplies everyday items for all your shopping needs."

214

The supervisor, pleased with himself, thrust back his shoulders and stuck out his chest, then took a look around the lecture hall.

"Let's say you go out to the market to buy something you use on a regular basis, something like socks or cosmetics. Not only will the prices be high, but there's a very good chance you'll end up being cheated. That's why we've set up a shop right here in the factory that offers you everything you'll ever need at wholesale prices. The place is for you and you alone. The factory, for its part, actually loses money by operating it."

The factory girls, their nerves on edge, now heaved a collective sigh of relief.

"But that's not all . . . for the benefit of all our employees, we have also set up a savings system. Savings is the light of the future! And that's why as long you work hard, we'll provide you with all the food and daily necessities you need and then deposit the remainder of your earnings in the bank for you. That way you can earn as much as you want to. All you have to do is hold onto that passbook of yours, and when you leave in three years' time, you'll have cash in the bank to pay for your weddings. How about that? Hah, ha . . ."

A vulgar smile appeared on the man's lips, but the factory girls giggled along with him.

"So stick it out for three years, and by the time you leave the factory, you'll be ready to set up a house, have a few children and enjoy the easy life. Now, all of you signed three-year contracts when you entered this factory, but those three years will go by faster than you could ever imagine. And when the time comes, you'll probably want to stay even longer. You see, the reason the factory wants to treat you so well is that each one of you has come with a guarantee from the police station, am I right? And I'm sure that you must all feel incredibly lucky to have been selected out of such a large pool of applicants. Tell me, have you ever heard of a place as good as a factory like this? Do you have any idea how many people are out there roaming the streets without jobs?"

At the memory of weeding the fields in the countryside with barely enough millet to keep themselves fed, the factory girls truly felt overwhelmed with their own good fortune. The supervisor's glasses flickered in the light from the electric lamps. He twisted the side of his mustache and continued.

"Here at this factory we also take it upon ourselves to maintain a strict code of moral discipline, so that none of our girls ends up spoiling her future prospects in life. And insofar as we prohibit you from leaving the factory grounds individually for this specific reason, all of you will no doubt miss contact with the outside world. But each year in the spring and fall we'll head out on a field trip with specially prepared box lunches. In fact, the office is right now making plans for the spring to provide you with new shoes at a discount and to take you all to Wŏlmido Island for a picnic . . ."

At these words, there seemed to be a glimmer of hope and joy in the eyes of all the factory girls. But Kannan wanted to jump to her feet and refute what the supervisor was saying—she was burning up inside.

"Here at this factory we also offer you a holiday every third Sunday, when we'll let you play sports and other games on the grounds out in front. This is of course for the sake of everyone's good health, and these holidays are one of the special advantages of working in this factory. Finally, I want you all to think of this factory as your very own factory. We have to keep it spotlessly clean, and work as efficiently as possible, so that you all can earn bonuses in addition to your regular salaries. Any slackers will pay penalties, mind you, so be forewarned!"

The audience stood up in unison, bowed to the supervisor, and slowly made their way out of the lecture hall in a huge crowd.

The bell rang once again. This being the bedtime bell, they all went to the toilet, returned to their rooms, and switched off the electric lights.

As she was tired, Kannan fell asleep for a while before rising in the middle of the night. Everything was completely still. All she could hear was the clamor of the machines coming from the factory floor. She went over to the window and wistfully stared outside. Just one day earlier she had been so excited, sitting there in front of Sinch'ŏl. But as she stood here alone now, thinking about all the work the future would hold for her, that future seemed awfully bleak. She knew of course that she had the support of more than enough comrades on the outside, but being locked up behind that jet-black wall made her feel terribly lonely. Outside her glass window there it stood—the wall encircling the athletic ground and soaring up so high into the air! Since the very minute she had entered the dormitory, that wall had been a source of deep concern for Kannan. And while she'd pinned her hopes on finding a hole at the base of it, the dark bricks had been stacked up extra-high at the top, and below them the surface of the wall had been cemented over with con-

216

crete to the height of several men. It seemed like an impenetrable sheet of iron—from here she couldn't see a single crack in it.

She got up quietly, opened the door, and came out into the corridor. At the other end of the hallway the moon cast a long beam of light through the window, making it look as though someone was actually standing there. Kannan froze in her tracks and quickly looked to either side. She heard the sound of a door opening, and pressed herself against the wall.

96

With bated breath Kannan looked in the direction of the creaking door. There seemed to be a single factory girl tiptoeing towards the room where the supervisor did night-duty. Drawn by a sudden curiosity, Kannan followed stealthily behind her.

The girl stopped in front of the duty room. She hesitated, then opened the door and went inside. Who could that be? wondered Kannan, but she didn't have the slightest clue. One thing was unmistakable—a factory girl had just entered the duty room for a tryst with the supervisor. Kannan remembered what Sinch'ŏl had told her the day before: it would only be a matter of time before many of the innocent young girls working in the factory would fall prey to the charms of the supervisors. She understood now why she had to open the eyes of these foolish girls as quickly as possible, and she truly felt a sense of responsibility for leading all one thousand girls into a collective fight for humane treatment and financial benefits. She remembered how, long ago, she had resigned herself to Tŏkho's immoral behavior. She broke into a cold sweat at the very thought of it. Having stood there lost in thought, she then tiptoed up to the duty room and put her ear to the door. She couldn't hear any voices. If it hadn't been for the importance of her own mission, oh, how she would have pounded on that door and made enough noise to turn this factory upside down in order to expose the truth to the other factory girls! Just then, the glass windows in the corridor started to rattle, and she saw the shadows of falling leaves floating downward. She quickly hid herself by running to the back door.

From the factory floor came the loud noise of the machinery. It was then that Kannan finally mustered the sort of do-or-die determination that was almost too much for her to bear. In a breath she had dashed outside, and began skirting the base of the wall in search of a hole. No matter how much she searched, however, her fingers felt nothing but cold bricks. Not even the tiniest of holes was she able to find. There were a few drainage vents at the base of the wall, but nothing else. She might be able to fit her hand through one of them, but of course a whole person would be unable to pass through. And since these vents were quite conspicuous to anyone's eye, it would be highly dangerous to make contact with somebody by means of them. On the other hand, it might very well be precisely these obvious vents that would be easy for others to overlook. After mulling it over for a while, Kannan decided to spend a few more days looking for an appropriate place, and then later come to a final decision. She made her way back inside, just as the clock in the lecture hall was striking three. When she slipped back under her covers, Sŏnbi rolled over onto her side.

"Did you go somewhere?"

"Yes. You're not asleep yet?"

"No, I fell asleep all right . . . But then I woke up and noticed you were gone."

"I just went the toilet."

"Oh."

"Sŏnbi. Did you believe everything the supervisor was saying earlier?"

Sŏnbi didn't know how she should answer under the circumstances, and she hesitated for a moment.

"Why are you asking me that all of a sudden?"

"I don't know . . . I was just wondering if what he said is really true."

"How am I supposed to know that . . ."

"Sŏnbi! You've got to make a point of knowing about it. Just think about it, here they are making us work, sometimes all through the night, and all they give us to eat is this imported rice. They're trying to pull the wool over our eyes with all this sweet talk about savings and bank accounts, but the fact is that they're just trying to make sure that we never see a single coin of our own money. They're only interested in getting as much work out of us as possible, even if it kills us. All this talk about protecting the girls' future by keeping them from going outside, and about distributing daily goods to us at discounted prices—I'm telling you it's in the interest of their profit margin alone that they're setting up all these regulations. And what about all this garbage about picnics and night school, and keeping our bodies fit by giving us a chance to exercise? I mean, it's complete nonsense, a total sham, meant to get as much out of us as possible . . ."

Sŏnbi couldn't understand why Kannan was going on like this. If she'd already known so much, well, they shouldn't have come to the factory in the first place. And, besides, they'd only just moved here from Seoul—why in the world was Kannan complaining like this when they'd hardly been there for a single day?

"Sŏnbi! I'm telling you, the supervisors who put us to work and all those people behind them—they're hundreds and thousands of times more frightening than Tŏkho."

Kannan wanted to tell Sŏnbi about the girl who had just snuck her way into the duty room, but she thought it better to wait a while before telling her too much. Sŏnbi herself had felt uneasy, even quite terrified of looking up at the tiger-like boss with that turned-up moustache, especially when he smiled at her with those ogling eyes. So when she heard Kannan mention him now, she could hardly keep the image of those his eyes out of her mind. She imagined the supervisor turning into Tŏkho, which almost plunged her into despair.

"Oh, Sŏnbi! You don't have the faintest idea what I'm talking about, do you? Well, you'll figure it out soon enough."

As Kannan spoke to Sŏnbi, she wrapped her arm around her waist and embraced her. Then she thought again about the girl who'd just snuck into the duty room.

97

Several days later Kannan tied a straw rope to the end of a long stick and pushed it through one of the drainage vents at the base of the wall behind the factory.

From then on, whenever the girls woke up in the morning, they found funny scraps of paper under their bedding and in the corners of their rooms. What the scraps of paper had scribbled on them, in easy-to-understand words, was a commentary on each point the supervisor had lectured on during night school the day before.

Each time they found a scrap of paper, the girls huddled together and read over it with delight.

"Girls, I don't know who put this note in here, but it sure does make sense! If the supervisor said that he was going to give out twenty chŏn a day in bonuses, why is it that no one's gotten any yet? That's nothing but lip service!" These were the words of one of the factory girls lying in bed in Room No. 4 on the top floor of the dormitory.

"That's right. I mean, Hyeyŏng is really good at her job, right? But from what I hear, she's never even once gotten a bonus . . . Why do you think they're telling us all these lies?"

"You know that new girl over in Room No. 7, the real pretty one? I heard she got a bonus alright."

"Someone actually got one?" asked another girl who was always laughing. "Who?"

"Shhh, someone will hear! Speak softer, will you?"

The girl who was always laughing giggled, stuck her hand beneath the covers, and poked the girl next to her.

"Who's going to hear us at this time of night?"

"Think about it! The supervisor makes rounds every night. Didn't you know that?"

"Oh, who cares if he make his rounds! How could anyone outside hear what we say under the covers? Anyway, who is this girl? Do you mean the cute one who just got here?

In the dormitory they always called Sŏnbi the cute one.

"Hey, so listen. Hyeyŏng was just telling me something. . . You know the new girl who sits just opposite of her? Well, Hyesŏng says the supervisor keeps standing right in front of her with a big smile on his face! Can you imagine? I can't stand the sight of him! He used to do the same thing to Yongnyŏ too, didn't he?"

"Hmph! Well, this new girl is much prettier than Yongnyŏ. She's really beautiful! If I was a man, I'd fall head over heels for her. Those eyes, and that nose—just take a good look at her sometime."

"Oh, what's so pretty about her? Have you seen her hands? I get the creeps just looking at them," chimed in a girl who was hard of hearing.

"Hey, deaf ears! You actually heard something . . . Hee-hee. . .Well, look at these hands here!" The laughing girl grabbed the hands of the girl hard of hearing. She'd been listening to them with her hands cupped behind her ears.

"Oh, stop laughing. I don't see what's so funny," said another girl, lying between them, who now put her hand over the mouth of the girl always laughing.

220

"Okay, Hyosun. Who do you think is leaving these notes in our room? They might have notes in other rooms, too, for all we know . . . I'll bet one of the girls here in the dorm is behind it all. In fact, I'm sure of it. In any case, what if all the factory girls got together like these notes say to do, and then . . ."

The girl who was hard of hearing went as far as this, but then seemed to be overcome with emotion. She pushed her bedding a bit and tried to catch her breath.

"Oh, don't start with that again. I used to work in a caramel factory in Seoul, you know, and our damn supervisor treated us cruelly, and hardly ever gave us our wages. So they tried to organize us all to strike, right? But some of the girls switched sides and ratted on us to the supervisor. And then what happened? He kicked almost everyone out of the factory. Somehow I was lucky and didn't get fired, but I hated that guy so much I couldn't stand it any longer, and got out. That's just how it is."

"Well, it's those snitches we've got to get rid of! You know the whole bunch of them are sleeping with the supers anyway . . ."

"Think about it. Here they are working us to death, and we don't even get to hold onto our own money. I mean, just look at us now! Our parents spoiled us as kids so so we could end up like this? I came within an inch of getting my hand ripped off by one of those reels today. Before we got here, who'd ever have dreamt it would be this bad?"

She put her hand to her cheek and then shuddered. She could almost see all the reels, still spinning furiously, in front of her.

"I wish I could talk to the person who planted these notes here! How about we keep watch?"

"Yeah, but what happens if it turns out to be some man we don't know?"

All of a sudden they felt a sense of shame and horror that sent a tingle across their breasts.

"Oh, now I'm scared!"

Instinctively they snuggled closer into each other's arms.

98

The workmen were shoveling stones into iron-mesh bags to build an embankment into the middle of the sea, while on the opposite side of it others were carrying dirt to dump into the marsh land. Ch'ŏtchae, too, mingled among them, carrying a load of dirt on his back. As he worked, he thought about his discussion with Sinch'ŏl the previous night, when they'd talked about organizing the day laborers.

Ever since meeting Sinch'ŏl, Ch'ŏtchae felt that there was nothing anymore that he didn't understand about the world. Everything that had puzzled him, immobilized him for half his lifetime, he could now understand clearly, as clearly as he saw this newly built road spread out before him. Even the path his life would take in the future now seemed as clear and as smooth as the newly built road. His once heavy heart was filled with a hope as bright as the sunshine that shone off the sea.

"Hey, man, take a look at that! Today must be a holiday, with all those students out here!"

Ch'ŏtchae quickly looked back. Several hundred schoolgirls were walking toward them in a single file. He then remembered what Sinch'ŏl had told him the day before, after getting the report from the Taedong Spinning Mill. Maybe they're actually factory girls. They'd been given new shoes to wear for some outing to a shrine, hadn't they? he remembered, as he plodded off once again.

"All right, get back to work. And stop staring!"

Startled by the voice of their foreman, the workmen stooped over again to carry their loads.

"Holy shit! They're all chicks."

"Well, why don't you go fetch one for yourself and run off with her." One of them laughed out loud.

The men shot glances at each other and joked around as they caught sight of the passing procession. The girls were dressed alike in black skirts and white blouses, and they even had black shoes. As Ch'ŏtchae made his way along, groaning under the burden of his load of dirt, he kept looking over at the procession with an indescribable pleasure, and wondering if they might really be factory girls. Then Ch'ŏtchae's eyes met with those of one of the girls. He staggered back in surprise.

"Sŏnbi?"

The woman he was staring at shot him a look of surprise. She froze in her tracks before slowly walking forward again, swept along by the others in line. Ch'ŏtchae wanted to throw off his load of dirt and follow her in order to find out if she was really Sŏnbi. It had been so long since he'd seen her, he couldn't be quite sure. Before he was even conscious of it, his feet had taken several steps in her direction.

222

"Hey, you! Get the hell back to work!"

Ch'ŏtchae tried his best to hold back the unbearable sadness rising within him, and when he looked back at his boss, he could feel his heart pounding. Slowly he retraced his steps. Sŏnbi? But how could she have gotten here? Did Tŏkho send her to school? But why would he do that? And who knows what could have happened to her? She's so pretty, maybe sending her to school is Tŏkho's way of getting her to like him. No, that can't be it! I mean, but hell, what else could it be? She's got to be married by now anyway . . . With this, Ch'ŏtchae took another look over at the girls. He remembered what Sinch'ŏl had told him last night, and realized that, indeed, these must be the factory girls from the spinning mill. Maybe Sŏnbi was working at the mill! All sorts of thoughts now raced through Ch'ŏtchae's mind. He made his way to the marsh land, dumped his dirt, and when he looked up again, the procession of girls, now just a line of black dots in the distance, was disappearing into the gateway to Wŏlmido. Sŏnbi? A factory girl? Could they really all be factory girls? Well, let's just wait and see! They might pass by again on their way back, for all I know . . . Judging from the way they were dressed, they hadn't seemed a bit like factory girls to Ch'ŏtchae.

As he gazed out at the red roof of the salt bath on Wŏlmido, in plain view on the other side of the marsh, two questions kept circling his mind. Were they factory girls? And was that really Sŏnbi? He kept his eyes peeled just in case the procession passed by again on the way back.

"Hey, man, snap out of it. You see a few factory girls and you get that worked up?"

"Factory girls? Do you know for sure they're factory girls?"

"What, are you crazy? Of course they're factory girls. What the hell else are they?"

"So they're not students going to school?"

"Hell, man! You have your head in the clouds? Known throughout all of Inch'ŏn for his treachery, the tiger boss with the twisted moustache—he just passed by, and you missed him?"

Ch'ŏtchae listened to the man, then he looked over at Wŏlmido once again. Factory girls . . . Now that he knew they were factory girls, he was certain that the woman who'd caught his attention was indeed Sŏnbi.

"Shit, you're smitten, aren't ya? Hah, ha . . . But you need some of this, you know."

His buddy made the sign of a coin with his fingers. As Ch'ŏtchae strapped his load of dirt onto his back and then rose to his feet with a grunt, he looked into the distance at the smokestack of the Taedong Spinning Mill. From the top of it, as always, streamed out puff after puff of thick, black smoke.

99

That smokestack! Rising up into the air as though it was about to pierce the sky . . . Staring at it was enough to make Ch'ŏtchae feel dizzy. He had worked there almost every day as a laborer while the mill was being built. When they'd put up the main building of the factory itself, he hadn't thought the work very dangerous. But as he recalled carrying up all those bricks to construct the smokestack, he felt dizzy even now, and everything seemed to spin in a circle around him.

Making his way up those rickety wooden ramps with three dozen bricks on his back, he'd been in a constant state of fear that the planks might collapse. When he looked down to the ground hundreds of feet below him, he felt like he was staring into a deep pool that was spinning round and round. He could feel his legs trembling beneath him and every hair on his head stood up on end. And even after he managed to pull himself together, he had only to start climbing once again to feel the smokestack swaying back and forth. Perhaps it was simply an effect of the perceived danger, but the higher up the smokestack he climbed, the more clearly he could actually see it sway. And each time he thought he saw it move, he was convinced that it was on the verge of collapse, and that he, too, was going to tumble to his death.

Knowing full well the danger involved, Ch'ŏtchae never failed to climb up that wooden path each morning. And each time he did, he'd think, Oh, no, I've done it again!

As Ch'ŏtchae recalled climbing the stairs, he froze in his tracks without realizing it—it was as though he had just climbed to the top of the smokestack. The dirt on his back felt the same as a load of bricks, and the sweat streamed down his lower back. His arms and legs started to tremble, and only after taking a good look around him and closing his eyes for a moment did he finally manage to bring himself to his senses. He realized that he'd probably never be able to get this smokestack out of his mind, not until the day he died. Oh, that terrifying smokestack!

224

He was so sick and tired of seeing it in his dreams. He couldn't count the number of times he'd had nightmares of falling from the top of it. How many of my friends have fallen to their deaths! How many of us have given our lives to these people—have no other choice but to wager our very lives for the sake of a single day's pay!

Ch'ŏtchae's thoughts drifted again to the factory girls, and to Sŏnbi. He'd had a picture of Sŏnbi in his head all day long. He made it back to the streets of Inch'ŏn quite late after he'd finished work. By the time he entered the soup shop, his buddies were already back from the labor market, eating their meals and drinking *makkŏlli* as they whiled away their time joking amongst themselves. Nothing was more comforting than this soup shop for these men. It gave them the chance to hang out with friends with a good buzz off the rice wine.

Ch'ŏtchae had a cup of *makkŏlli* and then downed a bubbling hot bowl of soup almost in a single gulp. He stole a few glances around the room, very carefully, so as to escape any notice. Ever since he met Sinch'ŏl, he always worried that there might be a spy or two lurking in these places where so many people gathered. Outside, the same sort of thought would invariably cross his mind when he saw a man in a suit or someone particularly well dressed. In any case, it had come to the point where, besides Sinch'ŏl and a few buddies of his who worked at the docks, Ch'ŏtchae looked at almost everyone with suspicion.

Only after checking out the shop for a while did he feel enough at ease to enter the inner room. He wanted to sleep a while in the heated room that was available to the shop's clients before heading back to his own place. It was boiling hot inside the room, and the stench of booze was almost as thick as smoke. He went to the warmest part of the floor and found a wooden pillow to rest his head on, but as soon as he lay down, that long line of factory girls came into his mind, followed by an image of Sŏnbi. Just then, he heard one of his buddies come in from outside shouting.

"Just look at him! Already dead asleep, are ya? Come on, wake up!"

Ch'ŏtchae opened his eyes, but only when his friend kicked him in the backside.

"What the hell! Just leave me alone, will you? I'm trying to get some sleep."

His friend was drunk and staggering, and now he scowled at Ch'ŏtchae.

"What's your problem anyway, man? Not paying for drinks any-more . . . How much you make today, anyway? Just buy me one drink, will ya? Hand over some money, man, mon-ey!"

His head swayed from side to side, and he finally collapsed to the ground. The sand caught in the folds of his clothes poured out onto the floor.

"Ha, ha . . . Oh, man! Those factory chicks sure are something . . . all those girls . . . they're killing me! Hah, ha . . .

Oh, dong-dong, one autumn night
The moon, dong-dong, is shining bright
Of my love, dong-dong, my thoughts
Way up there, dung-dung, are caught

Fall is here, my boy, and the moon is shinin'. Now, don't tell me you ain't got no girl! Hah, ha . . . Or wait, you aren't hitched yet, are ya?"

100

Ch'ŏtchae stared at him without a word in reply. His friend's eyes were red and seemed to glimmer at the mention of the opposite sex. Ch'ŏtchae imagined Sŏnbi for a moment but then felt something he wasn't used to feeling. His heart was now racing, and he jumped to his feet despite himself. His friend stared at him as he got up to go.

"Hey, man. Why won't you answer me?"

Instead of replying, Ch'ŏtchae smiled and made his way out to the kitchen. The woman running the place had been busy working her way around the kitchen when she happened to notice Ch'ŏtchae coming out.

"Mister, you owe me money today."

Ch'ŏtchae stopped. "How much altogether?"

"Well . . . fifty chŏn." She turned up a face with flat features as she softly studied the expression on his. The tables just behind them were still surrounded by workers slurping away at their soup.

"Here, take thirty for now."

"You're coming back tomorrow?"

"We'll see. I'll get you your money, sooner or later."

"Yes, well . . ."

226

The soup lady clearly wanted her remaining twenty chŏn now, but Ch'ŏtchae ignored her and called out to his friend, who was also getting up to go.

"You're drunk, man. Just lay down and sleep it off."

"You mean you're not going to buy me a drink?"

"Some other time, I promise. Today I'm flat broke."

"Broke? Oh, come on."

His friend kept clinging to him, but Ch'ŏtchae finally managed to drive him off and make his way outside. Would men like him ever develop a class consciousness? Ch'ŏtchae wondered. Before he'd met Sinch'ŏl, he himself had bought alchohol the very instant any money fell into his hands. When he wasn't drunk, his mind always felt clouded and his feelings boxed-in, which he found unbearable. The others had hard lives, too, but they had women and children at home, and after a day's work they had the comfort of hearing: "Daddy's home!" or "Honey, go get some rice with that money." But Ch'ŏtchae had no one to share his feelings with, and when he got home all he could do was stare at the wall. It was no wonder he used to get angry with himself and rush to the tavern. But now that he had met Sinch'ŏl, Ch'ŏtchae had given up both smoke and the bottle. He tried to avoid all the idle chatter, and was more likely to be found retreating into his own mind, even though his friends gave him a hard time. "Hey man," they'd joke. "What's the matter with you? Did some girl make you go dry?"

Ch'ŏtchae walked slowly down the street, ever aware of his immediate surroundings. For fear that a spy might be following him, he paid careful attention to each alleyway as he made his way back to his landlord's house.

Without a single light turned on to greet him, Ch'ŏtchae's room seemed rather lonely. And tonight, for some reason, he felt confined in this room and particularly bored, so he toyed with the idea of going out to see Sinch'ŏl. He figured that Sinch'ŏl probably wasn't at home, though, so he simply sat down and leaned against the wall. He always went to bed without lighting a lamp. Because he had grown up in dark rooms as a child, he truly enjoyed sitting in the dark like this. And if for some reason he did have to turn on a light, he would grow restless, and his eyes would start to sting—he hated it.

Oh, Sŏnbi! Was that really her? Maybe she's even seen the notes that I deliver there every day. But then again, can she even read? Not likely! They did say there's a night school in the factory, though, didn't they? Who knows, maybe she has learned the Korean alphabet . . . As these thoughts now raced through his mind, so too came another—he should learn how to read too. There had to be some place they'd teach him! Maybe he could even ask Sinch'ŏl. This thought made Ch'ŏtchae break out into a smile. That a full-grown man going on thirty should repeat the letters of the alphabet in front of Sinch'ŏl seemed quite silly. And more than that, he didn't have the need for it or the time to spare.

Ch'ŏtchae slept soundly for some time, and then gently rose out of bed. He felt completely reenergized. As he opened the door and quietly made his way outside, the clock in the neighbor's house struck two. Like clockwork, he always walked out of the gate at two a.m.

The usually lively streets of Inch'ŏn had come to a complete standstill, and only the occasional light from a lantern flickered here and there in the darkness. He stood outside his gate for some time, carefully taking in his surroundings, when suddenly he felt a rush of emotion and was struck with an indescribable sense of excitement. He heard the faint sound of a foghorn from a steamship far off in the distance, softly echoing through the city streets. He set off without letting his guard down for even an instant. When he finally made it to Sinch'ŏl's boarding house, Sinch'ŏl gave him a hearty welcome and invited him inside. Ch'ŏtchae could tell that Sinch'ŏl had just gotten home after finishing his work. He could see the exhausted look in his narrowed eyes. Sinch'ŏl rubbed his eyes and took a good look at Ch'ŏtchae. There was a flicker of anxiety in Ch'ŏtchae's darkened face, but there was also a certain dignity to it, something more courageous that glowed.

101

Back when Sinch'ŏl had first met Ch'ŏtchae, he had thought of him as nothing more than a simple, honest worker—or rather, Ch'ŏtchae had been so unbelievably naïve that Sinch'ŏl had taken him for something of a fool. Yet in the course of only a few months, Ch'ŏtchae seemed like a completely different person. When Sinch'ŏl sat face to face with him, as he was doing now, he even found himself feeling somewhat intimidated.

"You'll have to be careful, my friend," he said to Ch'ŏtchae. It seems the police have begun a crack down by following the trail of our leaflets—so you've got to be extra cautious."

Ch'ŏtchae had been staring straight at Sinch'ŏl with wide-open eyes, but now he shifted his gaze to the ground. It seemed as though they both might be arrested before long. He hoped that only the uneducated people like him would be arrested, those unable to take on the more important roles. If by any chance important figures like Sinch'ŏl were captured, the future looked quite bleak for the laborers in Inch'ŏn, who were only just on the point of coming into class consciousness. If Ch'ŏtchae or the other laborers were arrested, they would most likely be able to put up with the beatings—no matter how bad they were. But could Sinch'ŏl and the others? With such soft, white flesh? This worried Ch'ŏtchae more than anything.

Whenever Sinch'ŏl sat face to face with Ch'ŏtchae, whenever he had an important mission for him to carry out, he always phrased it like this: "This is what we've got to do"—the we meaning we, the workers. Yet the way Ch'ŏtchae saw things, Sinch'ŏl was the one person who seemed different from the others. Whenever Sinch'ŏl spoke to him, Ch'ŏtchae almost always felt a rush of emotion that was hard to describe: He's doing all this for our sake, working so hard to help us open our eyes . . .

"They've decided reports should be made once a month from now on, so why don't you come again on the fifteenth of next month? You've got to watch out, though, you understand? Stay on your guard around friends, and of course you know very well to stay away from anything like alcohol or women, so I won't say anything more about that . . ."

Sinch'ŏl tried to read the expression on Ch'ŏtchae's face. He sat there unflinchingly. On the one hand he seemed like a well-behaved ox, the very picture of loyalty, and yet on the other hand, there was something else, something unwavering about him that ran much deeper. Sinch'ŏl could see it there in him.

"Well then! Time for you to go!"

Sinch'ŏl got up and Ch'ŏtchae followed him outside. With a quick but firm gesture, Sinch'ŏl placed a sheaf of manifestos into his hands.

"Be careful now!"

Ch'ŏtchae took the pamphlets and shoved them down his pants. Then he shook Sinch'ŏl's hand firmly. He pulled down his hunting cap over his brow and headed out the main gate.

His nerves were on edge now because of what Sinch'ŏl had told him. His concentration was such that he'd become all eyes and ears. And by the time he finally arrived at the Taedong Spinning Mill his heart was

229

racing. First, he made a loop around the compound. Someone might have come to spy on him, he feared, so he kept his eyes peeled for anything that looked suspicious. He could hear the clamor of the factory generators. Out of that black smokestack rising into the sky came a stream of smoke, turned white now in the light of the moon.

He made his way back into the alley. There wasn't a trace of human life in sight—everything was completely still. This time he slowly emerged from the shadows and headed straight for the northeast corner of the factory compound, where he pressed himself up against the wall. He pulled the pamphlets out of his pants, quickly shoved them into the drainage pipe, and then turned around to go. Breathlessly, he dashed to the corner of the house opposite him, but his eyes were still fixed on the pipe. Again he saw that long line of factory girls in his mind and, then in the midst of them all, Sŏnbi. Oh, Sŏnbi! he cried silently, almost despite himself. Was that really you? Could you really be spinning thread in there now? Or maybe sleeping? It seemed like she was looking straight into my eyes . . . But had she even recognized me?

He hoped Sŏnbi was reading all those notes he'd been leaving in the factory. He wanted so much for her to be smart, not just pretty and gentle, like the old Sŏnbi used to be. If only she took that one step forward and became a strong, committed woman. That was the only way he'd ever be able to trust her and to walk with her side by side.

All human beings, after all, had to make a point of understanding what class they belonged to, and furthermore, it was those who struggled for the historical development of human society who were, in the truest sense, human beings—this is what Sinch'ŏl had told him.

102

Having finished night class and returned to Room No. 3, Sŏnbi lay down on her bedding before she'd even taken off her clothes. Back when she was in Room No. 7 with Kannan, they used to snuggle under the covers as soon as night school was over, and talk late into the night. But now that Sŏnbi had been moved, she felt like a guest in someone else's house, and she was never really comfortable—perhaps because she wasn't very close to her new roommates. What was that idiot of a supervisor thinking anyway? That she was going to give him favors if he moved her in here? There was something fishy about the move, to be sure. Maybe Kannan was right, and he was just trying to keep a better eye on her. But maybe I'm right, thought Sŏnbi, and the fool has actually fallen for me.

Along with these thoughts, an image of Ch'ŏtchae's face appeared in her mind's eye. It was on the way to Wŏlmido, on that cobblestone street on the wharf—they'd actually stared right into each other's eyes. But had that really been Ch'ŏtchae?

Having caught this glimpse of him so unexpectedly, Sŏnbi couldn't help but think about Ch'ŏtchae at night. She remembered the time when she'd climbed up the hill to collect wild herbs, and Ch'ŏtchae had stolen some of her sourstem, and she had run back down the hill in tears. And then there was the time when her mother was sick—the day when at the crack of dawn he'd brought them sumac roots! She knew she'd failed to appreciate what he'd tried to do for her. What a precious gift those sumac roots seemed to her now, and how grateful she felt for them! Proof of Ch'ŏtchae's sincerity, his pure heart, had been right there in those freshly dug roots still moist with soil, and yet at the time she'd completely failed to see it. What had she done with those roots? Roots he had surely spent all night digging? Roots that no doubt symbolized his true feelings? What she should have been grateful for she had tossed into the back corner! The more she thought about it, the more angry, the more ashamed she felt about her behavior.

Oh, if only just once! Was it really impossible for her to meet him again? Sŏnbi rolled onto her side and let out a deep sigh. She felt the warmth of her breath coming back into her face. But this triggered yet a different memory: of Tŏkho breathing heavily whenever he grabbed her. She shuddered at the thought of it. She had lost something now, it seemed, something without which she'd never be able to meet Ch'ŏtchae again. She felt absolutely helpless and horribly ashamed. The chastity she had guarded for twenty years had been stolen from her by that pumpkin-faced old Tŏkho, and the more she thought about it, the more enraged she became. She'd been so traumatized at the time that she hadn't even had the wherewithal to get upset about it. But as she lay in bed and pondered it now, she knew that Tŏkho had ruined her life forever, and her face flushed with shame. She tried to paint a picture of Ch'ŏtchae's face in her mind. Judging from his expression the other day, he'd seemed quite surprised to see her, which must have meant that he had recognized her. Even though their eyes had met for only the briefest instant, Sŏnbi could tell that Ch'ŏtchae hadn't forgotten her. Somewhere, in some corner of his mind, he had kept a memory of her alive.

Perhaps his eyes had lit up the way they did because Sŏnbi herself had stared at him with such excitement. In any event, it seemed certain that Ch'ŏtchae had recognized her. Sŏnbi had felt such a rush of emotions, first of sadness and then of joy, that her heart had simply trembled under their sway. She didn't ever want to leave Ch'ŏtchae's sight. And yet people had backed up behind her, and were pressing her on. Like a flash of lightning their paths had crossed, and like a flash of lightning myriad memories had suddenly swept through her mind. She'd had no choice but to move on.

Ch'ŏtchae's body was so big and strong now, she could hardly recognize it, and with his features so rugged, it was only those sparkling eyes that she recognized for sure—eyes that had smiled at her so long ago, those of a boy chewing on a piece of stolen sourstem. In those eyes she could now see something troubled by the world, as well as something of their earlier innocence and vitality. But in the very pupils of his eyes she could also see a powerful, almost terrifying glow! And it was this, and this alone, she knew, that would free her from her hatred of Tŏkho.

Then she remembered something that Kannan was always telling her—that the world was full of enemies, people just like Tŏkho. If we want to stand up to them, we have to do it together. Somehow Sŏnbi felt suddenly empowered. Only by doing what Kannan had taught her could she ever imagine taking Ch'ŏtchae's hand into her own. That strong back of Ch'ŏtchae's that must have carried so many loads of dirt! Her own hands that were blistered from spinning so much thread! There was no other choice but to bring together all those backs and all those hands and to join together in a fight against all the Tŏkhos of the world. This was the only path Sŏnbi could now see before her.

"Ahem!" At the sound of someone coughing, Sŏnbi flinched.

103

Sŏnbi listened with bated breath. When she heard the cough again, she realized that it had come from the supervisor in the night duty room. There was nothing but a single wall separating her and the super as they lay there side by side—the very thought of this made her uncomfortable. Sŏnbi remembered what Kannan had told her about Yongnyŏ.

232

Sure enough, the supervisor had moved Sǒnbi into this room hoping to make her into his next Yongnyǒ, but she would never let him get his way with her. And if he ever did come after her and try to make a plaything out of her like Yongnyǒ, she thought, well, I'd make a complete fool out of him and then just get out of here. Aren't there other factories out there besides this one?

In spite of her determination to avoid Yongnyǒ's fate, Sǒnbi's mind was plagued by a sense of foreboding about her future, which was no little cause for distress. If only Kannan were still in the same room with her, she might have said something to comfort Sǒnbi at a time like this. She wanted to make contact with Kannan and to discuss a plan of action, so that they could take a stand against this supervisor who kept throwing himself onto the girls. For some time now she'd been wanting to talk with Kannan, but it hadn't been easy to find the chance. They were both busy all day long, and had to work the night shift every other day, and if ever they had a single moment to spare, they'd have to use it to sew their clothes. If she didn't take advantage of nights like these, months, even years, might pass by before she found even a minute to sit down face to face with Kannan.

And yet judging from the fact that the supervisor had just coughed, it seemed he hadn't yet fallen asleep. At the sound of a door opening he'd most likely come chasing after her. Oh, to heck with it, I'll talk to her some other time! she thought. Why should it have to be today?

Then she heard a door open. Sǒnbi quickly looked at her door. It wasn't hers but rather, it seemed, the door to the supervisor's night-duty room. There was a sound of soft footsteps coming from outside. Sǒnbi flinched in fear that her body was in imminent danger. She pulled the blanket over her head and held her breath. She could hear the sound of footsteps no longer. But in her mind the supervisor was standing right outside her door, trying to guess whether the girls inside were sleeping or not. Sǒnbi's heart was racing a mile a minute for fear that he might any second now enter the room and force himself upon her. She was on the point of waking up her roommate, who was sleeping soundly beside her, oblivious to everything.

Sǒnbi slowly pulled down her blanket and tried listening for the sound of footsteps or the sound of a door. The girl next to her popped her head out of her blankets and looked at Sǒnbi.

"That was a door, wasn't it?"

Sŏnbi was so glad to hear that someone else was awake that she quickly moved closer to her, rustling her covers.

"You awake, too?

"Yes, whose door was that, anyway? It sounded like it came from the supervisor's room, didn't it?"

"It sure seems like it did."

The girl next to Sŏnbi put her lips up close to Sŏnbi's ear.

"This all just started a couple of days ago, you know . . . but the supervisor doesn't sleep at night any more. He actually goes out on patrol. Haven't you seen all those funny pieces of paper lying around recently?"

Sŏnbi feigned innocence.

"No . . . What kind of paper?"

"Well, I don't know about the other rooms, but when we wake up in the morning we've been finding these little notes scattered around the room. They have all sorts of stuff about the factory written on them. You know those shoes we all got when we went to Wŏlmido the other day?"

"Yes."

"Well, those shoes were . . . Look, I'll explain later."

After glancing over at the door, her roommate cut herself short. But since Sŏnbi had already heard the story from Kannan, she didn't press her any further. Besides, she feared the supervisor might have overheard what they were saying, and her heart was now practically in her throat. Thank goodness she'd stopped! But so many of the factory girls were now caught up in the mystery of those little paper notes that Sŏnbi knew for sure that it had to be Kannan who'd somehow managed to spread them around. Even though she had never mentioned them to her before, judging from her words and behavior she could tell that the mystery person had to be Kannan. And there were certainly others involved on the inside as well. Kannan wasn't normally someone to keep any secrets from her, but she was almost certain that on this matter Kannan was hiding something. Whatever it was all about, and whoever was directing things behind the scenes, wasn't quite clear to Sŏnbi, whose initial suspicions were only gradually taking shape into a better sense of what was going on. Sŏnbi wasn't yet ready to confirm her guesswork however—she hadn't quite pieced everything together.

Then, without warning, the door quietly swung open, and the beam of a flashlight streamed into the room.

234

104

They quickly pulled their bedding over their heads and pretended to be asleep. The door closed again softly and the sound of footsteps grew closer. Sŏnbi had her hands clutched tight against her chest and her head buried beneath her pillow. She was holding her breath, but her heart was pounding wildly. She couldn't help thinking that he'd actually heard what they were saying from the other side of the door, and was now coming after them to give them a piece of his mind.

A moment later, Sŏnbi felt the supervisor's hand touch her bedding, and instantly the blanket was ripped off of her. She recoiled in fear, her chin pulled in close to her chest.

"Why aren't you girls asleep?"

The supervisor's terrifying voice echoed in the room. Sŏnbi gave not a word in reply.

"How do you expect to get your work done tomorrow without a good night's sleep, huh?"

The supervisor quickly stretched out his hand and touched her face, but Sŏnbi instinctively pushed it away from her. Then she grabbed her covers and pulled them back over her.

"Tell me, have you found any notes scattered around this room? You hand them over to me, if you do, you hear?"

This time he tapped Sŏnbi on the head a couple of times. If Sŏnbi had thought her roommate beside her was asleep, she would have surely been scared out of her wits, but she knew full well that the girl was wide awake, which made it a little less scary. It was still horribly embarrassing, however, to know that the girl next to her had seen the supervisor stroke her cheek like that and then tap her on the head. What she really wanted to do was to stand right up and sock him in the face. But as it was, she could hardly bring herself to wiggle her finger. Just then Sŏnbi had a flashback to the moment when Tŏkho had stolen her virginity, and she started to tremble.

After standing there idly for some time, the supervisor gave her blankets a tug and covered her up completely.

"Now, stop all this nonsense and get back to sleep."

With this, the supervisor turned around and left the room. Sŏnbi let out her breath, laid her head on her pillow and stretched out again more comfortably. But that spot where the super's hand had touched her face felt like an insect still crawling on her. For a long time the unpleasant feeling wouldn't go away.

Several days later, Sŏnbi was called into the supervisor's office. Sitting at his desk, the man was examining one of the little manifestos. He glanced up at Sŏnbi.

"Take a seat right there . . ."

He pointed to a chair beside his desk. Sŏnbi hesitated.

"You've got some of these too, don't you, Sŏnbi?"

The supervisor was staring at her unblinkingly, as though staring straight into her soul. Sŏnbi's face went a deep red.

"No, I don't."

"What do you mean you don't? Don't lie to me, Sŏnbi. There's not a room in this dormitory where these notes haven't been found, so how am I supposed to believe you don't have any? Tell me the truth."

Her head down, Sŏnbi thought about the notes that she had stuffed deep into her socks. Was he asking her these questions because he'd seen her put them there? She panicked.

"Now, come over here."

The supervisor drew his hand through his combed back hair and then moved his chair a little closer.

"Listen. If you have any of these notes, you need to rip them right up and forget everything written on them. You're the only one I can really be sure of, Sŏnbi, so quiet and gentle, ha, ha . . . Anyway, you know that girl Kannan, the one who comes from the same village as you do? You haven't by any chance seen her going out at night, have you?"

This question took Sŏnbi by surprise. How could the supervisor, she wondered, actually suspect something that she herself, who had roomed with Kannan, wasn't even sure of? But Kannan might very well end up being kicked out because of these notes, so she thought it worthwhile to try to dispel the supervisor's suspicions. Since the supervisor held her in his good graces, it was probably still possible to defend Kannan, so long as he had no explicit evidence against her.

"She'd never do anything like that," replied Sŏnbi, mustering all her courage.

A smile drifted across the supervisor's lips, and he moved back a little in his chair.

"You're both from the same village, so I know you're trying to protect her . . . Now, sit down! You hear me?"

236

Her whole body was clenched as tight as a fist. Ever so slightly she backed away from him. The supervisor glanced probingly into Sŏnbi's eyes and took a drag on his cigarette.

"How old are you, Sŏnbi?"

The man tapped away the ashes from his cigarette. Sŏnbi felt an unbearable tightness in her chest: she just wanted to get out of there.

105

Seeing how Sŏnbi was fidgeting, the supervisor took on a slight air of authority.

"Now, what did I say? Just sit down, will you? I've got plenty to ask you. Right there . . ."

He pointed to the chair. Sŏnbi was at a loss as to what to do. She felt an imminent sense of danger pressing upon her, and she knew that somehow or other she simply had to get out of that room. She was finding it difficult to breathe, as though even the air in the room was closing in upon her. She remembered how Tŏkho had first raped her, and it became clear to her exactly what the supervisor was planning.

"I, um . . . I was actually in the middle of working on something, so I . . ."

"Working on something?"

The supervisor looked sideways at Sŏnbi's flushing cheeks and smiled suggestively.

"Yes, well, a jacket . . ."

"A jacket? You should try to make more money and pay someone else to do that. Hah, ha, ha . . . Now listen, Sŏnbi, I just want to make sure that you're not tempted by these notes into believing any lies. We've planned everything in this factory with the interests of our girls in mind, so I really don't see how anyone can take these notes seriously. I think it's ungrateful. Now, if you find any of these notes, Sŏnbi, I want you to bring them to me, okay? Will you do that for me?"

"Yes, I will," replied Sŏnbi promptly, happy to have him change the subject.

"Do you know who writes these notes and plants them around the dormitory? They're just a group of out-of-work idiots, jealous that we actually earn our own living. And Sŏnbi I just don't want you to get mixed up with these losers. So, I tell you what. You do what I say, and I'll give you a bonus every day of the week. I'll even make you a supervisor, so that you can boss around the factory girls as much as you want. How about that, huh? You could be my representative, so to speak. Know what I mean?"

The supervisor smiled as though satisfied with how he'd put it. Sŏnbi looked down at her feet.

"I think you're a great girl, Sŏnbi, so just do what I say and all this power is yours for the taking."

Sŏnbi could hardly wait for him to finish talking—but he kept going on and on with all this insincerity. As she stood there silently, it dawned on her that he didn't really have anything to say, and that he was just going to keep her there listening to the exact same things over and over again—until who knew when. Sŏnbi lifted her head.

"I should get back to my work now."

"Well, actually I uh . . ."

As she turned around to leave the room, he was still trying to stop her. But she pretended not to hear him, and finally made her way outside. When she came back to her own room, she found that Kannan was there. They heard the office door slam shut and the supervisor's footsteps going down the stairs. Happily, Kannan and her roommates heaved a sigh of relief and looked over at Sŏnbi, hoping she would fill them in. Sŏnbi was glad to have their attention, but she was also somewhat embarrassed.

"Hey, let's go work in my room," said Kannan after a while. She picked up the pieces of cloth they were working on and handed them to Sŏnbi one by one. Gathering them together, Sŏnbi followed her out of the room.

"Where'd everyone else go?" asked Sŏnbi, as she entered Kannan's room. Once inside, however, she thought, what a perfect chance!

"Well, where do you think? They all went off to work the night shift . . . Alright, Sŏnbi, so what did he say?"

Sŏnbi blushed, and then collected her thoughts for a moment.

"Okay, well, first of all he tells me to stay away from you. And then . . ."

Sŏnbi put her lips to Kannan's ear and then whispered into it for a while. Kannan nodded.

"Hmm, I suspected as much . . . Oh, Sŏnbi!" cried Kannan, the expression on her face suddenly grave.

238

Sŏnbi opened her eyes wide in concern, but Kannan couldn't bring herself to explain her sudden outburst. As Kannan looked up at Sŏnbi, it broke her heart to think that Sŏnbi hadn't become a trustworthy friend yet. If only Sŏnbi had a true class consciousness, she'd be able to accomplish so much. With just a little enticement, she thought, she'd have the supervisors eating out of the palm of her hand. Kannan had wanted to be able to entrust Sŏnbi with all of her important work, so that she might be able to leave the factory in case something urgent came up. And now Kannan had learned that she wouldn't be able to work in this factory for much longer, which made her sad. It was a moment of weakness that made her cry out Sŏnbi's name, hoping to tell her everything, but she knew that Sŏnbi still needed more time.

"What's the matter, Kannan? Come on, just tell me."

The rims of Kannan's eyes were red.

"Someday, okay, Sŏnbi? Someday!"

106

Inch'ŏn at dawn.

The crisp, fragrant air and the dark, blue-gray sky carried news in their silence of the spring to come.

Thousands of laborers had already gathered shoulder to shoulder on the wharf. They were gazing out to the eastern sky where morning was about to break, each one of them firm in their determination.

With his red bands in hand, Nickel-rims whipped his head this way and that, glaring at the laborers, as always, with those bulging eyes. On any other day the scene would have been an utter free-for-all, the workers vying with each other to get their hands on one of those red bands. But today, not a single one of them even blinked an eye as Nickel-rims paraded back and forth in front of them, showing off the red bands attached to his arms. Nickel-rims thought it strange and also somewhat frightening. He pretended not to notice, and called out to one of laborers with whom he was on friendly terms.

"Come over here! I've got a work band for you."

Just then the electric lights flickered out.

"I'm not going to work!"

Nickel-rims scratched his head and climbed onto the deck of a boat.

A steamship entered the harbor and docked itself against the wharf.

239

But the workers just stared at it without moving a muscle. Then several of them went into the office of the Land and Sea Transportation Cooperative with the intent of submitting a list of conditions they were demanding as representatives of the laborers. The workers stood there in formation, staring intently at the office.

The steamships in the harbor sat there, sending out puff after puff of smoke. The sailors lined up on their decks, staring at the unusual sight. Normally by this time the harbor looked like a swarm of bees with all those men unloading the ships of cargo, but today it felt almost deserted. Even Nickel-rims, whose eyes were usually shifting faster than the spinning wheels of a wagon, today stood off in a corner, his head hung, like a bird with a broken wing.

The sun rose a brilliant red. And as the workers watched the sun rise, they learned how mighty a force their collective strength truly was. In their eyes the sun was casting forth its glorious rays to witness their solidarity. Those brilliant waves out at sea, glowing in the rays of sun, now seemed to cradle them in their embrace. Everything that caught their eyes appeared to them fresh and new. And they who had felt so powerless, who had known no glory, today at this very moment, held all the power, all the power to control the world. They had come together as one and succeeded—the broken-spirited Nickel-rims, the cranes on the steam ships, even all those sailors—everything and everyone else had lost the ability to move an inch.

"Hey, those factory girls over at the rice mill are a rough and rowdy bunch! They say all hell just broke loose over there. They took control of the siren and started getting violent."

The man talking turned to look at Ch'ŏtchae. Ch'ŏtchae looked at him and smiled.

"Well, the same thing goes here," the man continued. "If they don't come through for us and give us what we want, we sure as hell aren't going to just sit here!"

He made a tight fist and showed Ch'ŏtchae the fire in his eyes. Ch'ŏtchae looked back at him, his eyes narrowed in reply. But just then they saw off in the distance a throng of police in uniform rushing towards the wharf. Half of them surrounded the office of the Land and Sea Transportation Cooperative, and the other half ran up to the workers and set up a guard around the crowd. The very sight of the policemen sparked the flame of resistance within the men. But they were still

240

waiting for news from their friends inside the office, so whatever their frustration, they patiently waited it out.

The sharp-eyed policemen wove their way through the crowds, never letting down their guard for an instant in the hope of finding an agitator among them.

The citizens of Inch'ŏn poured into the side streets in order to catch a glimpse of the longshoremen and their newfound solidarity. An endless stream of policemen sped to the scene on motorbikes. Throughout the area surrounding the wharf, the air was thick with tension—everyone could sense it.

One by one steamships loaded with freight pressed into the harbor, but they just sat there idly. Then the laborers who had entered the Land and Sea Transportation Cooperative with their list of demands came back outside escorted by policemen.

"They haven't accepted our demands!"

"*Kaisan*! Clear out!"

Before the full report had even been delivered, this order to disperse came from a police officer standing in the street, a man with several golden stripes attached to his shoulder. A horrible sound of angry movement filled the air.

1 07

The crowd grew excited and tried to demonstrate through the streets of Inch'ŏn, but countless people ended up being arrested. When Ch'ŏtchae made it back to his house, his landlady came out to greet him.

"Somebody just stopped by to see you."

Ch'ŏtchae had been running and was short of breath.

"Who was it?" he asked, still winded. "What sort of clothes was he wearing?"

Was it a cop? Or was it maybe Sinch'ŏl? thought Ch'ŏtchae. The old woman smiled.

"Let's see. How was he dressed? Well, I don't quite remember ... But he did say that he'd come right back, and that you should stay here and wait for him ..."

"So he said to wait?"

Judging from recent developments, Ch'ŏtchae could only imagine the worst scenario, and a frown settled over his brow. Who was it, I

241

wonder? Maybe it was Sinch'ŏl with an urgent message. Just then his door swung open. Ch'ŏtchae looked over in alarm. It was a man he recognized from the docks, who he'd met a few times over at Sinch'ŏl's.

"My friend," said the man, entering his room. "Are you Ch'ŏtchae?"

Ch'ŏtchae was at a loss as to what was happening, and looked around the room nervously before answering.

"Well, yes . . ."

He shook the hand extended toward him.

"Something terrible has happened, my friend."

Ch'ŏtchae stared at him searchingly, wondering what he meant by this.

"Sinch'ŏl was arrested today, at about one o'clock this afternoon."

Ch'ŏtchae's eyes opened wide.

"Arrested? Where?"

"They got him at home, so now the whole area around his place is under tight surveillance. You're going to have to move too. I've found a place you can stay for the time being, but you'll have to move again soon to a more suitable house. Now, come on, we've got to move quickly."

He took a quick glance around the room and then stood up to go. But Ch'ŏtchae was still in shock from the news of Sinch'ŏl's arrest. Of course he knew that he had countless other friends besides Sinch'ŏl who were working behind the scenes, but having learned under Sinch'ŏl's guidance, Ch'ŏtchae felt like a child who'd lost his mother—no words could describe how heartbroken he felt. And now he'd been caught before we even finished our mission, thought Ch'ŏtchae, hanging his head. His new friend whispered something into his ear, then left the room. Ch'ŏtchae followed him with his things to the new house where he sat alone in an unfamiliar room, his heart pounding with each thought that raced through his mind.

The sun seemed to set in no time at all. Ch'ŏtchae lay down on the floor facing the ceiling. The scene of the dockworkers demonstrating kept coming to mind, and then he pictured Sinch'ŏl tied up with rope . . .*

---

*The words "censored" appear here in the original text, marking a deletion of unknown length.

After letting his mind wander like this, he looked around and found that night had already darkened the room. Suddenly the door was quietly opening. Ch'ŏtchae jumped to his feet.

"Why don't you have a light on in here?"

"Oh, it's you . . ."

Had it been anyone else but his friend, Ch'ŏtchae would have thrown himself on top of him. For some reason he felt he might be able to curtail his grief by wrestling it out of himself in a good brawl. But instead, he collapsed to the floor.

"What happened?" asked Ch'ŏtchae softly. "I mean, with the dockworkers?"

His friend turned on the light and then came to Ch'ŏtchae's side with the bread he had bought for him.

"Here, have some! We have other friends in charge of the longshoremen's strike, so just sit back and relax for a while!"

Ch'ŏtchae picked up the bread and took a big bite out of the loaf, nodding his head in reply. Each time their eyes met they felt a warmth of affection in the shared silence between them.

"Now, how about getting some sleep?"

His friend stood up. Ch'ŏtchae saw him off without a word of farewell, turned out the light, and then finished eating his bread. As he sat there in the darkness, Ch'ŏtchae imagined the future victory of the workers on the docks, and he smiled. Then he pictured the Taedong Spinning Mill in his mind's eye, and wondered why they hadn't joined the strike. That really got to him! His thoughts then turned to Sŏnbi once again. If only she could open her eyes to the truth . . . But then Ch'ŏtchae remembered that Sinch'ŏl had been arrested, and his chest tightened. He could feel the warmth rushing into his head.

108

Sŏnbi was on her way out of the factory, having just finished the nightshift, when she felt something being slipped into her hand. Looking up, she saw Kannan pass by with a strange look on her face. She closed her fist tightly as soon as she realized it was Kannan, for now she knew what was in her hand. She looked over to see if Hyoae, who was pushing through the crowd with her, had noticed. But as usual, Hyoae was going on about something or other in a voice far too soft to be heard.

"Um . . . um . . . I know," replied Sŏnbi, though she hadn't caught a word.

"Well, make sure you do it tomorrow, okay?" said Hyoae, entering her room.

Though Sŏnbi had no idea what Hyoae wanted her to do, she turned around to go without asking for clarification. She raced up the stairs and dashed into her room. Luckily none of her roommates had come back yet. Her heart racing, she unfolded the tiny piece of paper.

"Meet me in outhouse—1:00 tonight."

Afraid that someone might see the note, Sŏnbi popped it into her mouth and swallowed it. She could hear the clamor of footsteps making their way up the stairs. Sŏnbi was spreading out the bedding when the door opened and her roommates came inside.

"You're already here, Sŏnbi? Boy, are you fast!" said one of her roommates with a smile.

"Thanks for spreading out my bed, too!"

The third roommate looked at Sŏnbi as she plopped down onto the floor.

"Hey! How many reels did you spin today?"

This was the sort of question they all asked each other as they threw off their clothes and lay down to bed. Sŏnbi pretended not to hear them, however, and pulled the covers over her head—she kept thinking that Kannan must have received another message from someone on the outside. Then she remembered how the supervisor had stood in front of her all day while she worked, with that ear-to-ear smile fixed on his face. Oh, she could have just died! The nerve of him to stand in front of her like that all day long—how humiliating!

Sŏnbi had just dozed off when she heard the clock in the night duty room strike one. She jumped up in alarm. She picked up some pillows and placed them inside her bedding so that it looked like someone was still sleeping there, and snuck out the door. She opened the front door carefully so as not to make any noise, and made her way outside.

The bright electric light left on above the entrance to the dormitory exposed her whole body. Taken by surprise, Sŏnbi quickly fled into the darkness for cover. She scanned her surroundings, then hesitated for some time for fear that the supervisor might be out there somewhere. Nothing caught her eye, though, so she set out once again. When she made it to the outhouse, she found Kannan inside.

"Have you been waiting long?" asked Sŏnbi, as she stepped in. Kannan put her lips to Sŏnbi's ear.

"The supervisor just walked by a second ago."

Sŏnbi flinched, then slowly looked behind her for fear that he had followed her. She and Kannan sat facing each other, but didn't say anything for some time.

"I'm going outside to see if the coast is clear, but I'll be right back, so stay put," said Kannan.

Sŏnbi stood there, her ear bent toward the door. Soon Kannan came back inside.

"I just saw the supervisor go inside the dorm," gasped Kannan, completely out of breath. "Listen, Sŏnbi. On orders from the XX,* I am to hand over everything to you and leave the factory tonight!"

Kannan grasped Sŏnbi's hand tightly and stared straight into her face, lit up by the faint electric light in the outhouse. Sŏnbi was stunned by this unexpected news, and as she looked at Kannan, she could feel a heaviness descend upon her.

"But why so suddenly? Why tonight?"

Just then, something made a rustling sound outside. Their conversation broke off, and they both listened at the door. It was the sound of the wind, but the noise coming from the factory suddenly seemed louder as well.

"It's an urgent directive, Sŏnbi. It seems like something big has happened on the outside."

Sŏnbi's legs were trembling and her heart was beating with terrifying speed. Kannan had been like an older sister to her as well as her best friend, and now she was leaving her behind—the thought of it was far too depressing.

"Sŏnbi, we've got to fight to the very end—even if it kills us! You made a pledge, didn't you?"

Kannan's eyes were turning red now. She brought her cheek up against Sŏnbi's.

"Don't worry about me!" insisted Sŏnbi. Just take care of yourself once you're out there!"

---

*This common mark of censorship, whether inserted here by an editor or the writer herself, most likely is replacing the words 'Communist Party' or 'Party member'.

She gave Kannan a hug and Kannan wiped away Sŏnbi's tears.

"Sŏnbi! No matter what happens, you can't lose heart. You've got to fight, you hear? So none of this crying. Be strong, Sŏnbi. Now, come on, I have to go."

They made their way out of the outhouse.

109

Kannan and Sŏnbi crept to the base of the wall. Then Kannan pulled a rope out from her pants.

"I'm going to climb up on your shoulders, so keep steady. And I want you to hold tightly onto this rope."

A gust of wind swept by. They quickly looked behind them, thinking it was the sound of someone's footsteps. The wind blew again, though, gradually gathering more speed. While they were relieved to realize it was only the wind, they were now both short of breath and their hearts were racing. Each gust that blew still sounded like the supervisor making a mad dash towards them, or like a pair of hands about to grab them. A cold sweat poured down the small of their backs.

Sŏnbi crouched so Kannan could climb onto her shoulders; then Sŏnbi grabbed the wall and tried to get to her feet. It felt as though her collar bone was about to snap in half, and no matter how hard she pushed, she couldn't manage to stand up. Only after several failed attempts was she able, just barely, to get to her feet. Though her own legs were unsteady, Kannan somehow managed with great effort to stand up straight and grab the very top of the wall. But Kannan found it impossible to leap up off of Sŏnbi's shoulders. She put the rope between her teeth, and with both hands firmly gripping the top of the wall, tried to lift herself over it. But all her efforts were in vain. Her sweaty hands slipped and she almost lost her balance.

As Kannan tried again to push off from Sŏnbi's shoulders, Sŏnbi finally tumbled over backward to the ground. With a loud shriek, Kannan, too, came crashing down on top of her. Sŏnbi quickly helped Kannan get up and glanced behind her. Still, the only sound she heard was the wind, blowing fiercely. That wind seemed to be blowing for their sake alone.

"Now, when I get out, toss these shoes over for me, okay?"

Sŏnbi nodded and crouched on the ground again, this time with her hands against the wall. But just as soon as Kannan had climbed up onto Sŏnbi's shoulders and grabbed the top of the wall, she was startled by a whistling sound. With bated breath Kannan listened carefully to see if the sound was coming from inside the factory walls or from the outside. At first the whistling seemed to come from inside the factory wall, but then it seemed to be coming from the other side. But then again perhaps it was just the wind. Kannan still hadn't managed to pull herself over the wall, and now she was at a loss as to what she should do. Again a gust of spring wind blew with a terrifying force. She pressed her cheek tightly against the wall so as not to lose her balance, and she listened all the while, still trying to make out the whistling sound and where it had come from.

A moment later, more certain that what she had heard was the wind, Kannan tried again with all her might to hoist herself over the wall. She simply couldn't do it. She finally managed to rise off Sŏnbi's shoulders, but she couldn't get onto the top of the wall. Sŏnbi stood on her tiptoes and gave Kannan's feet a push from below. After struggling for more than an hour, Kannan finally scaled the wall. Sŏnbi then took a firm grip on the rope. She felt several tugs on it, and then saw Kannan disappear over the wall. Sŏnbi quickly tied the rope to the shoes and tossed them over. The rope disappeared into the darkness. Amidst the howling of the wind, she could hear the faint sound of something hitting the ground. Sŏnbi wiped the sweat off her brow and took a careful look around. She let out a deep sigh and pressed herself against the wall, anxious that Kannan might have hurt herself, and hoping to catch the sound of her footsteps running off into the distance. At the same time, Sŏnbi kept her eyes peeled for anyone lurking on this side of the wall who might have seen them. She could feel the warm wind blow against her flushed face, but she heard nothing except a faint sound coming from the factory. Yet she felt more afraid than ever, for getting back to her room would be no easy feat. She could almost feel the supervisor's eyes glaring at her from the darkness and she could almost hear the sound of his footsteps as she imagined him swaggering toward her. Only after clinging, weak-willed, to the wall for some time did she finally set off.

She made it back to her room without incident and lay down in her bed. When her cheek touched the fresh pillow, she was surprised to find tears rolling down her face. Though she'd made it back to her room safely and was back in her bed, each time the wind rattled the glass window she kept thinking someone might barge through the door any minute, screaming, You little bitches! You helped Kannan escape, didn't you? She could just imagine how he'd threaten them. At the same time, she thought of Kannan bracing herself against that terrifying wind. Where could she be rushing off to? she wondered.

"Oh, Kannan! Kannan!"

Sŏnbi cried out to Kannan several times in her heart. She couldn't help feeling that she'd never see Kannan again. Her work at the factory would be more difficult now. And there were still so many questions she wanted to ask Kannan.

110

The next morning it seemed as though something major had happened in the dormitory.

Rumor had it that all the girls who'd had anything to do with Kannan had been called in by their supervisors and been threatened, some even beaten. People were whispering to each other in each corner of the dormitory.

Sŏnbi was certain that the supervisor was going call her in, and all day long she could feel her heart racing. She couldn't concentrate on her work, and her threads kept breaking. All the girls who had been close to Kannan were called in by the supervisor, even the girls in the neighboring rooms. But for some reason no one called Sŏnbi. This made her even more nervous. The whole dorm knew that she and Kannan had been close friends—even the supervisors knew that much—so anyone would have thought that she'd be the first person to be questioned. But as the day drew to a close, she still had heard no word from any of the supervisors, and she thought it all so strange that she started to feel very scared.

"I say good for Kannan! What's the use of being in here anyway?"

"You can say that again. But only the devil knows how she did it."

"Who knows, maybe she fell in love with some man? Someone must have helped her escape, right . . . ?"

"Even if she had a boyfriend, though, how could she have climbed over a wall that high? And where would she have gone?"

Kannan had caused something of a sensation among the girls who discussed it as they ate in the cafeteria; they knew that even if the skies collapsed, they wouldn't be able to escape.

"Hey, Sŏnbi, I bet you know all the details. Kannan must have told you she was leaving. She did, didn't she?" It was the girl who was always joking.

Sŏnbi was afraid the girl had some way of knowing what had actually happened. Her faced flushed and she bent her head down. But after pretending to pick out a stone from her bowl of rice, she lifted her head up and smiled.

"Actually, just before Kannan escaped, she asked me to go with her. But since I like working here in the factory so much, I turned down her offer."

All of them burst into a peal of laughter.

"The truth is, I'd be the first one to pick up and leave this place if I ever had the chance, that's for sure. I mean, why should anyone have to put up with this?"

"Well, I heard from Kannan that she wasn't getting along with Sŏnbi any longer. You want to hear what she said?"

Speaking with her mouth full, a girl with thin eyelids looked Sŏnbi square in the face. While at one time Sŏnbi would have blushed to hear such a thing, she now felt quite pleased that the factory girls had come up with this interpretation.

"Well, d'you want to hear about it, or not?" said the thin-lidded girl with a grin.

"Look, if you want to say something, just come out and say it," exclaimed a long-faced girl. "Why try to torture us like this, reading into everything we say, when the most you're going to tell us is that the supervisor has the hots for Sŏnbi. Am I right? Well, why pretend it's such a big secret? Hell, the whole dorm knows that much."

The long-faced girl spoke as though she wasn't interested in the slightest, and she continued to stuff herself with rice. Sŏnbi felt uncomfortable hearing "the whole dorm knows," but her feelings were so confused that it would have been hard for her to explain herself. She forced herself to smile.

Once Sŏnbi came back upstairs from the cafeteria, the supervisor called to her from his office.

She could feel a lump in her throat. All the answers she'd spent the whole night preparing in case the supervisor were to question her seemed to disappear into thin air. She didn't know what to do and just stood there blankly.

"Well, if you haven't done anything wrong, then what's there to worry about," said one of her roommates beside her. Sŏnbi's legs were trembling.

Only after he called a second time did Sŏnbi get up to go. She made her way out of her room and rubbed her flushed face. She tried to calm herself, but her heart kept racing. She took one step forward, and then one step back.

"How will I ever be able to carry out my work here acting like this? I've got to be strong! I've got to make my lies sound convincing in front of them!" she thought. It was as though she were shouting these words to herself as she opened the door to the supervisor's office and walked inside.

The man took a drag on his cigarette, and smiled as soon he saw Sŏnbi. She stood silently, gathering all the courage she possibly could. He cleared his throat and started to speak.

111

"Have you been sick recently?"

At the unanticipated question, Sŏnbi was unsure if she understood what he'd actually said. When she lifted her head just enough to look at him, she saw that it wasn't the Tiger Supervisor, with those hatefully shifting eyes, but rather Supervisor Ko, the one they'd all nicknamed the Clown. Sŏnbi's nerves were put somewhat at ease. Ko had less of an attitude. He may have joked around a little too much, but he was always quick to sense somebody's feelings. For this reason the girls treated him more kindly than any of the other supervisors.

"Sŏnbi, you're looking a little pale. You should take better care of yourself."

Supervisor Ko cleared his throat loudly, then looked at Sŏnbi's down-cast face. Here was the girl that all his co-workers had been secretly feuding over! There was always something new about her beauty to appreciate. It was still up in the air whose hands she would fall into at the end of the day. His co-workers were all fiercely jealous of each other, and while none of them had yet gotten their way with this one, they were all trying as hard as they could to curry her favor. That was why each one of them enjoyed doing dormitory duty and regretted having to go home in the morning.

"Take a seat. Come on, sit down."

The Clown lifted up a chair and moved it over next to her. Sŏnbi sat down and smoothed out the folds in her skirt. She wanted him to get on with his questions about Kannan so she could answer them and get out of there. Whenever she found herself facing one of the supervisors she felt awkward, almost as though she were overcome by that same unpleasantness she felt when facing Tŏkho.

"So, Sŏnbi, you come from the same village as this girl Kannan who just escaped, don't you?"

"Yes."

"You don't happen to remember anything she might have said to you before she left, do you?"

Sŏnbi knew that the Clown was sharp, and assumed that he was asking her these questions in full knowledge of what had actually happened. The color rushed into her face. She set her wits to work to come up with an answer.

"Well . . . I wasn't paying much attention to what she said, so I don't really remember."

The Clown blinked his eyes several times.

"It doesn't have to be anything important . . . Let's say, for example, maybe she was complaining about how hard the work was in the factory, or how one of the supervisors was treating her badly?"

"I don't really remember."

"Hmm."

Staring at Sŏnbi's apple-colored cheeks, the Clown could hardly control himself. He felt hot all over: Damn, she's . . . He wanted to jump forward right now and sweep her in his arms. But he was afraid that if any one of his co-workers found out about it, he'd be reported to his superiors, which meant his own job might be on the line.

"Well, what do you think about Kannan leaving like that?"

Judging from how well-behaved she normally was, the Clown had no real suspicions about her. Besides, they were sleeping in separate rooms, so she probably didn't know anything about it, he figured. He'd called her in and was asking her all these questions, for no other reason than to sit down with her face to face. He watched her expressions carefully in order to gauge exactly how friendly she was toward him.

"I believe her conduct was immoral."

Sŏnbi just barely came out with these words that her heart did not own. The supervisor smiled at her.

"Well! Of course her conduct was immoral. No factory girl could get out of here on her own. She must have planned her escape with a man. And where could she have gone all alone, anyway? Did Supervisor Yi by any chance mention something to you?"

Judging from this, it seemed as though the supervisors were becoming suspicious of each other.

"Well, did he?" he pressed her.

Sŏnbi put her hand up to her mouth and coughed softly. Then she let out a soft sigh of relief, now that she was confident the supervisor wasn't suspicious of her.

"Why won't you answer me? Now, tell me, did he say anything to you?"

"Yes!"

"Oh, come on, you keep saying yes, yes, yes, without thinking about what I'm actually asking you. Now, tell me, did he ask you anything about all this?"

That pest, Supervisor Yi, had sure enough called her in several days ago and asked her something or other about Kannan, but since Supervisor Ko was pretending he didn't know this, Sŏnbi now wondered whether he had already compared notes with Supervisor Yi. Just then Sŏnbi suddenly remembered what Kannan used to always tell her: "Don't always look so sulky when you talk with the supervisors. You have to at least pretend to smile. That way you'll really keep them guessing." Sŏnbi smiled, thinking how funny Kannan's comment was. Just then, they heard the sound of someone climbing the stairs . . .

112

The supervisor now looked serious. "Hell, you don't know a thing about Kannan, do you? Go on, get out!"

Sŏnbi left as soon as the words crossed his lips. Once in her room, she could hear muddled voices coming from the supervisor's office. Her roommates stared at her, ready to hang on her every word.

"So . . . what did he say?"

Sŏnbi took out her bedding and spread it on the floor. "What do you mean, what did he say? It's always the same old story."

"Well, aren't you coming to night school?"

"No, I'm not feeling so well."

"What's the matter?"

"I don't know . . . I'm just really tired."

Seeing that Sŏnbi was in such low sprits, the others assumed the supervisor had given her a horrible scolding. They all left the room with fear in their eyes: would the supervisor call them in, too?

Sŏnbi felt sick. She couldn't remember how long she had felt like this, but whenever she tried to relax, she felt chills throughout her body and her forehead broke out into a terrible sweat. When this happened, she couldn't stop thinking about the heated floor she'd once slept on. That grass hut where she and her mother had once lived together! Stoke the fire with just a half a bundle of wood and how toasty warm it would be . . . If only she could snuggle under the covers and sweat out her cold on a heated floor like that. In no time at all she'd feel as good as new.

She fell asleep for a while, then awoke at some point to find a full moon shining in through the glass window. She wiped the beads of sweat from her forehead and lay back down facing the moon. Judging from what the supervisor had asked her, she was fairly sure that he wasn't suspicious of her. But while she was relieved of much of the anxiety that Kannan's escape had caused her, she now bore on her shoulders the heavy burden of her mission, and she was overwhelmed with the almost impossible task of carrying it out. Everything that Kannan had taught her flashed into her mind: the factory cells, the organization guidelines, the way she'd have to be in contact with comrades on the outside, the secret way of distributing leaflets and other notes that came from the outside. Oh, if only Kannan had waited just a little longer before she left, I wouldn't be in this mess, she thought, after trying for a while to make sense of it all. But had Kannan even made it out safely? And what could have happened out there for Kannan to be called out so suddenly? Maybe some of them were arrested, she thought, struck with a keen sense of unease. And what kind of people were these comrades of hers, anyway, who she hadn't even met yet? Were they people like Ch'ŏtchae? Maybe Ch'ŏtchae was one of them? But judging from the time she'd seen him on her way to Wŏlmido, Ch'ŏtchae seemed to be working as some sort of day laborer, instead of in a factory. Most likely he had never met one of the leaders . . . Sŏnbi assumed that Ch'ŏtchae was simply trying to keep himself busy, and hadn't yet found the path which would lead him out of the darkness. And when Sŏnbi thought about Ch'ŏtchae in this way, she wanted to meet him more than ever. More than anything she wanted to bring him into class consciousness. She knew he was likely to become a fearsome fighter, far stronger than anyone she knew.

While Sŏnbi couldn't be certain, she wondered if this had something to do with that fact that Ch'ŏtchae had suffered bitter moments in his past that were incomparable with her own. Was he still stealing from people? But when she thought about it, she clearly understood why he had started stealing to begin with and how this related to his being the son of a prostitute. She wanted to meet Ch'ŏtchae as soon as possible and to teach him to fight alongside the masses, not just act as an individual.

Could he still be in Inch'ŏn? Maybe he's gone off somewhere else? And why on earth was I so scared of him back in the countryside? As Sŏnbi's thoughts raced on like this, she remembered once again how she'd tossed away the sumac roots Ch'ŏtchae had dug up for her, and yet stashed under her bed Tŏkho's money. Looking down at herself now, she felt so ashamed, so mortified, that she could feel cold sweat running down her back. But that wasn't the least of it! Hadn't she wept when Tŏkho had stolen her virginity! Hadn't she wished she were dead time after time! How utterly childish of her and how stupid she had been! The Sŏnbi who had once looked into Tŏkho's eyes and cried "Father! Oh, Father!"—that Sŏnbi was no longer the person she was now. And with this thought, so too came another: that of her own father's death, about which she had always held suspicions. Granny Sŏbun was right! Sŏnbi jumped to her feet hardly knowing what she was doing. A sharp pain ran through her fingers. She pressed them up against her cheeks. Having barely managed to escape from Tŏkho, here she was in the clutches of human beings far more terrifying—she could feel this in her bones. But the Sŏnbi of today was no longer that Sŏnbi of the past . . . she wanted to cry this out at the top of her lungs.

113

Visiting hours with his father were over now, and as he stepped back into his cell, Sinch'ŏl felt his heart shudder at the sound of his cell door closing shut. He collapsed to the floor, completely exhausted. The first time he'd entered this cell, the sound of that closing door had damaged his pride, but at the same time it had sparked enough resistance in him to make him firm in his decision to stick it out to the end, however difficult. And yet now the sound of the door made Sinch'ŏl realize that pride had been a falsehood, a mere pretension all along. He clutched his head in his hands and screwed up his face. It was painful thinking about how worn-down his father had looked. Whether it was because of Sinch'ŏl, or because of the difficult life he was now living, his father seemed like a completely different person than the man he had known only two years earlier. The clothes that his father was wearing, and that haggard, gaunt expression on his face! And then those red-rimmed eyes that stared at him blankly—a father unable to speak to his son! Sinch'ŏl could sense in his heart his father's true feelings, even though the man hadn't spoken. The clock ticked on and on, and neither father nor son could bring himself to utter a word to the other.

"Yŏngch'ŏl's doing well?" Sinch'ŏl asked eventually.

His father's eyes filled with tears.

"Uh-huh," he replied, distractedly, and then turned his face away. As Sinch'ŏl listened to this vague response from his father, he suddenly felt a heaviness in his chest. The thought that the boy might have died struck him like a bolt of lightning.

"Gimme some caramels!" Would he never hear that voice again? Sinch'ŏl leaned up against the wall, and closed his eyes tight.

"You met Judge Pak, didn't you?" his father had finally said to him. "Just do what Judge Pak tells you to do. Don't be stubborn, because it won't get you anywhere . . ."

Visiting hours had ended with these parting words. Oh, how his father's voice had trembled! The man had almost been begging Sinch'ŏl, and those words now seemed to pierce right through his heart, through the core of his beliefs, and into other thoughts buried deep in the recesses of his mind. What do I do now? Go along with what Pyŏngsik said yesterday?

Pyŏngsik was the student who Sinch'ŏl had thought so stupid, so contemptible on that last day he'd been studying in the library. Pyŏngsik was the one memorizing *The Compendium of the Six Laws*. He had already become a judge over preliminary hearings.

Sinch'ŏl had betrayed some surprise when he first saw Pyŏngsik, but his pride had quickly set itself into action. Or rather, Sinch'ŏl had forced himself to draw on that pride. Even though he could have easily turned a deaf ear to Pyŏngsik's advice, it was his pride that had made sitting face to face with him so unpleasant. And it was his pride that had helped him turn away from Pyŏngsik and refuse to answer any of his questions. In any case, Pyŏngsik had been courteous to him, insofar as his official duties were concerned, possibly because they'd once been friends.

In fact, now that he thought about it, Sinch'ŏl was sure his father had sought out Pyŏngsik and had entreated him to come here—indeed, there was no mistaking it. With this new revelation, Sinch'ŏl remembered word for word what Pyŏngsik had gone on about so excitedly.

"First of all let me just say that, personally speaking, I don't think that everything about capitalist society is fair. You know, it makes perfect sense to me that there are going to be brave people out there, fighting against the system and trying to build a new society. But doesn't history have a long way to go before we actually get rid of the system? You of all people should know that it's going to take a lot of time and a hell of a sacrifice before that ever happens. But to go so far as making an individual sacrifice all for the sake of justice? Now, I suppose for a man there's a sort of thrill in it all, but just think about it for a minute. No matter how much I think my sacrifice is going to contribute to the cause, a revolution isn't going to happen today or tomorrow because of what I do, nor will a revolution fail to come about because of what I don't do. We're born once in this world and that's it, so what's the point of ignoring yourself as an individual? And besides, hasn't your family fallen into pretty dire straights, just like mine has? Without us, they'd be out on the streets, begging from door to door in just a matter of time. Think about the sacrifices they'll have to make if you're locked up in here for a decade, or however long it takes . . . Now, you know very well that all the XX* Party big shots have converted now—even in Japan—

*Communist

256

and I'm sure they put a lot of thought into their decisions. What do you think about what I've said?"

Pyŏngsik's face seemed lit with pathos as he looked at Sinch'ŏl. But that Pyŏngsik would attempt to win him over with this selfish theory of individualism struck Sinch'ŏl as both amusing and beyond contempt. He refused to give Pyŏngsik a reply.

"Well," said Pyŏngsik, reading Sinch'ŏl's mind. "Go back in there and think about this very carefully. I have a job to do here, but I'll do my best to support you, since the two of us go way back."

Just then, the guard standing beside them shouted out an order.

"On your feet!"

114

How weak he had been today, how very pathetic his sense of determination, as he listened to his father pleading with him, and as he looked into his father's hollowed eyes. Sinch'ŏl let out a deep sigh. He thought of his friend Pamsongi, and then one by one he saw the faces of all his fellow comrades who were locked up in this very same prison. But then it was Ch'ŏtchae, back in Inch'ŏn, whose face in particular kept flashing into his mind, blown up to a frightening size. It was to avoid seeing that face that Sinch'ŏl now opened his eyes. Only last night he'd thought of Ch'ŏtchae with such fondness, but now that same face was somehow terrifying.

Shining through the window like red skeins of thread, the rays of the sun cast an elaborate pattern on the wall. The glass, the iron bars, the thick metal netting and the fine wire mesh, and making its way through all four layers was that sunlight! This was Sinch'ŏl's one and only friend. Each time the guard looked through the *mihari* hole, Sinch'ŏl asked him the time and made marks on the wall following the sun's path of movement. Sinch'ŏl now looked at that ray of sunlight and calculated that it was just about half past eleven. I bet Father's home by now, he thought. He must be going through sheer hell. It looked as though his father had lost his job at the school. And with several members of his extended family still relying on him for support, Sinch'ŏl could easily understand, even without seeing it for himself, the sort of poverty their life must have been reduced to.

What should he do? Judging from the situation back home, there was no question that he simply had to get out of here, but more importantly, it was his own weak state of health that made it impossible for him to stay. He thought back to how he'd been tortured at that first police station, and shuddered. That was one thing he could never go through twice in his lifetime. Not knowing what you were in for was one thing, but once you'd had a good taste of it, it was better to drop dead right on the spot than ever go through something like that again.

Though he didn't know for sure, it seemed as though it would take one or two years for his case to come up for deliberation. And a decision might take ten or twenty years—though he had no way of being sure even of that. In any case, it all would take far more than a decade. He might even end up spending his whole life in prison. Thinking about it was simply overwhelming. Sinch'ŏl thought about Pyŏngsik. He went over very carefully again what his friend had told him.

He'd refused to listen to Pyŏngsik's sickening spiel, but now less than twenty-four hours later what Pyŏngsik had told him seemed to make sense. But even so, he had far too much pride to hang his head in front of Pyŏngsik. He let out a deep sigh and glanced down at his feet. He noticed an ant climbing up and down his toes. With great delight Sinch'ŏl picked up the ant and placed it in the palm of his hand. The ant was oblivious to what had happened to it, and quickly tried to crawl away. But Sinch'ŏl caught it, placed it back in his palm, and stared down at it again.

The longer Sinch'ŏl stared at the ant, the more it seemed that he, too, was wasting all his efforts. The ant hadn't known what he was getting into when he entered this cell, for there was no reason to visit a dreary prison cell without a scrap of food to munch on. Today would be rough for the ant, for he'd been captured and he wouldn't get a thing to eat. And so, too, for Sinch'ŏl. It wasn't just that he'd willingly suffered by giving up the means to any income, or that he had ended up here in jail. Even if he were lucky enough to make it out alive in a couple of decades, he'd be so far behind the others that he wouldn't be able to relate to either side. And in the end there'd be nothing left for him to do but become someone like Ilp'o and Kiho —a stuffy, fallen intellectual.

But could he just up and leave this place? Sinch'ŏl started shaking his head. There was, however, precious little effort put in the gesture, and Sinch'ŏl realized that his head was moving side to side very, very slowly.

258

Fading in and out of range, Sinch'ŏl then caught the sound of a willow flute, and he jumped to his feet.

115

Sinch'ŏl quickly turned away from the *mihari* hole. He tried to catch the sound of the guard's footsteps, then moved in front of the window. The windowsill was just higher than jaw-level and came up even with his lips. He stared out at Mount Inwang. It was bathed in the warm rays of the sun and stood up crisply against the sky . . . Just then a bird called out from somewhere close by and Sinch'ŏl shifted his gaze.

There was a small pond outside the window, and beside that, a perfectly-sized weeping willow, whose branches draped softly down, one over the other, like a woman's let-down hair. The willow's leaves were a vivid bluish-green. Though the branches of the tree had been bare of leaves, and had been swept by the early spring winds when he'd first laid eyes upon them, in no time at all its leaves had turned into a beautiful color. How many times a day had he looked out onto that willow tree! And each time he looked, he met it with a new set of feelings. He would think of Wŏnso Pond in Yongyŏn and then, by association, of Sŏnbi. But his vision was somehow that of a different Sŏnbi than before—a Sŏnbi from whom he now felt distanced. What remained in his mind were his memories of Okchŏm. Oh, Okchŏm! he thought. Could she still be single? Still be waiting for me? Not likely! I bet she's somebody's wife by now! But I doubt she'll ever forget me . . . He stared blankly out onto the pond. The shadows of the willow branches seem to cast themselves here and there deep into the blue water. Just like his scattered memories of Okchŏm's face, which lay deeply buried within his heart.

Suddenly Sinch'ŏl heard the eerie sound of the willow flute again. It was a tune from his childhood, "The Widow's Cry," played with one hand over the tip of the flute so as to twist the sound of each note. He looked up to see where the sound was coming from: Mount Inwang in springtime . . . He could see children, and men and women in the flower of their youth carefully walking up the mountain shoulder to shoulder. He could hear the cheerful voices of the children, as clearly as the skylarks chirping beneath the blue sky. It seemed like just yesterday that he'd climbed that mountain with his own friends . . . Sinch'ŏl felt so sorry for himself that he was practically ready to stamp his feet

259

on the ground. He deeply regretted not having listened to his father in the first place. He knew that it was dirty and vulgar for him to entertain these thoughts, but he couldn't help it. It drove him to his wit's end to think that because of these empty visions and idle dreams, the flower of his youth was going to rot behind these metal bars. And why should he alone make this sacrifice? It would be meaningless . . . As Sinch'ŏl looked out onto the men and women climbing Mount Inwang, in his heart he was deeply torn. For he knew full well that all this anguish and pain was not his alone—there were so, so many others locked up in here with him.

The sound of the flute gradually grew fainter. Should he compare it to the point of a needle, piercing in and out of his troubled mind with each twist and turn of his thoughts? Or a razor-sharp sword slicing effortlessly through the chambers of his heart? Oh, the sounds of that flute, drifting through the blue sky like so many wisps of smoke! Without thinking, he clutched his head in his arms. He scowled at the iron bars that crisscrossed darkly before his eyes. He longed for the world outside, just as his throat thirsted for water. He wanted to feel the air in his lungs beneath that blue sky.

Suddenly the sound of a metal clank took Sinch'ŏl by surprise, and he quickly sat down.

"What do you think you're doing!"

His heart shuddered at the guard's thundering voice.

"Get over here and sit down!"

Sinch'ŏl had no choice but to take a seat closer to the door.

"Don't look outside! Next time that happens, you'll pay a price for it!"

The anger was surging up at the base of his throat, and Sinch'ŏl just barely managed to hold it back. All he could do was to sit there in silent exasperation. The guard stayed for a moment glaring at him, then closed the peephole shut with a clank. Sinch'ŏl leaned against the wall, and let out his breath in sheer anguish. He opened his hand and found that the ant had disappeared. Having lost his friend the ant, he grabbed the *Lotus Sutra*, placed there beside him, and he opened it.

116

Sŏnbi had lost her appetite. She skipped dinner before coming onto the factory floor with several of her co-workers. It was Sŏnbi's turn on the night shift. All the factory girls hated working at night, and whenever their turn came up, they twisted their faces and shook their heads back and forth. The factory girls on friendly terms with the male workers, however, liked the night shift. Of course there was always a supervisor on the job, but they worked on several different shifts throughout the night. And each time a shift change came around, the girls managed to exchange eye contact with the men who carried in the barrels of silk cocoons. The supervisors didn't watch over them as vigilantly as they did during the day, so it was at night that these girls tried hardest to flirt with the male workers.

Recently there had been more than a few cases in which a male worker and a factory girl had illicit intercourse and then left the factory. Even though the supervisors were supposed to keep a close watch, this sort of thing went on quite frequently.

Sŏnbi came up to cauldron No. 603 and tapped lightly on her friend's shoulder.

"I'm on now. You can go."

Her friend was in the middle of cleaning out the cauldron.

"I'll clean it up," said Sŏnbi.

"Oh, you're a dear . . . Hey, are you feeling any better now?"

Sŏnbi watched the girl pull off her reels of silk, place them into her pail, and turn to leave.

Sŏnbi picked up the brush, and after giving the cauldron a quick scrub, she dumped the stale water out and filled it up with fresh water again. Even as Sŏnbi cleaned out the machine, however, it remained in operation. All the girls in this factory came to understand that a machine was something that never stopped moving. In fact, they were all so afraid they might get their hair or clothing caught in the machines that they tied their hair up with towels and made black, full-length aprons for themselves that covered them from head to toe. They had never worn these sorts of things before, but last spring one of the girls had gotten her hair caught, and had died a gruesome death when she was twisted up into a machine. Inside the factory this was a closely guarded secret, and no one was allowed to talk about it. But since many of the girls had witnessed the horrible scene, the story had spread throughout the entire factory. After the accident they were all given strict orders from above to wear uniforms and kerchiefs. But of course the factory didn't actually give them these clothes. They forced the girls to make them themselves.

Sŏnbi took the boiled cocoons the male worker had carried to her and poured them into her cauldron. The bubbling water started to fizz and froth and the cocoons in the cauldron each began spinning around on their sides. Sŏnbi felt a chill run through her shoulders, and she began shivering. She fell into a fit of coughing that lasted for some time. Try as she might to close her mouth firmly and hold her breath to stop the coughing, she felt an unbearable itch at the base of her throat, try- ing its hardest to work its way out. As Sŏnbi fought back the urge to cough, she picked up her little broom and pushed down on the boiling cocoons a few times. Then she pulled off the silk filaments that stuck to the broom and wrapped them around her left hand. She could feel her face flushing in the steam billowing from the cauldron and her fingers had already begun to sting. And yet, strangely, she still felt chills run- ning through her body. Though Sŏnbi had felt like this ever since the spring, she'd figured it was just a case of fatigue that a little time would cure. But now that it was already well into summer, her symptoms had persisted and she'd also developed this nasty cough. And while she had indeed become somewhat worried, by no means did she want to be seen by a doctor.

Sŏnbi put down her broom and with lightning speed fed the tip of each of the silk filaments in her left hand through a porcelain needle. If too many filaments were fed through the same needle the silk thread would be too thick, so she couldn't use more that five per needle. Once the filaments passed through the porcelain needle—just like a thread fed through the needle of a sewing machine—they were twisted together and then drawn up above her, where the thread was spun onto one of many reels. Next to each reel was a glass hook suspended in the air, which moved back and forth guiding the thread so that each reel was wound evenly.

The electric lights made it as bright as day and the glare from the glass windows and glass ceiling above was almost blinding. The noise from the generator seemed to block her ears, muffling her hearing. Cough after cough, Sŏnbi struggled to keep up the pace, hardly able to sit for a moment in her chair. For she alone was operating twenty reels, and without such an effort the task would have been simply impossible. What had earlier been chills, however, now turned into a burning fever, and she began sweating so heavily that her clothes seemed to cling to her body. Beads of sweat were dripping from her forehead like raindrops, but she had no idea what to do about it. She was frightfully short of breath, almost gasping. And her fingers were now so scalding hot that she gradually lost all feeling in them. Whether those hands in front of her belonged to her or to somebody else she couldn't even tell.

117

Sŏnbi's threads started to cut off in several places. She pressed down on the pedal to stop the machine, and then quickly started picking up the ends of the threads. The supervisor beside her shouted, "Hurry up and tie those! What's gotten into you, Sŏnbi?"

The supervisor cracked his whip at the reels, making the machine spin back into operation again. This sent the reels spinning round again, even though the threads hadn't been tied back into place. Sŏnbi now wanted to cry. All the work she'd done throughout the night was basically wasted. When a supervisor spun your reels like this, it meant a twenty-chŏn penalty. Sŏnbi was at a loss as to what to do, and after staring at the spinning reels for a while, she tried her best to find the loose ends of the threads. Everything in front of her was a blur now and she couldn't even control her coughing.

"What's gotten into that head of yours? How about taking your work a bit more seriously, huh?"

Sŏnbi's heart was suddenly gripped by fear, and she tried her best to gather her wits together. Had they found out about her? she wondered. Maybe that was why they'd been picking on her almost every day now. Sŏnbi's heart shuddered with ever greater intensity, and she frantically set her limbs into action.

Within a few minutes she finally managed to tie together all the loose ends. But the supervisor was already writing something down in his notebook. He stole a few glances at her out of the corner of his eye, stuffed his notebook inside his pocket, and walked away. Sŏnbi finally let out a sigh of relief. Then she heaved a violent cough. She quickly turned around to see if the supervisor had heard her. He was standing in front of one of the new girls, chatting her up with a smile. Then he gave her a slap on her firm backside.

"Keep up the good work! That's how you'll make your bonus."

The girl twisted her body flirtatiously and when she caught the man's eye she smiled at him with half-lowered lids. She had this habit of closing her eyes whenever she smiled. Sŏnbi was glad that the supervisor left her alone now that he had shifted his attentions to this new girl. But she was afraid that the secret mission entrusted to her might come to light because of this change. The supervisor had from time to time given her a bonus, but never had he whipped her reels or chewed her out like this before. And ever since this new girl had begun to curry the supervisor's favors, his attitude toward Sŏnbi had become quite cold. Today was the third time she'd been hit with a fine. Sŏnbi quickly set her fingers back into motion and let out a deep sigh. Her body ached more than ever, her coughing never let up, and now she felt a tightness in her chest. While earlier she'd at least held out the hope of earning a few dozen chŏn, now that faint hope had vanished, and all that welled up inside her was pain and sorrow. She remembered again what Kannan had told her, and regretted not having made at least something of an effort to kiss up to her supervisors.

Sŏnbi couldn't bear the coughing any longer, and in an effort to stop she quickly grabbed her broom and tried concentrating on fishing out the silk cocoons. In the light of the electric lamps, the water in the cauldron glistened like gold, and out of it, drawn up endlessly into the air, was all that silk thread! Tens of thousands of reels of that thread were spun in a single day.

Sŏnbi fished out a cocoon and held it between her lips; then she lifted up her head to take a look at the reels. They were spinning furiously, drawing up the thread like a white rainbow through those porcelain needles, then whirling it round and round! The first time she'd ever set her eyes on those reels, they had somehow captured a piece of her heart. And nothing could have described the feeling of satisfaction she'd once experienced upon taking those reels out, loading them into the box she kept at her station, and carrying them into the appraisal office. But as she looked at those reels now, they seemed like giant insects slowly gnawing away at her very existence.

Sŏnbi sensed that the supervisor was coming her way again, and she looked back down. She picked off a thread from one of the cocoons and fastened it to a porcelain needle. This time the supervisor passed by without giving her a second glance. Sŏnbi was so relieved that she again let her thoughts wander.

But then she heard the loud voice of the supervisor and looked out the corner of her eye: he was whipping the reels of the girl beside her.

The girl's face went a deep red as she frantically tried to tie her loose threads . . . Those arms! And those fingers! For all the world Sŏnbi couldn't bear to watch. She wiped the sweat from her brow and then looked at her own fingers again. That scalded, red hand! And those five white fingers, swollen by the boiling water! They seemed like dead fingers dangling from a living hand. She felt goosebumps at the thought of how many more dead fingers were gathered inside this factory alone!

Spin reels, spin reels
Round and round. . . .

The song rose and fell amid the clamor of the generators.

118

Sŏnbi soon joined in the singing.

Spin reels, spin reels
Round and round
Spin real good, that bonus is mine.
Spin real bad, I pay that fine.

But it was barely even a whisper that crossed Sŏnbi's lips as her eyes grew hot and tears began to roll down her cheeks. This song they sang to forget their suffering! It was supposed to make their work more fun, but to Sŏnbi it meant nothing. Her whole body was roasting over the intense heat of the cauldron. Her throat was parched, her heart was throbbing, even her sinuses and the sockets of her eyes felt like they were on fire. If she had her way she would have lain down right there and rested for a few minutes. Several times already Sŏnbi had heard the supervisor's footsteps behind her, and each time she'd wanted to tell him that she just couldn't work any longer because of the pain. But her lips had always remained tightly sealed, and the words simply never came out. In the past, Sŏnbi had found herself somewhat tongue-tied when she'd met face to face with one of the supervisors, but now that she was in such physical pain it was even harder.

Sŏnbi hadn't thought her condition very serious until recently. But it was the blood she coughed up, the little red threads of it mixed in with her phlegm that made her more and more concerned. Tomorrow I'll go to the infirmary for sure! she'd say to herself. But then she'd calculate how much money would be subtracted from what was written in her savings passbook. It had already been a full year since she'd entered the factory. And over that period of time they'd subtracted her board, as well the cost of her shoes and her toiletries, so that now there was only about three wŏn fifty left in her account. If she went to the infirmary at this point, it actually meant having to go into debt. And who in their right mind would pay three wŏn each time they were sick? Give me a wŏn's worth of the best medicine out there and I'll be fine, she figured.

She looked over at the giant clock mounted to the wall to the far side of her. It was already ten past two. As anxious as she was to get out of there, this gave her at least a modicum of pleasure, even a glimmer of hope.

Then one of her threads broke and floated up into the air, so Sŏnbi quickly set herself to refastening it. But when she looked up to see if the supervisor had noticed, she grew dizzy and almost fainted. In her confusion, she let her right hand slip into the cauldron.

"Ah!" she cried, and with a jerk pulled out her hand. She hadn't been alert enough to feel the pain at first when it had fallen into the boiling water, but before long her whole arm began to sting so much that she thought she might die.

"Burn yourself badly?"

Sŏnbi looked up. When she realized the person speaking to her was one of the men carrying over a barrel of cocoons, it was the image of Ch'ŏtchae's face that immediately flashed in her mind. With tears streaming down her cheeks, she turned away. The man stood there staring at her for a while, but then turned around to leave. Normally she would have died of embarrassment from this sort of encounter, but today with her whole body aching and her hand scalded up to her wrist, she wasn't embarrassed in the slightest and instead felt a strong urge to call out to the man. If this man had only been Ch'ŏtchae, Sŏnbi wouldn't have hesitated even for an instant to entrust her frail body into his arms. She couldn't bear the pain any longer. She held her wrist against her tongue. Then she stole a glance back at the man who'd just walked away—through her tears she could only faintly make out his face. At this rate there was no way she would make it through the night shift. She looked up at the clock and decided to tell the supervisor that she had to stop the next time he came by.

Off in the distance the faint image of the supervisor flickered before her eyes, and she tried to gather her wits. When it seemed as though he was passing by her, she opened her mouth and tried to say something. But just then she let out a violent cough again, and as the phlegm rose up from her chest, she quickly put her hand to her mouth. The coughs persisted, coming one after another, and as Sŏnbi tried her best to control them, through the five fingers she had raised to her mouth came several trickles of bright red blood. Sŏnbi collapsed right there on the spot.

119

It was like the inside of a cave, this room where Ch'ŏtchae sat day after day simply twiddling his thumbs. For someone used to doing physical labor almost every single day of his entire life, nothing could have been more frustrating, more agonizing, than to sit around idly like this. But circumstances required him to stay out of sight, so Ch'ŏtchae stayed put and let his friends bring him everything he needed to survive.

He had never before been guilty of idle thinking, but now he let his imagination run wild, for he had nothing else to do all day long. What he thought about most was Sinch'ŏl. Occasionally he heard news of him from Ch'ŏlsu, though the news was never very comforting. Oh, if only Sinch'ŏl could get out quickly, so we could get back to work, hand-in-hand, just like we always used to . . . And with this thought, Ch'ŏtchae again pictured that long line of factory girls walking out toward Wŏlmido. Then that startled expression on Sŏnbi's face came to his mind. It seemed likely that he might see her again someday, if it really had been her. He felt the sudden urge to find out about the report from the Taedong Spinning Mill that should have made its way to Ch'ŏlsu last night. He was burning up inside now and couldn't stand being indoors for even a minute longer, so he decided to go to Ch'ŏlsu's room.

"I've heard some news about Sinch'ŏl from a friend in Seoul," said Ch'ŏlsu, lowering his voice.

Ch'ŏtchae looked up at him. His eyes were as round as saucers.

"Apparently they dropped the charges against him and he got out of prison . . . on grounds of ideological conversion."

"Conversion?"

Ch'ŏtchae took in the meaning of these words, but he couldn't make sense of them. Could he believe them? Was it right to believe them?

Suddenly Ch'ŏtchae felt an indescribable tightness spread throughout his chest. Ch'ŏlsu could see how hard Ch'ŏtchae was taking the news.

"My friend! It's no surprise Sinch'ŏl converted. What do you expect from the so-called intellectual class? From what I hear, he found a job in Manchuria and married some rich girl just as soon as he got out of prison."

Found a job . . . married some rich girl? With these new words, something pierced Ch'ŏtchae's mind like a thunderbolt.

Just then, they heard the sound of footsteps rushing toward them. A door flew open and both men jumped to their feet.

120

It was Kannan. Ch'ŏlsu glared at her disapprovingly. Kannan had to catch her breath before speaking.

"You . . . you've got to come now. Okay? Just hurry."

Kannan had barely finished her sentence before she spun around and ran off again. Their hearts were still racing from the surprise. Kannan had looked quite familiar to Ch'ŏtchae when he'd seen her there for the first time, but it hadn't dawned on him immediately who exactly she'd been. Ch'ŏlsu looked back at Ch'ŏtchae.

"Come on, let's go . . . It looks like she might die!"

Ch'ŏtchae studied the expression on Ch'ŏlsu's face and followed him out the door.

"Last night one of our women comrades was dismissed from the Taedong Spinning Mill on account of illness . . ." Ch'ŏlsu told him.

Just then a bicycle sped by, and the stench of fish hit the air. Catching a glipse of the fish peddler, Ch'ŏtchae repeated to himself the words Ch'ŏlso had just spoken. Then he felt a sudden tightness in his chest.

"It's her lungs," said Ch'ŏlsu, letting out a deep sigh.

His tiny eyes narrowed as he glanced over at Ch'ŏtchae, and his lips tightened. Ch'ŏtchae was looking out into the distance at the smokestack of the Taedong Spinning Mill, visible just beyond a grove of trees. It kept spewing out puffs of jet-black smoke. Could Sŏnbi have caught a disease like that too? he wondered.

When they reached Kannan's house, she came out to meet them. Her lips were quivering and she tried to put something into words, but her voice cracked and neither of them could understand what she was

268

saying. They hurried into the room. Ch'ŏlsu rushed to the patient's side and shook her.

"Comrade! Snap out of it, my friend!"

The patient's body was already stone cold and her face was deathly pale. Ch'ŏlsu let out a deep sigh and turned around to look at Ch'ŏtchae. He was standing anxiously to the side of Ch'ŏlsu, that then took one step closer. And then he saw her.

"Sŏnbi!" he cried, standing paralyzed at the sight of her.

The whole world began to spin in front of him—he'd been booted off a cliff and was tumbling far below into the darkness. This was his Sŏnbi, whom he'd loved since he was a boy. This was his Sŏnbi, whom he had so longed to see again . . . And there she was right in front of him, dead and gone forever! Ch'ŏlsu's comments about Sinch'ŏl now struck him like a flash of lightening.

"He married some rich girl and found a good job . . ."

That's it! Sinch'ŏl always had that luxury of choice! And that's what led him to an ideological conversion. But what about me? What choice do I have? What choice did I ever have? Sinch'ŏl has many paths to follow. That's what makes us different people!

Ch'ŏtchae looked down at Sŏnbi again. Sŏnbi, whom he had loved since he was a little child! Sŏnbi, whom he had so longed to marry and have children with! Never once had he been able to talk to her. And in the end she'd become a corpse, laid out before his very own eyes!

It was as though someone had simply tossed her to him. Here, take her, now that she's dead!

And with this, a fire seemed to burn in Ch'ŏtchae's eyes.

He trembled violently. His line of vision was fixed on Sŏnbi's terrifying corpse as it gradually transformed into a dark mass that swept before his eyes.

This dark mass! Slowly expanding in size, blackening out everything before him, indeed everything in the path of all human beings. If this wasn't the very essence of all human problems, what else could be?

These human problems! More than anything we need to find a solution to them. People have fought for hundreds and thousands of years in an effort to solve them. But still no one has come up with a solution! And if that's the case, just which human beings will actually solve these problems in the future? Just who?

Glossary

Korean and Japanese words

chŏn (K.) a unit of currency; one hundredth of a wŏn.

donburi (J.) a Japanese dish made with a base of rice.

geta (J.) Japanese wooden clogs, elevated several centimeters from the ground.

intelli (J./K.) a pejorative term for intellectuals.

kake udon (J.) a bowl of thick Japanese noodles, served hot.

kimchi (K.) a spicy pickled vegetable, often made with cabbage.

kisaeng (K.) a traditional Korean entertainer or courtesan.

li (K.) a unit of currency; one tenth of a chŏn.

makkŏlli (K.) a milky-white Korean alcoholic beverage.

mihari (J.) a peephole in a prison door.

nyang (K.) an older unit of currency, equivalent in the provinces to one chŏn.

Shikishima (J.) a brand of expensive Japanese cigarettes; an ancient name for Japan.

torii (J.) a Japanese gateway, made of wood or stone, located outside a Shinto shrine.

tubu tchigae (K.) spicy tofu stew.

waku (J.) the reel on a spinning machine on which thread is spun.

wŏn (K.) a unit of currency, equivalent to approximately two days labor on the docks.

yakiguri (J.) roasted chestnuts.

yukata (J.) a Japanese robe.

270

Place Names

Ch'anggyŏng Park (Ch'anggyŏng kongwŏn) Once an imperial palace, turned into a zoo by the Japanese colonial government. Now called the Piwŏn, or the "Secret Garden."

Chosŏn Sin'gung (Chōsen jingu) The Shrine of Korea, built by the colonial government on Namsan, but removed after liberation.

Chosŏn An older word for Korea, still used in North Korea and the area of northeastern China and Japan populated by Koreans.

Hwanggŭm-jŏng The area now called Ŭljiro in Seoul.

Kyŏngsŏng Imperial University Now called Seoul National University. During the colonial period and for sometime afterward it was located in the north of Seoul.

Man'guk Park (Man'guk kongwŏn) Now called Chayu kongwŏn, or Freedom Park, in Inchŏn.

Mitsukoshi Department One of the first modern department stores in Seoul, it once occupied the six-story building where the Sinsegye Department Store is found today.

Monggŭmp'o Beach Once a well-known holiday destination in Hwanghae Province, now part of the Democratic People's Republic of Korea.

Mount Inwang (Inwangsan) A mountain west of the Kyŏngbok Palace in Seoul, and east of the Sŏdaemun Prison.

Mount Pugak (Pugaksan) A mountain situated directly behind Kyŏngbok Palace.

Mount Pult'a (Pult'asan) A mountain in Hwanghae Province, now in the DPRK.

Namdaemun The Southern Gate in Seoul.

Namsan A mountain located in central Seoul between the Han river and the Chongno district.

P'yŏngyang A center of industry during the Japanese occupation. Obliterated by American napalming during the Korean War, it has been rebuilt into the modern capital of the DPRK.

Pagoda Park The site in central Seoul where thousands of Koreans gathered for a historic independence march in 1918, which ultimately proved unsuccessful.

Pon-jŏng Honmachi in Japanese, the area now called Ch'ungmuro in Seoul.

Posŏng College Founded in 1905, it is now called Korea University (Koryŏ Daehakkyo).

Seoul The capital city of South Korea. Officially called Kyŏngsŏng (or in Japanese, Keijō) during the colonial period.

Sup'yo Bridge A small bridge now re-built over the reconstructed Ch'ŏnggye River in Seoul.

Taedong Spinning Mill Most likely refers to the Tongyang Spinning Mill in Inchŏn.

Umigwan A popular movie theater in Seoul.

Wŏlmido A small island off of Inchŏn popular for its amusement park and salt-water baths.

Yongsan District in Seoul where Japanese military bases were located.

Acknowledgments

So many friends and colleagues have helped me shape this translation into a book—sharing their enthusiasm, their editorial assistance, and their practical advice—that I find it difficult to think of this project as anything but a collective effort.

The initial stages of this work would have been impossible without the philological expertise and generous mentorship of fellow translator Yu Youngnan. My deepest appreciation goes to her for reading early drafts of my translation in close consultation with the original Korean. I also want to acknowledge the crucial support of both Kyeong-Hee Choi, who introduced me to Kang Kyŏng-ae's fiction during my graduate training at the University of Chicago, and Janet Poole, who first encouraged me to take on the translation of Kang's novel.

I especially want to thank fellow Korean literature scholars Choi Wŏnshik at Inchŏn University, Lee Sunok at Sookmyung Women's University, and Lee Sangkyung at KAIST (Korea Advanced Institute of Science and Technology) for the expertise and kindness they extended to me in Seoul during the early stages of this project. For their inspirational work as translators and for the value they have placed on translation as an intellectual and creative practice, I am deeply grateful to my professors of Japanese literature, Bill Sibley and Norma Field at the University of Chicago. I want to thank Jihong Pak, Chŏn Hye-sŏn, and Ch'oe Chun-ho for their assistance in clarifying parts of the original Korean novel. And to my students and colleagues in the Department of East Asian Studies at Brown University, I am deeply thankful for the welcoming and supportive environment in which I managed to complete the final stages of this manuscript during my first year of teaching.

Preliminary work on this translation was made possible through a Graduate Translation Fellowship from the International Communications Foundation, and later through a generous grant from the Korea Literature Translation Institute. Additional funding to support this publication was provided by the Korea Institute at Harvard University as well as the Korea Literature Translation Institute. I would like to thank David McCain and Susan Laurence, in particular, for their support of this project while I was a postdoctoral fellow at the Korea Institute and the Reischauer Institute for Japanese Studies at Harvard University.

The cover art of Inch'ŏn harbor by Yoshida Hatsusaburō was first shown to me by the staff of the Incheon Foundation for Arts & Culture, and a digital copy was generously provided by the Map Communications Museum in Japan.

My deepest gratitude also goes to The Feminist Press for agreeing to oversee the editing and publication of *From Wŏnso Pond*, and for helping to bring Kang's novel to a far wider audience than it might have had otherwise. Florence Howe first gave her support for this project after what must have seemed like unrelenting appeals from me. Her support was graciously followed by the editorial assistance of Gloria Jacobs, Theresa Noll, and Jeanann Pannasch, whom I thank for their patience in dealing with a first-time author.

Finally, to Kang Kyŏng-ae, whose fortitude and creativity have helped sustain me for so long, my thanks are everlasting.

CPSIA information can be obtained
at www.ICGtesting.com
Printed in the USA
JSHW031452250821
18137JS00005B/3